AT THE MOUSE CIRCUS
—Harlan Ellison

A mysterious, enigmatic, haunting story. . . . I found it irresistible: beautifully written, marvelously controlled, wondrously hallucinatory. I'm proud to have published it.

NOBODY'S HOME
—Joanna Russ

I regard this story with awe, for it seems to me one of the most vivid and plausible depictions of the daily life of the future ever written.

THE PSYCHOLOGIST WHO WOULDN'T DO AWFUL THINGS TO RATS
—James Tiptree, Jr.

If I were allowed to claim as my work just one of the whole hundred-odd stories I've published in *New Dimensions*, this is the one I would take.

—Robert Silverberg

THE BEST OF NEW DIMENSIONS

Edited by
Robert Silverberg

PUBLISHED BY POCKET BOOKS NEW YORK

Another *Original* publication of POCKET BOOKS

POCKET BOOKS, a Simon & Schuster division of
GULF & WESTERN CORPORATION
1230 Avenue of the Americas, New York, N.Y. 10020

ISBN: 0-671-82976-9

First Pocket Books printing November, 1979

10 9 8 7 6 5 4 3 2 1

Trademarks registered in the United States and other countries.

Printed in the U.S.A.

Contents

Introduction

I REMEMBER TELLING MYSELF, BACK WHEN I WAS twenty-three or so, that it must be a whole lot easier to be an editor than a writer. A writer must conceive ideas, get them down on paper in properly publishable form, convey them somehow to the attention of a sympathetic editor, and, once having found a purchaser for his material, endure the harrowing process of collecting his check. Whereas an editor, as I imagined it, placidly sorts through his mail, selecting enough stories to fill his current issue, and sends the rest back —a filter, nothing much more. And a filter who gets a paycheck every Friday, too.

Of course, this was nonsense, and I knew it even then. Editors don't have to bear the creative and financial risks that writers do, but otherwise their jobs are no sinecures. Aside from the little matter of commuting to some Manhattan office every day—a bother from which writers are spared—there's the burden of maintaining standards, the need to catch flak from high-strung writers, the risk of losing the job around which one's security is built, etc., etc. And though some editors are content to be mere filters, the best of them—John W. Campbell, Horace Gold, Anthony Boucher, at that time—are involved in a constant exhausting enterprise of exhorting writers, cajoling them, instructing them, browbeating them, whatever is necessary in order to extract copy from them worthy of the gifts they have. Editors, in their way, work just as hard as writers, with rather less in the way of financial reward. (At least, as a twenty-three-year-old writer I was earning rather more than even the most important of the editors I dealt with. I was knocking myself silly to do it, though, which is probably why I found myself envying them their roles in the publishing world.)

My own brushes with editing had been occasional and casual. In summer camp I had edited the camp newspaper; in high school I had edited the school newspaper; from 1949 to 1955 I had edited an amateur science-fiction magazine, which at first was a strikingly incompetent publication but which eventually came to command considerable respect in its field. And at the age of eighteen or nineteen, after attempting with only spotty success to launch a career as a writer of science fiction, I had indicated to friends that I hoped some day to edit a professional science-fiction magazine. It seemed, just then, my only chance of earning a living doing something I enjoyed—for the writing wasn't going particularly well. I remember telling a friend, after a spate of particularly discouraging rejection slips, that I thought my talents were primarily critical rather than creative, so that editing was really the most sensible path.

By the time I was twenty I was a successful professional author, producing stories as fast as I could type and selling them even faster, and that was the end of the notion of going into editing. I might have, in moments of fatigue, envied the life of an editor, but when I was rational I knew full well that I was in the right end of the business. And so it went for a decade or so. Eventually I did drift into a sort of editing—compiling anthologies of my favorite science-fiction stories—but that was pleasant part-time work, virtually a hobby, done at home in spare moments, a means of drawing on my expertise in the genre and, incidentally, of getting paid for it. The real center of my career was still writing, and as the years went along it became altogether inconceivable that I would ever exchange the perquisites and delights of the free-lance writer's life for the constraints of an editor's. Editors, after all, are *employees*. They report to an office; they wear shoes when they work; they must pay heed to sales figures and the whims of popular taste.

Even so, in the late 1960's I felt vague fugitive twitches of the desire to work with other writers on original material. I had strong notions about the nature of science fiction and an equally strong technical grounding in the craft of writing. I felt that most of the editors of the science-fiction magazines of the day were on the wrong track. (Gold had retired, Boucher was dead, Campbell had lost interest in his work. Among active editors, Fred Pohl and Ed Ferman were capable enough, surely, but were forced by monthly deadlines to cut too many corners, and Damon Knight, with whose tastes I had been most nearly in sympathy, had lately veered much too far, I felt, in the direction of avant-garde experimentalism.) And finally I decided to enter the editorial ring myself.

Not as an employee, though, and not with a monthly magazine. The concept of the anthology of original fiction, pioneered by Frederik Pohl with his *Star* series in 1952, had lately been revived by Damon Knight with *Orbit*. Pohl's *Star* had been an extraordinary publication. (Imagine a first-issue contents page with such names as Asimov, Bradbury, Clarke, del Rey, Gold, Kornbluth, Kuttner and Moore, Leiber, Leinster, Merril, Sheckley, Simak, Tenn, Wyndham!) Pohl had done it by making use of his extensive contacts with other authors, by outbidding the existing magazines, and by being unwilling to settle for anything less than the best. I saw no reason why I couldn't do the same. With some book publisher to back me, I would edit in unhurried fashion an annual volume of new short stories. I would pay the highest rate in the field (three cents a word was tops then—this was 1968) and work carefully and thoughtfully with my writers.

At the 1968 science-fiction convention in Oakland, California, I took the matter up with George Ernsberger, the sensitive and perceptive science-fiction editor of Avon Books. He had recently purchased my novels *Nightwings* and *The Man in the Maze;* we trusted and respected one another; and we had markedly similar tastes in science fiction. He was immediately enthusiastic about the *New Dimensions* proposal, with only one reservation: the cost of the project.

I wanted to publish a fine fat book, 80,000 words, and pay five cents a word for my material. That was $4000 right there—to which I meant to add an editorial fee for myself of $1000. But a $5000 advance was a bit outlandish for 1968, when 95% of all science-fiction books were bought for guarantees of $3000 or less. Months passed while we endeavored to find a way around this problem. Since I refused to reduce the editorial budget (there was no point in doing the book unless I could offer higher word-rates than the conventional s-f magazines, and thus demanding more careful writing and rewriting) it became necessary to call in a co-publisher, and in time one was procured: Walker & Company, which then had a program of reprinting in hard cover outstanding paperback science-fiction novels. A complex arrangement was worked out by which Avon agreed to pay me $5000, then would collect $1500 from Walker, who would do a hardbound edition in advance of the Avon publication. I signed the contract on September 15, 1969.

By that time I had already been editing *New Dimensions* in an unofficial way for many months. Well in advance of the contract, on Ernsberger's verbal commitment alone, I had quietly sent out requests for material to a select group of writer and agents. I did *not* notify *Writers' Digest* or any of the other traditional disseminators of market news, for I dreaded being inundated by amateur manuscripts. (I had my own main career to handle, after all; this was supposed to be part-time work.) A typical letter was this one to agent Virginia Kidd in December, 1968:

"My inclinations are slightly to left of center in the Old Wave/New Wave thing, and I intend to be pretty tough about what I buy. . . . I mean to be fussy, even if I look conservative; I'm not going to make loud noises about 'storytelling,' by which the Old Wavers mean lots of chase sequences and laser duels, but I'm going to hold out for a high level of literacy. What I want, I suppose, is the sort of tight, cerebrum-in-gear writing that is characteristic of Bester, Blish, Kuttner, Kornbluth, Budrys, Pohl. I'm willing to buy flamboyance of the Zelazny type or wild soaring Lafferty stuff—but I've got to have the feeling that the author is in charge of his material, that he understands what a short story is, what the elements of his material are. . . . I'm trying to define a position here, and in a way it's a classicist's position: I will buy any kind of story that touches my imagination, even if it violates the Hal Clement rules [of hard science]; I'm open to surrealism, to grotesquerie, to black humor, but I want professionalism too, and will not happily buy an amateurish story that shows flashes of brilliance."

What I wanted, actually, were stories worthy of Fred Pohl's early issues of *Star*—early 1950's craftsmanship, late 1960's sensibility.

The grapevine was efficient and soon stories started coming in—too soon, for the Avon-Walker contractual waltz was going on and on, nothing was signed, and I had no way of paying for material. The first acceptable story reached me on February 7, 1969—from two beginners, Alex and Phyllis Eisenstein. I bought it instantly, but warned them I might not be able to pay for it for a few months; then, while the negotiations with the publishers continued interminably, I had to keep those poor people waiting almost all year for their first professional writing check! (I finally paid them in October.)

There were more embarrassments ahead. In a leisurely way I went on buying stories all during 1969 and early 1970. Some of the writers I had most hoped to see material from sent nothing—no Blish, no Zelazny, no Dick, no Vance, no Budrys, no Bester —but I did get stories of the level I was seeking from such professionals as Ursula Le Guin and Philip José Farmer and such newcomers as Gardner Dozois and Ed Bryant. From Thomas Disch came a brilliant segment of his novel-in-progress *334*. From Barry Malzberg, Harry Harrison, Harlan Ellison—well, the issue came together swiftly and pleasingly. But I did get into one bad row with Le Guin that almost cost me her story after I had accepted it, because my acceptance was only moderately enthusiastic and a garbled report of my opinion got back to her. We patched that up. I got into difficulties with another well-known writer about revisions; we didn't patch that one up, and the story went elsewhere. And then, somehow, Walker backed out of the co-publishing deal.

I don't know how that happened. Apparently someone failed to draw up a binding contract between Avon and Walker, and, when Avon finally noticed it, Walker had changed editors and no longer cared to do the book. This left Avon stuck with the whole $5000 advance, an impossible economic burden at the time. I had already bought the stories, so the first issue would appear; but it appeared as though the first would also be the last. Since no other co-publishing scheme seemed feasible, I sent out word in the autumn of 1970 that I had ceased to solicit manuscripts.

Help arrived from a most unexpected source. On October 29, 1970, Diane Cleaver of Doubleday wrote me, "All the fanzines are informing us that *New Dimensions* has folded. Would you be interested in bringing it to Doubleday on an annual basis? If you are, let's talk."

That was a surprise. Doubleday and I were on friendly terms and they had published many of my novels; but still, here was an offer out of the blue for an unpublished anthology, sight unseen. I found that flattering. Could anything be worked out, though? I doubted that. Avon already owned the book; Doubleday would have to buy it in a subsidiary position; and Doubleday never ever did things like that. This time they did. The intricacies of the deal would numb the mind if I were to recount them here; it need only be said that all went well, and *New Dimensions 1* appeared as a Doubleday book on October 1, 1971, just three years and a month after I had first broached the idea to George Ernsberger of Avon.

The subsequent publishing history of the book proved to be as wondrously complex as its origins. Doubleday and Avon co-published the second issue, but were unable to agree among themselves on terms for the third, and neither would go it alone; ultimately I had to take the book to another house entirely, New American Library, which published numbers three and four as paperback originals. Then my relationship with NAL grew bumpy, and when Harper & Row offered to undertake publication of *New Dimensions* I happily shifted it there as of number five. Harper intended to do its own paperback edition, but did so only for one year; issues six through ten, though handsomely published in hard covers by Harper, had no paperbacks at all. (There was a stillborn deal for reprints of issues six, seven, and eight by Pinnacle Books of Los Angeles.) The lack of a paperback edition eventually made it unfeasible for Harper to go on, and with the forthcoming eleventh issue *New Dimensions* shifts again, to Pocket Books. With the same issue I begin to share editorial duties with Marta Randall, and I use "sharing" euphemistically, for her responsibilities as co-editor will be increasingly heavy ones. After eleven years, I think the time has come to began easing myself out of the editorial chair: all editors go stale in time, even the immortal John Campbell, and what was a driving passion for me in 1969 now has become a routine chore. That is unfair to readers, writers, and me—and, having found a co-editor whose ideas about science fiction are harmonious with those I held at the founding of *New Dimensions,* I have started to withdraw from active control.

But I found my decade as editor an exciting one, and not merely because seven publishers had to be dealt with in the course of getting out eleven issues. There was the delightful experience, many times repeated, of helping an author make his first sale. There was the pleasure of having some altogether magnificent manuscript arrived unsolicited in the mailbox from an unknown contributor. There was the joy of seeing two out of three Hugo awards for short fiction at the 1974 World Science Fiction Convention go to stories from *New Dimensions.* There was the reward of hearing writers express particular satisfaction at having sold something to *New Dimensions,* because I was so demanding an editor.

I wouldn't do it again. But I'm glad to have done it when I did; and I regret only that this collection of the best stories from *New Dimensions* is not five times as long as it is. Arbitrarily I have limited each writer to one selection, which rules out some choice pieces by regular contributors; I have had to eliminate most of the longer stories I published; and I have left out others because of arcane copyright restrictions. Nevertheless, I think this collection fairly represents my intentions with *New Dimensions,* and I think I did accomplish, to a reasonable degree, what I had hoped to do when I first suggested the idea of the book in 1968.

—Robert Silverberg
Oakland, California
April, 1979

THE
BEST OF
NEW
DIMENSIONS

A Special Kind
of Morning

GARDNER R. DOZOIS

In the summer of 1969, during that curious interregnum after the existence of *New Dimensions* had been announced but before any publishers' contracts had been signed, a manuscript came to me from a writer whose name was not only unfamiliar to me at the time but also unpronounceable: Gardner Dozois. ("Do-*zwah*," I quickly found out.) His eloquent and amusing covering letter began, "Several people have suggested that I submit something to an anthology you're editing for Avon called *New Dimensions*. I thought that this was a fine idea; the state of perpetual starvation in which I exist renders me highly susceptible to suggestions of this sort." The story was called "The Sound of Muzak." I didn't buy it, but I sent the most enthusiastic rejection letter I could: "I wish I could buy this," I said, "because the prose is sensitive and intelligent, and I want to encourage that. You write very well, and I don't mean that as the standard rejection-slip crap." But the story, I insisted, wasn't true science fiction. "What's going for it, really, other than its excellent writing? Style isn't enough. The reader should be enlightened, enlarged, transformed. Shown things he's never seen before and can't think up for himself. I admire style, which is rarer than it ought to be in s-f,

1

but I want an honest s-f theme underneath it, since that's the commodity I'm offering the public. Note that I don't mean I want Buck Rogers *writing:* just s-f *thinking.* I don't find much of it in 'Sound of Muzak'. But please do let me see something else. The book is wide open, new names are welcome, and there's a nickel a word waiting for you."

That was in August. In November I met Dozois for the first time, at a convention—he turned out to be a skinny, soft-spoken, hippie-looking sort with a lot of hair—and he told me a second story was in the works. Around Christmas I received it, a hideously sloppy manuscript looking like the work of a subliterate teenager. I began reading it, and read on and on, enthralled, and on the afternoon of December 30, 1969, wrote him, "You may be the lousiest speller this side of the Rockies. But you are one hell of a writer, and you have a sale, man. An exciting hour for me—reading your story tensely, wondering if you were going to sustain the promise of the first few pages or let it all go driveling away into slush, as so many of the other new writers who've been sending me stuff have done . . . thereby wasting my time and depriving me of a story. But no. The thing held up, it grew from page to page in inventiveness, the style remained vivid and supple—go have a swelled head for an evening. You've earned it. Now I know what editors talk about when they speak of the thrill of having something come in from an unknown that turns them on. But your spelling sure is awful."

Dozois' "A Special Kind of Morning" was the first story in the first issue of *New Dimensions*—I always tried to lead with my strongest item—and it was the first story chosen for *The Best Of New Dimensions.* It was a Hugo and Nebula nominee and belongs in all sorts of *Best* anthologies. All by itself, it made having edited *New Dimensions* worthwhile.

The Doomsday Machine is the human race.
—graffito in New York subway, 79th St. station

DID Y'EVER HEAR THE ONE ABOUT THE OLD MAN AND the sea?

Halt a minute, lordling; stop and listen. It's a fine story, full of balance and point and social pith; short and direct. It's not mine. Mine are long and rambling and parenthetical and they corrode the moral fiber right out of a man. Come to think, I won't tell you that one after all. A man of my age has a right to prefer his own material, and let the critics be damned. I've a prejudice now for webs of my own weaving.

Sit down, sit down: butt against pavement, yes; it's been done before. Everything has, near about. Now that's not an expression of your black pessimism, or your futility, or what have you. Pessimism's just the common-sense knowledge that there's more ways for something to go wrong than for it to go right, from our point of view anyway—which is not necessarily that of the management, or of the mechanism, if you prefer your cosmos depersonalized. As for futility, everybody dies the true death eventually; even though executives may dodge it for a few hundred years, the hole gets them all in the end, and I imagine that's futility enough for a start. The philosophical man accepts both as constants and then doesn't let them bother him any. Sit down, damn it; don't pretend you've important business to be about. Young devil, you are in the enviable position of having absolutely nothing to do because it's going to take you a while to recover from what you've just done.

There. That's better. Comfortable? You don't look it; you look like you've just sat in a puddle of piss and're wondering what the socially appropriate reaction is. Hypocrisy's an art, boy; you'll improve with age. Now you're bemused, lordling, that you let an old soak chivy you around, and now he's making fun of you. Well, the expression on your face is worth a chuckle; if you could see it you'd laugh yourself. You will see it years from now too, on some other young man's face—that's the only kind of mirror that ever shows it clear. And *you'll* be an old soak by that time, and you'll laugh and insult the young buck's dignity, but you'll be laughing more at the reflection of the man you used to be than at that particular stud himself. And you'll probably have to tell the buck just what I've told you to cool him down, and there's a laugh in that too; listen for the echo of a million and one laughs behind you. I hear a million now.

How do I get away with such insolence? What've I got to lose, for one thing? That gives you a certain perspective. And I'm socially instructive in spite of myself—I'm valuable as an object lesson. For that matter, why is an arrogant young aristo like you sitting there and putting up with my guff? Dont' even bother to answer; I knew the minute you came whistling down the street, full of steam and strut. Nobody gets up this early in the morning any more, unless they're old as I am and begrudge sleep's dry-run of death— or unless they've never been to bed in the first place. The world's your friend this morning, a toy for you to play with and examine and stuff in your mouth to taste, and you're letting your benevolence slop over onto the old degenerate you've met on the street. You're even happy enough to listen, though you're being quizzical about it, and you're sitting over there feeling benignly superior. And I'm sitting over *here* feeling benignly superior. A nice arrangement, and everyone content. Well, then; mornings make you feel that way. Especially if you're fresh from a night at the Towers, the musk of Lady Ni still warm on your flesh.

A blush—my buck, you *are* new-hatched. How did I know? Boy, you'd be surprised what I know; I'm occasionally startled myself, and I've been working longer to get it catalogued. Besides, hindsight is a comfortable substitute for omnipotence. And I'm not blind yet. You have the unmistakable look of a cub who's just found out he can do something else with it besides piss. An incredible revelation, as I recall. The blazing significance of it will wear a little with the years, though not all that much, I suppose; until you get down to the brink of the Ultimate Cold, when you stop worrying about the identity of warmth, or demanding that it pay toll in pleasure. Any hand of clay, long's the blood still runs the tiny degree that's just enough for difference. Warmth's the only definition between you and graveyard dirt. But morning's not for graveyards, though it works the other way. Did y'know they also used to use that to make babies? 's'fact, though few know it now. It's a versatile beast. Oh *come*—buck, cub, young clocksman—stop being so damn surprised. People ate, slept, and fornicated before you were born, some of them anyway, and a few will probably even find the courage to keep on at it after you die. You don't have to keep it secret; the thing's been circulated in this region once or twice before. You weren't the first to learn how to make the beast do its trick, though I *know* you don't believe that. *I* don't believe it concerning myself, and I've had a long time to learn.

You make me think, sitting there innocent as an egg and twice as vulnerable; yes, you are definitely about to make me think, and I believe I'll have to think of some things I always regret having thought about, just to keep me from growing maudlin. Damn it, boy, you *do* make me think. Life's strange—wet-eared as you are, you've probably had that thought a dozen times already, probably had it this morning as you tumbled out of your fragrant bed to meet the rim of the sun; well, I'm four times your age, and have a ream more experience, and I still can't think of anything better to sum up the world: life's strange, 's been said, yes. But *think,* boy, how strange: the two of us talking, you coming, me going; me knowing where you've got to go, you suspecting where I've been, and the same destination for both. O strange, very strange. Damn it, you're a deader already if you can't see the strangeness of that, if you can't sniff the poetry; it reeks of it, as of blood. And I've smelt blood, buck. It has a very distinct odor; you know it when you smell it. You're bound for blood; for blood and passion and high deeds and all the rest of the business, and maybe for a little understanding if you're lucky and have eyes to see. Me, I'm bound for nothing, literally. I've come to rest here in Kos, and while the Red Lady spins her web of colors across the sky I sit and weave my own webs of words and dreams and other spider stuff—

What? Yes, I do talk too much; old men like to babble, and philosophy's a cushion for old bones. But it's my profession now, isn't it, and I've promised you a story. What happened to my leg? That's a bloody story, but I said you're bound for blood; I know the mark. I'll tell it to you then; perhaps it'll help you to understand when you reach the narrow place, perhaps it'll even help you to think, although that's a horrible weight to wish on any man. It's customary to notarize my card before I start, keep you from running off at the end without paying. Thank you, young sir. Beware of some of these beggars, buck; they have a credit tally at Central greater than either of us will ever run up. They turn a tidy profit out of poverty. I'm an honest pauper, more's the pity, exist mostly on the subsidy, if you call that existing—Yes, I know. The leg.

We'll have to go back to the Realignment for that, more than half a century ago, and half a sector away, at World. This was before World was a member of the Commonwealth. In fact, that's what the Realignment was about, the old Combine overthrown by the Quaestors, who then opted for amalgamation and forced World into the Commonwealth. That's where and when the story starts.

Start it with waiting.

A lot of things start like that, waiting. And when the thing you're waiting for is probable death, and you're lying there loving life and suddenly noticing how pretty everything is and listening to the flit hooves of darkness click closer, feeling the iron-shod boots strike relentless sparks from the surface of your mind, knowing that death is about to fall out of the sky and that there's no way to twist out from under

—then, waiting can take time. Minutes become hours, hours become unthinkable horrors. Add enough horrors together, total the scaly snouts, and you've got a day and a half I once spent laying up in a mountain valley in the Blackfriars on World, almost the last day I ever spent anywhere.

This was just a few hours after D'kotta. Everything was a mess, nobody really knew what was happening, everybody's communication lines cut. I was just a buck myself then, working with the Quaestors in the field, a hunted criminal. Nobody knew what the Combine would do next, we didn't know what *we'd* do next, groups surging wildly from one place to another at random, panic and riots all over the planet, even in the Controlled Environments.

And D'kotta-on-the-Blackfriars was indescribable, a seventy-mile swath of smoking insanity, capped by boiling umbrellas of smoke that eddied ashes from the ground to the stratosphere and back. At night it pulsed with molten scum, ugly as a lanced blister, lighting up the cloud cover across the entire horizon, visible for hundreds of miles. It was this ugly glow that finally panicked even the zombies in the Environments, probably the first strong emotion in their lives.

It'd been hard to sum up the effects of the battle. We thought that we had the edge, that the Combine was close to breaking, but nobody knew for sure. If they weren't as close to folding as we thought, then we were probably finished. The Quaestors had exhausted most of their hoarded resources at D'kotta, and we certainly couldn't hit the Combine any harder. If they could shrug off the blow then they could wear us down.

Personally, I didn't see how anything could shrug *that* off. I'd watched it all and it'd shaken me considerably. There's an old-time expression, "put the fear of God into him." That's what D'kotta had done for me. There wasn't any God anymore, but I'd seen fire vomit from the heavens and the earth ripped wide for rape, and it'd been an impressive enough surrogate.

Few people ever realized how close the Combine and the Quaestors had come to destroying World between them, there at D'kotta.

We'd crouched that night—the team and I—on the high stone ramparts of the tallest of the Blackfriars, hopefully far away from anything that could fall on us. There were twenty miles of low, gnarly foothills between us and the rolling savannahland where the city of D'kotta had been minutes before, but the ground under our bellies heaved and quivered like a sick animal, and the rock was hot to the touch: feverish.

We could've gotten farther away, should have gotten farther away, but we had to watch. That'd been decided without anyone saying a word, without any question about it. It was impossible *not* to watch. It never even occurred to any of us to take another safer course of action. When reality is being turned inside out like a dirty sock, you watch, or you are less than human. So we watched it all from beginning to end: two hours that became a single second lasting for eons. Like a still photograph of time twisted into a scream—the scream reverberating on forever and yet taking no duration at all to experience.

We didn't talk. We *couldn't* talk—the molecules of the air itself shrieked too loudly, and the deep roar of explosions was a continual drumroll—but we wouldn't have talked even if we'd been able. You don't speak in the presence of an angry God. Sometimes we'd look briefly at each other. Our faces were all nearly identical: ashen, waxy, eyes of glass, blank, and lost as pale driftwood stranded on a beach by the tide. We'd been driven through the gamut of expressions into *extremus–rictus*: faces so contorted and strained they ached—and beyond to the quietus of shock: muscles too slack and flaccid to respond any more. We'd only look at each other for a second, hardly focusing, almost not aware of what we were seeing, and then our eyes would be dragged back as if by magnetism to the Fire.

At the beginning we'd clutched each other, but as the battle progressed we slowly drew apart, huddling into individual agony; the thing so big that human warmth meant nothing, so frightening that the instinct to gather together for protection was reversed, and the presence of others only intensified the realization of how ultimately naked you were. Earlier we'd set up a scattershield to filter the worst of the hard radiation— the gamma and intense infrared and ultraviolet—blunt some of the heat and shock and noise. We thought we had a fair chance of surviving, then, but we couldn't have run anyway. We were fixed by the beauty of horror/horror of beauty, surely as if by a spike driven through our backbones into the rock.

And away over the foothills, God danced in anger, and his feet struck the ground to ash.

What was it like?

Kos still has oceans and storms. Did y'ever watch the sea lashed by high winds? The storm boils the water into froth, whips it white, until it becomes an ocean of ragged lace to the horizon, whirlpools of milk, not a fleck of blue left alive. The land looked like this at D'kotta. The hills *moved*. The Quaestors had a discontinuity projector there, and under its lash the ground stirred like sluggish batter under a baker's spoon; stirred, shuddered, groaned, cracked, broke: acres heaved themselves into new mountains, other acres collapsed into canyons.

Imagine a giant asleep just under the surface of the earth, overgrown by fields, dreaming dreams of rock and crystal. Imagine him moving restlessly, the long rhythm of his dreams touched by nightmare, tossing, moaning, tremors signaling unease in waves up and down his miles-long frame. Imagine him catapulted into waking terror, lurching suddenly to his knees with the bawling roar of ten million burning calves: a steaming claw of rock and black earth raking for the sky. Now, in a wink, imagine the adjacent land hurtling downward, sinking like a rock in a pond, opening a womb a thousand feet wide, swallowing everything and grinding it to powder. Then, almost too quick to see, imagine the mountain and the crater switching, the mountain collapsing all at once and washing the feet of the older Blackfriars with a tidal wave of earth, then tumbling down to make a pit; at the same time the sinking earth at the bottom of the other crater reversing itself and erupting upward into a quaking fist of rubble. Then they switch again, and keep switching. Like watching the same filmclip continuously run forward and backward. Now multiply that by a million and spread it out so that all you can see to the horizon is a stew of humping rock. D'y'visualize it? Not a tenth of it.

Dervishes of fire stalked the chaos, melting into each other, whirlpooling. Occasionally a tactical-nuclear explosion would punch a hole in the night, a brief intense flare that would be swallowed like a candle in a murky snowstorm. Once a tacnuke detonation coincided with the upthrusting of a rubble mountain, with an effect like that of a firecracker exploding inside a swinging sack of grain.

The city itself was gone; we could no longer see a trace of anything man-made, only the stone maelstrom. The river Delva had also vanished, flash-boiled to steam; for a while we could see the gorge of its dry bed stitching across the plain, but then the ground heaved up and obliterated it.

It was unbelievable that anything could be left alive down there. Very little was. Only the remainder of the heavy weapons sections on both sides continued to survive, invisible to us in the confusion. Still protected by powerful phasewalls and scattershields, they pounded blindly at each other—the Combine somewhat ineffectively with biodeths and tacnukes, the Quaestors responding by stepping up the discontinuity projector. There was only one, in the command module—the Quaestor technicians were praying it wouldn't be wiped out by a random strike—and it was a terraforming device and not actually a "weapon" at all, but the Combine had been completely unprepared for it, and were suffering horribly as a result.

Everything began to flicker, random swatches of savannah-land shimmering and blurring, phasing in and out of focus in a jerky, mismatched manner: that filmstrip run through a spastic projector. At first we thought it must be heat eddies caused by the fires, but then the flickering increased drastically in frequency and tempo, speeding up until it was impossible to keep anything in focus even for a second, turning the wide veldt into a mad kaleidoscope of writhing, interchanging shapes and color-patterns from one horizon to the other. It was impossible to watch it for long. It hurt the eyes and filled us with an oily, inexplicable panic that we were never able to verbalize. We looked away, filled with the musty surgings of vague fear.

We didn't know then that we were watching the first practical application of a process that'd long been suppressed by both the Combine and the Commonwealth, a process based on the starship dimensional "drive" (which isn't a "drive" at all, but the word's passed into the common press) that enables a high-cycling discontinuity projector to throw time out of phase within a limited area, so that a spot *here* would be a couple of minutes ahead or behind a spot a few inches away, in continuity sequence. That explanation would give a psychophysicist fits, since "time" is really nothing at all like the way we "experience" it, so the process "really" doesn't do what I've said it does—doing something abstruse[10] instead—but that's close enough to what it does on a practical level, 'cause even if the time distortion is an "illusionary effect"—like the sun seeming to rise and set—they still used it to kill people. So it threw time out of phase, and kept doing it, switching the dislocation at random: so that in any given square foot of land there might be four or five discrepancies in time sequence that kept interchanging. Like, *here* might be one minute "ahead" of the base "now," and then a second later (language breaks down hopelessly under this stuff; you need the math) *here* would be two minutes behind the now, then five minutes behind, then three ahead, and so on. And all the adjacent zones in that square foot are going through the same switching process at the same time (Goddamn this language!). The Combine's machinery tore itself to pieces. So did the people: some died of suffocation because of a five-minute discrepancy between an inhaled breath and oxygen received by the lungs, some drowned in their own blood.

It took about ten minutes, at least as far as we were concerned as unaffected observers. I had a psychophysicist tell me once that "it" had both continued to "happen" forever and had never "happened" at all, and that neither statement canceled out the validity of the other, that *each* statement in fact was both "applicable" and "non-applicable" to the same situation consecutively—and I did not understand. It took ten minutes.

At the end of that time, the world got very still.

We looked up. The land had stopped churning. A tiny star appeared amongst the rubble in the middle distance, small as a pinhead but incredibly bright and clear. It seemed to suck the night into it like a vortex, as if it were a pinprick through the worldstuff into a more intense reality, as if it were gathering a great breath for a shout.

We buried our heads in our arms as one, instinctively.

There was a very bright light, a light that we could feel through the tops of our heads, a light that left dazzling after-images even through closed and shrouded lids. The mountain leaped under us, bounced us into the air again and again, battered us into near unconsciousness. We never even heard the roar.

After a while, things got quiet again, except for a continuous low rumbling. When we looked up, there were thick, sluggish tongues of molten magma oozing up in vast flows across the veldt, punctuated here and there by spectacular shower-fountains of vomited sparks.

Our scattershield had taken the brunt of the blast, borne it just long enough to save our lives, and then overloaded and burnt itself to scrap; one of the first times *that's* ever happened.

Nobody said anything. We didn't look at each other. We just lay there.

The chrono said an hour went by, but nobody was aware of it.

Finally, a couple of us got up, in silence, and started to stumble aimlessly back and forth. One by one, the rest crawled to their feet. Still in silence, still trying not to look at each other, we automatically cleaned ourselves up. You hear someone say "it made me shit my pants," and you think it's an expression; not under the right stimuli. Automatically, we treated our bruises and lacerations, automatically we tidied the camp up, buried the ruined scatterfield generator. Automatically, we sat down again and stared numbly at the lightshow on the savannah.

Each of us knew the war was over—we knew it with the gut rather than the head. It was an emotional reaction, but very calm, very resigned, very passive. It was a thing too big for questioning; it became a self-evident fact. After D'kotta there could be nothing else. Period. The war was over.

We were almost right. But not quite.

In another hour or so a man from field HQ came up over the mountain shoulder in a stolen vacform and landed in camp. The man switched off the vac, jumped down, took two steps toward the parapet overlooking hell, stopped. We saw his stomach muscles jump, tighten. He took a stumbling half-step back, then stopped again. His hand went up to shield his throat, dropped, hesitated, went back up. We said nothing. The HQ directing the D'kotta campaign had been sensibly located behind the Blackfriars: they had been shielded by the mountain-chain and had seen nothing but glare against the cloud cover. This was his first look at the city; at where the city had been. I watched the muscles play in his back, saw his shoulders hunch as if under an upraised fist. A good many of the Quaestor men involved in planning the D'kotta operation committed suicide immediately after the Realignment; a good many didn't. I don't know what category this one belonged in.

The liaison man finally turned his head, dragged himself away. His movements were jerky, and his face was an odd color, but he was under control. He pulled Heynith, our team leader, aside. They talked for a half hour. The liaison man showed Heynith a map, scribbled on a pad for Heynith to see, gave Heynith some papers. Heynith nodded occasionally. The liaison man said good-by, half-ran to his vacform. The vac lifted with an erratic surge, steadied, then disappeared in a long arc over the gnarled backs of the Blackfriars. Heynith stood in the dirtswirl kicked up by the backwash and watched impassively.

It got quiet again, but it was a little more apprehensive.

Heynith came over, studied us for a while, then told us to get ready to move out. We stared at him. He repeated it in a quiet, firm voice; unendurably patient. Hush for a second, then somebody groaned, somebody else cursed, and the spell of D'kotta was partially broken, for the moment. We awoke enough to ready our gear; there was even a little talking, though not much.

Heynith appeared at our head and led us out in a loose travel formation, diagonally across the face of the slope, then up toward the shoulder. We reached the notch we'd found earlier and started down the other side.

Everyone wanted to look back at D'kotta. No one did.

Somehow, it was still night.

We never talked much on the march, of course, but tonight the silence was spooky: you could hear boots crunch on stone, the slight rasp of breath, the muted jangle of knives occasionally bumping against thighs.

You could hear our fear; you could smell it, you could see it.

We could touch it, we could taste it.

I was a member of something so old that they even had to dig up the name for it when they were rooting through the rubble of ancient history, looking for concepts to use against the Combine: a "commando team." Don't ask me what it means, but that's what it's called. Come to think, I know what it means in terms of flesh: it means ugly. Long ugly days and nights that come back in your sleep even uglier, so that you don't want to think about it at all because it squeezes your eyeballs like a vise. Cold and dark and wet, with sudden death looming up out of nothing at any time and jarring you with mortality like a rubber glove full of ice water slapped across your face. Living jittery high all the time, so that everything gets so real that it looks fake. You live in an anticipation that's pain, like straddling a fence with a knifeblade for a top rung, waiting for something to come along in the dark and push you off. You get so you like it. The pain's so consistent that you forget it's there, you forget there ever was a time when you didn't have it, and you live on the adrenalin.

We liked it. We were dedicated. We *hated*. It gave us something to do with our hate, something tangible we could see. And nobody'd done it but us for hundreds of years; there was an exultation to that. The Scholars and Antiquarians who'd started the Quaestor movement—left fullsentient and relatively unwatched so they could better piece together the muddle of prehistory from generations of inherited archives—they'd been smart. They knew their only hope of baffling the Combine was to hit them with radical concepts and tactics, things they didn't have instructions for handling, things out of the Combine's experience. So they scooped concepts out of prehistory, as far back as the archives go, even finding *written* records somewhere and having to figure out how to use them.

Out of one of these things, they got the idea of "guerrilla" war. No, I don't know what that means either, but what it *means* is playing the game by your own rules instead of the enemy's. Oh, you let the enemy keep playing by *his* rules, see, but you play by your own. Gives you a wider range of moves. You *do* things. I mean, *ridiculous* things, but so ancient they don't have any defense against it because they never thought they'd have to defend against *that*. Most of the time they never even knew *that* existed.

Like, we used to run around with these projectile weapons they'd copied from old plans and mass-produced in the autfacs on the sly by stealing computer time. The things worked by a chemical reaction inside the mechanism that would spit these tiny missiles out at high velocity. The missile would hit you so hard it would actually lodge itself in your body, puncture internal organs, kill you. I know it sounds like an absurd concept, but there were advantages.

Don't forget how tightly controlled a society the Combine's was; even worse than the Commonwealth in its own way. We couldn't just steal energy weapons or biodeths and use them, because all those things operated on broadcast power from the Combine, and as soon as one was reported missing the Combine would just cut the relay for that particular code. We couldn't make them ourselves because unless you used the Combine's broadcast power you'd need a ton of generator equipment with each weapon to provide enough energy to operate it, and we didn't have the technology to miniaturize that much machinery. (Later some genius figured out a way to make, say, a functioning biodeth with everything but the energy source and then cut into and tap Combine broadcast power without showing up on the coding board, but that was toward the end anyway, and most of them were stockpiled for the shock troops at D'kotta.) At least the "guns" worked. And there were even un-expected advantages. We found that tanglefields, scat-tershields, phasewalls, personal warders, all the usual defenses, were unable to stop the "bullets" (the little missiles fired by the "guns")—they were just too sophisticated to stop anything as crude as a lump of metal moving at relatively sluggish ballistic speeds. Same with "bombs" and "grenades"—devices designed to have a chemical reaction violent enough to kill in an enclosed place. And the list went on and on. The Combine thought we couldn't move around because all vehicles were coded and worked on broadcast power. Did you ever hear of "bicycles"? They're devices for translating mechanical energy into motion, they ride on wheels that you actually make revolve with physical labor. And the bicycles didn't have enough metal/mass to trigger sentryfields or show up on sweep probes, so we could go undetected to places they thought nobody could reach. Communicate? We used mirrors to flash messages, used puffs of smoke as code, had people actually carry messages from one place to another.

More important, we personalized war. That was the most radical thing, that was the thing that turned us from kids running around and having fun breaking things into men with bitter faces, that was the thing that took the heart out of the Combine more then anything else. That's why people still talk about the Realignment with horror today, even after all these years, especially in the Commonwealth.

We killed people. We did it, ourselves. We walked up and stabbed them. I mentioned a knife before, boy, and I knew you didn't know what it was; you bluff well for a kid—that's the way to a reputation for wisdom: look sage and always keep your mouth shut about your ignorance. Well, a knife is a tapering piece of metal with a handle, sharpened on the sides and very sharp at the tapered end, sharp enough so that when you strike someone with it the metal goes right into their flesh, cuts them, rips them open, *kills* them, and there is blood on your hands which feels wet and sticky and is hard to wash off because it dries and sticks to the little hairs on the backs of your wrists. We learned how to hit people hard enough to kill them, snap the bones inside the skin like dry sticks inside oiled cloth. We did. We strangled them with lengths of wire. You're shocked. So was the Combine. They had grown used to killing at a great distance, the push of a button, the flick of a switch, using vast, clean, impersonal forces to do their annihilation. *We* killed people. We killed *people*—not statistics and abstractions. We heard their screams, we saw their faces, we smelled their blood, and their vomit and shit and urine when their systems let go after death. You have to be crazy to do things like that. We were crazy. We were a good team.

There were twelve of us in the group, although we mostly worked in sections of four. I was in the team leader's section, and it had been my family for more than two years.

Heynith, stocky, balding, leatherfaced; a hard, fair man; brilliant organizer.

Ren, impassive, withdrawn, taciturn, frighteningly competent, of a strange humor.

Goth, young, tireless, bullheaded, given to sudden enthusiasms and depressions; he'd only been with us for about four months, a replacement for Mason, who had been killed while trying to escape from a raid on Cape Itica.

And me.

We were all warped men, emotional cripples one way or the other.

We were all crazy.

The Combine could never understand that kind of craziness, in spite of the millions of people they'd killed or shriveled impersonally over the years. They were afraid of that craziness, they were baffled by it, never could plan to counter it or take it into account. They couldn't really believe it.

That's how we'd taken the Blackfriars Transmitter, hours before D'kotta. It had been impregnable— wrapped in layer after layer of defense fields against missile attack, attack by chemical or biological agents, transmitted energy, almost anything. We'd walked in. They'd never imagined anyone would do that, that it was even possible to attack that way, so there was no defense against it. The guardsystems were designed to meet more esoteric threats. And even after ten years of slowly escalating guerrilla action, they still didn't *really* believe anyone would use his body to wage war. So we walked in. And killed everybody there. The staff was a sentient techclone of ten and an executive foreman. No nulls or zombies. The ten identical technicians milled in panic, the foreman stared at us in disbelief, and what I think was distaste that we'd gone so far outside the bounds of procedure. We killed them like you kill insects, not really thinking about it much, except for that part of you that always thinks about it, that records it and replays it while you sleep. Then we blew up the transmitter with chemical explosives. Then, as the flames leaped up and ate holes in the night, we'd gotten on our bicycles and rode like hell toward the Blackfriars, the mountains hunching and looming ahead, as jagged as black snaggle-teeth against the industrial glare of the sky. A tangle-field had snatched at us for a second, but then we were gone.

That's all that I personally had to do with the "historic" Battle of D'kotta. It was enough. We'd paved the way for the whole encounter. Without the Transmitter's energy, weapons, and transportation systems —including liftshafts, slidewalks, iris-doors, and windows, heating, lighting, waste disposal—were inoperable; D'kotta was immobilized. Without the station's broadcast matter, thousands of buildings, industrial complexes, roadways, and homes had collapsed into chaos, literally collapsed. More important, without broadcast nourishment, D'kotta's four major Cerebrums—handling an incredible complexity of military/industrial/administrative tasks—were knocked out of operation, along with a number of smaller Cerebrums—the synapses need constant nourishment to function, and so do the sophont ganglion units, along with the constant flow of the psychocybernetic current to keep them from going mad from sensory deprivation, and even the nulls would soon grow intractable as hunger stung them almost to self-awareness, finally to die after a few days. Any number of the lowest-ranking sentient clones—all those without stomachs or digestive systems; mostly in the military and industrial castes—would find themselves in the same position as the nulls; without broadcast nourishment they would die within days. And without catarcs in operation to duplicate the function of atrophied intestines, the build-up of body wastes would poison them anyway, even if they could somehow get nourishment. The independent food dispensers for the smaller percentage of fullsentients and higher clones simply could not increase their output enough to feed that many people, even if converted to intravenous systems. To say nothing of the zombies in the Environments scattered throughout the city.

There were backup failsafe systems, of course, but they hadn't been used in centuries, the majority of them had fallen into disrepair and didn't work, and other Quaestor teams made sure the rest of them wouldn't work either.

Before a shot had been fired, D'kotta was already a major disaster.

The Combine had reacted as we'd hoped, as they'd been additionally prompted to react by intelligence reports of Quaestor massings in strength around D'kotta that it'd taken weeks to leak to the Combine from unimpeachable sources. The Combine was pouring forces into D'kotta within hours, nearly the full strength of the traditional military caste and a large percentage of the militia they'd cobbled together out of industrial clones when the Questors had begun to get seriously troublesome, plus a major portion of their heavy armament. They had hoped to surprise the Quaestors, catch them between the city and the inaccessible portion of the Blackfriars, quarter the area with so much strength it'd be impossible to dodge them, run the Quaestors down, annihilate them, break the back of the movement.

It had worked the other way around.

For years the Quaestors had stung and run, always retreating when the Combine advanced, never meeting them in conventional battle, never hitting them with anything really heavy. Then, when the Combine had risked practically all of its military resources on one gigantic effort calculated to be effective against the usual Quaestor behavior, we had suddenly switched tactics. The Quaestors had waited to meet the Combine's advance and had hit the Combine forces with everything they'd been able to save, steal, hoard, and buy clandestinely from sympathizers in the Commonwealth in over fifteen years of conspiracy and campaign aimed at this moment.

Within an hour of the first tacnuke exchange, the city had ceased to exist, everything leveled except two of the Cerebrums and the Escridel Creche. Then the Quaestors activated their terraforming devices, which I believe they bought from a firm here on Kos, as a matter of fact. This was completely insane—terraforming systems used indiscriminately can destroy entire planets—but it was the insanity of desperation, and they did it anyway. Within a half hour, the remaining Combine Heavy Armaments battalions and the two Cerebrums ceased to exist. A few minutes later, the supposedly invulnerable Escridel Creche ceased to exist, the first time in history a creche had ever been destroyed. Then, as the cycling energies got out of hand and filterfeedback built to a climax, everything on the veldt ceased to exist.

The carnage had been inconceivable.

Take the vast population of D'kotta as a base, the second largest city on World, one of the biggest even in this sector of the Commonwealth. The subfleets had been in, bringing the betja harvest and other goods up the Delva; river traffic was always heaviest at that time of year. The mines and factories had been in full swing, and the giant sprawl of the Westernese Shipyards and Engine Works. Add the swarming inhabitants of the six major Controlled Environments that circled the city. Add the city-within-a-city of Admin South, in charge of that hemisphere. Add the twenty generations of D'kotta Combine fullsentients whose discorporate ego-patterns had been preserved in the mountain of "indestructible" micromolecular circuitry called the Escridel Creche. (Those executives had died the irreversible true death, without hope of resurrection this time, even as disembodied intellects housed within artificial mind-environments: the records of their brain's unique pattern of electrical/chemical/psychocybernetic rhythms and balances had been destroyed, and you can't rebuild consciousness from a fused puddle of slag. This hit the Combine where they lived, literally, and had more impact than anything else.) Add the entire strength of both opposing forces; all of our men—who suspected what would happen—had been suicide volunteers. Add all of the elements together.

The total goes up into the multiples of billions.

The number was too big to grasp. Our minds fumbled at it while we marched, and gave up. It was too big.

I stared at Ren's back as we walked, a nearly invisible mannequin silhouette, and tried to multiply that out to the necessary figure. I staggered blindly along, lost and inundated beneath thousands of individual arms, legs, faces; a row of faces blurring off into infinity, all screaming—and the imagining nowhere near the actuality.

Billions.

How many restless ghosts out of that many deaders? Who do they haunt?

Billions.

Dawn caught us about two hours out. It came with no warning, as usual. We were groping through World's ink-dark, moonless night, watched only by the million icy eyes of evening, shreds of witchfire crystal, incredibly cold and distant. I'd watched them night after night for years, scrawling their indecipherable hieroglyphics across the sky, indifferent to man's incomprehension; now, as always, the night sky reminded me of a computer punch card, printed white on black. I stopped for a second on a rise, pushing back the infrared lenses, staring at the sky. What program was printed there, suns for ciphers, worlds for decimal points? An absurd question—I was nearly as foolish as you once, buck—but it was the first fully verbalized thought I'd had since I'd realized the nakedness of flesh, back there on the parapet as my life tore itself apart. I asked it again, half-expecting an answer, watching my breath turn to plumes and tatters, steaming in the silver chill of the stars.

The sun came up like a meteor. It scuttled up from the horizon with that unsettling, deceptive speed that even natives of World never quite get used to. New light washed around us, blue and raw at first, deepening the shadows and honing their edges. The sun continued to hitch itself up the sky, swallowing stars, a watery pink flush wiping the horizon clear of night. The light deepened, mellowed into gold. We floated through silver mist that swirled up around the mountain's knobby knees. I found myself crying silently as I walked the high ridge between mist and sky, absorbing the morning with a new hunger, grappling with a thought that was still too big for my mind and kept slipping elusively away, just out of reach. There was a low hum as our warmsuits adjusted to the growing warmth, polarizing from black to white, bleeding heat back into the air. Down the flanks of the Blackfriars and away across the valley below—visible now as the mists pirouetted past us to the summits—the night plants were dying, shriveling visibly in mile-long swaths of decay. In seconds the Blackfriars were gaunt and barren, turned to hills of ash and bone. The sun was now a bloated yellow disk surrounded by haloes of red and deepening scarlet, shading into the frosty blue of rarefied air. Stripped of softening vegetation, the mountains looked rough and abrasive as pumice, gouged by lunar shadows. The first of the day plants began to appear at our feet, the green spiderwebbing, poking up through cracks in the dry earth.

We came across a new stream, tumbling from melting ice, sluicing a dusty gorge.

An hour later we found the valley.

Heynith led us down onto the marshy plain that rolled away from mountains to horizon. We circled wide, cautiously approaching the valley from the lowlands. Heynith held up his hand, pointed to me, Ren, Goth. The others fanned out across the mouth of the valley, hid, settled down to wait. We went in alone. The speargrass had grown rapidly; it was chest-high. We crawled in, timing our movements to coincide with the long soughing of the morning breeze, so that any rippling of the grass would be taken for natural movement. It took us about a half hour of dusty, sweaty work. When I judged that I'd wormed my way in close enough, I stopped, slowly parted the speargrass enough to peer out without raising my head.

It was a large vacvan, five-hundred-footer, equipped with waldoes for self-loading.

It was parked near the hill flank on the side of the wide valley.

There were three men with it.

I ducked back into the grass, paused to make sure my "gun" was ready for operation, then crawled laboriously nearer to the van.

It was very near when I looked up again, about twenty-five feet away in the center of a cleared space. I could make out the hologram pictograph that pulsed identification on the side: the symbol for Urheim, World's largest city and Combine Seat of Board, half a world away in the Northern Hemisphere. They'd come a long way; still thought of as long, though ships whispered between the stars—it was still long for feet and eyes. And another longer way: from fetuses in glass wombs to men stamping and jiggling with cold inside the fold of a mountain's thigh, watching the spreading morning. That made me feel funny to think about. I wondered if they suspected that it'd be the

last morning they'd ever see. That made me feel fun-
nier. The thought tickled my mind again, danced
away. I checked my gun a second time, needlessly.

I waited, feeling troubled, pushing it down. Two
of them were standing together several feet in front
of the van, sharing a mild narcotic atomizer, sucking
deeply, shuffling with restlessness and cold, staring out
across the speargrass to where the plain opened up.
They had the stiff, rumpled, puff-eyed look of people
who had just spent an uncomfortable night in a
cramped place. They were dressed as fullsentients uncloned, junior officers of the military caste, probably
hereditary positions inherited from their families, as
is the case with most of the uncloned cadet executives.
Except for the cadre at Urheim and other major cities
they must have been some of the few surviving clans-
men; hundreds of thousands of military cadets and
officers had died at D'kotta (along with uncounted
clones and semisentients of all ranks), and the caste
had never been extremely large in the first place. The
by-laws had demanded that the Combine maintain a
Security Force, but it had become mostly traditional
with minimum function, at least among the uncloned
higher ranks, almost the last stronghold of old-
fashioned nepotism. That was one of the things that
had favored the Quaestor uprising, and had forced
the Combine to take the unpopular step of impressing
large levies of industrial clones into a militia. The most
junior of these two cadets was very young, even
younger than me. The third remained inside the van's
cab. I could see his face blurrily through the windfield,
kept on against the cold though the van was no longer
in motion.

I waited. I knew the others were maneuvering into
position around me. I also knew what Heynith was
waiting for.

The third man jumped down from the high cab.
He was older, wore an officer's hologram: a full executive. He said something to the cadets, moved a few
feet toward the back of the van, started to take a piss.

The column of golden liquid steamed in the cold air.

Heynith whistled.

I rolled to my knees, parted the speargrass at the edge of the cleared space, swung my gun up. The two cadets started, face muscles tensing into uncertain fear. The older cadet took an involuntary step forward, still clutching the atomizer. Ren and Goth chopped him down, firing a stream of "bullets" into him. The guns made a very loud metallic rattling sound that jarred the teeth, and fire flashed from the ejector ends. Birds screamed upward all along the mountain flank. The impact of the bullets knocked the cadet off his feet, rolled him so that he came to rest belly-down. The atomizer flew through the air, hit, bounced. The younger cadet leaped toward the cab, right into my line of fire. I pulled the trigger; bullets exploded out of the gun. The cadet was kicked backwards, arms swinging wide, slammed against the side of the cab, jerked upright as I continued to fire, spun along the van wall and rammed heavily into the ground. He tottered on one shoulder for a second, then flopped over on his back. At the sound of the first shot, the executive had whirled—penis still dangling from pantaloons, piss spraying wildly—and dodged for the back of the van, so that Heynith's volley missed and screamed from the van wall, leaving a long scar. The executive dodged again, crouched, came up with a biodeth in one hand and swung right into a single bullet from Ren just as he began to fire. The impact twirled him in a staggering circle, his finger still pressing the trigger; the carrier beam splashed harmlessly from the van wall, traversed as the executive spun, cut a long swath through the speargrass, the plants shriveling and blackening as the beam swept over them. Heynith opened up again before the beam could reach his clump of grass, sending the executive —somehow still on his feet—lurching past the end of the van. The biodeth dropped, went out. Heynith kept firing, the executive dancing bonelessly backwards on his heels, held up by the stream of bullets. Heynith released the trigger. The executive collapsed: a heap of arms and legs at impossible angles.

When we came up to the van, the young cadet was still dying. His body shivered and arched, his heels drummed against the earth, his fingers plucked at nothing, and then he was still. There was a lot of blood.

The others moved up from the valley mouth. Heynith sent them circling around the rim, where the valley walls dipped on three sides.

We dragged the bodies away and concealed them in some large rocks.

I was feeling numb again, like I had after D'kotta.

I continued to feel numb as we spent the rest of the morning in frantic preparation. My mind was somehow detached as my body sweated and dug and hauled. There was a lot for it to do. We had four heavy industrial lasers, rock-cutters; they were clumsy, bulky, inefficient things to use as weapons, but they'd have to do. This mission had not been planned so much as thrown together, only two hours before the liaison man had contacted us on the parapet. Anything that could possibly work at all would have to be made to work somehow; no time to do it right, just do it. We'd been the closest team in contact with the field HQ who'd received the report, so we'd been snatched; the lasers were the only things on hand that could even approach potential as a heavy weapon, so we'd use the lasers.

Now that we'd taken the van without someone alerting the Combine by radio from the cab, Heynith flashed a signal mirror back toward the shoulder of the mountain we'd quitted a few hours before. The liason man swooped down ten minutes later, carrying one of the lasers strapped awkwardly to his platvac. He made three more trips, depositing the massive cylinders as carefully as eggs, then gunned his platvac and screamed back toward the Blackfriars in a maniac arc just this side of suicidal. His face was still gray, tight-pressed lips a bloodless white against ash, and he hadn't said a word during the whole unloading procedure. I think he was probably one of the Quaestors who followed the Way of Atonement. I never saw him again. I've sometimes wished I'd had the courage to follow his example, but I rationalize by telling myself that I have atoned with my life rather than my death, and who knows, it might even be somewhat true. It's nice to think so anyway.

It took us a couple of hours to get the lasers into position. We spotted them in four places around the valley walls, dug slanting pits into the slopes to conceal them and tilt the barrels up at the right angle. The hardest thing was figuring out elevation and trajectory, but we finally got them all zeroed on a spot about a hundred feet above the center of the valley floor, the muzzle arrangement giving each a few degrees of leeway on either side. That's where she'd have to come down anyway if she was a standard orbot, the valley being just wide enough to contain the boat and the vacvan, with a safety margin between them. Of course, if they brought her down on the plain outside the valley mouth, things were going to get very hairy; in that case we might be able to lever one or two of the lasers around to bear, or, failing that, we could try to take the orbot on foot once it's landed, with about one chance in eight to making it. But we thought that they'd land her in the valley; that's where the vacvan had been parked, and they'd want the shelter of the high mountain walls to conceal the orbot from any Quaestor eyes that might be around. If so, that gave us a much better chance. About one out of three.

When the lasers had been positioned, we scatterd, four men to an emplacement, hiding in the camouflaged trenches alongside the big barrels. Heynith led Goth and me toward the laser we'd placed about fifty feet up the mountain flank, directly behind and above the vacvan. Ren stayed behind. He stood next to the the van—shoulders characteristically slouched, thumbs hooked in his belt, face carefully void to expression—and watched us out of sight. Then he looked out over the valley mouth, hitched up his gun, spat in the direction of Urheim and climbed up into the van cab.

The valley was empty again. From our positions the vacvan looked like a shiny toy, sundogs winking across its surface as it baked in the afternoon heat. An abandoned toy, lost in high weeds, waiting in loneliness to be reclaimed by owners who would never come.

Time passed.

The birds we'd frightened away began to settle back onto the hillsides.

I shifted position uneasily, trying half-heartedly to get comfortable. Heynith glared me into immobility. We were crouched in a trench about eight feet long and five feet deep, covered by a camouflage tarpaulin propped open on the valley side by pegs, a couple of inches of vegetation, and topsoil on top of the tarpaulin. Heynith was in the middle, straddling the operator's saddle of the laser. Goth was on his left, I was on his right. Heynith was going to man the laser when the time came; it only took one person. There was nothing for Goth and me to do, would be nothing to do even during the ambush, except take over the firing in the unlikely event that Heynith was killed without the shot wiping out all of us, or stand by to lever the laser around in case that became necessary. Neither was very likely to happen. No, it was Heynith's show, and we were superfluous and unoccupied.

That was bad.

We had a lot of time to think.

That was worse.

I was feeling increasingly numb, like a wall of clear glass had been slipped between me and the world and was slowly thickening, layer by layer. With the thickening came an incredible isolation (isolation though I was cramped and suffocating, though I was jammed up against Heynith's bunched thigh—I couldn't touch him, he was miles away) and with the isolation came a sick, smothering panic. It was the inverse of claustrophobia. My flesh had turned to clear plastic, my bones to glass, and I was naked, ultimately naked, and there was nothing I could wrap me in. Surrounded by an army, I would still be alone; shrouded in iron thirty feet underground, I would still be naked. One portion of my mind wondered dispassionately if I were slipping into shock; the rest of it fought to keep down the scream that gathered along tightening muscles. The isolation increased. I was unaware of my surroundings, except for the heat and the pressure of enclosure.

I was seeing the molten spider of D'kotta, lying on its back and showing its obscene blotched belly, kicking legs of flame against the sky, each leg raising a poison blister where it touched the clouds.

I was seeing the boy, face runneled by blood, beating heels against the ground.

I was beginning to doubt big, simple ideas.

Nothing moved in the valley except wind through grass, spirits circling in the form of birds.

Spider legs.

Crab dance.

The blocky shadow of the vacvan crept across the valley.

Suddenly, with the intensity of vision, I was picturing Ren sitting in the van cab, shoulders resting against the door, legs stretched out along the seat, feet propped up on the instrument board, one ankle crossed over the other, gun resting across his lap, eyes watching the valley mouth through the windfield. He would be smoking a cigarette, and he would take it from his lips occasionally, flick the ashes onto the shiny dials with a fingernail, smile his strange smile, and carefully burn holes in the plush fabric of the upholstery. The fabric (real fabric; not plastic) would smolder, send out a wisp of bad-smelling smoke, and there would be another charred black hole in the seat. Ren would smile again, put the cigarette back in his mouth, lean back, and puff slowly. Ren was waiting to answer the radio signal from the orbot, to assure them that all was well, to talk them down to death. If they suspected anything was wrong, he would be the first to die. Even

if everything went perfectly, he stood a high chance
of dying anyway; he was the most exposed. It was almost certainly a suicide job. Ren said that he didn't
give a shit; maybe he actually didn't. Or at least had
convinced himself that he didn't. He was an odd man.
Older than any of us, even Heynith, he had worked
most of his life as a cadet executive in Admin
at Urheim, devoted his existence to his job, sub-
jugated all of his energies to it. He had been passed
over three times for promotion to executive status,
years of redoubled effort and mounting anxiety between each rejection. With the third failure he had
been quietly retired to live on the credit subsidy he
had earned with forty years of service. The next morning, precisely at the start of his accustomed work period, he stole a biodeth from a security guard in the
Admin Complex, walked into his flowsector, killed
everyone there, and disappeared from Urheim. After
a year on the run, he had managed to contact the
Quaestors. After another year of training, he was serving with a commando team in spite of his age. That
had been five years ago; I had known him for two.
During all that time, he had said little. He did his job
very well with a minimum of waste motion, never
made mistakes, never complained, never showed emotion. But occasionally he would smile and burn a
hole in something. Or someone.

The sun dived at the horizon, seeming to crash into
the plain in an explosion of flame. Night swallowed
us in one gulp. Black as a beast's belly.

It jerked me momentarily back into reality. I had
a bad moment when I thought I'd gone blind, but then
reason returned and I slipped the infrared lenses down
over my eyes, activated them. The world came back
in shades of gray. Heynith was working cramped legs
against the body of the laser. He spoke briefly, and
we gulped some stimulus pills to keep us awake; they
were bitter, and hard to swallow dry as usual, but they
kicked up a familiar acid churning in my stomach,
and blood began to flow faster. I glanced at Heynith.

He'd been quiet, even for Heynith. I wondered what he'd been thinking. He looked at me, perhaps reading the thought, and ordered us out of the trench.

Goth and I crawled slowly out, feeling stiff and brittle, slapped our thighs and arms, stamped to restore circulation. Stars were sprinkling across the sky, salt spilled on black porcelain. I still couldn't read them, I found. The day plants had vanished, the day animals had retreated into catalepsy. The night plants were erupting from the ground, fed by the debris of the day plants. They grew rapidly, doubling, then tripling in height as we watched. They were predominately thick, ropy shrubs with wide, spearhead leaves of dull purple and black, about four feet high. Goth and I dug a number of them up, root-systems intact, and placed them on top of the tarpaulin to replace the day plants that had shriveled with the first touch of bitter evening frost. We had to handle them with padded gloves; the leaf surfaces greedily absorbed the slightest amount of heat and burned like dry ice.

Then we were back in the trench, and it was worse than ever. Motion had helped for a while, but I could feel the numbing panic creeping back, and the momentary relief made it even harder to bear. I tried to start a conversation, but it died in monosyllabic grunts, and silence sopped up the echoes. Heynith was methodically checking the laser controls for the nth time. He was tense; I could see it bunch his shoulder muscles, bulge his calves into rock as they pushed against the footplates of the saddle. Goth looked worse than I did; he was somewhat younger, and usually energetic and cheerful. Not tonight.

We should have talked, spread the pain around; I think all of us realized it. But we couldn't; we were made awkward by our own special intimacy. At one time or another every one of us had reached a point where he *had* to talk or die, even Heynith, even Ren. So we all had talked and all had listened, each of us switching roles sooner or later. We had poured our fears and dreams and secret memories upon each other, until now we knew each other too well. It made us afraid. Each of us was afraid that he had exposed too much, let down too many barriers. We were afraid of vulnerability, of the knife that jabs for the softest fold of the belly. We were all scarred men already, and twice-shy. And the resentment grew that others had seen us that helpless, that vulnerable. So the walls went back up, intensified. And so when we needed to talk again, we could not. We were already too close to risk further intimacy.

Visions returned, ebbing and flowing, overlaying the darkness.

The magma churning, belching a hot breath that stinks of rotten eggs.

The cadet, his face inhuman in the death rictus, blood running down in a wash from his smashed forehead, plastering one eye closed, bubbling at his nostril, frothing around his lips, the lips tautening as his head jerks forward and then backwards, slamming the ground, the lips then growing slack, the body slumping, the mouth sagging open, the rush of blood and phlegm past the tombstone teeth, down the chin and neck, soaking into the fabric of the tunic. The feet drumming at the ground a final time, digging up clots of earth.

I groped for understanding. I had killed people before, and it had not bothered me except in sleep. I had done it mechanically, routine backed by hate, hate cushioned by routine. I wondered if the night would ever end. I remembered the morning I'd watched from the mountain. I didn't think the night would end. A big idea tickled my mind again.

The city swallowed by stone.

The cadet falling, swinging his arms wide.

Why always the cadet and the city in conjunction? Had one sensitized me to the other, and if so, which? I hesitated.

Could both of them be equally important?

One of the other section leaders whistled.

We all started, somehow grew even more tense.

The whistle came again, warbling, sound floating on silence like oil on water. Someone was coming. After a while we heard a rustling and snapping of underbrush approaching downslope from the mountain. Whoever it was, he was making no effort to move quietly. In fact he seemed to be blundering along, bulling through the tangles, making a tremendous thrashing noise. Goth and I turned in the direction of the sound, brought our guns up to bear, primed them. That was instinct. I wondered who could be coming *down* the mountain toward us. That was reason. Heynith twisted to cover the opposite direction, away from the noise, resting his gun on the saddle rim. That was caution. The thrasher passed our position about six feet away, screened by the shrubs. There was an open space ten feet farther down, at the head of a talus bluff that slanted to the valley. We watched it. The shrubs at the edge of the clearing shook, were torn aside. A figure stumbled out into starlight.

It was a null.

Goth sucked in a long breath, let it hiss out between his teeth. Heynith remained impassive, but I could imagine his eyes narrowing behind the thick lenses. My mind was totally blank for about three heartbeats, then, surprised: a null! and I brought the gun barrel up, then, uncomprehending: a null? and I lowered the muzzle. Blank for a second, then: how? and trickling in again: how? Thoughts snarled into confusion, the gun muzzle wavered hesitantly.

The null staggered across the clearing, weaving in slow figure-eights. It almost fell down the talus bluff, one foot suspended uncertainly over the drop, then lurched away, goaded by tropism. The null shambled backward a few paces, stopped, swayed, then slowly sank to its knees.

It kneeled; head bowed, arms limp along the ground, palms up.

Heynith put his gun back in his lap, shook his head. He told us he'd be damned if he could figure out where it came from, but we'd have to get rid of it. It could spoil the ambush if it was spotted. Automatically, I raised my gun, trained it. Heynith stopped me. No noise, he said, not now. He told Goth to go out and kill it silently.

Goth refused. Heynith stared at him speechlessly, then began to flush. Goth and Heynith had had trouble before. Goth was a good man, brave as a bull, but he was stubborn, tended to follow his own lead too much, had too many streaks of sentimentality and touchiness, *thought* too much to be a really efficient cog.

They had disagreed from the beginning, something that wouldn't have been tolerated this long if the Quaestors hadn't been desperate for men. Goth was a devil in a fight when aroused, one of the best, and that had excused him a lot of obstinacy. But he had a curious squeamishness, he hadn't developed the layers of numbing scar-tissue necessary for guerrilla work, and that was almost inevitably fatal. I'd wondered before, dispassionately, how long he would last.

Goth was a hereditary fullsentient, one of the few connected with the Quaestors. He'd been a cadet executive in Admin, gained access to old archives that had slowly soured him on the Combine, been hit at the psychologically right moment by increasing Quaestor agitprop, and had defected; after a two-year proving period, he'd been allowed to participate actively. Goth was one of the only field people who was working out of idealism rather than hate, and that made us distrust him. Heynith also nurtured a traditional dislike for hereditary fullsentients. Heynith had been part of an industrial sixclone for over twenty years before joining the Quaestors. His Six had been wiped out in a production accident, caused by standard Combine negligence. Heynith had been the only survivor. The Combine had expressed mild sympathy, and told him that they planned to cut another clone from him to replace the destroyed Six; he of course would be placed in charge of the new Six, by reason of his seniority. They smiled at him, not seeing any reason why he wouldn't want to work another twenty years with biological replicas of his dead brothers and sisters, the men, additionally, reminders of what he'd been as a youth, unravaged by years of pain. Heynith had thanked them politely, walked out and kept walking, crossing the Voninx Waste on foot to join the Quaestors.

I could see all this working in Heynith's face as he raged at Goth. Goth could feel the hate too, but he stood firm. The null was incapable of doing anybody any harm; he wasn't going to kill it. There'd been enough slaughter. Goth's face was bloodless, and I could see D'kotta reflected in his eyes, but I felt no sympathy for him, in spite of my own recent agonies. He was disobeying orders. I thought about Mason, the man Goth had replaced, the man who had died in my arms at Itica, and I hated Goth for being alive instead of Mason. I had loved Mason. He'd been an Antiquarian in the Urheim archives, and he'd worked for the Quaestors almost from the beginning, years of vital service before his activities were discovered by the Combine. He'd escaped the raid, but his family hadn't. He'd been offered an admin job in Quaestor HQ, but had turned it down and insisted on field work in spite of warnings that it was suicidal for a man of his age. Mason had been a tall, gentle, scholarly man who pretended to be gruff and hard-nosed, and cried alone at night when he thought nobody could see. I'd often thought that he could have escaped from Itica if he'd tried harder, but he'd been worn down, sick and guilt-ridden and tired, and his heart hadn't really been in it; that thought had returned to puzzle me often afterward. Mason had been the only person I'd ever cared about, the one who'd been more responsible than anybody for bringing me out of the shadows and into humanity, and I could have shot Goth at that moment because I thought he was betraying Mason's memory.

Heynith finally ran out of steam, spat at Goth, started to call him something, then stopped and merely glared at him, lips white. I'd caught Heynith's quick glance at me, a nearly invisibile head-turn, just before he'd fallen silent. He'd almost forgotten and called Goth a zombie, a wide-spread expletive on World that had carefully not been used by the team since I'd joined. So Heynith had never really forgotten, though he'd treated me with scrupulous fairness. My fury turned to a cold anger, widened out from Goth to become a sick distaste for the entire world.

Heynith told Goth he would take care of him later, take care of him good, and ordered me to go kill the null, take him upslope and out of sight first, then conceal the body.

Mechanically, I pulled myself out of the trench, started down-slope toward the clearing. Anger fueled me for the first few feet, and I slashed the shrubs aside with padded gloves, but it ebbed quickly, leaving me hollow and numb. I'd known how the rest of the team must actually think of me, but somehow I'd never allowed myself to admit it. Now I'd had my face jammed in it, and coming on top of all the other anguish I'd gone through the last two days, it was too much.

I pushed into the clearing.

My footsteps triggered some response in the null. It surged drunkenly to its feet, arms swinging limply, and turned to face me.

The null was slightly taller than me, built very slender, and couldn't have weighed too much more than a hundred pounds. It was bald, completely hairless. The fingers were shriveled, limp flesh dangling from the club of the hand; the hand never been used. The toes had been developed to enable technicians to walk nulls from one section of the Cerebrum to another, but the feet had never had a chance to toughen or grow callus: they were a mass of blood and lacerations. The nose was a rough blob of pink meat around the nostrils, the ears similarly atrophied. The eyes were enormous, huge milky corneas and small pupils, like those of a nocturnal bird; adapted to the gloom of the Cerebrum, and allowed to function to forestall sensory deprivation; they aren't cut into the psycho-cybernetic current like the synapses or the ganglions. There were small messy wounds on the temples, wrists, and spine-base where electrodes had been torn loose. It had been shrouded in a pajama-like suit of non-conductive material, but that had been torn almost completely away, only a few hanging tatters remaining. There were no sex organs. The flesh under the rib-cage was curiously collapsed; no stomach or digestive tract. The body was covered with bruises, cuts, gashes, extensive swatches sun-baked to second-degree burns, other sections seriously frostbitten or marred by bad coldburns from the night shrubs.

My awe grew, deepened into archetypical dread.

It was from D'kotta, there could be no doubt about it. Somehow it had survived the destruction of its Cerebrum, somehow it had walked through the boiling hell to the foothills, somehow it had staggered up to and over the mountain shoulder. I doubted if there'd be any predilection in its actions: probably it had just walked blindly away from the ruined Cerebrum in a straight line and kept walking. Its actions with the talus bluff demonstrated that; maybe earlier some dim instinct had helped it fumble its way around obstacles in its path, but now it was exhausted, baffled, stymied. It was miraculous that it had made it this far. And the agony it must have suffered on its way was inconceivable. I shivered, spooked. The short hairs bristled on the back of my neck.

The null lurched toward me.

I whimpered and sprang backwards, nearly falling, swinging up the gun.

The null stopped, its head lolling, describing a slow semi-circle. Its eyes were tracking curiously, and I doubted if it could focus on me at all. To it, I must have been a blur of darker gray.

I tried to steady my ragged breathing. It couldn't hurt me; it was harmless, nearly dead anyway. Slowly,

I lowered the gun, pried my fingers from the stock, slung the gun over my shoulder.

I edged cautiously toward it. The null swayed, but remained motionless. Below, I could see the vacvan at the bottom of the bluff, a patch of dull gunmetal sheen. I stretched my hand out slowly. The null didn't move. This close, I could see its gaunt ribs rising and falling with the effort of its ragged breathing. It was trembling, an occasional convulsive spasm shuddering along its frame. I was surprised that it didn't stink; nulls were rumored to have a strong personal odor, at least according to the talk in field camps—bullshit, like so much of my knowledge at that time. I watched it for a minute, fascinated, but my training told me I couldn't stand out here for long; we were too exposed. I took another step, reached out for it, hesitated. I didn't want to touch it. Swallowing my distaste, I selected a spot on its upper arm free of burns or wounds, grabbed it firmly with one hand.

The null jerked at the touch, but made no attempt to strike out or get away. I waited warily for a second, ready to turn my grip into a wrestling hold if it should try to attack. It remained still, but its flesh crawled under my fingers, and I shivered myself in reflex. Satisfied that the null would give me no trouble, I turned and began to force it upslope, pushing it ahead of me.

It followed my shove without resistance, until we hit the first of the night shrubs, then it staggered and made a mewing, inarticulate sound. The plants were burning it, sucking warmth out of its flesh, raising fresh welts, ugly where bits of skin had adhered to the shrubs. I shrugged, pushed it forward. It mewed and lurched again. I stopped. The null's eyes tracked in my direction, and it whimpered to itself in pain. I swore at myself for wasting time, but moved ahead to break a path for the null, dragging it along behind me. The branches slapped harmlessly at my warmsuit as I bent them aside; occasionally one would slip past and lash the null, making it flinch and whimper, but it was spared the brunt of it. I wondered vaguely at my motives for doing it. Why bother to spare someone (some*thing,* I correct nervously) pain when you're going to have to kill him (*it*) in a minute? What difference could it make? I shelved that and concentrated on the movements of my body; the null wasn't heavy, but it wasn't easy to drag it uphill either, especially as it'd stumble and go down every few yards and I'd have to pull it back to its feet again. I was soon sweating, but I didn't care, as the action helped to occupy my mind, and I didn't want to have to face the numbness I could feel taking over again.

We moved upslope until we were about thirty feet above the trench occupied by Heynith and Goth. This looked like a good place. The shrubs were almost chest-high here, tall enough to hide the null's body from an aerial search. I stopped. The null bumped blindly into me, leaned against me, its breath coming in rasps next to my ear. I shivered in horror at the contact. Gooseflesh blossomed on my arms and legs, swept across my body. Some connection sent a memory whispering at my mind, but I ignored it under the threat of rising panic. I twisted my shoulder under the null's weight, threw it off. The null slid back downslope a few feet, almost fell, recovered.

I watched it, panting. The memory returned, gnawing incessantly. This time it got through:

Mason scrambling through the sea-washed rocks of Cape Itica toward the waiting ramsub, while the fire sky-whipping behind picked us out against the shadows; Mason, too slow in vaulting over a stone ridge, balancing too long on the razor-edge in perfect silhouette against the night; Mason jerking upright as a fusor fired from the high cluff puddled his spine, melted his flesh like wax; Mason tumbling down into my arms, almost driving me to my knees; Mason, already dead, heavy in my arms, *heavy in my arms;* Mason torn away from me as a wave broke over us and deluged me in spume; Mason sinking from sight as Heynith screamed for me to come on and I fought my way through the chest-high surf to the ramsub—

That's what supporting the null had reminded me of: Mason, heavy in my arms.

Confusion and fear and nausea.

How could the null make me think of Mason?

Sick self-anger that my mind could compare Mason, gentle as the dream-father I'd never had, to something as disgusting as the null.

Anger novaed, trying to scrub out shame and guilt. I couldn't take it. I let it spill out onto the null.

Growling, I sprang forward, shook it furiously until its head rattled and wobbled on its limp neck, grabbed it by the shoulders and hammered it to its knees.

I yanked my knife out. The blade flamed suddenly in starlight.

I wrapped my hand around its throat to tilt its head back.

Its flesh was warm. A pulse throbbed under my palm.

All at once, my anger was gone, leaving only nausea.

I suddenly realized how cold the night was. Wind bit to the bone.

It was looking at me.

I suppose I'd been lucky. Orphans aren't as common as they once were—not in a society where reproduction has been relegated to the laboratory, but they still occur with fair regularity. I had been the son of an uncloned junior executive who'd run up an enormous credit debit, gone bankrupt, and been forced into insolvency. The Combine had cut a clone from him so that their man/hours would make up the bank discrepancy, burned out the higher levels of his brain and put him in one of the nonsentient penal Controlled Environments. His wife was also cloned, but avoided brainscrub and went back to work in a lower capacity in Admin. I, as a baby, then became a ward of the State and was sent to one of the institutional Environments. Imagine an endless series of low noises, repeating over and over again forever, no high or low spots, everything level: MMMMMMMMMMMMMMM MMMMMMMMMMMMMMMMMMMMMMMMMMMMMM MMMMMM. Like that. That's the only way to describe the years in the Environments. We were fed, we were kept warm, we worked on conveyor belts piecing together miniaturized equipment, we were put to sleep electronically, we woke with our fingers already busy in the monotonous, rhythmical motions that we couldn't remember learning, motions we had repeated a million times a day since infancy. Once a day we were fed a bar of food-concentrates and vitamins. Occasionally, at carefully calculated intervals, we would be exercised to keep up muscle tone. After reaching puberty, we were occasionally masturbated by electric stumulation, the seed saved for sperm banks. The administrators of the Environment were not cruel; we almost never saw them. Punishment was by machine shocks; never severe, very rarely needed. The excutives had no need to be cruel. All they needed was MMMMMMM MMMMMMMMMMMMMMMMMMMMMMMM. We had been taught at some early stage, probably by shock and stimulation, to put the proper part in the proper slot as the blocks of equipment passed in front of us. We had never been taught to talk, although an extremely limited language of several mood-sounds had independently developed among us; the executives never spoke on the rare intervals when they came to check the machinery that regulated us. We had never been told who we were, where we were; we had never been told anything. We didn't care about any of these things, the concepts had never formed in our minds, we were only semi-conscious at best anyway. There was nothing but MMMMMMMMMMMMMMMMMMMM MMMM. The executives weren't concerned with our spiritual development, there was no graduation from the Environment; there was no place else for us to go in a rigidly stratified society. The Combine had discharged its obligation by keeping us alive, in a place where we could even be minimally useful. Though our

jobs were sinecures that could have been more efficiently performed by computer, they gave the expense
of our survival a socially justifiable excuse, they put us
comfortably in a pigeon-hole. We were there for life.
We would grow up from infancy, grow old, and die,
bathed in MMMMMMMMMMMMMMMMMMMMMMM.
The first real, separate and distinct memory of my life
is when the Quaestors raided the Environment, when
the wall of the assembly chamber suddenly glowed red,
buckled, collapsed inward, when Mason pushed out of
the smoke and debris-cloud, gun at the ready, and
walked slowly toward me. That's hindsight. At the
time, it was only a sudden invasion of incomprehen-
sible sounds and lights and shapes and colors, too
much to possibly comprehend, incredibly alien. It was
the first discordant note ever struck in our lives: MM
MMMMMMMMM!!!! shattering our world in an instant, plunging us into another dimension of existence. The Quaestors kidnaped all of us, loaded us onto
vacvans, took us into the hills, tried to undo some of
the harm. That'd been six years ago. Even with the
facilities available at the Quaestor underground complex—hypno-trainers and analysis computers to plunge
me back to childhood and patiently lead me out again
step by step for ten thousand years of subjective time,
while my body slumbered in stasis—even with all of
that, I'd been lucky to emerge somewhat sane. The
majority had died, or been driven into catalepsy. I'd
been lucky even to be a Ward of the State, the way
things had turned out. Lucky to be a zombie. I could
have been a low-ranked clone, without a digestive
system, tied forever to the Combine by unbreakable
strings. Or I could have been one of the thousands of
tank-grown creatures whose brains are used as
organic-computer storage banks in the Cerebrum ge-
stalts, completely unsentient: I could have been a null.

Enormous eyes staring at me, unblinking.

Warmth under my fingers.

I wondered if I was going to throw up.

Wind moaned steadily through the valley with a sound like MMMMMMMMMMMMMM.

Heynith hissed for me to hurry up, sound riding the wind, barely audible. I shifted my grip on the knife. I was telling myself: it's never been really sentient anyway. Its brain has only been used as a computer unit for a biological gestalt, there's no individual intelligence in there. It wouldn't make any difference. I was telling myself: it's dying anyway from a dozen causes. It's in pain. It would be kinder to kill it.

I brought up the knife, placing it against the null's throat. I pressed the point in slowly, until it was pricking flesh.

The null's eyes tracked, focused on the knifeblade.

My stomach turned over. I looked away, out across the valley. I felt my carefully created world trembling and blurring around me, I felt again on the point of being catapulted into another level of comprehension, previously unexpected. I was afraid.

The vacvan's headlights flashed on and off, twice.

I found myself on the ground, hidden by the ropy shrubs. I had dragged the null down with me, without thinking about it, pinned him flat to the ground, arm over back. That had been the signal that Ren had received a call from the orbot, had given it the proper radio code reply to bring it down. I could imagine him grinning in the darkened cab as he worked the instruments.

I raised myself on an elbow, jerked the knife up, suspending it while I looked for the junction of spine and neck that would be the best place to strike. If I was going to kill him (*it*), I would have to kill him (*it!*) now. In quick succession, like a series of slides, like a computer equation running, I got: D'kotta—the cadet—Mason—the null. *It* and *him* tumbled in selection. Came up *him*. I lowered the knife. I couldn't do it. He was human. Everybody was.

For better or worse, I was changed. I was no longer the same person.

I looked up. Somewhere up there, hanging at the

edge of the atmosphere, was the tinsel collection of forces in opposition called a starship, delicately invulnerable as an iron butterfly. It would be phasing in and out of "reality" to hold its position above World, maintaining only the most tenuous of contacts with this continuum. It had launched an orbot, headed for a rendezvous with the vacvan in this valley. The orbot was filled with the gene cultures that could be used to create hundreds of thousands of nonsentient clones who could be imprinted with behavior patterns and turned into computer-directed soldiers; crude but effective. The orbot was filled with millions of tiny metal blocks, kept under enormous compression: when released from tension, molecular memory would reshape them into a wide range of weapons needing only a powersource to be functional. The orbot was carrying, in effect, a vast army and its combat equipment, in a form that could be transported in a five hundred-foot vacvan and slipped into Urheim, where there were machines that could put it into use. It was the Combine's last chance, the second wind they needed in order to survive. It had been financed and arranged by various industrial firms in the Commonwealth who had vested interests in the Combine's survival on World. The orbot's cargo had been assembled and sent off before D'kotta, when it had been calculated that the reinforcements would be significant in insuring a Combine victory; now it was indispensable. D'kotta had made the Combine afraid that an attack on Urheim might be next, that the orbot might be intercepted by the Quaestors if the city was under siege when it tried to land. So the Combine had decided to land the orbot elsewhere and sneak the cargo in. The Blackfriars had been selected as a rendezvous, since it was unlikely the Quaestors would be on the alert for Combine activity in that area so soon after D'kotta, and even if stopped, the van might be taken for fleeing survivors and ignored. The starship had been contacted by esper in route, and the change in plan made.

Four men had died to learn of the original plan.

Two more had died in order to learn of the new landing site and get the information to the Quaestors in time.

The orbot came down.

I watched it as in a dream, coming to my knees, head above the shrubs. The null stirred under my hand, pushed against the ground, sat up.

The orbot was a speck, a dot, a ball, a toy. It was gliding silently in on gravs, directly overhead.

I could imagine Heynith readying the laser, Goth looking up and chewing his lip the way he always did in stress. I knew that my place should be with them, but I couldn't move. Fear and tension were still there, but they were under glass. I was already emotionally drained. I could sum up nothing else, even to face death.

The orbot had swelled into a huge, spherical mountain. It continued to settle, toward the spot where we'd calculated it must land. Now it hung just over the valley center, nearly brushing the mountain walls on either side. The orbot filled the sky, and I leaned away from it instinctively. It dropped lower—

Heynith was the first to fire.

An intense beam of light erupted from the ground downslope, stabbed into the side of the orbot. Another followed from the opposite side of the valley, then the remaining two at once. The orbot hung, transfixed by four steady, unbearably bright columns.

For a while, it seemed as if nothing was happening.

I could imagine the consternation aboard the orbot as the pilot tried to reverse gravs in time.

The boat's hull had become cherry-red in four widening spots. Slowly, the spots turned white.

I could hear the null getting up beside me, near enough to touch. I had risen automatically, shading eyes against glare.

The orbot exploded.

The reactor didn't go, of course; they're built so that can't happen. It was just the conventional auxiliary engines, used for steering and for powering internal systems. But that was enough.

Imagine a building humping itself into a giant stone fist, and bringing that fist down on you: *squash*. Pain so intense that it snuffs your consciousness before you can feel it.

Warned by instinct, I had time to do two things. I thought, distinctly: so night will never end.

And I stepped in front of the null to shield him. Then I was kicked into oblivion.

I awoke briefly to agony, world a solid, blank red. Very, very far away, I could hear someone screaming. It was me.

I awoke again. The pain had lessened. I could see. It was day, and the night plants had died. The sun was dazzling on bare rock. The null was standing over me, seeming to stretch up for miles into the sky. I screamed in preternatural terror. The world vanished.

The next time I opened my eyes, the sky was heavily overcast and it was raining, one of those torrential southern downpours. A Quaestor medic was doing something to my legs, and there was a platvac nearby. The null was lying on his back a few feet away, a bullet in his chest. His head was tilted up toward the scuttling gray clouds. His eyes mirrored the rain.

That's what happened to my leg. So much nerve tissue destroyed that they couldn't grow me a new one, and I had to put up with this stiff prosthetic. But I got used to it. I considered it my tuition fee.

I'd learned two things; that everybody is human, and that the universe doesn't care one way or the other; only people do. The universe just doesn't give a damn. Isn't that wonderful? Isn't that a relief? It isn't out to get you, and it isn't going to help you either. You're on your own. We all are, and we all have to answer to ourselves. We make our own heavens and hells; we can't pass the buck any further. How much easier when we could blame our guilt or good-ness on God.

Oh, I could read supernatural significance into it all—that I was Spared because I'd spared the null, that some benevolent force was rewarding me—but what about Goth? Killed, and if he hadn't balked in the first place, the null wouldn't have stayed alive long enough for me to be entangled. What about the other team members, all dead—wasn't there a man among them as good as me and as much worth saving? No, there's a more direct reason why I survived. Prompted by the knowledge of his humanity, I had shielded him from the explosion. Three other men survived the ex-plosion, but they died from exposure in the hours before the med team got there, baked to death by the sun. I didn't die because the null stood over me during the hours when the sun was rising and frying the rocks, *and his shadow shielded me from the sun.* I'm not saying that he consciously figured that out, deliberately shielded me (though who knows), but I had given him the only warmth he'd known in a long nightmare of pain, and so he remained by me when there was nothing stopping him from running away—and it came to the same result. You don't need intelligence or words to respond to empathy, it can be communi-cated through the touch of fingers—you know that if you've ever had a pet, ever been in love. So that's why I was spared, warmth for warmth, the same reason anything good ever happens in this life. When the med team arrived, they shot the null down because they thought it was trying to harm me. So much for super-natural rewards for the Just.

So, empathy's the thing that binds life together; it's the flame we share against fear. Warmth's the only answer to the old cold questions.

So I went through life, boy; made mistakes, did a lot of things, got kicked around a lot more, loved a little and ended up on Kos, waiting for evening.

But night's a relative thing. It always ends. It does;

because even if you're not around to watch it, the sun always comes up, and someone'll be there to see.

It's a fine, beautiful morning.

It's always a beautiful morning somewhere, even on the day you die.

You're young—that doesn't comfort you yet.

But you'll learn.

The Sliced-Crosswise Only-on-Tuesday World

PHILIP JOSÉ FARMER

In *New Dimensions'* first year—and for that matter throughout my entire tenure as editor—relatively few submissions came in from the writers I thought of as Old Pros, the ones who had been doing the most notable work of the early 1950's when my own tastes in science fiction were being formed. Publishing newcomers like Dozois and Le Guin and Disch was fun, but I yearned to see some manuscripts from the likes of Vance and Dick and Bester and Farmer and Sheckley and my other heroes of 1952–54.

The only one who actually did send anything was Farmer, who early in 1970 sent me an ingenious and oddly moving little piece, marred only by some patches of blurry dialog and a few bits of heavy-handed exposition. I asked him to do some minor retouching, and three days later he sent me a sheaf of insert sheets, neatly handling the revisions I had requested and throwing in a few improvements that had occurred to him upon second look at the manuscript. Thus it is with Old Pros; and that's how they get to be Old Pros. The story provided a usefully big name for the contents page of the first *New Dimensions,* and went on to be selected for two best-science-fiction-of-the-year anthologies.

GETTING INTO WEDNESDAY WAS ALMOST IMPOSSIBLE.

Tom Pym had thought about living on other days
of the week. Almost everybody with any imagination
did. There were even TV shows speculating on this.
Tom Pym had even acted in two of these. But he had
no genuine desire to move out of his own world. Then
his house burned down.

This was on the last day of the eight days of spring.
He awoke to look out the door at the ashes and the
firemen. A man in a white asbestos suit motioned for
him to stay inside. After fifteen minutes, another man
in a suit gestured that it was safe. He pressed the button by the door, and it swung open. He sank down in
the ashes to his ankles; they were a trifle warm under
the inch-thick coat of water-soaked crust.

There was no need to ask what had happened, but
he did, anyway.

The fireman said, "A short-circuit, I suppose. Actually, we don't know. It started shortly after midnight,
between the time that Monday quit and we took over."

Tom Pym thought it must must be strange to be
a fireman or a policeman. Their hours are so different,
even though they were still limited by the walls of
midnight.

By then the others were stepping out of their stoners
or "coffins" as they were often called. That left sixty
still occupied.

They were due for work at 08:00. The problem
of getting new clothes and a place to live would have
to be put off until off-hours, because the TV studio
where they worked was behind in the big special it
was due to put on in 144 days.

They ate breakfast at an emergency center. Tom
Pym asked a grip if he knew of any place he could
stay. Though the government would find one for him,
it might not look very hard for a convenient place.

The grip told him about a house only six blocks
from his former house. A makeup man had died,
and as far as he knew the vacancy had not been filled.
Tom got onto the phone at once, since he wasn't

needed at the moment, but the office wouldn't be open until ten, as the recording informed him. The recording was a very pretty girl with red hair, tourmaline eyes, and a very sexy voice. Tom would have been more impressed if he had not known her. She had played some small parts in two of his shows, and the maddening voice was not hers. Neither was the color of her eyes.

At noon he called again, getting through after a ten minute wait, and asked Mrs. Bellefield if she would put through a request for him. Mrs. Bellefield reprimanded him for not having phoned sooner; she was not sure that anything could be done today. He tried to tell her his circumstances and then gave up. Bureaucrats! That evening he went to a public emergency place, slept for the required four hours while the inductive field speeded up his dreaming, woke up, and got into the upright cylinder of eternium. He stood for ten seconds, gazing out through the transparent door at other cylinders with their still figures, and then he pressed the button. Approximately fifteen seconds later he became unconscious.

He had to spend three more nights in the public stoner. Three days of fall were gone; only five left. Not that that mattered in California so much. When he had lived in Chicago, winter was like a white blanket being shaken by a madwoman. Spring was a green explosion. Summer was a bright roar and a hot breath. Fall was the topple of a drunken jester in garish motley.

The fourth day, he received notice that he could move into the very house he had picked. This surprised and pleased him. He knew of a dozen who had spent a whole year—forty-eight days or so—in a public station while waiting. He moved in the fifth day with three days of spring to enjoy. But he would have to use up his two days off to shop for clothes, bring in groceries and other goods, and get acquainted with his housemates. Sometimes, he wished he had not been born with the compulsion to act. TV'ers worked five days at a stretch, sometimes six, while a plumber, for instance, only put in three days out of seven.

The house was as large as the other, and the six extra blocks to walk would be good for him. It held eight people per day, counting himself. He moved in that evening, introduced himself, and got Mabel Curta, who worked as a secretary for a producer, to fill him in on the household routine. After he made sure that his stoner had been moved into the stoner room, he could relax somewhat.

Mabel Curta had accompanied him into the stoner room, since she had appointed herself his guide. She was a short, overly curved woman of about thirty-five (Tuesday time). She had been divorced three times, and marriage was no more for her unless, of course, Mr. Right came along. Tom was between marriages himself, but he did not tell her so.

"We'll take a look at your bedroom," Mabel said. "It's small but it's soundproofed, thank God."

He started after her, then stopped. She looked back through the doorway and said, "What is it?"

"This girl . . ."

There were sixty-three of the tall gray eternium cylinders. He was looking through the door of the nearest at the girl within.

"Wow! Really beautiful!"

If Mabel felt any jealousy, she suppressed it.

"Yes, isn't she!"

The girl had long, black, slightly curly hair, a face that could have launched him a thousand times times a thousand times, a figure that had enough but not too much, and long legs. Her eyes were open; in the dim light they looked a purplish-blue. She wore a thin silvery dress.

The plate by the top of the door gave her vital data. Jennie Marlowe. Born 2031 A.D., San Marino, California. She would be twenty-four years old. Actress. Unmarried. Wednesday's child.

"What's the matter?" Mabel said.

"Nothing."

How could he tell her that he felt sick in his stomach from a desire that could never be satisfied? Sick from beauty?

> For will in us is over-ruled by fate.
> Who ever loved, that loved not at first sight?

"What?" Mabel said, and then, after laughing, "You must be kidding!"

She wasn't angry. She realized that Jennie Marlowe was no more competition than if she were dead. She was right. Better for him to busy himself with the living of this world. Mabel wasn't too bad, cuddly, really, and, after a few drinks, rather stimulating.

They went downstairs afterward after 18:00 to the TV room. Most of the others were there, too. Some had their ear plugs in; some were looking at the screen but talking. The newscast was on, of course. Everybody was filling up on what had happened last Tuesday and today. The Speaker of the House was retiring after his term was up. His days of usefulness were over and his recent ill health showed no signs of disappearing. There was a shot of the family graveyard in Mississippi with the pedestal reserved for him. When science someday learned how to rejuvenate, he would come out of stonerment.

"That'll be the day!" Mabel said. She squirmed on his lap.

"Oh, I think they'll crack it," he said. "They're already on the track; they've succeeded in stopping the aging of rabbits."

"I don't mean that," she said. "Sure, they'll find out how to rejuvenate people. But then what? You think they're going to bring them all back? With all the people they got now and then they'll double, maybe triple, maybe quadruple, the population? You think they won't just leave them standing out there?" She giggled, and said, "What would the pigeons do without them?"

He squeezed her waist. At the same time, he had a

vision of himself squeezing *that* girl's waist. Hers would be soft enough but with no hint of fat.

Forget about her. Think of now. Watch the news.

A Mrs. Wilder had stabbed her husband and then herself with a kitchen knife. Both had been stonered immediately after the police arrived, and they had been taken to the hospital. An investigation of a work slowdown in the county government offices was taking place. The complaints were that Monday's people were not setting up the computers for Tuesday's. The case was being referred to the proper authorities of both days. The Ganymede base reported that the Great Red Spot of Jupiter was emitting weak but definite pulses that did not seem to be random.

The last five minutes of the program was a precis devoted to outstanding events of the other days. Mrs. Cuthmar, the housemother, turned the channel to a situation comedy with no protests from anybody.

Tom left the room, after telling Mabel that he was going to bed early—alone, and to sleep. He had a hard day tomorrow.

He tiptoed down the hall and the stairs and into the stoner room. The lights were soft, there were many shadows, and it was quiet. The sixty-three cylinders were like ancient granite columns of an underground chamber of a buried city. Fifty-five faces were white blurs behind the clear metal. Some had their eyes open; most had closed them while waiting for the field radiated from the machine in the base. He looked through Jennie Marlowe's door. He felt sick again. Out of his reach; never for him. Wednesday was only a day away. No, it was only a little less than four and a half hours away.

He touched the door. It was slick and only a little cold. She stared at him. Her right forearm was bent to hold the strap of a large purse. When the door opened, she would step out, ready to go. Some people took their showers and fixed their faces as soon as they got up from their sleep and then went directly into the stoner. When the field was automatically radiated at

05:00, they stepped out a minute later, ready for the day.

He would like to step out of his "coffin", too, at the same time.

But he was barred by Wednesday.

He turned away. He was acting like a sixteen-year-old kid. He had been sixteen about one hundred and six years ago, not that that made any difference. Physiologically, he was thirty.

As he started up to the second floor, he almost turned around and went back for another look. But he took himself by his neck-collar and pulled himself up to his room. There he decided he would get to sleep at once. Perhaps he would dream about her. If dreams were wish-fulfillments, they would bring her to him. It still had not been "proved" that dreams always expressed wishes, but it had been proved that man deprived of dreaming did go mad. And so the somnium radiated a field that put man into a state in which he got all the sleep, and all the dreams, that he needed within a four-hour period. Then he was awakened and a little later went into the stoner where the field suspended all atomic and subatomic activity. He would remain in that state forever unless the activating field came on.

He slept, and Jennie Marlowe did not come to him. Or if she did, he did not remember. He awoke, washed his face, went down eagerly to the stoner where he found the entire household standing around, getting in one last smoke, talking, laughing. Then they would step into their cylinders and a silence like that at the heart of a mountain would fall.

He had often wondered what would happen if he did not go into the stoner. How would he feel? Would he be panicked? All his life, he had known only Tuesdays. Would Wednesday rush at him, roaring, like a tidal wave? Pick him up and hurl him against the reefs of a strange time?

What if he made some excuse and went back upstairs and did not go back down until the field had come on? By then, he could not enter. The door to his cylinder would not open again until the proper time. He could still run down to the public emergency stoners only three blocks away. But if he stayed in his room, waiting for Wednesday . . .

Such things happened. If the breaker of the law did not have a reasonable excuse, he was put on trial. It was a felony second only to murder to "break time," and the unexcused were stoned. All felons, sane or insane, were stoned. Or *mañanaed,* as some said. The *mañanaed* criminal waited in immobility and unconsciousness, preserved unharmed until science had techniques to cure the insane, the neurotic, the criminal, the sick. *Mañana*.

"What was it like in Wednesday?" Tom had asked a man who had been unavoidably left behind because of an accident.

"How would I know? I was knocked out except for about fifteen minutes. I was in the same city, and I had never seen the faces of the ambulance men, of course, but then I've never seen them here. They stonered me and left me in the hospital for Tuesday to take care of." .

He must have it bad, he thought. Bad. Even to think of such a thing was crazy. Getting into Wednesday was almost impossible. Almost. But it could be done. It would take time and patience, but it could be done.

He stood in front of his stoner for a moment. The others said, "See you! So long! Next Tuesday!" Mabel called, "Good night, lover!"

"Good night," he muttered.

"What?" she shouted.

"Good night!"

He glanced at the beautiful face behind the door. Then he smiled. He had been afraid that she might hear him say good night to a woman who called him lover.

He had ten minutes left. The intercom alarms were

whooping. Get going, everybody! Time to take the six-day trip! Run! Remember the penalties!

He remembered, but he wanted to leave a message. The recorder was on a table. He activated it, and said, "Dear *Miss* Jennie Marlowe. My name is Tom Pym, and my stoner is next to yours. I am an actor, too; in fact, I work at the same studio as you. I know this is presumptuous of me, but I have never seen anybody so beautiful. Do you have a talent to match your beauty? I would like to see some run-offs of your shows. Would you please leave some in room five? I'm sure the occupant won't mind. Yours, Tom Pym."

He ran it back. It was certainly bald enough, and that might be just what was needed. Too flowery or too pressing would have made her leery. He had commented on her beauty twice but not overstressed it. And the appeal to her pride in her acting would be difficult to resist. Nobody knew better than he about that.

He whistled a little on his way to the cylinder. Inside, he pressed the button and looked at his watch. Five minutes to midnight. The light on the huge screen above the computer in the police station would not be flashing for him. Ten minutes from now, Wednesday's police would step out of their stoners in the precinct station, and they would take over their duties.

There was a ten-minute hiatus between the two days in the police station. All hell could break loose in these few minutes and it sometimes did. But a price had to be paid to maintain the walls of times.

He opened his eyes. His knees sagged a little and his head bent. The activation was a million micro-seconds fast—from eternium to flesh and blood almost instantaneously and the heart never knew that it had been stopped for such a long time. Even so, there was a little delay in the muscles' response to a standing position.

He pressed the button, opened the door, and it was

as if his button had launched the day. Mabel had made herself up last night so that she looked dawn-fresh. He complimented her and she smiled happily. But he told her he would meet her for breakfast. Half-way up the staircase, he stopped, and waited until the hall was empty. Then he sneaked back down and into the stoner room. He turned on the recorder.

A voice, husky but also melodious, said, "Dear Mister Pym. I've had a few messages from other days. It was fun to talk back and forth across the abyss between the worlds, if you don't mind my exaggerating a little. But there is really no sense in it, once the novelty has worn off. If you become interested in the other person, you're frustrating yourself. That person can only be a voice in a recorder and a cold waxy face in a metal coffin. I wax poetic. Pardon me. If the person doesn't interest you, why continue to communicate? There is no sense in either case. And I *may* be beautiful. Anyway, I thank you for the compliment, but I am also sensible.

"I should have just not bothered to reply. But I want to be nice; I didn't want to hurt your feelings. So please don't leave any more messages."

He waited while silence was played. Maybe she was pausing for effect. Now would come a chuckle or a low honey-throated laugh, and she would say, "However, I don't like to disappoint my public. The run-offs are in your room."

The silence stretched out. He turned off the machine and went to the dining room for breakfast.

Siesta time at work was from 14:40 to 14:45. He lay down on the bunk and pressed the button. Within a minute he was asleep. He did dream of Jennie this time; she was a white shimmering figure solidifying out of the darkness and floating toward him. She was even more beautiful than she had been in her stoner.

The shooting ran overtime that afternoon so that he got home just in time for supper. Even the studio would not dare keep a man past his supper hour, especially since the studio was authorized to serve food only at noon.

He had time to look at Jennie for a minute before Mrs. Cuthmar's voice screeched over the intercom. As he walked down the hall, he thought, "I'm getting barnacled on her. It's ridiculous. I'm a grown man. Maybe . . . maybe I should see a psycher."

Sure, make your petition, and wait until a psycher has time for you. Say about three hundred days from now, if you are lucky. And if the psycher doesn't work out for you, then petition for another, and wait six hundred days.

Petition. He slowed down. Petition. What about a request, not to see a psycher, but to move? Why not? What did he have to lose? It would probably be turned down, but he could at least try.

Even obtaining a form for the request was not easy. He spent two nonwork days standing in line at the Center City Bureau before he got the proper forms. The first time, he was handed the wrong form and had to start all over again. There was no line set aside for those who wanted to change their days. There were not enough who wished to do this to justify such a line. So he had had to queue up before the Miscellaneous Office counter of the Mobility Section of the Vital Exchange Department of the Interchange and Cross Transfer Bureau. None of these titles had anything to do with emigration to another day.

When he got his form the second time, he refused to move from the office window until he had checked the number of the form and asked the clerk to double-check it. He ignored the cries and the mutterings behind him. Then he went to one side of the vast room and stood in line before the punch machines. After two hours, he got to sit down at a small rolltop desk-shaped machine, above which was a large screen. He inserted the form into the slot, looked at the projection of the form, and punched buttons to mark the proper spaces opposite the proper questions. After that, all he had to do was to drop the form into a slot and hope it did not get lost. Or hope he would not have to go through the same procedure because he had improperly punched the form.

That evening, he put his head against the hard metal and murmured to the rigid face behind the door, "I must really love you to go through all this. And you don't even know it. And, worse, if you did, you might not care one bit."

To prove to himself that he had kept his gray stuff he went out with Mabel that evening to a party given by Sol Voremwolf, a producer. Voremwolf had just passed a civil service examination giving him an A-13 rating. This meant that, in time, with some luck and the proper pull, he would become an executive vice-president of the studio.

The party was a qualified success. Tom and Mabel returned about half an hour before stoner time. Tom had managed to refrain from too many blowminds and liquor, so he was not tempted by Mabel. Even so, he knew that when he became unstonered, he would be half-loaded and he'd have to take some dreadful counter-activities. He would look and feel like hell at work, since he had missed his sleep.

He put Mabel off with an excuse, and went down to the stoner room ahead of the others. Not that that would do him any good if he wanted to get stonered early. The stoners only activated within narrow time limits.

He leaned against the cylinder and patted the door. "I tried not to think about you all evening. I wanted to be fair to Mabel, it's not fair to go out with her and think about you all the time."

All's fair in love . . .

He left another message for her, then wiped it out. What was the use? Besides, he knew that his speech was a little thick. He wanted to appear at his best for her.

Why should he? What did she care for him?

The answer was, he did care, and there was no reason or logic connected with it. He loved this forbidden, untouchable, faraway-in-time, yet-so-near woman.

Mabel had come in silently. She said, "You're sick!"

Tom jumped away. Now why had he done that? He had nothing to be ashamed of. Then why was he so angry with her? His embarrassment was understandable but his anger was not.

Mabel laughed at him, and he was glad. Now he could snarl at her. He did so, and she turned away and walked out. But she was back in a few minutes with the others. It would soon be midnight.

By then he was standing inside the cylinder. A few seconds later, he left it, pushed Jennie's backward on its wheels, and pushed his around so that it faced hers. He went back in, pressed the button, and stood there. The double doors only slightly distorted his view. But she seemed even more removed in distance, in time, and in attainability.

Three days later, well into winter, he received a letter. The box inside the entrance hall buzzed just as he entered the front door. He went back and waited until the letter was printed and had dropped out from the slot. It was the reply to his request to move to Wednesday.

Denied. Reason: he had no reasonable reason to move.

That was true. But he could not give his real motive. It would have been even less impressive than the one he had given. He had punched the box opposite No. 12. REASON: TO GET INTO AN ENVIRONMENT WHERE MY TALENTS WILL BE MORE LIKELY TO BE ENCOURAGED.

He cursed and he raged. It was his human, his civil right to move into any day he pleased. That is, it should be his right. What if a move did cause much effort? What if it required a transfer of his I.D. and all the records connected with him from the moment of his birth? What if . . . ?

He could rage all he wanted to, but it would not change a thing. He was stuck in the world of Tuesday.

Not yet, he muttered. Not yet. Fortunately, there is no limit to the number of requests I can make in my own day. I'll send out another. They think they can wear me out, huh? Well, I'll wear them out. Man against the machine. Man against the system. Man against the bureaucracy and the hard cold rules.

Winter's twenty days had sped by. Spring's eight days rocketed by. It was summer again. On the second day of the twelve days of summer, he received a reply to his second request.

It was neither a denial nor an acceptance. It stated that if he thought he would be better off psychologically in Wednesday because his astrologer said so, then he would have to get a psycher's critique of the astrologer's analysis. Tom Pym jumped into the air and clicked his sandaled heels together. Thank God that he lived in an age that did not classify astrologers as charlatans! The people—the masses—had protested that astrology was a necessity and that it should be legalized and honored. So laws were passed, and, because of that, Tom Pym had a chance.

He went down to the stoner room and kissed the door of the cylinder and told Jennie Marlowe the good news. She did not respond, though he thought he saw her eyes brighten just a little. That was, of course, only his imagination, but he liked his imagination.

Getting a psycher for a consultation and getting through the three sessions took another year, another forty-eight days. Doctor Sigmund Traurig was a friend of Doctor Stelhela, the astrologer, and so that made things easier for Tom.

"I've studied Doctor Stelhela's chart carefully and analyzed carefully your obsession for this woman," he said. "I agree with Doctor Stelhela that you will always be unhappy in Tuesday, but I don't quite agree with him that you will be happier in Wednesday. However, you have this thing going for this Miss Marlowe, so I think you should go to Wednesday. But only if you sign papers agreeing to see a psycher there for extended therapy."

Only later did Tom Pym realize that Doctor Traurig might have wanted to get rid of him because he had too many patients. But that was an uncharitable thought.

He had to wait while the proper papers were transmitted to Wednesday's authorities. His battle was half-won. The other officials could turn him down. And if he did get to his goal, then what? She could reject him without giving him a second chance.

It was unthinkable, but she could.

He caressed the door and then pressed his lips against it.

"Pygmalion could at least touch Galatea," he said. "Surely, the gods—the dumb bureaucrats—will take pity on me, who can't even touch you. Surely."

The psycher had said that he was incapable of a true and lasting bond with a woman, as so many men were in this world of easy-come-easy-go liaisons. He had fallen in love with Jennie Marlowe for several reasons. She may have resembled somebody he had loved when he was very young. His mother, perhaps? No? Well, never mind. He would find out in Wednesday—perhaps. The deep, the important, truth was that he loved Miss Marlowe because she could never reject him, kick him out, or become tiresome, complain, weep, yell, insult and so forth. He loved her because she was unattainable and silent.

"I love her as Achilles must have loved Helen when he saw her on top of the walls of Troy," Tom said.

"I wasn't aware that Achilles was ever in love with Helen of Troy," Doctor Traurig said drily.

"Homer never said so, but I *know* that he must have been! Who could see her and *not* love her?"

"How the hell would I know? I never saw her! If I had suspected these delusions would intensify . . ."

"I am a poet!" Tom said.

"Overimaginative, you mean! Hmmm. She must be a douser! I don't have anything particular to do this evening. I'll tell you what . . . my curiosity is aroused . . . I'll come down to your place tonight and take a look at this fabulous beauty, your Helen of Troy."

Doctor Traurig appeared immediately after supper, and Tom Pym ushered him down the hall and into the stoner room at the rear of the big house as if he were a guide conducting a famous critic to a just-discovered Rembrandt.

The doctor stood for a long time in front of the cylinder. He hummed several times and checked her vital-data plate several times. Then he turned and said, "I see what you mean, Mr. Pym. Very well. I'll give the go-ahead."

"Ain't she something?" Tom said on the porch. "She's out of this world, literally and figuratively, of course."

"Very beautiful. But I believe that you are facing a great disappointment, perhaps heartbreak, perhaps, who knows, even madness, much as I hate to use that unscientific term."

"I'll take the chance," Tom said. "I know I sound nuts, but where would we be if it weren't for nuts? Look at the man who invented the wheel, at Columbus, at James Watt, at the Wright brothers, at Pasteur, you name them."

"You can scarcely compare these pioneers of science with their passion for truth with you and your desire to marry a woman. But, as I have observed, she is strikingly beautiful. Still, that makes me exceedingly cautious. Why isn't she married? What's wrong with her?"

"For all I know, she may have been married a dozen times!" Tom said. "The point is, she isn't now! Maybe she's disappointed and she's sworn to wait until the right man comes along. Maybe . . ."

"There's no maybe about it, you're neurotic," Traurig said. "But I actually believe that it would be more dangerous for you *not* to go to Wednesday than it would be *to* go."

"Then you'll say yes!" Tom said, grabbing the doctor's hand and shaking it.

"Perhaps. I have some doubts."

The doctor had a faraway look. Tom laughed and released the hand and slapped the doctor on the shoulder. "Admit it! You were really struck by her! You'd have to be dead not to!"

"She's all right," the doctor said. "But you must think this over. If you do go there and she turns you down, you might go off the deep end, much as I hate to use such a poetical term."

"No, I won't. I wouldn't be a bit the worse off. Better off, in fact. I'll at least get to see her in the flesh."

Spring and summer zipped by. Then, a morning he would never forget, the letter of acceptance. With it, instructions on how to get to Wednesday. These were simple enough. He was to make sure that the technicians came to his stoner sometime during the day and readjusted the timer within the base. He could not figure out why he could not just stay out of the stoner and let Wednesday catch up to him, but by now he was past trying to fathom the bureaucratic mind.

He did not intend to tell anyone at the house, mainly because of Mabel. But Mabel found out from someone at the studio. She wept when she saw him at supper time, and she ran upstairs to her room. He felt badly, but he did not follow to console her.

That evening, his heart beating hard, he opened the door to his stoner. The others had found out by then; he had been unable to keep the business to himself. Actually, he was glad that he had told them. They seemed happy for him, and they brought in drinks and and many rounds of toasts. Finally, Mabel came downstairs, wiping her eyes, and she said she wished him luck, too. She had known that he was not really in love with her. But she did wish someone would fall in love with her just by looking inside her stoner.

When she found out that he had gone to see Doctor Traurig, she said, "He's a very influential man. Sol Voremworf had him for his analyst. He says he's even got influence on other days. He edits the *Psyche Cross-currents*, you know, one of the few periodicals read by other people."

Other, of course, meant those who lived in Wednesdays through Mondays.

Tom said he was glad he had gotten Traurig. Perhaps he had used his influence to get the Wednesday authorities to push through his request so swiftly. The walls between the worlds were seldom broken, but it was suspected that the very influential did it when they pleased.

Now, quivering, he stood before Jennie's cylinder again. The last time, he thought, that I'll see her stonered. Next time, she'll be warm, colorful, touchable flesh.

"*Ave atque vale!*" he said aloud. The others cheered. Mabel said, "How corny!" They thought he was addressing them, and perhaps he had included them.

He stepped inside the cylinder, closed the door, and pressed the button. He would keep his eyes open, so that . . .

And today was Wednesday. Though the view was exactly the same, it was like being on Mars.

He pushed open the door and stepped out. The seven people had faces he knew and names he had read on their plates. But he did not know them.

He started to say hello, and then he stopped.

Jennie Marlowe's cylinder was gone.

He seized the nearest man by the arm.

"Where's Jennie Marlowe?"

"Let go. You're hurting me. She's gone. To Tuesday."

"*Tuesday! Tuesday?*"

"Sure. She'd been trying to get out of here for a long time. She had something about this day being unlucky for her. She was unhappy, that's for sure. Just two days ago, she said her application had finally been accepted. Apparently, some Tuesday psycher had used his influence. He came down and saw her in her stoner and that was it, brother."

The walls and the people and the stoners seemed to be distorted. Time was bending itself this way and that. He wasn't in Wednesday; he wasn't in Tuesday. He wasn't in *any* day. He was stuck inside himself at some crazy date that should never have existed.

"She can't do that!"

"Oh, no! She just did that!"

"But . . . you can't transfer more than once!"

"That's her problem."

It was his, too.

"I should never have brought him down to look at her!" Tom said. "The swine! The unethical swine!"

Tom Pym stood there for a long time, and then he went into the kitchen. It was the same environment, if you discounted the people. Later, he went to the studio and got a part in a situation play which was, really, just like all those in Tuesday. He watched the newscaster that night. The President of the U.S.A. had a different name and face, but the words of his speech could have been those of Tuesday's President. He was introduced to a secretary of a producer; her name wasn't Mabel, but it might as well have been.

The difference here was that Jennie was gone, and oh, what a world of difference it made to him.

At the Mouse Circus

HARLAN ELLISON

Already a big name a decade ago, but hardly an Old Pro (if he were to write for the next hundred years, Harlan would never be an Old Pro to me), Harlan Ellison was one of the first writers to offer a story to *New Dimensions*. It was something called "A Boy and His Dog," and I wrote him on January 18, 1969, that I was willing to publish it, but only with what amounted to a total rewrite. I didn't like the style, I didn't like the fascination with sadistic violence, I thought the ending was bungled, I wanted about 3500 words cut altogether; and I sent him a single-spaced two-page letter explaining how he could save the story. As I suspected, Harlan chose not to listen to me. He sold it somewhere else as it stood; it won a Nebula the following year, has been reprinted many times, and eventually was made into a motion picture, none of which has led me to believe that the story has any merit whatever. I'd send it back again just as fast today, even *knowing* it was going to win an award, become a movie, et cetera, et cetera. (An editor has to have the courage of his convictions. I once rejected a Gordon Eklund story that I wished later I had bought, and I did the same dumb thing to Christopher Priest. Otherwise I have no misgivings about editorial decisions, however misgiven they may look to others.)

With "A Boy and His Dog" going elsewhere, Ellison's desire to have a story in *New Dimensions,* and mine to have one from him, went frustrated for over a year; but early in 1970 he shipped me the mysterious, enigmatic, haunting story reprinted here. I had a hard time justifying it to myself as science fiction, despite a time-travel sequence complete with dinosaurs; it was straight surrealism, far more experimental than I considered appropriate for *New Dimensions'* intended middle-of-the-road policy. But I found it irresistible: beautifully written, marvelously controlled, wondrously hallucinatory. I decided to risk it, since most of the rest of the first issue was relatively straightforward in manner. It didn't win any awards and has not yet been bought for filming, and reader response was a bit on the baffled side; but I'm proud to have published it. (An editor has to have the courage of his convictions.) Over the next seven or eight years Harlan frequently spoke of submitting other stories to me, but somehow he never did: somebody else's pressing deadline always got in the way. I'm glad I did get one of his best into the book right at the outset.

THE KING OF TIBET WAS HAVING HIMSELF A FAT white woman. He had thrown himself down a jelly tunnel, millennia before, and periodically, as he pumped her, a soft pink-and-white bunny rabbit in weskit and spats trembled through, scrutinizing a turnip watch at the end of a heavy gold-link chain. The white woman was soft as suet, with little black eyes thrust deep under prominent brow ridges. Honkie bitch groaned in unfulfilled ecstasy, trying desperately and knowing she never would. For she never had. The King of Tibet had a bellyache. Oh, to be in another place, doing another thing, alone.

The land outside was shimmering in waves of fear that came radiating from mountaintops far away. On the mountaintops, grizzled and wizened old men considered ways and means, considered runes and portents, considered whys and wherefores . . . ignored them all . . . and set about sending more fear to farther places. The land rippled in the night, beginning to quake with terror that was greater than the fear that had gone before.

"What time is it?" he asked, and received no answer.

Thirty-seven years ago, when the King of Tibet had been a lad, there had been a man with one leg—who had been his father for a short time—and a woman with a touch of the tar brush in her, and she had served as mother.

"You can be anything, Charles," she had said to him. "Anything you want to be. A man can be anything he can do. Uncle Wiggly, Jomo Kenyatta, the King of Tibet, if you want to. Light enough or black, Charles, it don't mean a thing. You just go your way and be good and *do*. That's all you got to remember."

The King of Tibet had fallen on hard times. Fat white women and cheap cologne. Doodad, he had lost the horizon. Exquisite, he had dealt with surfaces and been dealt with similarly. Wasted, he had done time.

"I got to go," he told her.

"Not yet, just a little more. Please."

So he stayed. Banners unfurled, lying limp in absence of breezes from Camelot, he stayed and suffered. Finally, she turned him loose, and the King of Tibet stood in the shower for forty minutes. Golden skin pelted, drinking, he was never quite clean. Scented, abluted, he still knew the odors of wombats, hallway musk, granaries, futile beakers of noxious fluids. If he was a white mouse, why could he not see his treadmill?

"Listen, baby, I got need of fi'hunnerd dollahs. I know we ain't been together but a while, but I got this *bad* need." She went to snap-purses and returned.

He hated her more for doing than not doing.

And in her past, he knew he was no part of any recognizable future.

"Charlie, when'll I see you again?" Stranger, never!

Borne away in the silver flesh of Cadillac, the great beautiful mother Hog, plunging wheelbased at one hundred and twenty (bought with his semen) inches, Eldorado god-creature of four hundred horsepower, displacing recklessly 440 cubic inches, thundering into forgetting weighing 4550+ pounds, goes . . . went . . . Charlie . . . Charles . . . the King of Tibet. Golden brown, cleaned as best as he could, five hundred reasons and five hundred aways. Driven, driving into the outside.

Forever inside, the King of Tibet, going outside.

Along the road. Manhattan, Jersey City, New Brunswick, Trenton. In Norristown, having had lunch at a fine restaurant, Charlie was stopped on a street corner by a voice that went *pssst* from a mailbox. He opened the slit and a small boy in a pullover sweater and tie thrust his head and shoulders into the night. "You've got to help me," the boy said. "My name is Batson. Billy Batson. I work for radio station WHIZ and if I could only remember the right word, and if I could only *say* it, something wonderful would happen. S is for the wisdom of Solomon, H is for the strength of Hercules, A is for the stamina of Atlas, Z is for the power of Zeus . . . and after that I go blank . . ."

The King of Tibet slowly and steadily thrust the head back into the mailslot, and walked away. Reading, Harrisburg, Mt. Union, Altoona, Nanty Glo.

On the road to Pittsburgh there was a four-fingered mouse in red shorts with two big yellow buttons on the front, hitch-hiking. Shoes like two big boxing gloves, bright eyes sincere, forlorn, and way lost, he stood on the curb with meaty thumb and he waited. Charlie whizzed past. It was not his dream.

Youngstown, Akron, Canton, Columbus, and hungry once more in Dayton.

O.

Oh aitch eye oh. Why did he ever leave. He had never been there before. This was the good place. The river flowed dark, and the day passed overhead like some other river. He pulled into a parking space and did not even lock the god-mother Eldorado. It waited patiently, knowing its upholstered belly would be filled with the King of Tibet soon enough.

"Feed you next," he told the sentient vehicle, as he walked away toward the restaurant.

Inside—dim and candled at high noon—he was shown to a heavy wood booth, and there he had laid before him a pure white linen napkin, five pieces of silver, a crystal goblet in which fine water waited, and a promise. From the promise he selected nine-to-five winners, a long shot and the play number for the day.

A flocked-velvet witch perched on a bar stool across from him turned, exposed thigh, and smiled. He offered her silver, water, a promise, and they struck a bargain.

Charlie stared into her oiled teakwood eyes through the candle flame between them. All moistened Saran-wrap was her skin. All thistled gleaming were her teeth. All mystery of cupped hollows beneath cheek-bones was she. Charlie had bought a television set once, because the redhead in the commercial was part of his dream. He had bought an electric tooth-brush because the brunette with her capped teeth had indicated she, too, was part of his dream. And his great Eldorado, of course. *That* was the dream of the King of Tibet.

"What time is it?" But he received no answer and, drying his lips of the last of the *pêche flambée,* he and the flocked-velvet witch left the restaurant: he with his dream fraying, and she with no product save one to sell.

There was a party in a house on a hill.

When they drove up the asphalt drive, the blacktop beneath them uncoiled like the sooty tongue of a great primitive snake. "You'll like these people," she said, and took the sensitive face of the King of Tibet be-tween her hands and kissed him deeply. Her finger-nails were gunmetal silvered and her palms were faintly moist and plump, with expectations of tactile enrichments.

They walked up to the house. Lit from within, every window held a color facet of light. Sounds swelled as they came toward the house. He fell a step behind her and watched the way her skin flowed. She reached out, touched the house, and they became one.

No door was opened to them, but holding fast to her hair he was drawn behind her, through the flesh of the house.

Within, there were inlaid ivory boxes that, when opened, revealed smaller boxes within. He became fascinated by one such box sitting high on a pedestal in the center of an om rug. The box was inlaid with teeth of otters and puff adders and lynx. He opened the first box and within was a second box frosted with rime. Within the frost-box was a third, and it was decorated with mirrors that cast back no reflections. And next within was a box whose surface was a mass of intaglios, and they were all fingerprints, and none of Charlie's fit, and only when a passing man smiled and caressed the lid did it open, revealing the next, smaller box. And so it went, till he lost count of the boxes and the journey ended when he could not see the box that fit within the dust-mote-size box that was within all the others. But he knew there were more, and he felt a great sadness that he could not get to them.

"What is it, precisely, you want?" asked an older woman with very good bones. He was leaning against a wall whose only ornamentation was a gigantic wooden crucifix on which a Christ-figure hung, head bowed, shoulders twisted as only shoulders can be whose arms have been pulled from sockets; the figure was made of massive pieces of wood, all artfully stained: chunks of doors, bedposts, rowels, splines, pintles, joists, crossties, rabbet-joined bits of massive frames.

"I want . . ." he began, then spread his hands in confusion. He knew what he wanted to say, but no one had ever ordered the progression of words properly.

"Is it Madelaine?" the older woman asked. She smiled as Aunt Jemima would smile, and targeted a finger across the enormous living room, bull's-eyed on the flocked-velvet witch all the way over there by the fireplace. "She's here."

The King of Tibet felt a bit more relaxed.

"Now," the older woman said, her hand on Charlie's cheek, "what is it you need to know? Tell me. We have all the answers here. Truly."

"I want to know—"

The television screen went silver and cast a pool of light, drawing Charlie's attention. The possibilities were listed on the screen. And what he had wanted to know seemed inconsequential compared to the choices he saw listed.

"That one," he said. "That second one. How did the dinosaurs die."

"Oh, fine!" She looked pleased he had selected that one. "Shefti . . . ?" she called to a tall man with gray hair at the temples. He looked up from speaking to several women and another man, looked up expectantly and she said, "He's picked the second one. May I?"

"Of course, darling," Shefti said, raising his wine glass to her.

"Do we have time?"

"Oh, I think so," he said.

"Yes . . . what time *is* it?" Charlie asked.

"Over here," the older woman said, leading him firmly by the forearm. They stopped beside another wall. "Look."

The King of Tibet stared at the wall, and it paled, turned to ice, and became translucent. There was something imbedded in the ice. Something huge. Something dark. He stared harder, his eyes straining to make out the shape. Then he was seeing more clearly, and it was a great saurian, frozen at the moment of pouncing on some lesser species.

"*Gorgosaurus,*" the older woman said, at his elbow. "It rather resembles *Tyrannosaurus,* you see; but the forelimbs have only two digits. You see?"

Thirty-two feet of tanned gray leather. The killing teeth. The nostriled snout, the amber smoke eyes of the eater of carrion. The smooth sickening tuber of balancing tail, the crippled forelimbs carried tragically withered and useless. The musculature . . . the pulsing beat of iced blood beneath the tarpaulin hide. The . . . beat . . .

It lived.

Through the ice went the King of Tibet, accompanied by Circe-eyed older woman, as the shellfish-white living room receded back beyond the ice-wall. Ice went, night came.

Ice that melted slowly from the great hulk before him. He stood in wonder. "See," the woman said.

And he saw as the ice dissolved into mist and night-fog, and he saw as the earth trembled, and he saw as the great fury lizard moved in shambling hesitancy, and he saw as the others came to cluster unseen nearby. *Scolosaurus* came. *Trachodon* came. *Stephanosaurus* came. *Protoceratops* came. And all stood, waiting.

The King of Tibet knew there were slaughterhouses where the beef was hung upside down on hooks, where the throats were slit and the blood ran thick as motor oil. He saw a golden thing hanging, and would not look. Later, he would look.

They waited. Silently, for its coming.

Through the Cretaceous swamp it *was* coming. Charlie could hear it. Not loud, but coming steadily closer. "Would you light my cigarette, please," asked the older woman.

It was shining. It bore a pale white nimbus. It was stepping through the swamp, black to its thighs from the decaying matter. It came on, its eyes set back under furred brow-ridges, jaw thrust forward, wide nostrils sniffing at the chill night, arms covered with matted filth and hair. Savior man.

He came to the lizard owners of the land. He walked around them and they stood silently, their time at hand. Then he touched them, one after the other, and the plague took them. Blue fungus spread from the five-pronged marks left on their imperishable hides; blue death radiating from impressions of opposed thumbs, joining, spreading cilia and rotting the flesh of the great gone dinosaurs.

The ice re-formed and the King of Tibet moved back through pearly cold to the living room.

He struck a match and lit her cigarette.

She thanked him and walked away.

The flocked-velvet witch returned. "Did you have a nice time?" He thought of the boxes-within-boxes.

"Is that how they died? Was he the first?"

She nodded. "And did Nita ask you for anything?"

Charlie had never seen the sea. Oh, there had been the Narrows and the East River and the Hudson, but he had never seen the sea. The real sea, the thunder sea that went black at night like a pane of glass. The sea that could summon and the sea that could kill, that could swallow whole cities and turn them into myth. He wanted to go to California.

He suddenly felt a fear he would never leave this thing called Ohio here.

"I asked you: did Nita ask you for anything?"

He shivered.

"What?"

"Nita. Did she *ask* you for anything?"

"Only a light."

"Did you give it to her?"

"Yes."

Madelaine's face swam in the thin fluid of his sight. Her jaw muscles trembled. She turned and walked across the room. Everyone turned to look at her. She went to Nita, who suddenly took a step backward and threw up her hands. "No, I didn't—"

The flocked-velvet witch darted a hand toward the older woman and the hand seemed to pass into her neck. The silver-tipped fingers reappeared, clenched around a fine sparkling filament. Then Madelaine snapped it off with a grunt.

There was a terrible minor sound from Nita, then she turned, watery, and stood silently beside the window, looking empty and hopeless.

Madelaine wiped her hand on the back of the sofa and came to Charlie. "We'll go now. The party is over."

He drove in silence back to town.

"Are you coming up?" he asked, when they parked the Eldorado in front of the hotel.

"I'm coming up."

He registered them as Professor Pierre and Marja Sklodowska Curie, and for the first time in his life he was unable to reach a climax. He fell asleep sobbing over never having seen the sea, and came awake hours later with the night still pressing against the walls. She was not there.

He heard sounds from the street, and went to the window.

There was a large crowd in the street, gathered around his car.

As he watched, a man went to his knees before the golden Eldorado and touched it. Charlie knew *this* was his dream. He could not move; he just watched, as they ate his car.

The man put his mouth to the hood and it came away bloody. A great chunk had been ripped from the gleaming hide of the Cadillac. Golden blood ran down the man's jaws.

Another man draped himself over the top of the car and even through the window the King of Tibet could hear the terrible sucking, slobbering sounds. Furrows were ripped in the top.

A woman pulled her dress up around her hips and backed, on all fours, to the rear of the car. Her face trembled with soft expectancy, and then it was inside her and she moved on it.

When she came, they all moved in on the car and

he watched as his dream went inside them, piece by piece, chewed and eaten as he stood by helpless.

"That's all, Charlie," he heard her say, behind him. He could not turn to look at her, but her reflection was superimposed over his own in the window. Out there in darkness now, they moved away, having eaten.

He looked, and saw the golden thing hanging upside down in the slaughterhouse, its throat cut, its blood drained away in onyx gutters.

Afoot, in Dayton, Ohio, he was dead of dreams.

"What time is it?" he asked.

Nobody's Home

JOANNA RUSS

One gifted writer who didn't make it into the first *New Dimensions,* though I very much wanted her there, was Joanna Russ. In the spring of 1969 her agent sent me a piece called "When It Changed," which I wanted to buy if she would add one more 500-word scene, sketching out the next phase in the conflict between men and women that was at the heart of the story: I felt that the ending as it stood was abrupt and undramatic. I had some other minor suggestions, too; but Joanna, though she revised the final lines of the story to meet my objections, did not want to add the 500-word scene, and I chose to stand firm. So she sold the story to Harlan Ellison's *Again, Dangerous Visions* instead, and it won a Nebula. Looking at "When It Changed" now, I begin to think I could have published it as it stood without doing undue harm to my sense of the fitness of things, but I'm still glad I rejected it, for in its place I received what I consider a far superior story, "Nobody's Home." That one I bought pronto, and to this day I regard it with awe, for it seems to me one of the most vivid and plausible depictions of the daily life of the future ever written. It arrived too late for *New Dimensions 1,* but that allowed me to give it the premier position in the second issue, which appeared in October, 1972. Some short stories demand to be read in a single sitting and in no other way: this is one of them.

AFTER SHE HAD FINISHED HER WORK AT THE NORTH Pole, Jannina came down to the Red Sea refineries, where she had family business, jumped to New Delhi for dinner, took a nap in a public hotel in Queensland, walked from the hotel to the station, bypassed the Leeward Islands (where she thought she might go, but all the stations were busy), and met Charley to watch the dawn over the Carolinas.

"Where've you *been,* dear C?"

"Tanzania. And you're married."

"No."

"I heard you were married," he said. "The Lees told the Smiths who told the Kerguelens who told the Utsumbés and we get around, we Utsumbés. A new wife, they said. I didn't know you were especially fond of women."

"I'm not. She's my husbands' wife. And we're not married yet, Charley. She's had hard luck: a first family started in '35, two husbands burned out by an overload while arranging transportation for a concert—of all things, pushing papers, you know!—and the second divorced her, I think, and she drifted away from the third (a big one), and there was some awful quarrel with the fourth, people chasing people around tables, I don't know."

"Poor woman."

In the manner of people joking and talking lightly they had drawn together, back to back, sitting on the ground and rubbing together their shoulders and the backs of their heads. Jannina said sorrowfully, "What lovely hair you have, Charley Utsumbé, like metal mesh."

"All we Utsumbés are exceedingly handsome." They linked arms. The sun, which anyone could chase around the world now, see it rise or set twenty times a day, fifty times a day—if you wanted to spend your life like that—rose dripping out of the cypress swamp. There was nobody around for miles. Mist drifted up from the pools and low places.

"My God," he said, "it's summer! I have to be at Tanga now."

"What?" said Jannina.

"One loses track," he said apologetically. "I'm sorry, love, but I have unavoidable business at home. Tax labor."

"But why summer, why did its being summer—"

"Train of thought! Too complicated" (and already they were out of key, already the mild affair was over, there having come between them the one obligation that can't be put off to the time you like, or the place you like; off he'd go to plug himself into a road-mender or a doctor, though it's of some advantage to mend all the roads of a continent at one time).

She sat cross-legged on the station platform, watching him enter the booth and set the dial. He stuck his head out the glass door.

"Come with me to Africa, lovely lady!"

She thumbed her nose at him. "You're only a passing fancy, Charley U!" He blew a kiss, enclosed himself in the booth, and disappeared. (The transmatter field is larger than the booth, for obvious reasons; the booth flicks on and off several million times a second and so does not get transported itself, but it protects the machinery from the weather and it keeps people from losing elbows or knees or slicing the ends off a package or a child. The booths at the cryogenics center at the North Pole have exchanged air so often with those of warmer regions that each has its own micro-climate; leaves and seeds, plants and earth are piled about them. Don't Step on the Grass!—say the notes pinned to the door—Wish to Trade Pawlownia Sapling for Sub-arctic Canadian Moss; Watch Your Goddamn Bare Six-Toed Feet!; Wish Amateur Cellist for Quartet, Six Months' Rehearsal Late Uhl with Reciter; I Lost a Squirrel Here Yesterday, Can You Find It

Before It Dies? Eight Children Will be Heartbroken—
Cecilia Ching, Buenos Aires.)

Jannina sighed and slipped on her glass woolly;
nasty to get back into clothes, but home was cold. You
never knew where you might go, so you carried them.
Years ago (she thought) I came here with someone in
the dead of winter, either an unmatched man or someone's starting spouse—only two of us, at any rate—
and we waded through the freezing water and danced
as hard as we could and then proved we could sing
and drink beer in a swamp at the same time, Good
Lord! And then went to the public resort on the Ile de
la Cité to watch professional plays, opera, games—
you have to be good to get in there!—and got into
some clothes because it was chilly after sundown in
September—no, wait, it was Venezuela—and watched
the lights come out and smoked like mad at a café table and tickled the robot waiter and pretended we
were old, really old, perhaps a hundred and fifty. . . .
Years ago!,

But *was* it the same place? she thought, and dismissing the incident forever, she stepped into the booth,
shut the door, and dialed home: the Himalayas. The
trunk line was clear. The branch stop was clear. The
family's transceiver (located in the anteroom behind
two doors, to keep the task of heating the house within
reasonable limits) had damn well better be clear, or
somebody would be blown right into the vestibule.
Momentum- and heat-compensators kept Jannina
from arriving home at seventy degrees Fahrenheit
internal temperature (seven degrees lost for every
mile you teleport upward) or too many feet above
herself (rise to the east, drop going west, to the north
or south you are apt to be thrown right through the
wall of the booth). Someday (thought Jannina) everybody will decide to let everybody live in decent cli-
mates. But not yet. Not this everybody.

She arrived home singing "The World's My Back
Yard, Yes, the World Is My Oyster," a song that had

been popular in her first youth, some seventy years before.

The Komarovs' house was hardened foam with an automatic inside line to the school near Naples. It was good to be brought up on your own feet. Jannina passed through; the seven-year-olds lay with their heads together and their bodies radiating in a six-personed asterisk. In this position (which was supposed to promote mystical thought) they played Barufaldi, guessing the identity of famous dead personages through anagrammatic sentences, the first letters of the words of which (unscrambled into aphorisms or proverbs) simultaneously spelled out a moral and a series of Goedel numbers (in a previously agreed-upon code) which—

"Oh, my darling, how felicitous is the advent of your appearance!" cried a boy (hard to take, the polysyllabic stage). "Embrace me, dearest maternal parent! Unite your valuable upper limbs about my eager person!"

"Vulgar!" said Jannina, laughing.

"Non sum filius tuus?" said the child.

"No, you're not my body-child; you're my godchild. Your mother bequeathed me to you when she died. What are you learning?"

"The eternal parental question," he said, frowning. "How to run a helicopter. How to prepare food from its actual, revolting, raw constituents. Can I go now?"

"Can you?" she said. "Nasty imp!"

"Good," he said. "I've made you feel guilty. Don't *do* that," and as she tried to embrace him, he ticklishly slid away. "The robin walks quietly up the branch of the tree," he said breathlessly, flopping back on the floor.

"That's not an aphorism." (Another Barufaldi player.)

"It is."

"It isn't."

"It is."

"It isn't."

"It is."

"It—"

The school vanished; the antechamber appeared. In the kitchen Chi Komarov was rubbing the naked back of his sixteen-year-old son. Parents always kissed each other; children always kissed each other. She touched foreheads with the two men and hung her woolly on the hook by the ham radio rig. Someone was always around. Jannina flipped the cover off her wrist chronometer: standard regional time, date, latitude-longitude, family computer hookup clear. "At my age I ought to remember these things," she said. She pressed the computer hookup: Ann at tax labor in the schools, bit-a-month plan, regular Ann; Lee with three months to go, five years off, heroic Lee; Phuong in Paris, still rehearsing; C.E. gone won't say where, spontaneous C.E.; Ilse making some repairs in the basement, not a true basement, really, but the room farthest down the hillside. She went up the stairs and then came down and put her head round at the living-and-swimming room. Through the glass wall one could see the mountains. Old Al, who had joined them late in life, did a bit of gardening in the brief summers, and generally stuck around the place. Jannina beamed. "Hullo, Old Al!" Big and shaggy, a rare delight, his white body hair. She sat on his lap. "Has she come?"

"The new one? No," he said.

"Shall we go swimming?"

He made an expressive face. "No, dear," he said. "I'd rather go to Naples and watch the children fly helicopters. I'd rather go to Nevada and fly them myself. I've been in the water all day, watching a very dull person restructure coral reefs and experiment with polyploid polyps."

"You mean *you* were doing it."

"One gets into the habit of working."

"But you didn't have to!"

"It was a private project. Most interesting things are."

She whispered in his ear.

With happily flushed faces, they went into Old Al's inner garden and locked the door.

Jannina, temporary family representative, threw the computer helmet over her head and, thus plugged in, she cleaned house, checked food supplies, did a little of the legal business entailed by a family of eighteen adults (two triplet marriages, a quad, and a group of eight). She felt very smug. She put herself through by radio to Himalayan HQ (above two thousand meters) and hooking computer to computer—a very odd feeling, like an urge to sneeze that never comes off—extended a formal invitation to one Leslie Smith ("Come stay, why don't you?"), notifying every free Komarov to hop it back and fast. Six hikers might come for the night—back-packers. More food. First thunderstorm of the year in Albany, New York (North America). Need an extra two rooms by Thursday. Hear the Palnatoki are moving. Can't use a room. Can't use a kitten. Need the geraniums back, Mrs. Adam, Chile. The best maker of hand-blown glass in the world has killed in a duel the second-best maker of hand-blown glass for joining the movement toward ceramics. A bitter struggle is foreseen in the global economy. Need a lighting designer. Need fifteen singers and electric pansensicon. Standby tax labor xxxxxpj through xxxyq to Cambaluc, great tectogenic—

With the guilty feeling that one always gets gossiping with a computer, for it's really not reciprocal, Jannina flipped off the helmet. She went to get Ilse. Climbing back through the white foam room, the purple foam room, the green foam room, everything littered with plots and projects of the clever Komarovs or the even cleverer Komarov children, stopping at the baby room for Ilse to nurse her baby. Jannina danced staidly around studious Ilse. They turned on the nursery robot and the television screen. Ilse drank beer in the swimming room, for her milk. She worried her way through the day's record of events—faults in the foundation, some people who came from Chichester and couldn't find C.E. so one of them burst into tears, a new experiment in genetics coming round the gossip circuit, an execrable set of equations from some imposter in Bucharest.

"A duel!" said Jannina.

They both agreed it was shocking. And what fun. A new fashion. You had to be a little made to do it. Awful.

The light went on over the door to the tunnel that linked the house to the antechamber, and very quickly, one after another, as if the branch line had just come free, eight Komarovs came into the room. The light flashed again; one could see three people debouch one after the other, persons in boots, with coats, packs, and face masks over their woollies. They were covered with snow, either from the mountain terraces above the house or from some other place, Jannina didn't know. They stamped the snow off in the antechamber and hung their clothes outside; "Good heavens, you're not circumcised!" cried someone. There was as much handshaking and embracing all around as at a wedding party. Velet Komarov (the short, dark one) recognized Fung Pao-yu and swung her off her feet. People began to joke, tentatively stroking one another's arms. "Did you have a good hike? Are you a good hiker, Pao-yu?" said Velet. The light over the antechamber went on again, though nobody could see a thing since the glass was steamed over from the collision of hot with cold air. Old Al stopped, halfway into the kitchen. The baggage receipt chimed, recognized only by family ears—upstairs a bundle of somebody's things, ornaments, probably, for the missing Komarovs were still young and the young are interested in clothing, were appearing in the baggage receptacle. "Ann or Phuong?" said Jannina. "Five to three, anybody, Match me!" but someone strange opened the door of the booth and peered

out. Oh, a dizzying sensation. She was painted in a
few places, which was awfully odd because really it
was old-fashioned; and why do it for a family evening? It was a stocky young woman. I was an awful
mistake (thought Jannina). Then the visitor made her
second mistake. She said:

"I'm Leslie Smith." But it was more through clum-
siness than being rude. Chi Komarov (the tall, blond
one) saw this instantly and, snatching off his old-
fashioned spectacles, he ran to her side and patted
her, saying teasingly:

"Now, haven't we met? Now, aren't you married to
someone I know?"

"No, no," said Leslie Smith, flushing with pleasure.

He touched her neck. "Ah, you're a tightrope
dancer!"

"Oh, no!" exclaimed Leslie Smith.

"*I'm* a tightrope dancer," said Chi. "Would you believe it?"

"But you're too—too *spiritual*," said Leslie Smith
hesitantly.

"Spiritual, how do you like that, family, spiritual?"
he cried, delighted (a little more delighted, thought
Jannina, than the situation really called for) and he
began to stroke her neck.

"What a lovely neck you have," he said.

This steadied Leslie Smith. She said, "I like tall
men," and allowed herself to look at the rest of the
family. "Who are these people?" she said, though one
was afraid she might really mean it.

Fung Pao-yu to the rescue: "Who are these people?
Who are they, indeed! I doubt if they are anybody.
One might say, 'I have met these people,' but has one?
What existential meaning would such a statement convey? I myself, now, I have met them. I have been introduced to them. But they are like the Sahara; it is
all wrapped in mystery; I doubt if they even have
names," etc. etc. Then lanky Chi Komarov disputed
possession of Leslie Smith with Fung Pao-yu, and
Fung Pao-yu grabbed one arm and Chi the other; and

she jumped up and down fiercely; so that by the time the lights dimmed and the food came, people were feeling better—or so Jannina judged. So embarrassing and delightful to be eating fifteen to a room! "We Komarovs are famous for eating whatever we can get whenever we can get it," said Velet proudly. Various Komarovs in various places, with the three hikers on cushions and Ilse at full length on the rug. Jannina pushed a button with her toe and the fairy lights came on all over the ceiling. "The children did that," said Old Al. He had somehow settled at Leslie Smith's side and was feeding her so-chi from his own bowl. She smiled up at him. "We once," said a hiking companion of Fung Pao-yu's, "arranged a dinner in an amphitheater where half of us played servants to the other half, with forfeits for those who didn't show. It was the result of a bet. Like the bad old days. Did you know there were once *five billion people* in this world?"

"The gulls," said Ilse, "are mating on the Isle of Skye." There were murmurs of appreciative interest. Chi began to develop an erection and everyone laughed. Old Al wanted music and Velet didn't; what might have been a quarrel was ended by Ilse's furiously boxing their ears. She stalked off to the nursery.

"Leslie Smith and I are both old-fashioned," said Old Al, "because neither of us believes in gabbing. Chi—your theater?"

"We're turning people away." He leaned forward, earnestly, tapping his fingers on his crossed knees. "I swear, some of them are threatening to commit suicide."

"It's a choice," said Velet reasonably.

Leslie Smith had dropped her bowl. They retrieved it for her.

"Aiy, I remember—" said Pao-yu. "What I remember! We've been eating dried mush for three days, tax-issue. Did you know one of my dads killed himself?"

"No!" said Velet, surprised.

"Years ago," said Pao-yu. "He said he refused to live to see the time when chairs were reintroduced. He also wanted further genetic engineering, I believe, for even more intelligence. He did it out of spite, I'm sure. I think he wrestled a shark. Jannina, is this tax-issue food? Is it this year's style tax-issue sauce?"

"No, next year's," said Jannina snappishly. Really, some people! She slipped into Finnish, to show up Pao-yu's pronunciation. "Isn't that so?" she asked Leslie Smith.

Leslie Smith stared at her.

More charitably Jannina informed them all, in Finnish, that the Komarovs had withdrawn their membership in a food group, except for Ann, who had taken out an individual, because what the dickens, who had the time? And tax-issue won't kill you. As they finished, they dropped their dishes into the garbage field and Velet stripped a layer off the rug. In that went, too. Indulgently Old Al began a round:

"Red."

"Sun," said Pao-yu.

"The Red Sun Is," said one of the triplet Komarovs.

"The Red Sun Is—High," said Chi.

"The Red Sun Is High, The," Velet said.

"The Red Sun Is High, The Blue—" Jannina finished. They had come to Leslie Smith, who could either complete it or keep it going. She chose to declare for complete, not shyly (as before) but simply by pointing to Old Al.

"The red sun is high, the blue," he said. "Subtle! Another: Ching."

"Nü."

"Ching nü ch'i."

"Ching nü ch'i ch'u."

"Ssu."

"Wo."

"Ssu wo yü." It had got back to Leslie Smith again. She said, "I can't do that." Jannina got up and began to dance—I'm nice in my nasty way, she thought. The others wandered toward the pool and Ilse reappeared on the nursery monitor screen, saying, "I'm coming down." Somebody said, "What time is it in Argentina?"

"Five A.M."

"I think I want to go.'

"Go then."

"I go."

"Go well."

The red light over the antechamber door flashed and went out.

"Say, why'd you leave your other family?" said Ilse, settling near Old Al where the wall curved out. Ann, for whom it was evening, would be home soon; Chi, who had just got up a few hours back in western America, would stay somewhat longer; nobody ever knew Old Al's schedule and Jannina herself had lost track of the time. She would stay up until she felt sleepy. She followed a rough twenty-eight-hour day, Phuong (what a nuisance that must be at rehearsals!) a twenty-two-hour one, Ilse six hours dozing. Jannina nodded, heard the question, and shook herself awake.

"I didn't leave them. They left me."

There was a murmur of sympathy around the pool.

"They left me because I was stupid," said Leslie Smith. Her hands were clasped passively in her lap. She looked very genteel in her blue body paint, a stocky young woman with small breasts. One of the triplet Komarovs, flirting in the pool with the other two, choked. The non-aquatic members of the family crowded around Leslie Smith, touching her with little, soft touches; they kissed her and exposed to her all their unguarded surfaces, their bellies, their soft skins. Old Al kissed her hands. She sat there, oddly unmoved. "But I *am* stupid," she said. "You'll find out." Jannina put her hands over her ears: "A masochist!" Leslie Smith looked at Jannina with a curious, stolid look. Then she looked down and absently began to rub one blue-painted knee. "Luggage!" shouted Chi, clapping his hands together, and the triplets dashed for the stairs. "No, I'm going to bed," said Leslie Smith; "I'm

tired," and quite simply, she got up and let Old Al
lead her through the pink room, the blue room, the
turtle-and-pet room (temporarily empty), the trash
room, and all the other rooms, to the guest room with
the view that looked out over the cold hillside to the
terraced plantings below.

"The best maker of hand-blown glass in the world,"
said Chi, "has killed in a duel the second-best maker
of hand-blown glass in the world."

"For joining the movement to ceramics," said Ilse,
awed. Jannina felt a thrill: this was the bitter stuff under the surface of life, the fury that boiled up. A bitter struggle is foreseen in the global economy. Good
old tax-issue stuff goes toddling along, year after year.
She was, thought Jannina, extraordinarily grateful to
be living now, to be in such an extraordinary world,
to have so long to go before her death. So much to do!

Old Al came back into the living room. "She's in
bed."

"Well, which of us—?" said the triplet-who-had-
choked, looking mischievously round from one to the
other. Chi was about to volunteer, out of his usual con-
scientiousness, thought Jannina, but then she found
herself suddenly standing up, and then just as suddenly sitting down again. "I just don't have the nerve,"
she said. Velet Komarov walked on his hands toward
the stairs, then somersaulted, and vanished, climbing.
Old Al got off the hand-carved chest he had been sitting on and fetched a can of ale from it. He levered
off the top and drank. Then he said, "She really is
stupid, you know." Jannina's skin crawled.

"Oooh," said Pao-yu. Chi betook himself to the
kitchen and returned with a paper folder. It was
coated with frost. He shook it, then impatiently
dropped it in the pool. The redheaded triplet swam
over and took it. "Smith, Leslie," she said. "Adam
Two, Leslie. Yee, Leslie. Schwarzen, Leslie."

"What on earth does the woman *do* with herself
besides get married?" exclaimed Pao-yu.

"She drove a hovercraft," said Chi, "in some out-of-the-way places around the Pacific until the last underground stations were completed. Says when she was a child she wanted to drive a truck."

"Well, you can," said the redheaded triplet, "can't you? Go to Arizona or the Rockies and drive on the roads. The sixty-mile-an-hour road. The thirty-mile-an hour road. Great artistic recreation."

"That's not work," said Old Al.

"Couldn't she take care of children?" said the redheaded triplet. Ilse sniffed.

"Stupidity's not much of a recommendation for that," Chi said. "Let's see—no children. No, of course not. Overfulfilled her tax work on quite a few routine matters here. Kim, Leslie. Went to Moscow and contracted a double with some fellow, didn't last. Registered as a singleton, but that didn't last, either. She said she was lonely and they were exploiting her."

Old Al nodded.

"Came back and lived informally with a theater group. Left them. Went into psychotherapy. Volunteered for several experimental, intelligence-enhancing programs, was turned down—hm!—sixty-five come the winter solstice, muscular coordination average, muscular development above average, no overt mental pathology, empathy average, prognosis: poor. No, wait a minute, it says, 'More of the same.' Well, that's the same thing.

"What I want to know," added Chi, raising his head, "is who met Miss Smith and decided we needed the lady in this Ice Palace of ours?"

Nobody answered. Jannina was about to say, "Ann, perhaps?" but as she felt the urge to do so—surely it wasn't right to turn somebody off like that, *just* for that!—Chi (who had been flipping through the dossier) came to the last page, with the tax-issue stamp absolutely unmistakable, woven right into the paper.

"The computer did," said Pao-yu and she giggled idiotically.

"Well," said Jannina, jumping to her feet, "tear it up, my dear, or give it to me and I'll tear it up for you. I think Miss Leslie Smith deserves from us the same we'd give to anybody else, and I—for one—intend to go *right up there*—"

"After Velet," said Old Al dryly.

"*With* Velet, if I must," said Jannina, raising her eyebrows, "and if you don't know what's due a guest, Old Daddy, I do, and I intend to provide it. Lucky I'm keeping house this month, or you'd probably feed the poor woman nothing but seaweed."

"You won't like her, Jannina," said Old Al.

"I'll find that out for myself," said Jannina with some asperity, "and I'd advise you to do the same. Let her garden with you, Daddy. Let her squirt the foam for the new rooms. And now"—she glared round at them—"I'm going to clean *this* room, so you'd better hop it, the lot of you," and dashing into the kitchen, she had the computer helmet on her head and the hoses going before they had even quite cleared the area of the pool. Then she took the helmet off and hung it on the wall. She flipped the cover off her wrist chronometer and satisfied herself as to the date. By the time she got back to the living room there was nobody there, only Leslie Smith's dossier lying on the carved chest. There was Leslie Smith; there was all of Leslie Smith. Jannina knocked on the wall cupboard and it revolved, presenting its openable side; she took out chewing gum. She started chewing and read about Leslie Smith.

Q: What have you seen in the last twenty years that you particularly liked?

A: I don't . . . the museum, I guess. At Oslo. I mean the . . . the mermaid and the children's museum, I don't care if it's a children's museum.

Q: Do you like children?

A: Oh no.

(No disgrace in *that*, certainly, thought Jannina.)

Q: But you liked the children's museum.

A: Yes, sir. . . . Yes. . . . I liked those animals, the fake ones, in the—the—

Q: The crèche?

A: Yes. And I liked the old things from the past, the murals with the flowers on them, they looked so real.

(Dear God!)

Q: You said you were associated with a theater group in Tokyo. Did you like it?

A: No . . . yes. I don't know.

Q: Were they nice people?

A: Oh yes. They were awfully nice. But they got mad at me, I suppose. . . . You see . . . well, I don't seem to get things quite right, I suppose. It's not so much the work, because I do that all right, but the other . . . the little things. It's always like that.

Q: What do you think is the matter?

A: You . . . I think you know.

Jannina flipped through the rest of it: normal, normal, normal. Miss Smith was as normal as could be. Miss Smith was stupid. Not even very stupid. It was too damned bad. They'd probably have enough of Leslie Smith in a week, the Komarovs; yes, we'll have enough of her (Jannina thought), never able to catch a joke or a tone of voice, always clumsy, however willing, but never happy, never at ease. You can get a job for her, but what else can you get for her? Jannina glanced down at the dossier, already bored.

Q: You say you would have liked to live in the old days. Why is that? Do you think it would have been more adventurous or would you like to have had lots of children?

A: I . . . you have no right . . . You're condescending.

Q: I'm sorry. I suppose you mean to say that then you would have been of above-average intelligence. You would, you know.

A: I know. I looked it up. Don't condescend to me.

Well, it *was* too damned bad! Jannina felt tears rise in her eyes. What had the poor woman done? It was just an accident, that was the horror of it, not even a tragedy, as if everyone's forehead had been stamped with the word "Choose" except for Leslie Smith's. She needs money, thought Jannina, thinking of the bad old days when people did things for money. Nobody could take to Leslie Smith. She wasn't insane enough to stand for being hurt or exploited. She wasn't clever enough to interest anybody. She certainly wasn't feeble-minded; they couldn't very well put her into a hospital for the feeble-minded or the brain-injured; in fact (Jannina was looking at the dossier again) they had tried to get her to work there and she had taken a good, fast swing at the supervisor. She had said the people there were "hideous" and "revolting." She had no particular mechanical aptitudes. She had no particular interests. There was not even anything for her to read or watch; how could there be? She seemed (back at the dossier) to spend most of her time either working or going on public tours of exotic places, coral reefs and places like that. She enjoyed aqualung diving, but didn't do it often because that got boring. And that was that. There was, all in all, very little one could do for Leslie Smith. You might even say that in her own person she represented all the defects of the bad old days. Just imagine a world made up of such creatures! Jannina yawned. She slung the folder away and padded into the kitchen. Pity Miss Smith wasn't good-looking, also a pity that she was too well balanced (the folder said) to think that cosmetic surgery would make that much difference. Good for you, Leslie, you've got some sense, anyhow. Jannina, half asleep, met Ann in the kitchen, beautiful, slender Ann reclining on a cushion with her so-chi and melon. Dear old Ann. Jannina nuzzled her brown shoulder. Ann poked her.

"Look," said Ann, and she pulled from the purse she wore at her waist a tiny fragment of cloth, stained rusty brown.

"What's that?"

The second-best maker of hand-blown glass—oh, you know about it—well, this is his blood. When the best maker of hand-blown glass in the world had stabbed to the heart the second-best maker of hand-blown glass in the world, and cut his throat, too, some small children steeped handkerchiefs in his blood and they're sending pieces all over the world."

"Good God!" cried Jannina.

"Don't worry, my dear," said lovely Ann; "it happens every decade or so. The children say they want to bring back cruelty, dirt, disease, glory, and hell. Then they forget about it. Every teacher knows that." She sounded amused. "I'm afraid I lost my temper today, though, and walloped your godchild. It's in the family, after all."

Jannina remembered when she herself had been much younger and Annie, barely a girl, had come to live with them. Ann had played at being a child and had put her head on Jannina's shoulder, saying, "Jannie, tell me a story." So Jannina now laid her head on Ann's breast and said, "Annie, tell me a story."

Ann said: "I told my children a story today, a creation myth. Every creation myth has to explain how death and suffering came into the world, so that's what this one is about. In the beginning, the first man and the first woman lived very contentedly on an island until one day they began to feel hungry. So they called to the turtle who holds up the world to send them something to eat. The turtle sent them a mango and they ate it and were satisfied, but the next day they were hungry again.

" 'Turtle,' they said, 'send us something to eat.' So the turtle sent them a coffee berry. They thought it was pretty small, but they ate it anyway and were satisfied. The third day they called on the turtle again and this time the turtle sent them two things: a banana and a stone. The man and woman did not know which to choose, so they asked the turtle which thing it was they should eat. 'Choose,' said the turtle. So they chose the banana and ate that, but they used the stone for a game of catch. Then the turtle said, 'You should have chosen the stone. If you had chosen the stone, you would have lived forever, but now that you have chosen the banana, Death and Pain have entered the world, and it is not I that can stop them."

Jannina was crying. Lying in the arms of her old friend, she wept bitterly, with a burning sensation in her chest and the taste of death and ashes in her mouth. It was awful. It was horrible. She remembered the embryo shark she had seen when she was three, in the Auckland Cetacean Research Center, and how she cried then. She didn't know what she was crying about. "Don't, don't!" she sobbed.

"Don't what?" said Ann affectionately. "Silly Jannina!"

"Don't, don't," cried Jannina, "don't, it's true, it's true!" and she went on in this way for several more minutes. Death had entered the world. Nobody could stop it. It was ghastly. She did not mind for herself but for others, for her godchild, for instance. He was going to die. He was going to suffer. Nothing could help him. Duel, suicide, or old age, it was all the same. "This life!" gasped Jannina. "This awful life!" The thought of death became entwined somehow with Leslie Smith, in bed upstairs, and Jannina began to cry afresh, but eventually the thought of Leslie Smith calmed her. It brought her back to herself. She wiped her eyes with her hand. She sat up. "Do you want a smoke?" said beautiful Ann, but Jannina shook her head. She began to laugh. Really, the whole thing was quite ridiculous.

"There's this Leslie Smith," she said, dry-eyed. "We'll have to find a tactful way to get rid of her. It's idiotic, in this day and age."

And she told lovely Annie all about it.

Eurema's Dam

R. A. LAFFERTY

R. A. Lafferty had a story ("Sky") in the first *New Dimensions,* another ("Eurema's Dam") in the second, one more ("Days of Grass, Days of Straw") in the third, and, I think, several more farther along the way. All of them are lovely idiosyncratic pixyish fables, sinewy and lilting, and since I had arbitrarily chosen to include only one story by each author in this collection, I picked "Eurema's Dam" above the other Laffertys at my disposal mainly because it had won a Hugo. (In 1973, at Toronto.) I am not all that awed by stories that win awards, nor all that scornful of those that don't—among those that didn't win in 1973, though they were on the final ballot, were Russ' "When It Changed," which I had rejected, and Silverberg's "When We Went to See the End of the World," which I had written—but Lafferty's feat of winning a Hugo for "Eurema's Dam" deserves some commemoration. Virtually all Hugo-winning stories are first published in science-fiction magazines or in paperback anthologies, cheap and easily available to a wide segment of the electorate. But *New Dimensions 2* had appeared only in an expensive hardcover edition that had sold perhaps 6000 copies. (The paperback reprint did not emerge until long after the awards had been handed out.) How, given that handicap, Lafferty's story had ever reached enough people to get the required number of votes, I have no idea. Yet it won, just beating out my own story. I will not pretend that I would not have preferred it the other way around; but I was undilutedly delighted that so fine and special a writer as Lafferty had carried off his first trophy with a story I had published.

HE WAS ABOUT THE LAST OF THEM.

What? The last of the great individualists? The last of the true creative geniuses of the century? The last of the sheer precursors?

No. No. He was the last of the dolts.

Kids were being born smarter all the time when he came along, and they would be so forevermore. He was about the last dumb kid ever born.

Even his mother had to admit that Albert was a slow child. What else can you call a boy who doesn't begin to talk till he is four years old, who won't learn to handle a spoon till he is six, who can't operate a doorknob till he is eight? What else can you say about one who put his shoes on the wrong feet and walked in pain? And who had to be told to close his mouth after yawning?

Some things would always be beyond him—like whether it was the big hand or the little hand of the clock that told the hours. But this wasn't something serious. He never did care what time it was.

When, about the middle of his ninth year, Albert made a breakthrough at telling his right hand from his left, he did it by the most ridiculous set of mnemonics ever put together. It had to do with the way dogs turn around before lying down, the direction of whirlpools and whirlwinds, the side a cow is milked from and a horse is mounted from, the direction of twist of oak and sycamore leaves, the maze patterns of rock moss and tree moss, the cleavage of limestone, the direction of a hawk's wheeling, a shrike's hunting, and a snake's coiling (remembering that the Mountain Boomer is an exception), the lay of cedar fronds and balsam fronds, the twist of a hole dug by a skunk and by a badger (remembering pungently that skunks sometimes use old badger holes). Well, Albert finally learned to remember which was right and which was left, but an observant boy would have learned his right hand from his left without all that nonsense.

Albert never learned to write a readable hand. To get by in school he cheated. From a bicycle speedometer, a midget motor, tiny eccentric cams, and batteries stolen from his grandfather's hearing aid Albert made a machine to write for him. It was small as a doodle bug and fitted onto pen or pencil so that Albert could conceal it with his fingers. It formed the letters beautifully as Albert had set the cams to follow a copybook model. He triggered the different letters with keys no bigger than whiskers. Sure it was crooked, but what else can you do when you're too dumb to learn how to write passably?

Albert couldn't figure at all. He had to make another machine to figure for him. It was a palm-of-the-hand thing that would add and subtract and multiply and divide. The next year when he was in the ninth grade they gave him algebra, and he had to devise a flipper to go on the end of his gadget to work quadratic and simultaneous equations. If it weren't for such cheating Albert wouldn't have gotten any marks at all in school.

He had another difficulty when he came to his fifteenth year. People, that is an understatement. There should be a stronger word than "difficulty" for it. He was afraid of girls.

What to do?

"I will build me a machine that is not afraid of girls," Albert said. He set to work on it. He had it nearly finished when a thought came to him: "But *no* machine is afraid of girls. How will this help me?"

His logic was at fault and analogy broke down. He did what he always did. He cheated.

He took the programming rollers from an old player

piano in the attic, found a gear case that would serve, used magnetized sheets instead of perforated music rolls, fed a copy of Wormwood's *Logic* into the matrix, and he had a logic machine that would answer questions.

"What's the matter with me that I'm afraid of girls?" Albert asked his logic machine.

"Nothing the matter with you," the logic machine told him. "It's logical to be afraid of girls. They seem pretty spooky to me too."

"But what can I do about it?"

"Wait for time and circumstance. They sure are slow. Unless you want to cheat—"

"Yes, yes, what then?'   '

"Build a machine that looks just like you, Albert, and talks just like you. Only make it smarter than you are, and not bashful. And, ah, Albert, there's a special thing you'd better put into it in case things go wrong. I'll whisper it to you. It's dangerous."

So Albert made Little Danny, a dummy who looked like him and talked like him, only he was smarter and not bashful. He filled Little Danny with quips from *Mad* magazine and from *Quip,* and then they were set.

Albert and Little Danny went to call on Alice.

"Why, he's wonderful!" Alice said. "Why can't you be like that, Albert? Aren't you wonderful, Little Danny? Why do you have to be so stupid, Albert, when Little Danny is so wonderful?"

"I, uh, uh, I don't know," Albert said, "uh, uh, uh."

"He sounds like a fish with the hiccups," Little Danny said.

"You do, Albert, really you do!" Alice screamed. "Why can't you say smart things like Little Danny does, Albert? Why are you so stupid?"

This wasn't working out very well, but Albert kept with it. He programmed Little Danny to play the ukulele and to sing. He wished that he could program himself to do it. Alice loved everything about Little

Danny, but she paid no attention to Albert. And one day Albert had had enough.

"Wha- wha- what do we need with this dummy?" Albert asked. "I just made him to am- to amu- to make you laugh. Let's go off and leave him."

"Go off with you, Albert?" Alice asked. "But you're so stupid. I tell you what. Let's you and me go off and leave Albert, Little Danny. We can have more fun without him."

"Who needs him?" Little Danny asked, "Get lost, Buster."

Albert walked away from them. He was glad that he'd taken his logic machine's advice as to the special thing to be built into Little Danny. He walked fifty steps. A hundred. "Far enough," Albert said, and he pushed a button in his pocket.

Nobody but Albert and his logic machine ever did know what that explosion was. Tiny wheels out of Little Danny and small pieces of Alice rained down a little later, but there weren't enough fragments for anyone to identify.

Albert had learned one lesson from his logic machine: never make anything that you can't unmake.

Well, Albert finally grew to be a man, in years at least. He would always have something about him of a very awkward teen-ager. And yet he fought his own war against those who were teen-agers in years, and defeated them completely. There was enmity between them forever. He hadn't been a very well-adjusted adolescent, and he hated the memory of it. And nobody ever mistook him for an adjusted man.

Albert was too awkward to earn a living at an honest trade. He was reduced to peddling his little tricks and contrivances to shysters and promoters. But he did back into a sort of fame, and he did become burdened with wealth.

He was too stupid to handle his own monetary affairs, but he built an actuary machine to do his investing and became rich by accident; he built the damned thing too good and he regretted it.

Albert became one of that furtive group that has saddled us with all the mean things in our history. There was that Punic who couldn't learn the rich variety of hieroglyphic characters and who devised the crippled short alphabet for wan-wits. There was the nameless Arab who couldn't count beyond ten and who set up the ten-number system for babies and idiots. There was the double-Dutchman with his movable type who drove fine copy out of the world. Albert was of their miserable company.

Albert himself wasn't much good at anything. But he had in himself a low knack for making machines that were good at everything.

His machines did a few things. You remember that anciently there was smog in the cities. Oh, it could be drawn out of the air easily enough. All it took was a tickler. Albert made a tickler machine. He would set it fresh every morning. It would clear the air in a circle three hundred yards around his hovel and gather a little over a ton of residue every twenty-four hours. This residue was rich in large polysyllabic molecules which one of his chemical machines could use.

"Why can't you clear all the air?" the people asked him.

"This is as much of the stuff as Clarence Deoxyribonucleiconibus needs every day," Albert said. That was the name of this particular chemical machine.

"But we die from the smog," the people told him. "Have mercy on us."

"Oh, all right," Albert said. He turned it over to one of his reduplicating machines to make as many copies as were necessary.

You remember that once there was a teen-ager problem? You remember when those little buggers used to be mean? Albert got enough of them. There was something ungainly about them that reminded him too much of himself. He made a teen-ager of his own. It was rough. To the others it looked like one of themselves, the ring in the left ear, the dangling side-locks, the brass knucks and the long knife, the guitar pluck to jab in the eye. But it was incomparably rougher than the human teen-agers. It terrorized all in the neighborhood and made them behave, and dress like real people. There was one thing about the teen-age machine that Albert made. It was made of such polarized metal and glass that it was invisible except to teen-ager eyes.

"Why is your neighborhood different?" the people asked him. "Why are there such good and polite teen-agers in your neighborhood and such mean ones everywhere else? It's as though something had spooked all those right around here."

"Oh, I thought I was the only one who didn't like the regular kind," Albert said.

"Oh no, no," the people said. "If there is anything at all you can do about it—"

So Albert turned his mostly invisible teen-ager machine over to one of his reduplicating machines to make as many copies as were necessary, and set up one in every neighborhood. From that day to this the teen-agers have all been good and polite and a little bit frightened. But there is no evidence of what keeps them that way except an occasional eye dangling from the jab of an invisible guitar pluck.

So the two most pressing problems of the latter part of the twentieth century were solved, but accidentally and to the credit of no one.

As the years went by, Albert felt his inferiority most when in the presence of his own machines, par-ticularly those in the form of men. Albert just hadn't their urbanity or sparkle or wit. He was a clod beside them, and they made him feel it.

Why not? One of Albert's devices sat in the Presi-dent's Cabinet. One of them was on the High Council of World-Watchers that kept the peace everywhere.

One of them presided at Riches Unlimited, that private-public-international instrument that guaranteed reasonable riches to everyone in the world. One of them was the guiding hand in the Health and Longevity Foundation that provided those things to everyone. Why should not such splendid and successful machines look down on their shabby uncle who had made them?

"I'm rich by a curious twist," Albert said to himself one day, "and honored through a mistake of circumstance. But there isn't a man or a machine in the world who is really my friend. A book here tells how to make friends, but I can't do it that way. I'll make one my own way."

So Albert set out to make a friend.

He made Poor Charles, a machine as stupid and awkward and inept as himself. "Now I will have a companion," Albert said, but it didn't work. Add two zeros together and you still have zero. Poor Charles was too much like Albert to be good for anything.

Poor Charles! Unable to think, he made a—(*but wait a moleskin-gloved minute here, Colonel, this isn't going to work at all*)—he made a machi—(*but isn't this the same blamed thing all over again?*)—he made a machine to think for him and to—

Hold it, hold it! That's enough. Poor Charles was the only machine that Albert ever made that was dumb enough to do a thing like that.

Well, whatever it was, the machine that Poor Charles made was in control of the situation and of Poor Charles when Albert came onto them accidentally. The machine's machine, the device that Poor Charles had constructed to think for him, was lecturing Poor Charles in a humiliating way.

"Only the inept and the deficient will invent," that damned machine's machine was droning. "The Greeks in their high period did not invent. They used neither adjunct power nor instrumentation. They used, as intelligent men or machines will always use, slaves. They did not descend to gadgets. They, who did the difficult with ease, did not seek the easier way.

"But the incompetent will invent. The insufficient will invent. The depraved will invent. And knaves will invent."

Albert, in a seldom fit of anger, killed them both. But he knew that the machine of his machine had spoken the truth.

Albert was very much cast down. A more intelligent man would have had a hunch as to what was wrong. Albert had only a hunch that he was not very good at hunches and would never be. Seeing no way out, he fabricated a machine and named it Hunchy.

In most ways this was the worst machine he ever made. In building it he tried to express something of his unease for the future. It was an awkward thing in mind and mechanism, a misfit.

His more intelligent machines gathered around and hooted at him while he put it together.

"Boy! Are you lost!" they taunted. "That thing is a primitive! To draw its power from the ambient! We talked you into throwing that away twenty years ago and setting up coded power for all of us."

"Uh—someday there may be social disturbances and all centers of power and apparatuses seized," Albert stammered. "But Hunchy would be able to operate if the whole world were wiped smooth."

"It isn't even tuned to our information matrix," they jibed. "It's worse than Poor Charles. That stupid thing practically starts from scratch."

"Maybe there'll be a new kind of itch for it," said Albert.

"It's not even housebroken!" the urbane machines shouted their indignation. "Look at that! Some sort of primitive lubrication all over the floor."

"Remembering my childhood, I sympathize," Albert said.

"What's it good for?" they demanded.

"Ah—it gets hunches," Albert mumbled.

"Duplication!" they shouted. "That's all you're good for yourself, and not very good at that. We suggest an election to replace you as—pardon our laughter—head of these enterprises."

"Boss, I got a hunch how we can block them there," the unfinished Hunchy whispered.

"They're bluffing," Albert whispered back. "My first logic machine taught me never to make anything I can't unmake. I've got them there, and they know it. I wish I could think up things like that myself."

"Maybe there will come an awkward time and I will be good for something," Hunchy said.

Only once, and that rather late in life, did a sort of honesty flare up in Albert. He did one thing (and it was a dismal failure) on his own. That was the night in the year of the double millennium when Albert was presented with the Finnerty-Hochmann Trophy, the highest award that the intellectual world could give. Albert was certainly an odd choice for it, but it had been noticed that almost every basic invention for thirty years could be traced back to him or to the devices with which he had surrounded himself.

. You know the trophy. Atop it was Eurema, the synthetic Greek goddess of invention, with arms spread as though she would take flight. Below this was a stylized brain cut away to show the convoluted cortex. And below this was the coat of arms of the Academicians: Ancient Scholar rampant (argent); the Anderson Analyzer sinister (gules); the Mondeman Space-Driver dexter (vair). It was a very fine work by Groben, his ninth period.

Albert had the speech composed for him by his speech-writing machine, but for some reason he did not use it. He went on his own, and that was a disaster. He got to his feet when he was introduced, and he stuttered and spoke nonsense:

"Ah—only the sick oyster produces nacre," he said, and they all gaped at him. What sort of beginning for a speech was that? "Or do I have the wrong creature?" Albert asked weakly.

"Eurema does not look like that!" Albert gawked out and pointed suddenly at the trophy. "No, no, that isn't her at all. Eurema walks backward and is blind. And her mother is a brainless hulk."

Everybody was watching him with pained expression.

"Nothing rises without a leaven," Albert tried to explain, "but the yeast is itself a fungus and a disease. You be regularizers all, splendid and supreme. But you cannot live without the irregulars. You will die, and who will tell you that you are dead? When there are no longer any deprived or insufficient, *who will invent?* What will you do when there are none of us defectives left? Who will leaven your lump then?"

"Are you unwell?" the master of ceremonies asked him quietly. "Should you not make an end of it? People will understand."

"Of course I'm unwell. Always have been," Albert said. "What good would I be otherwise? You set the ideal that all should be healthy and well adjusted. No! No! Were we all well adjusted, we would ossify and die. The world is kept healthy only by some of the unhealthy minds lurking in it. The first implement made by man was not a scraper or celt or stone knife. It was a crutch, and it wasn't devised by a hale man."

"Perhaps you should rest," a functionary said in a low voice, for this sort of rambling nonsense talk had never been heard at an awards dinner before.

"Know you," said Albert, "that it is not the fine bulls and wonderful cattle who make the new paths. Only a crippled calf makes a new path. In everything that survives there must be an element of the incongruous. Hey, you know the woman who said, 'My husband is incongruous, but I never liked Washington in the summertime.'"

Everybody gazed at him in stupor.

"That's the first joke I ever made," Albert said lamely. "My joke-making machine makes them lots better than I do." He paused and gaped, and gulped a big breath. "Dolts!" he croaked out fiercely then. "What will you do for dolts when the last of us is gone? How will you survive without us?"

Albert had finished. He gaped and forgot to close his mouth. They led him back to his seat. His publicity machine explained that Albert was tired from overwork, and then the thing passed around copies of the speech that Albert was supposed to have given.

It had been an unfortunate episode. How noisome it is that the innovators are never great men. And the great men are never good for anything but just being great men.

In that year a decree went forth from Caesar that a census of the whole country should be taken. The decree was from Cesare Panebianco, the President of the country; it was the decimal year proper for the census, and there was nothing unusual about the decree. Certain provisions, however, were made for taking a census of the drifters and decrepits who were usually missed, to examine them and to see why they were so. It was in the course of this that Albert was picked up. If any man ever looked like a drifter and a decrepit, it was Albert.

Albert was herded in with other derelicts, sat down at a table, and asked tortuous questions. As:

"What is your name?"

He almost muffed that one, but he rallied and answered, "Albert."

"What time is it by that clock?"

They had him there in his old weak spot. Which hand was which? He gaped and didn't answer.

"Can you read?"

"Not without my—" Albert began. "I don't have with me my— No, I can't read very well by myself."

"Try."

They gave him a paper to mark with true and false questions. Albert marked them all true, believing that he would have half of them right. But they were all false. The regularized people are partial to false-hood. Then they gave him a supply-the-word test on proverbs.

"— — — — — — is the best policy" didn't mean a thing to him. He couldn't remember the names of the companies that he had his own policies with.

"A— — — — — in time saves nine" contained more mathematics than Albert could handle. "There appear to be six unknowns," he told himself, "and only one positive value, nine. The equating verb 'saves' is a vague one. I cannot solve this equation. I am not even sure that it is an equation. If only I had with me my—"

But he hadn't any of his gadgets or machines with him. He was on his own. He left half a dozen more proverb fill-ins blank. Then he saw the chance to re-coup. Nobody is so dumb as not to know one answer if enough questions are asked.

"— — — — — — — — is the mother of invention," it said.

"Stupidity," Albert wrote in his weird ragged hand. Then he sat back in triumph. "I know that Eurema and her mother," he snickered. "Man, how I do know them!"

But they marked him wrong on that one too. He had missed every answer to every test. They began to fix him a ticket to a progressive booby hatch where he might learn to do something with his hands, his head being hopeless.

A couple of Albert's urbane machines came down and got him out of it. They explained that, while he was a drifter and derelict, yet he was a rich drifter and derelict and that he was even a man of some note.

"He doesn't look it, but he really is—pardon our laughter—a man of some importance;" one of the fine machines explained. "He has to be told to close his mouth after he has yawned, but for all that he is the winner of the Finnerty-Hochmann Award. We will be responsible for him."

Albert was miserable as his fine machines took him out, especially when they asked that he walk three or four steps behind them and not seem to be with them. They gave him some pretty rough banter and turned him into a squirming worm of a man. Albert left them and went to a little hide-out he kept.

"I'll blow my crawfishing brains out," he swore. "The humiliation is more than I can bear. Can't do it myself, though. I'll have to have it done."

He set to work building a device in his hide-out.

"What you doing, boss?" Hunchy asked him. "I had a hunch you'd come here and start building something."

"Building a machine to blow my pumpkin-picking brains out," Albert shouted. "I'm too yellow to do it myself."

"Boss, I got a hunch there's something better to do. Let's have some fun."

"Don't believe I know how to," Albert said thoughtfully. "I built a fun machine once to do it for me. He had a real revel till he flew apart, but he never seemed to do anything for me."

"This fun will be for you and me. Consider the world spread out. What is it?"

"It's a world too fine for me to live in any longer," Albert said. "Everything and all the people are perfect, and all alike. They're at the top of the heap. They've won it all and arranged it all neatly. There's no place for a clutter-up like me in the world. So I get out."

"Boss, I've got a hunch that you're seeing it wrong. You've got better eyes than that. Look again, real canny, at it. Now what do you see?"

"Hunchy, Hunchy, is that possible? Is that really what it is? I wonder why I never noticed it before. That's the way of it, though, now that I look closer."

"Six billion patsies waiting to be took! Six billion patsies without a defense of any kind! A couple of guys out for some fun, man, they could mow them down like fields of Albert-Improved Concho Wheat!"

"Boss, I've got a hunch this is what I was made for. The world sure has been getting stuffy. Let's tie into it and eat off the top layer. Man, we can cut a swath!"

"We'll inaugurate a new era!" Albert gloated. "We'll call it the Turning of the Worm. We'll have fun, Hunchy. We'll gobble them up like goobers. How come I never saw it like that before? Six billion patsies!"

The twenty-first century began on this rather odd note.

$$f(x) = (11/15/67)$$
$$x = her, f(x) = o$$

GEORGE ALEC EFFINGER

George Alec Effinger was one of the brightest and most gifted of the new young writers who turned up in science fiction at the beginning of the Seventies. His perceptions were unmistakably his own, his cool, clear style was poised and elegant, and his method of storytelling combined classic structural strength with a very contemporary playfulness. The science-fiction world has never been very kind to that sort of writer; to those raised on flat-footed, ham-fisted magazine prose, someone as sly and aloof as Effinger seems subversive and disturbing, for it is difficult for such readers to tell whether they are being entertained or mocked. So there were no Hugos for Effinger, not even any Nebulas (which were more plausible, since he's undeniably a writer's writer, and that sort often gets Nebulas.) In time he drifted away from writing science fiction, though he still checks in occasionally; the last I heard he was writing mainstream novels, and doing fairly well at it between bouts of dismaying medical problems. Our loss, surely. I published four of his stories in the first six issues of *New Dimensions,* of which this is marginally my favorite, though on alternate days I think I might have chosen "Target: Berlin" from number six.

OFTENTIMES WE SPEAK OF THE "PRIVILEGE OF SCI-
ence." Now, just what does this phrase mean?
"Science," our dictionary tells us, concerns the observation and classification of natural phenomena. Now,
already we are losing touch with the personal involvement that enables each of us, as individuals, to identify and communicate with our environment and our
time. "Natural phenomena." What does that actually
mean, how are we to grab hold of such a nebulous
concept (an idea which in two words encompasses
everything that comes to pass within the confines of
the universe) so that it represents a concrete and vir-
tual process? I intend by no means to suggest that all
such groups of jargon words be eliminated in favor
of pragmatic terms, but I *do* wish, at the outset, to
avoid creating a mistaken impression in the mind of
the reader.

So, to begin. Over three years ago our department
began an experiment. The whole idea grew out of a
discussion we had been continuing during our lunch
break for some time. Indeed, the head of our department was aware of the high caliber of insights that
were made during the informal bull sessions. He
guessed that it had something to do with the contrast
between the rigorous hours of the morning and the
relaxed surroundings during lunch. In any event,
someone (I believe it was Dr. Green) made an off-
hand remark about what we could do if we had the
proper equipment. I said that even with the facilities
he envisioned it would be impossble. Dr. Nelson disagreed. For four days our staff argued, in ever more
heated tones. Research was done in our spare time.
Authorities were consulted for outside opinions. Anal-
ogies were constructed, attacked, and defended. All
of this was done extracurricularly; never did our regular tasks suffer.

On the morning of November 15, 1967, I arrived
at the lab early. Somehow I knew that it was going
to be a special day. Though I went to my locker
nearly half an hour before my usual time, I found al-

most every one of my associates already dressed and ready for work. The green blackboard in the locker room had been freshly washed (some black wet spots were still fading from view) and a mysterious quotation had been written high up on the board. The writing was a masculine scrawl, beginning in the upper left corner and slanting down to about the middle of the board. The message was: *"Direct lies told to the world are as dust in the balance when weighed against the falsehoods of inaccuracy; and accuracy can be taught."* *Sir Arthur Helps.*

I was mystified. "What does this mean?" I asked Dr. Johnson.

"I don't know," he said, stifling a yawn with the back of his hand. His wristwatch protruded from the sleeve of his lab coat and gleamed under the locker room's fluorescents. His other hand held his clipboard.

"Is he weighing lies against falsehoods?" asked Dr. Green.

"I suppose," said Dr. Johnson.

"Which would be heavier?" said Dr. Nelson. "What's so significant about dust in the balance? A gram is still a gram."

"It's very strange," I said, shaking my head.

"Perhaps this will straighten things out," said the deep voice of the department head. We all turned around quickly, startled, and saw our superior standing in the entrance to the tunnel that leads to our work area. He was leaning against the doorjamb and smiling. His smile is an unsettling thing: small, forced, generally reserved for unpleasant occasions. But now we knew that he had an agreeable surprise for us. He held a large glass apparatus in his hands.

"A Fleischer retort!" said Dr. Green. "And a hypostasis unit! How ever did you wangle that out of the commissioners?"

"My secret, gentlemen," said the department head softly. "As you no doubt realize, this equipment is very sophisticated, very expensive, and very necessary to that project you've all been mooning about for the last week. I've received permission to suspend the current experiments for as long as it takes for you to gather your data. Have a good time, gentlemen, but be careful! These things are fragile." Surely he knew that such a warning was unnecessary to men of our background, but I suppose that he was actually suggesting that the future of our department might rest with our conduct and our results in this spontaneous enterprise. I know for certain that his own position was in jeopardy. But we could never let him down; this was not the first time that our department head had taken such a risk for us.

"This is the way that science operates," said Dr. Green musingly, staring at Sir Arthur's quotation.

"Co-operation," said Dr. Johnson, clapping him on the back and putting his other arm around my shoulder as we started down the tunnel to the lab. "If we work together, we can build something that will endure for all time. If we bicker, if we let our petty feelings in the way, it'll be pure hell."

"Let's do it," said Dr. Nelson behind us. "Let's do it for the department head."

"Right," said Dr. Green.

And that's the way the project began. Of course, as yet we had little idea of the work before us, or even the general direction that it would be necessary to explore. Each of us had his own idea of the proper hypothesis or the proper method. Even though we wanted desperately to begin the actual experimentation, we knew from experience that that stage was still some months away. Now was the time for more research, serious contemplation, and independent study in our particular field of strength. Later our data would be collated and evaluated, and our department head would guide us in directing our energies along what appeared to be the most profitable avenues.

Imagination is the lifeblood of science, as research and experimentation are its nerves and sinews. The scientist as artist: no mere contradiction in terms, but a true picture of the necessary role of the creative spark in the pageant of technological development. At Science Seminary in Iowa we were trained in many of the techniques used by the other schools, particularly the liberal arts branches. We read by candlelight. We were made to stare blankly from attic windows, our instructors walking among us to position our fingers in thoughtful attitudes on our chins and cheeks. We learned to use hunger and frustration effectively. Perhaps this is the reason that today those of us who made it through the Seminary are apt to be more dependably *erratic,* or spontaneous, or whatever constitutes true originality. Though (no doubt, no doubt!) we are harder to work with.

How large a part imagination plays in the cavalcade of scientific endeavor: that which is not accidental discovery is instead the result of careful preparation. Careful preparation in turn is the product of thought and reasoned discourse, which proceed from a train of related insights, which develop from a single, momentary, creative inspiration. The continued encouragement of an open-minded, receptive (and, therefore, productive), and enthusiastic outlook is essential. For years I signed my letters with this exhortation: *Do not stultify!* until I realized that it was pretentious.

As we began our work our interpersonal relationships became more complex. We were all great chums as it was, but now again we felt ourselves to be members of the same team, all working together, pulling as one, co-operating in a true spirit of Christian fellowship. Then one day our department head introduced the new member, Dr. Short (or, as we all called her, Janet). Far from being resented, she was immediately welcomed and made to feel at home. We did our best to include her in our group feeling as well as in our work, pausing now and then to give her a chance to voice whatever opinion she might have.

Janet was beautiful; even in her white lab coat she

was the loveliest woman that I had ever seen. Her hair fell about her shoulders like rippling waves of sunshine. Her eyes were twin pools of limpid blue, and I never tired of staring into them. And, fortunately, she enjoyed that too. We used to stand about the lab, each of us by his own gas jet, staring into her eyes from our scattered work areas. She would smile and turn slowly, giving each of us his turn at falling directly into her line of sight. Her features were finely shaped, classically beautiful. Her bearing suggested that she was accustomed to command. We all gazed wistfuly at the way her pendulous alabaster globes strained at the thin material of the sweater beneath the lab coat. On those rare occasions when we caught a glimpse of her thigh, we noticed that it was as creamy white and smooth as we hoped. Not one of us failed to feel the stirring in his loins when she came, in each morning to chat with us in the locker room. But it was given only to Dr. Nelson to enjoy her special favor. Not that we overly envied his fortune or thought ill of them. Indeed, we were overjoyed at their happiness, for it seemed to knit our little group even closer. We took delight in their joy, and often.

The process of maturing is the recurring task of learning discipline. This lesson becomes more and more difficult, for as we grow older and more set in our ways we become less willing to be refashioned in new molds for new outlooks. The final rigidity, the final inability to follow instructions, is death. Nothing else is worth worrying about. And so it is in science: the imagination is vital, of course, but only insofar as it is disciplined. We must recognize standards.

Was that Dr. Short's function? Was she the unifying touchstone of caution that held us together, that kept us from flying off like excited children lost among the phantoms of scientific speculation? Or was she rather a scheme of our department head, to maintain Dr. Nelson's shaky equilibrium? Surely Dr. Nelson's instability was no secret; we discussed it often enough in his absence. But with Janet—Dr. Short—Dr. Nelson seemed to find his spiritual anchor. And everyone knew his weakness for trim ankles and faint mustaches.

While the exotic apparatus collected dust and held down papers on the desk of the department head, we compiled our facts. One by one the hypotheses were abandoned as hard facts contradicted premises. We celebrated the death of each theory at lunch. Someone would bring a radio and we'd dance, drawing lots while Janet, the only partner, sat apart and smiled tightly. She had a light dusting of freckles across her nose; I'll always remember that.

During the summer of 1968, Drs. Nelson and Short became better and better acquainted. Janet bought him a pair of boots, and he gave her several necklaces and pendants. It became a morning ritual to stand about the lockers with their pasted-up pictures of Jane Fonda or Johnny Bench and the color shot clipped from *Life*, blown-up photos taken through an electron microscope of a virus or refractions from molecular arrangements and comment on them (the various necklaces and pendants, one of which Dr. Short would wear each day). We would laugh quietly and some of us would smoke until the bell rang. Then we'd all start off down the tunnel, ready for another day at the slate-topped work tables. The department head spoke to us each morning, just as we reached the end of the tunnel and emerged into the laboratory proper. We would ply him with questions concerning the meaning of that day's cryptic quotation, but he never gave us a hint. He believed that his daily mystery aided us in expanding our horizons, increasing our mental agility, combating the creeping conservatism that is inimical to progress, and so forth. He was apart from us, being admin., but in his own way he was always truly one of us. We never did really resent him.

I believe that it was Dr. Johnson who first remarked on the parallel courses of our experiment and Drs. Nelson's and Short's burgeoning relationship. "Even

as we grope blindly," said Dr. Johnson, and Janet
blushed endearingly, "feeling about for new laws for
old events, so too are you, our very dear colleagues,
discovering the most charming and novel variations of
the age-old 'love' situation. Certainly you realize that
this has been done many times before, but are you not
still amazed at how fresh and new it seems? We are
learning as we go, creating the rules and discovering
the operations as they become necessary. So are you.
I am curious to see who will win."

And this was very true. Dr. Nelson ceased shaking
and mumbling, habits which, good friend though he
was, often made him impossible to get along with. He
found security at last, after nearly fifty years in the
field. Janet made sure to touch an elbow patch of his
lab coat every time she passed his work table. Dr.
Nelson would look up and smile, the familiar old
vagueness gone from his eyes. And soon he began to
make important contributions, just as he did long before I was born. And Janet—that is, Dr. Short—
gained from their alliance too. She took to carrying a
small spiral notebook with her, to copy down such
vocabulary words or aphorisms as Dr. Nelson might
pronounce. She began to wear tight blouses, unbut-
toned in a suggestive manner.

And then, after a year, we came into the locker
room on November 15, 1968. On the blackboard, as
usual, was a quotation: *"There are not many joys in
human life equal to the joy of the sudden birth of a
generalization illuminating the mind after a long period of patient research." Prince Kropotkin.*

Dr. Johnson turned to me, his speckled face transformed with expectation. "Are you ready?" he asked.

"Gee, I don't know," I said. I certainly didn't feel
any differently.

"But today's the day, apparently," said Dr. Green.
"I wonder who it'll be."

Dr. Johnson looked across the room at Drs. Nelson
and Short. "I sort of hope it's Dr. Nelson. That would
vindicate the department head."

We all stared with Dr. Johnson, and the rightness of his sentiment was undeniable. I think that each of us secretly decided to shirk that day, in order not to deprive Dr. Nelson of the opportunity of making the Big Breakthrough by himself. None of us wanted to beat him accidentally to the key discovery. Consequently, after filing into the laboratory, we pretended to work as usual, but spent a good deal of time tying shoelaces and sharpening pencils. Dr. Johnson and Dr. Green played "dots." I called the other six associates (whom I have yet to mention by name; they were very silent) together for a review of our previous year's work, ostensibly as an anniversary celebration. Dr. Nelson was so engrossed in his analyses that he failed to notice us.

About noon Dr. Nelson called out to Dr. Johnson, "Do you think that the reduced amount of ultraviolet let through by the denser atmosphere could have been the stimulating factor?" Dr. Johnson said that he wasn't sure. Dr. Nelson went back to his work. In an hour he announced that he believed that he had a unified hypothesis that covered every one of the contingencies that we had specified in the last twelve months. We congratulated him, and Janet led him away to get a bit of lunch. We didn't see them again for several days, but we were so relieved that the initial phase was completed that we just chuckled indulgently.

When circumstances had returned to normal we met with the department head. He appointed Dr. Green to become obsessed with perfection. I was to be the pessimist. Dr. Johnson and one other were to question our motives. Dr. Nelson and Dr. Short had made their contributions, but they were to do even more. We owed quite a bit to them. Without their continuing efforts and constant support, both intellectual and spiritual, our job could never have been accomplished. Now, our team scattered as it is to the four corners of the globe, we often think of our debt to those two oddly matched, dedicated workers. I doubt if I will ever see their like again. It would be a tiresome repetition.

Everyone but the experimenter himself has confidence in the results, for the technician is the only one aware of the amount of hedging that is done (yes, we all do it, even the noblest of us, for time is money). But the only one likely to be completely enthusiastic about a hypothesis is its originator. Thus, the department head tried to encourage us along lines which he himself believed to be best, while attempting to convince us that these choices were our own. We all knew what he was doing, but it made no difference.

When the working hypothesis was first put forward by Dr. Nelson (and soundly applauded), and modified by suggestions from Dr. Johnson and two of the others, we gathered together into a circle with the department head in the center. Those of us along the perimeter joined hands, and the department head made us promise that if the hypothesis proved unworkable we would not hold to it stubbornly. We gladly agreed. I recall very clearly walking back to my work area with Dr. Green. "Still," he said, "that does not mean that we must abandon the hypothesis after an initial failure or two."

"Right," I said. "As long as mere ideas do not take precedence over truths we shall be fine."

By this time, I believe, Drs. Nelson and Short were deeply and sincerely in love. They spoke to each other in lovers' terms, with few actual words, but many sentimentalized looks and gestures. We watched them approvingly, and a little enviously, for we had all forsworn happiness at the Seminary. I always got a bit of a twinge when I saw Dr. Nelson put his hand on Janet's knee when he thought no one was watching. The shadows and planes of her knees worked together to give the impression that one was viewing a photograph of a bust of Poseidon. No one ever mentioned this, though. It may be that I was the only one of us who thought so.

The two were inseparable. They wandered about

the lab together, they went out for a drink of water together, they sat together at lunch, he pressing his right calf against her left. They did little work, but we covered for them. Perhaps the department head realized that this was happening, but he said nothing as long as our tasks were completed according to our voluntary schedule. Dr. Short, when included in our conversations, would at one point or another remark on how brilliant Dr. Nelson's hypothesis was, and how much time it saved the entire project. Dr. Johnson reinforced his earlier observation thusly: "Our project is heading off in a definite direction now. We don't know yet if it is the correct one exactly, but the work we do will give us that information in just a matter of time. The structure is sound, built on sufficient mature thought. And so is your relationship. You are applying what you have learned about each other to form a long-lasting, internally consistent, mutually profitable arrangement."

Shortly after the actual research began we were stunned one morning to find *two* quotations on the board. I do not recall the uppermost sentiment (the one put there by the department head), but below it was scrawled in Dr. Nelson's hand: *"We must never be too absorbed by the thought we are pursuing."* *Claude Bernard*. We were shaken. Was this a denial of the significance of our work? Was it, even worse, an indication of his waning interest in Janet (Dr. Short)? We asked him about it at lunch; he denied putting it on the blackboard. We pressed him, and he admitted writing it there. But he was surprised at our outrage and curiosity. "I don't necessarily mean what Bernard suggests," he said, smiling. "It's just food for thought, gentlemen." We shook our heads in wonder. Even as old as he was, Dr. Nelson's mind moved through devious channels.

Research is to the progress of science as everything after the shuffling is to a game of canasta. There are two types of research: research done for its own sake or the sake of knowledge (*ad maiorem gloriam Dei*), and research done to solve a particular problem. Our present work was neither. "Is this applied research?" I asked.

"No," said Dr. Johnson, "I don't believe so. There is actually little commercial value in what we're doing."

"But does that mean then that we're doing straight abstract stuff?"

"That should follow," he said with a puzzled expression, "but in this case it doesn't."

"Perhaps we have stumbled on a third sort of research," said Dr. Green.

"Maybe that's it," said Dr. Johnson, dismissing the matter with a wave of his hand.

At the Science Seminary we were instructed in game theory, according to the supposition that proper scientific experimentation had its own strategies, as much so as any game of chance. It does not take much alteration of viewpoint to see science as competition between the researcher and the inscrutable forces of nature. There is even a sort of "box score" that may be used to outline the degree of success enjoyed by an experiment. Science has its teams, its goals, its penalties; reason is its referee. The war against disease, poverty, ignorance, and intolerance is being won on the playing fields of Cal Tech.

Well, the sides had been chosen, the ball field prepared, the coin tossed, but there were no spectators. Ours was a silent struggle. No bands played, no girls in blue and white shorts cheered us on. Just the long walk from the locker room through the tunnel to the "dugout" (the lab), where our "manager" would give us our daily pep talk. We, the home team, *Science* carved in big rock letters like the ads for *Ben Hur* out on the Seminary lawn so many years ago, we started out half an inning behind the opposition. But we would bat last. What a silly way for adults to spend their lives.

We were like children! It was like Christmas out of our distant past; we set up the delicate glassware in preparation for the first of the test runs. Flasks, retorts, induction coils, copper tubing, rubber tubing, glass tubing, stoppers and petcocks, all joined together like a malformed Xmas tree for chemists. Banks of electrophoresis apparatus stood ready to analyze the products of the experiment. Cables ran underfoot, twisting through furniture and doorways to end with red and green plastic viper heads. It seemed to me that I was transported back to my youth, trying to synthesize amino acids in the high school lab, with sparks in a piece of glassware simulating lightning. Again, we played God.

"Building, always building," murmured Dr. Green. I happened to be standing very near to him at the time.

"Dr. Nelson and Janet?" asked Dr. Johnson, who stood very near to Dr. Green on the other side.

"No," said Dr. Green, "I meant us, here, with all this. In a little while we'll have *learned* something."

"I suppose," said Dr. Johnson. "But those two," indicating Drs. Nelson and Short, "are building much more, and at a greater rate than we can hope to match. *They* are the ones doing beautiful things."

"Perhaps we should give up here and go out and do likewise," I said jokingly.

"Not so facetious a suggestion as you might think," said one of the other scientists.

"Just keeping ourselves open to whatever options present themselves should suffice," I said. "Have a goal, but take what comes."

"With dedication the password to success," said the voice of the department head. We turned around, startled and amazed at his unusual appearance in our realm so late in the day.

"Dedication," said the wheezing voice of Dr. Nelson, "ah, dedication is less than illusion. It is a fallacy." We all gasped at his contradiction of the department head. Dr. Nelson had struck at the very foundation of our belief. "No matter," he said, "I don't really mean that, either. The important thing to remember, though, is that *someone* does." Could he mean me? I thought anxiously.

Perhaps it was only my guilty mind that insisted that Dr. Nelson had directed his curious attack at me. I *was* guilty, because I worshiped Dr. Short. I was blind then. I did not see those shortcomings which became so painfully evident later on, after the reviews were printed: I was not aware of her pathological needs which masqueraded as concern, or the malleable, almost mercuric nature of her personality, which provided her with emotional camouflage. We never wondered why she avoided large groups of people; she could not assume a personality that would be proof against the potential threats of all the others. But, as I say, I saw none of this. I was entranced by the pellucidness, the apparent guilelessness, the graciousness, the exuberance that was merely immaturity. And I loved her and felt guilt, for she was not my woman.

"What is observed depends on who's looking." W. H. George. That was the quotation on the blackboard for November 15, 1969, the second anniversary of our project. Naturally, when each of us came in that morning we expected to be greeted by news of some major development that the department had had planned. It was one year ago that Dr. Nelson had made the necessary synthesis to begin our actual experiment. I felt that today might be the day when we would detect those products that signaled the final phase. But the quotation gave us little hope of such a step. In fact, the more we discussed it, the more it seemed to be actually negative in nature, as though we had been overlooking something vital and would have to begin again.

Dr. Green did not agree. "No," he said, "I think you're wrong there, barking up the wrong tree, so to speak. Your interpretation does not hold water. You're too quick to look at the gloomy side. I believe that the department head intends for us to see today as a rebirth of devotion, in a slightly altered direction. That is, if you take my meaning, that our outlook must no longer be so parochial, so narrow. We must grow with the project, if you follow me. We are in danger of getting in over our heads, and our only salvation will be to push back the frontiers of our trepidations, so that we may operate comfortably even though we're unsure what we're doing."

"That's very interesting," said Dr. Johnson.

"But aren't we all observing?" I asked innocently.

"Precisely," said Dr. Green.

"And aren't we all taking notes independently?" asked Dr. Johnson.

"Exactly," said Dr. Green.

"Well?" said Dr. Johnson.

"We're all approaching this wrong," said Dr. Green.

"We're viewing the thing passively, jotting down each development when it happens and not trying to anticipate. Something happens and we say, 'Look at that!' We should be trying to predict what will occur, and then watch for justification."

"Is he right?" I asked Dr. Johnson.

"Perhaps," he said.

So that day we began doing just that. It must have been the correct thing, because the department head beamed proudly. Later, Dr. Green told me in confidence that he was inspired to his singular interpretation by his observation of Drs. Nelson and Short. They had ceased to be astonished by their relationship; not to say that the wonder had vanished, but that they had enough confidence in themselves now that they could rather make plans with some assurance. The future, of course, was still unknown, but it worked within a framework that they had discovered within themselves and within each other. The two of them had gladly replaced the fire of their early passion with a mature and quiet faith.

Some days later Dr. Johnson was staring into the huge central apparatus. The contents of the glassware were bubbling and shifting as they had begun to do recently, sliding through color changes in no apparent pattern. The liquid contents roiled and surged in a thick, sexual way, while the gaseous products hung in slowly shifting clouds, occasionally rising out of or falling into the liquid. It was an incredibly gorgeous thing to see, and I wonder if the beauty of it didn't seduce our eyes from the purely scientific observation for which we were employed. Dr. Short, that is, Janet, came over to the central work area and stood beside Dr. Johnson. He never took his eyes from the huge glass bubble, but he knew that she was there.

"These are the words that I have for your love for Dr. Nelson," he said. "Opalescent, sustentative, radiant, crystalline, epicene, vibrant, adamantine, chatoyant. The devoutly-to-be-wished consummation."

Janet was silent for a moment. Then she laughed. "Golly," she said, "if you only knew!" She twisted a button on her blouse for a few seconds, then turned around and walked away. She went back to her table with Dr. Nelson and put her arm around him and called him "honey."

It was now early summer of 1970. We had formed a softball squad to play the research team from across the hall. At the first game I stood at the backstop with a few of the fellows from the opposing group. Dr. Short was taking her practice in the batter's box and was doing pretty well, hitting line drives over the in fielders' heads and sending the outfielders back in astonishment with some fairly long flies. One of the other group of fellows remarked on her surprising talent. I smiled and told them that she was involved with one of our number, and that the experiment we were conducting seemed to be paralleling their love affair. My audience chuckled, but stopped when I angrily repeated my strange statement. I was told that such a thing was very common, that they had had a similar experience themselves a few years ago. I said nothing more to these cloddish fellows. I watched Janet, now taking fielding practice in her long white lab coat. She seemed to me to be still afraid of hard ground balls.

Near the end of the summer things began to go bad. The first sign was the day we arrived to find no quotation on the blackboard. Hurrying worriedly through the tunnel, we discovered Dr. Short sitting at her work area, crying.

"What's wrong?" I asked her.

"Can we do anything?" asked one of the others.

Dr. Short (Janet) pointed in the direction of the experiment. Still weeping, she took Dr. Nelson's hand. "I don't know," she said, sobbing. "I don't know if I love you because of that thing or in spite of it." The department head had been summoned and now stood on the outside of our circle. We looked like Snow White and the seven dwarfs. He told her that she could have the rest of the day off. She shook her head, but followed him back down the tunnel to the locker room. We all told Dr. Nelson that everything would be all right. He watched helplessly.

Again the next day there was no quotation. We said nothing, but it was obvious that something terrible was happening. It was frustrating not to know what. The next morning I arrived half an hour early, so that I could write the quotation for the day. Someone already had: *"The patient investigation and accurate methods required to obtain desired results in the school of experimental and technical science cannot fail to impress, refine, and ennoble the characters of those who work in this direction." Sir William Mather.* It was not the handwriting of the department head. It seemed to have been put there by one of the nameless others. It certainly was the wrong sentiment; I was enraged. I took up a piece of chalk and printed "UP YOURS!" in very large letters. We were all feeling the effects of the tension.

It was learned that afternoon that the experiment was slowing down. There seemed to be less material in the glass bubble, although this seemed hardly possible. There was no way to measure the quantity of the contents without interrupting (and thus ending) the process. We could only observe anxiously. Weeks passed. It became definite: the liquid and gas in the bubble were somehow disappearing. We talked little, even at lunch. The department head spent a lot of time walking between our benches and silently patting our backs. We saw no more quotations.

At the same time we noticed that Drs. Short and Nelson also had little to say to each other. This was the most heartbreaking part, I believe. We had come this far, nearly three years, and we were committed to seeing it through. This was the test of maturity we had been warned about at the Seminary. I always thought that I could handle it; in theory I knew what I would do, that it was foolish to let adolescent emotions confuse your actions. But somehow I found myself as helpless as the others. There can be no preparation.

The third anniversary passed, officially unmarked. No one cared to mention that sad fact. More weeks passed; the contents of the glass bubble had dwindled to a few lumps of red-gold matter about the bottom and just a hint of greenish haze. I spent the days writing letters. Dr. Johnson and Dr. Green brought their guitars. Some of the others built models or touched each other secretly. On January 30, 1971, it was all over. A Saturday morning, bright and cold; we came into the lab and dressed wordlessly. When we passed through the tunnel we found the experiment completely dismantled. An old cleaning lady was just finishing up. The flasks, retorts, tubing, and special equipment rested upside down, washed and drying on the slate-topped table. We were taken aback; there was nothing else to do but turn around. We returned to the locker room, hung up the lab coats, and went home. I have never seen any of that gang since.

Science, now—well, science has its rewards. But it requires a certain detachment, I suppose; they tried to drill that into me at the Seminary, but I was too idealistic to believe it. You have to be able to keep your identity. These things don't *always* turn out to be grand *Scientific American* coups (how seldom they do!). And you have to be able to pick yourself up and clean out your crusted test tubes and do it again: *"The love of life and the love of science are nearly indistinguishable, as science is the willing pupil of life.*

Thus, the science of life, which is after all the purpose of all learning, and the science of love, the latter only just less than equal to the former, follow in their courses at the night the day."
Robert W. Hanson.

The Ones Who Walk Away from Omelas

URSULA K. LE GUIN

Ursula Le Guin's *The Left Hand of Darkness* was published in 1969 and received both Hugo and Nebula awards virtually by acclamation. Rarely has such instant fame come to a writer in the science-fiction field. (The only comparable cases I can think of are A.E. van Vogt, after the publication of "Black Destroyer" in 1939, and Philip José Farmer, in the aftermath of "The Lovers" in 1952.) When Le Guin's agent Virginia Kidd sent me a longish story called "Vaster Than Empires and More Slow" in January, 1970, I bought it instantly for the first *New Dimensions,* though not without some (very mild) reservations: as I told Virginia Kidd, the story, though "sensitive, beautifully written, intelligent," was, style aside, rather more traditional in theme and handling than I had in mind for the brand-new *New Dimensions.* This was merely intended to let an important agent and good friend know that I stood ready to publish farther-out material than that; but Ursula chose to interpret my remarks as meaning that I found the story "dull and derivative," and had bought it merely to fill a hole in my anthology, in which case she preferred not to let me publish it.

Some quick correspondence got all that straightened out to everybody's satisfaction; Ursula came to realize that I was not likely to buy a story I thought dull or derivative just to plug a gap in the book, and allowed it to remain; we have all been good friends ever since, and "Vaster" finished second in the following year's Nebula voting. I still think it's a fine story in the traditional exploration-team-story mode, and I'm not at all surprised that it's gone on to five or six later anthologizations. (I'm responsible for reprinting it once myself.)

It is not present in *The Best of New Dimensions*, however, because I happened to publish another Le Guin story in the third issue—a strange little fable called "The Ones Who Walk Away from Omelas." It picked up a Hugo in 1974—the second year in a row that a short story from *New Dimensions* had been so honored—and went on to become something of a classic. (And has been recorded by its author, in a supremely elegant reading for Caedmon Records.)

WITH A CLAMOR OF BELLS THAT SET THE SWALlows soaring, the Festival of Summer came to the city Omelas, bright-towered by the sea. The rigging of the boats in harbor sparkled with flags. In the streets between houses with red roofs and painted walls, between old moss-grown gardens and under avenues of trees, past great parks and public buildings, processions moved. Some were decorous: old people in long stiff robes of mauve and gray, grave master workmen, quiet, merry women carrying their babies and chatting as they walked. In other streets the music beat faster, a shimmering of gong and tambourine, and the people went dancing, the procession was a dance. Children dodged in and out, their high calls rising like the swallows' crossing flights over the music and the singing. All the procession wound toward the north side of the city, where on the great watermeadow called the Green Fields boys and girls, naked in the bright air, with mudstained feet and ankles and long, lithe arms, exercised their restive horses before the race. The horses wore no gear at all but a halter without bit. Their manes were braided with streamers of silver, gold, and green. They blew out their nostrils and pranced and boasted to one another; they were vastly excited, the horse being the only animal who has adopted our ceremonies as his own. Far off to the north and west the mountains stood up half-encircling Omelas on her bay. The air of morning was so clear that the snow still crowning the Eighteen Peaks burned with white-gold fire across the miles of sunlit air, under the dark blue of the sky. There was just enough wind to make the banners that marked the race course snap and flutter now and then. In the silence of the broad green meadows one could hear the music winding through the city streets, farther and nearer and ever approaching, a cheerful faint sweetness of the air that from time to time trembled and gathered together and broke out into the great joyous clanging of the bells.

Joyous! How is one to tell about joy? How describe the citizens of Omelas?

They were not simple folk, you see, though they were happy. But we do not say the words of cheer much any more. All smiles have become archaic. Given a description such as this one tends to make certain assumptions. Given a description such as this one tends to look next for the King, mounted on a splendid stallion and surrounded by his noble knights, or perhaps in a golden litter borne by great-muscled slaves. But there was no king. They did not use swords, or keep slaves. They were not barbarians. I do not know the rules and laws of their society, but I suspect that they were singularly few. As they did without monarchy and slavery, so they also got on without the stock exchange, the advertisement, the secret police, and the bomb. Yet I repeat that these were not simple folk, not dulcet shepherds, noble savages, bland utopians. They were not less complex than we. The trouble is that we have a bad habit, encouraged by pedants and sophisticates, of considering happiness as something rather stupid. Only pain is intellectual, only evil interesting. This is the treason of the artist: a refusal to admit the banality of evil and the terrible boredom of pain. If you can't lick 'em, join 'em. If it hurts, repeat it. But to praise despair is to condemn delight, to embrace violence is to lose hold of everything else. We have almost lost hold; we can no longer describe a happy man, nor make any celebration of joy. How can I tell you about the people of Omelas? They were not naive and happy children—though their children were, in fact, happy. They were mature, intelligent, passionate adults whose lives were not wretched. O miracle! But I wish I could describe it better. I wish I could convince you. Omelas sounds in my words like a city in a fairytale, long ago and far away, once upon a time. Perhaps it would be best if you imagined it as your own fancy bids, assuming it will rise to the occasion, for certainly I cannot suit you all. For instance, how about technology? I think that there would be no cars or helicopters in and above the streets; this follows from the fact that the people of Omelas are happy people. Happiness is based on a just discrimination of what is necessary, what is neither necessary nor destructive, and what is destructive. In the middle category, however—that of the unnecessary but undestructive, that of comfort, luxury, exuberance, etc.—they could perfectly well have central heating, subway trains, washing machines, and all kinds of marvelous devices not yet invented here, floating light-sources, fuelless power, a cure for the common cold. Or they could have none of that: it doesn't matter. As you like it. I incline to think that people from towns up and down the coast have been coming in to Omelas during the last days before the Festival on the very fast little trains and double-decked trams, and that the train station of Omelas is actually the handsomest building in town, though plainer than the magnificent Farmers Market. But even granted trains, I fear that Omelas so far strikes some of you as goody-goody. Smiles, bells, parades, horses, bleh. If so, please add an orgy. If an orgy would help, don't hesitate. Let us not, however, have tem-

ples from which issue beautiful nude priests and priest-
esses already half in ecstasy and ready to copulate
with whomsoever, man or woman, lover or stranger,
desires union with the deep godhead of the blood, although that was my first idea. But really it would be
better not to have any temples in Omelas—at least,
not manned temples. Religion yes, clergy no. Surely
the beautiful nudes can just wander about, offering
themselves like divine soufflés to the hunger of the
needy and the rapture of the flesh. Let them join the
processions. Let tambourines be struck above the cop-
ulations, and the glory of desire be proclaimed upon
the gongs, and (a not unimportant point) let the offspring of these delightful rituals be beloved and looked
after by all. One thing I know there is none of in
Omelas is guilt. But what else should there be? I
thought at first there were no drugs, but that is puri-
tanical. For those who like it, the faint insistent sweetness of *drooz* may perfume the ways of the city, *drooz*
which first brings a great lightness and brilliance to
the mind and limbs, and then after some hours a
dreamy languor, and wonderful visions at last of the
very arcana and inmost secrets of the Universe, as
well as exciting the pleasure of sex beyond all belief;
and it is not habit-forming. For more modest tastes
I think there ought to be beer. What else, what else
belongs in the joyous city? The sense of victory, surely,
the celebration of courage. But as we did without
clergy, let us do without soldiers. The joy built upon
successful slaughter is not the right kind of joy; it will
not do; it is fearful and it is trivial. A boundless and
generous contentment, a magnanimous triumph felt
not against some outer enemy but in communion with
the finest and fairest in the souls of all men everywhere
and the splendor of the world's summer: this is what
swells the hearts of the people of Omelas, and the victory they celebrate is that of life. I really don't think
many of them need to take *drooz*.

Most of the processions have reached the Green
Fields by now. A marvelous smell of cooking goes

forth from the red and blue tents of the provisioners. The faces of small children are amiably sticky; in the benign gray beard of a man a couple of crumbs of rich pastry entangled. The youths and girls have mounted their horses and are beginning to group around the starting line of the course. An old woman, small, fat, and laughing, is passing out flowers from a basket, and tall young men wear her flowers in their shining hair. A child of nine or ten sits at the edge of the crowd, alone, playing on a wooden flute. People pause to listen, and they smile, but they do not speak to him, for he never ceases playing and never sees them, his dark eyes wholly rapt in the sweet, thin magic of the tune.

He finishes, and slowly lowers his hands holding the wooden flute.

As if that little private silence were the signal, all at once a trumpet sounds from the pavillion near the starting line: imperious, melancholy, piercing. The horses rear on their slender legs, and some of them neigh in answer. Sober-faced, the young riders stroke the horses' necks and soothe them, whispering, "Quiet, quiet, there my beauty, my hope . . . " They begin to form in rank along the starting line. The crowds along the race course are like a field of grass and flowers in the wind. The Festival of Summer has begun.

Do you believe? Do you accept the festival, the city, the joy? No? Then let me describe one more thing.

In a basement under one of the beautiful public buildings of Omelas, or perhaps in the cellar of one of its spacious private homes, there is a room. It has one locked door, and no window. A little light seeps in dustily between cracks in the boards, secondhand from a cobwebbed window somewhere across the cellar. In one corner of the little room a couple of mops, with stiff, clotted, foul-smelling heads, stand near a rusty bucket. The floor is dirt, a little damp to the touch, as cellar dirt usually is. The room is about three paces long and two wide: a mere broom closet or disused toolroom. In the room a child is sitting. It might be a boy or a girl. It looks about six, but actually is nearly ten. It is feebleminded. Perhaps it was born defective, or perhaps it has become imbecile through fear, malnutrition, and neglect. It picks its nose and occasionally fumbles vaguely with its toes or genitals, as it sits hunched in the corner farthest from the bucket and the two mops. It is afraid of the mops. It finds them horrible. It shuts its eyes, but it knows the mops are still standing there; and the door is locked; and nobody will come. The door is always locked, and nobody ever comes, except that sometimes —the child has no understanding of time or interval —sometimes the door rattles terribly and opens, and a person, or several people, are there. One of them may come in and kick the child to make it stand up. The others never come close, but peer in at it with frightened, disgusted eyes. The food bowl and the water jug are hastily filled, the door is locked, and the eyes disappear. The people at the door never say anything, but the child, who has not always lived in the toolroom, and can remember sunlight and its mother's voice, sometimes speaks. "I will be good," it says. "Please let me out. I will be good!" They never answer. The child used to scream for help at night, and cry a good deal, but now it only makes a kind of whining, "eh-haa, eh-haa," and it speaks less and less often. It is so thin there are no calves to its legs; its belly protrudes; it lives on a half-bowl of cornmeal and grease a day. It is naked. Its buttocks and thighs are a mass of festered sores, as it sits in its own excrement continually.

They all know it is there, all the people of Omelas. Some of them have come to see it, others are content merely to know it is there. They all know that it has to be there. Some of them understand why, and some do not, but they all understand that their happiness, the beauty of their city, the tenderness of their friendships, the health of their children, the wisdom of their scholars, the skill of their makers, even the abundance of their harvest and the kindly weathers of their skies, depend wholly on this child's abominable misery.

This is usually explained to the children when they are between eight and twelve, whenever they seem capable of understanding; and most of those who come to see the child are young people, though often enough an adult comes, or comes back, to see the child. No matter how well the matter has been explained to them, these young spectators are always shocked and sickened at the sight. They feel disgust, which they had thought themselves superior to. They feel anger, outrage, impotence, despite all the explanations. They would like to do something for the child. But there is nothing they can do. If the child were brought up into the sunlight out of that vile place, if it were cleaned and fed and comforted, that would be a good thing, indeed; but if it were done, in that day and hour all the prosperity and beauty and delight of Omelas would wither and be destroyed. Those are the terms. To exchange all the goodness and grace of every life in Omelas for that single, small improvement: to throw away the happiness of thousands for the chance of the happiness of one: that would be to let guilt within the walls indeed.

The terms are strict and absolute; there may not even be a kind word spoken to the child.

Often the young people go home in tears, or in a tearless rage, when they have seen the child and faced this terrible paradox. They may brood over it for weeks or years. But as time goes on they begin to realize that even if the child could be released, it would not get much good of its freedom: a little vague pleasure of warmth and food, no doubt, but little more. It is too degraded and imbecile to know any real joy. It has been afraid too long ever to be free of fear. Its habits are too uncouth for it to respond to humane treatment. Indeed after so long it would probably be wretched without walls about it to protect it, and darkness for its eyes, and its own excrement to sit in. Their tears at the bitter injustice dry when they begin to perceive the terrible justice of reality, and accept it. Yet it is their tears and anger, the trying of their generosity and the acceptance of their helplessness, which are perhaps the true source of the splendor of their lives. Theirs is no vapid, irresponsible happiness. They know that they, like the child, are not free. They know compassion. It is the existence of the child, and their knowledge of its existence, that makes possible the nobility of their architecture, the poignancy of their music, the profundity of their science. It is because of the child that they are so gentle with children. They know that if the wretched one were not there sniveling in the dark, the other one, the fluteplayer, could make no joyful music as the young riders line up in their beauty for the race in the sunlight of the first morning of summer.

Now do you believe in them? Are they not more credible? But there is one more thing to tell, and this is quite incredible.

At times one of the adolescent girls or boys who go to see the child does not go home to weep or rage, does not, in fact, go home at all. Sometimes also a man or woman much older falls silent for a day or two, and then leaves home. These people go out into the street, and walk down the street alone. They keep walking, and walk straight out of the city of Omelas, through the beautiful gates. They keep walking across the farmlands of Omelas. Each one goes alone, youth or girl, man or woman. Night falls; the traveler must pass down village streets, between the houses with yellow-lit windows, and on out into the darkness of the fields. Each alone, they go west or north, toward the mountains. They go on. They leave Omelas, they walk ahead into the darkness, and they do not come back. The place they go toward is a place even less imaginable to most of us than the city of happiness. I cannot describe it at all. It is possible that it does not exist. But they seem to know where they are going, the ones who walk away from Omelas.

They Live on Levels

TERRY CARR

Terry Carr has been my friend for something over twenty years, and for the past decade we have been neighbors as well, in the hills facing San Francisco Bay. He edits an anthology called *Universe,* in which several of my stories have appeared; and I have used several of his in *New Dimensions*. Outsiders may quickly conclude from this that we run a nifty old-buddies arrangement whereby we blithely peddle stories to each other for cozy mutual benefit whenever we need a few extra dollars. And they would be wrong; for in fact I had to nag Carr for a year or more before he finally submitted "They Live on Levels" to me. He had tantalized me with a brief description, then successfully managed not to get around to writing it until I bludgeoned it out of him. Contrariwise, Terry has been waiting since 1973 for me to send him a short story whose scribbled outline he once saw on my desk, and I think he'll go on waiting a good many more years before I finally turn it in. If any sort of symbiosis has been going on in these hills, it involves other people's manuscripts—for one thing we have done, and frequently, is to pass on to each other stories that we have rejected but think the other might like to publish. This saves postage for authors and has frequently produced beneficial effects for an editor—as when Carr found himself unable to publish James Tiptree's "The Girl Who Was Plugged In" and turned it over to me for *New Dimensions 3*. It went on to win a Hugo in 1974. I returned the favor a couple of years later, to my chagrin, when I let Carter Scholz' Hugo nominee "The Ninth Symphony of Ludwig von Beethoven and Other Lost Songs" slip through my fingers and into *Universe*.

So much for behind-the-scenes gossip. As for "They Live on Levels," it's a lovely, joyous story of rare beauty, and I wish Carr would write some more just as good. But he doesn't seem to be writing any fiction at all these days—he says he's too busy editing anthologies. A pity, say I.

To Ram Manjari, Level Chandra, September 12, 2422:
Your talk diverts me beyond expression—I might fuse, as my old hygiene instructor liked to say. What an odd world is yours; you must take care not to make it too real for me or I should soon be there with you, and then what of our crosstalk?

Since I spoke last, we are immersed in sounds. A droning from the west comes each morning; chitterings and cymbals flit about our heads all day, and gay whoops fall periodically from the sky. Most peculiar, but agreeable. We feel no need for vocalizing, ourselves; everyone would seem most somber and close-mouthed to you, I'm sure. We are listening, we are bemused.

Hender leaves us tomorrow for Portsmouth, as he wishes very much to visit his focus there. He is better than when I last spoke, though still by no means peaceful. He will spend the week centering, and return to us only when his light has begun to reopen. Do you call your city Portsmouth too? It is on our western coast, and such an ancient city that it must have existed before the dispersal. (How near our worlds are, yet there are chasms between us!)

Anandaruth and Ruthanan have come again to live

with us. We had not expected them, therefore we were unprepared; but we made well upon fruits of the air, which seem to be stimulated by the great volume of sounds that wash them. The airspice will be blooming next; if the sounds last, we should have a most delightful season.

Ruthanan is not grown any more mindful than she was, nor Anandaruth at all more emotive. If they did not have each other I believe both would perish for want of understanding the world. But they will add to our echoing house, so I welcome them.

Speak to me again soon, please; I feel I have found a friend at last, and that is most wonderful to me. There are greater distances on Rose Level than scales can measure. Tell me of Level Chandra, your grounds and rocks and how they grind. Do you have these sounds too? One never knows the pervasive from the particular.

> Unhindered, unfiltered,
> Cass

"Our normal waking consciousness is but one special type of consciousness whilst all about it, parted from it by the flimsiest of screens, there lie potential forms of consciousness entirely different. No account of the universe in its totality can be final which leaves these other forms of consciousness quite disregarded."
—William James

To Cass Laureling, Rose Level, September 14, 2422:
Fascinating to hear of your air-sounds; there's nothing like that here, but we have more floating emotions than usual. You can be simply walking around, doing nothing in particular, and suddenly you find yourself skipping buoyantly, happy as leaves, for no reason. Keep walking and you leave that mood, but you could just as easily walk into a gloom. I stumbled into one yesterday so deep it actually dimmed the sun's light, and I could feel my pupils expand.

The thing to do when you get into one of those is to

keep walking, and you'll get out of the area; they're not big. A really deep gloom can make you want to lie down and moan, though, so you have to remember to keep going.

I had a childhood adventure with such a floating mood. I was only fourteen months, but I thought I was terribly smart. We had a very rainy season and I was cold and wet forever, it seemed (actually less than a month); I was in foul humor and never slept in the same bed twice. One day I wandered into a cloud of giggles, and began to bubble with them, joyfully and boisterously. I had a grand time. But they passed, and I was cold and wet again. I jumped up and looked around for the cloud, but of course you can't see them. I ran several steps in one direction, found nothing, ran in another direction, still nothing; I began to jump back and forth, thinking maybe I could surprise the thing. I got furious and began to hiss and curse. People who saw me say I spent over an hour trying to find the giggles again, and I got red in the face and wouldn't be dissuaded. I never found that patch again, of course, but I entertained a lot of people.

Anyway, we're absolutely inundated with floating moods now,. Most of them seem to be risers, but we do stumble into holes in the air sometimes. Virna, my mother this week, says she can see these moods by eye; I look where she points but never see anything. She says the risers have a faint silver cast, shimmering, and the holes are a sort of dim purple.

Virna and I have been talking about changing our relationship from mother-son to woman-man. We could do both, of course, but Virna likes to keep things simple. Can you offer any advice? Virna is forty-seven years old, petite, gamin-faced, with a bubbly aura. I've stayed with her as son frequently; we play hand games and sing together, and she likes my cooking. We hear each other's minds very well. I think she's attractive, but I'm a little afraid of the new relationship. I want so much from it. I suppose we could always keep it short, no more than a week the first time, but I have the feeling I need to do more.

Ram

They live on levels. There are twenty billion people on Earth today, but they still retain their parklands, their countrysides, farming areas, wildernesses of mountains and lakes. The oceans were cleared of their last pollutants during the century when the technologists were distilling even trace elements for desperately needed fuel. They ran out, of course, but technology had run its course anyway; it was time for progress in a new direction, and they were forced to it.

Huizinga said that culture began as an expression of our play instinct: we built new shapes, we imitated things we saw, we learned how to make other things do what we wanted. Not in the interests of building a civilization, only of getting a kick out of life. Civilization came with that, and the new shapes were standardized. Culture told us to do what it wanted, and we did. The play went out of it quickly.

That's why culture is for unhappy people. That's why the ecstatics always got off in the desert.

But when most of the fuel resources of the world were gone, technology faltered and people began to study new disciplines. The breakthrough into psychic space came shortly, and humanity discovered new worlds in the alternate realities of perception.

Here were universes that had seldom been glimpsed by men, and then only as shimmering dreams, Hai Brasils of the mind. Now, as people learned how to reach them, these new levels of perception offered space for the planet's aching cities. Landscapes assumed new lines, colors pulsed above, below and beside the familiar spectra. People found that they themselves looked other than they remembered. Natural laws seemed to change, or were augmented. And on each new level it was different, always different from the last, an infinity of new worlds. All it took was for people to follow their full natures, to live their own consciousnesses. Each to his own perception, to each his own reality.

So now they live on levels. No one knows how many levels there are, but there are enough to provide room for twenty billion people on this one planet.

Are you dubious? Even if they don't see people who live on different levels from them, that can't mean the others aren't there, can it? In reality there are more people on Earth than the planet can support, and nobody really has room to stretch his toes without stepping on someone else's. It's really that crowded, in reality, isn't it?

Maybe. What's "reality"? Maybe this isn't the twenty-fifth century after all, maybe it's the twentieth and they're in India and they're all starving.

But if so, they don't know it. You wouldn't want to bring them down, would you?

To Ram Manjari, Level Chandra, September 15, 2422:
We have had boomings from the west, and sharp crackling above, like sun-lightning. The chittering and whoops are still with us, but these deeper sounds begin to override them. We are all most amazed, and wondering what will come next: are we to live in the midst of an air symphony? The world is suddenly bombastic.

Ruthanan grows morose; she says these new sounds weigh on her with a physical presence. And I do see her shrink and tire when our booms are sounding, though chitterings sometimes cause her to smile. Yesterday I was with her when all of our sounds seemed to come at once, a quick rending sound followed by deep dull crashes, and with these a chittering and loud bells right in the room with us. What play of emotions on Ruthanan's face! She is so very emotive, far more than the rest of our home. We are all hoping the heavier sky sounds will pass quickly for her sake.

Our home is made emptier while Hender is away at Portsmouth, but we did have word from him today. He contacted Bard, of course, and she relayed much of their talk afterward. He feels quite excited by new powers and energies in his focus. Bard asked him to store some for us and he did promise it.

Your floating moods sound most intriguing; we have those so seldom here. We are a mere concrete level, I believe. I once felt a gloom-darkening such as you describe, but it was only in one room, it never moved. We opened the windows to air that room, but nothing availed for days, till finally we found a dead bird that had flown in and died behind a tape closet. The bird removed, the gloom passed.

How curious your relationship with Virna! Are mother-son ties different from those of man-woman? Or do you speak metaphorically? Surely you do not change shape as you assume new relationships. Is one relationship closer than others? Then choose the closest—space between people is wasted, as we say here. (It is only a wistful saying, however.)

Do you celebrate anniversaries of the dispersal? We used to, but the practice is unpopular now. Our world is so very slow in filling up, we begin to fear it will forever be a wilderness.

                    Unseen, unexplored,
                    Cass

They're born knowing all about sex. Why shouldn't they understand it?—they remember their former lives. Cellular memory isn't very complicated, perhaps, but it's clear and complete.

The only time they don't remember very well is when they are born into another level. On the cellular scale, things can still slip through; the screen between levels is no iron wall. Kids get born to women who haven't had relations with a man for years; kids get born to men, too. Five-year-olds have borne children and thought nothing of it.

The prevalence of crossbirth means people never are certain whose genes went into the kids they birth, so there's a lot less identification and they don't have a lot of expectations and demands to make. Most of the time a woman's child is hers and her lover's, as you'd expect, but they can't count on that and they don't. Flesh of my flesh doesn't mean anything when you don't know: blood ties become theoretical.

(When men or kids have children, they can figure it didn't happen on their level, they must have been around when a fertilized egg came through the screen. But that's just a certainty of uncertainty; the bearer knows he's *not* the genetic parent.)

Family systems are different on the different levels, and often there's a wide variety even on the same level. Most of them tend toward low intensities of involvement, usually expanded families or community parenthood: if a child is hungry, they feed him; if he wants to know something, they tell him. Affection gets spread more thinly than it was in nuclear families, but there are few traumas. Life is placid.

The kids are healthy and bright; they walk in five months and start talking soon after. They're sexually mature at seven or eight.

Cass Laureling is ten years old and Ram Manjari is nine.

To Cass Laureling, Rose Level, September 19, 2422:
I don't understand Virna. For days she spoke of man-womaning, so that I was seriously thinking about it, but suddenly she has no interest in emotions. She's all work and seriousness, is seldom home. She studies environment, and is presently very involved in our mood-weather. When we talk, it's about only that. I'm disappointed; I do want a strong emotional experience, and now I have no prospect.

Maybe there's a down mood in the room, but I don't think so. Since Virna pointed out that they can be seen, I've become adept at spotting them. There are so many, far more than I suspected a few days ago; I wonder if they're increasing or if I just never realized how much at the mercy of the air my own feelings were.

The good ones are silvery, and they dance in the air like heatwaves. They seem to fade in and out, and I can tell that they do drift around the room, sometimes very rapidly. When they leave, they go through the walls as often as through a window or doorway. The downs are darker colors, violet and mahogany and grayish blue, and they tend to move less. I avoid them, of course.

They're all the conversational rage now. Everyone has a theory about them. My body healer says they're drawn to where humans congregate, by some magnetic force in our nervous systems—and it's true that these clouds, these moods, seem much more plentiful in places where people live. I have an acquaintance who's an amuser, who gives public performances, and she claims she can dispel the darker moods and attract the silvery bubbling ones by the force of her own projections.

Virna's begun to hint that she knows where they come from, and she makes odd meaningful remarks which she won't elaborate. Her mind is always so roiling with thought and constructions that I can't see much of what she means.

One thing she said was, "They're more than moods. They're alive." And I think she may be right; I've been watching them and I think they do move with real purpose at times. But if they're really alive, how long have they been here? And do they see us?

You've spoken before of Hender's focus at Portsmouth. We do have a coastal town named Portsmouth, not far from here; it's a research center for mind-work. Is a focus anything like a self-augmenter? (Sometimes called a mind-plug.) A very powerful self-augmenter has just been completed at our Portsmouth, and Virna wants to go there to investigate more about mood-weather. Maybe I should go there myself, to strengthen my emotional abilities in the augmenter. I'm very serious about needing to relate closely with some. (I understand you very well about the space between people being wasted. And we have so *much* space on Level Chandra.)

Ram

Messages pass from one level to another by a process much like telepathy but far more tricky. There really is such a thing as etheric vibration, but it obeys its own rules and is hard to chart; sometimes the messages go through clearly and sometimes they have time-fade, so that words and phrases arrive seconds after they should. It requires getting used to and some extra concentration, but the communication is perfectly clear.

There are people who do this sort of work as their main function. It takes a lot of psychic energy, and these people are seldom very active in their own communities; most of their attention is spread through the levels and they hear murmurs and echoes even when no messages are actually coming or going. They're a special kind of people who live more in others than in themselves: switchboard operators, town eavesdroppers; they have great curiosity about people but they don't talk a great deal themselves.

Cass's homemate Bard is one of the people who pass crosslevel messages.

To Ram Manjari, Level Chandra, September 20, 2422:

How curious your talk of living air-moods! Bard read your letter across to me as I bathed her this morning; it is my week as her bodyservant. I pumiced and blew her as she recited, and we fancied we could see your ghostly forms moving about us, but it was only the fine pumice settling through sunbeams.

But all this talk of forms and moods in the air, and our own booming and chittering, is most odd indeed. Bard gives much weight to your reportage; and she has said that in crosstalk from dwellers on other levels than yours and ours, there is frequent word of strange occurrences. Anandarth, for instance, talks with a man on Form Level (they are both students of logic, which evidently varies from level to level); this man has told him that he feels pressures from the very air around him, and actual tactile sensations . . . as of unseen solid bodies brushing against him. Many on his level are in a fright about it. On other levels there are strange lights, daytime as well as night, and sometimes even voices. Yes, voices, though their words are not understandable.

How intriguing it all is, yet how foreboding! Our foremothers were so joyed to discover the new territory of the levels—it meant living space when there were too many of us in the single world. But now when we are still trying to become comfortable with our new space, are we to find that the levels were inhabited all along? Are we interlopers?

Yet we have not detected them till now, so I dare to hope that they are only lately arrived, that it is they who importune on us.

We have such noisy creatures in our air! Their chatter grows louder till they fairly screech, and their booms explode most frightfully at times. Ruthanan is terribly burdened by these sounds, and keeps to her pallet. I have tried to speak with her about them, but she remains mute and miserable. The sounds follow us indoors, droning or whistling sharply at our shoulders. We are invaded!

Hender has returned from Portsmouth to relieve some of our loneliness. He has gained much in confidence there; I believe you guess correctly in likening a focus to a self-augmenter. It is an area of concentrated energy which commands one's attention and informs the sensibilities for days or weeks after. Hender says he has never had such a successful time there, that the tenders of the site feel it is particularly powerful now. We are hoping to convince Ruthanan to make the trip, in hopes it will enable her to face these invading sounds.

I do not say a great deal about your relationship with Virna because I find myself strangely reticent in this area. Dear Ram, my thought are frequently with you, and they are warm ones; may you achieve closeness, whether with Virna or anyone else you choose. I do so much understand your wish for it. (The time I have spent serving Bard this week has been a closeness that has buoyed me; but with Hender returned her attention naturally goes to him.)

> Solitary warmth,
> Cass

To Cass Laureling, Rose Level, September 22, 2422:

They *are* alive, Cass, and they do see us! It's impossible to doubt it any more—Virna has managed to communicate with one of them!

We're at Portsmouth, and it happened our first morning here. The creature was silvery, very bright in the clear air of post-dawn. It drifted through a wall of our garden room and seemed to hover over the pool there. A tall, elongated shape, constantly shifting its form, like a ghostly amoeba. But it seemed to be facing us and it seemed to be watching, so Virna went toward it, holding out a hand and talking in a soothing tone. The form hung still in the air, bobbing slightly; when Virna reached the edge of the pool she stopped but continued to hold out her hand in invitation as she called softly to it. And after several minutes it came to her.

There was no mistaking its purpose, Cass. It came to her and touched her hand, and Virna shivered visibly; then it moved closer and covered the upper part of her body, and I heard her suddenly laugh in delight. The creature turned in the air, and Virna turned with it; as she faced me I saw wonder and joy on her face. The creature moved a bit aside, but still hovered near her; Virna called to it again, and again it came to cover her with silvery joy. She began to hum lightly, to sing without words, and to dance; and the creature followed her, hanging always close to her head and shoulders but sometimes bobbing to one side in time with Virna's movements.

It must have lasted several minutes. Eventually the creature retreated, or faded; it seemed to go back out the same wall it had entered by. Virna waved to it. All this time I had stood in awe and was a little frightened, not daring to call to Virna for fear I might startle the creature. But as soon as it was gone I blurted out questions: What was it like? Could you feel it? How did you know how to dance with it?

She said it felt like light in her mind, and bubbles up her spine. She had danced because that was how it made her feel. And she was sure the creature had been happy to contact her too; she had felt delight from it. "He'll come back before long," she told me. "I'm going to wait here till he does."

A few hours have passed since then, and though we've both seen the creatures drifting by outside and once inside, none had quite that silvery sheen of our morning's visitor and none seemed to notice Virna's calls. (I tried calling myself, but I didn't really know what to do.)

If they're invaders, they're welcome ones, Cass. But I don't think they're entirely new here. We've never had so many of them before, that's true, but remember that we have always had these floating moods, ever since I was a young child, and you said you'd once experienced something like it too. I think we must be the invaders, that we moved into worlds that were already populated only we couldn't see them. Now they're beginning to show themselves to us, and I think it means they've decided to trust us. (I hope so, anyway.)

As for Virna, she seems to have forgotten that we ever talked about man-womaning. All her attention goes to these creatures. I can't blame her, of course, but my loneliness is pervasive and I find myself going to her in the son-role for comfort. It's less than I need, but it's all I have.

I hope there'll be talk from you today. I have to find a crossmind here at Portsmouth right away. With

Virna's distant attitude, my closest human tie is with you—in another world!

Ram

Ram Manjari has no home. When he was seven he moved into a bright high room in a vacant house and began to acquire possessions: he collected colored stones and arranged them in patterns that flowed as the sun moved; he built chairs and wove a dining rug; he began to feed the animals of the neighborhood. On his eighth birthday he gave away the rug, scattered his stones and walked toward the sun till he found a woman who offered a mother-son week. This was Virna, and he lived with her more than ten weeks in the next year. The rest of the time he lived with fathers, sisters, once an old man who wanted him as grandson. On Level Chandra, people form family relationships to fill the needs of friendship.

Cass Laureling's home is a many-roomed house overlooking the River Quale. She moved in three years ago because she had been unhomed by a fire, and Andaruth and Ruthanan came with her from her previous home to this new one. There were four others then, including Hender; some moved out, others moved in; Rose Level homes exist in flux. Bard moved in to join with Hender a year ago. Homemates sleep with whom they want, and sex with whom they want, and sometimes there is love.

Outside the homes, on Rose Level or Level Chandra, there is space for trees, lakes, walking paths, streams. There is always room to be alone outside a house but people tend to huddle together within whatever walls they call homes.

To Ram Manjari, Level Chandra, September 22, 2422:

Ruthanan continues to bow beneath the weight of sounds; last night I heard her whimpering as she slept. Anandaruth was with her, but he hears nothing when he sleeps; he lies dreamless and is no comfort to her.

I crept to her pallet and held her till she quieted. This morning she thanked me and said her dreams were better when I was with her. To be truthful, I slept more fully myself . . . Bard, of course, was with Hender and I should otherwise have slept alone.

Later this morning Ruthanan faded again; we had a great booming over the river and then a sharp crack right in the very room with us. Ruthanan cried out and cowered, and began to cry. Anandaruth was just going out; he paused and tried to talk with her but she was not equal to his rationality and he retreated from the force of her fear. "They are only aural impressions," he said, "you are free to interpret them in comforting ways rather than manufacturing monsters." Anandaruth does not understand fear, it is not familiar to him.

He went out to an appointment and I went to Ruthanan. "Are you unhurt?" I asked her, to which she nodded vaguely, eyes wide and staring. "Will you travel with me to focus at Portsmouth?" I said. She shook her head violently and retreated beneath her blanket for some minutes. At last she came forth and said, "Do you think it will help?" So I knew she would change her mind, and I assured her that a day of focusing should greatly strengthen her understanding, and that all of us had agreed this was her best course. "Anandaruth too?" she asked, and I said yes, he too. He does not understand her and is no help to her but still she looks to him for guidance.

So I am making up an overnight pack and in an hour we shall leave for Portsmouth, whence I shall send my next message to you, assuming I can be heard despite our increasingly clamorous skies.

In hopeful transit,
Cass

To Cass Laureling, Rose Level, September 23, 2422:
I was so relieved to find our new crossmind last night; I was feeling terribly isolated, cut off. (All the familiar lonely feelings, here in the middle of a city

of thousands of people!) He's a gray man, with quiet eyes and a dry manner; he recites his messages as though he weren't hearing them himself. Did I ever tell you that our last crossmind was a berry-cheerful little man who would hop around and make flamboyant gestures as he read your words across? He gave a lot of joy to your messages . . . but I find from this new gray man that your own joy comes through with no need of a crossmind's acting.

I think you must be a rising bubble all by yourself, one of those pockets of happiness that we've been having in our air. Everything is metaphorical, all of life is a symbol of some other reality, and haven't we found that these air-moods are living creatures? You're a joyous bubble to me, Cass—if only I could chase you as easily as I used to chase giggles!

(I'm sorry; I'm starting to babble nonsense. I'll talk about something else.)

We've been visited again by our air-creatures, three of them this time, and Virna is beginning to establish a language of gestures. They become clearer to the eye each day; now we can see the movement of their limbs. They walk upright, and I think they have several arms—does that frighten you? They really don't seem at all menacing, and I could be wrong about their arms.

I've been talking with people at Portsmouth about them; everybody thinks they're becoming more and more numerous every day. A woman who tends the city's parks is very grumpy about all the hubbub. "They build this big *augmenter*," she complained to me, "an now evybody comes here to get bigger, they sleep in the grass and leave their odors behine. An that's not bad enough, now there's *ghosts* comin to haunt us! It was a happier town without this augmenter, but try an tell anything to these young snats with their *self-realization!*"

The town does have more people in it than there are beds for—not that that's any problem to anyone but a sour old woman. I was hoping I'd get to visit the augmenter myself, but there's always such a crowd there that the effects are diffused among them. And still more people arrive every day.

I manage to be lonely even among the crowds, though. I suppose loneliness is a part of us all. Your message yesterday cheered me, but it was frustrating too. So good to hear your words, surprising to know you've come to Portsmouth too . . . but you're not really here, are you, not here where I can see and touch you and look you in the eyes. If only we lived in the same world, so that I could travel to be with you, no matter how many days away! But to be in the same city and still be so far apart . . . ?

I can't think of anything more to say.

Ram

"I'm not trying to change you. It may happen that one day you may become a man of knowledge . . . but that will not change you. Some day perhaps you'll be able to *see* men in another mode and then you'll realize that there's no way to change anything about them."

—Don Juan

To Ram Manjari, Level Chandra, September 24, 2422:

Do you really think me so joyous, Ram, so light and bright? Oh I wish I were! But in truth I am a distressingly empty person; I need people around me or I am still as dust. I need to be stirred.

I am moved now, but not entirely pleasantly. We arrived in Portsmouth only to find the city besieged by the sounds of a teeming sky; the air is drenched in noise, so very clamorous that Ruthanan wanted to turn and leave immediately. I prevailed on her to stay, at least to visit a focus and try its effect. She has done so and is perhaps a bit better today.

I have been wondering the streets of old Portsmouth, in some awe at the great specificity of these surroundings. Such straight lanes, never wandering, and the

ancient Portsmouth trees placed almost geometrically
at the verges. It is a city planned in our eras of ration-
alism, one can apprehend this immediately, and its
beauties are rational. Quite appropriate for a great
center of mind-focus, of course, for the very geometry
of the city discourages a wandering mind.

Yet sharing these austere streets with us are the
gongs and cries of these new creatures. (Or these old
creatures who are new to us.) Portsmouth is a dreaming city of the past painfully roused to wakefulness
by alarums from emptiness. Leaves quail before blasts
of sound, and people try to go about their lives as
though nothing were at all anomalous.

Here too we are beginning to see these creatures.
One need only find the point from whence a ghost-
sound issues, and there will be a darkening of the air,
light that is mysteriously roiled and agitated, as though
the creatures are trying to pull themselves *through*.
And they must be succeeding, for only a few days ago
they could not be seen at all and now they are here;
they invade us in full force.

Perhaps I have caught Ruthanan's fears, for in truth
the creatures are frequently beautiful and their sounds
melodious. I believe some of those sounds are their
voices, that we seem to hear bells and hissing because
our senses must interpret only fractionally heard sounds
without referents. I met a man today who maintained
that these new creatures are gods, come to deliver us
from our isolation; that they are to be worshipped
and loved. He did believe it, I could hear as much
from his mind as from his voice and it was all joyful.
He said there are many others in Portsmouth who believe as he does, and that when they hear the voices
of these creatures they always sound musically, har-
moniously. And it is true that I see people walking the
streets and parks with eyes half-closed, listening in joy.

When I brought Ruthanan to her center of focus
last night she was told immediately that her first discipline would be that of silence: to create peace within
herself and to hear it in her surroundings. Afterward

she may hear the harmonies of this silence. Never once did her instructors mention the new creatures, but clearly what they are teaching is a response to them.

I confess that I welcome them, whether they are gods or monsters. They fill this world, and their sounds do not ring in hollowness, at the least. If they sometimes frighten me, and if I do not always hear them as melody, they do drown the incessant chatter of my inner cries.

Why should Portsmouth be such a target for these creatures, if not because of the great natural focus that exists here? They flock to a city where our minds are most open and capable, where we may be expected to be most receptive of the bizarre. Indeed, they fill the empty spaces of Portsmouth so that the very fruits of the air seem crowded and constricted. (This morning Ruthanan and I drank the light and wondered if we might thereby also be consuming a creature or two!) I am coming to believe that these beings appear so predominantly at this place because they are drawn to the vacuum of our loneliness, which is more openly felt at this point of focus; for those of us who are in need of gathering our selves are so very frequently driven to it by our inescapable isolation.

It is a fact, that I have not confided to anyone, that every person I meet seems only a reflection of myself, and therefore no relationship that I have had has been fully satisfying. We live in this level because this is who we are; but our very closeness makes our contact empty. And so we feel our closeness as isolation, and that is the irony of it.

Does this make sense to you, dear Ram, or am I only being fanciful? I feel that we have arrived at a turning point, but I cannot define its nature; something new is happening but what is it?

I do understand with all my heart when you speak of the frustration of being so near and so inescapably distant now that we are both in Portsmouth. But why should we feel this need to meet in the flesh? Why should we be drawn to each other rather than to those of our own worlds? I believe it is our very strangeness that in orms our attachment: for I feel you as an *other*, as not-me, to a degree impossible on my own level.

Perhaps we can meet yet, Ram, in a way. If we are truly in the same Portsmouth city, then let us try it. There is, in the Portsmouth I see, a long straight lane through South Park flanked by poplars and root-berries, with at the very south end a giant brooding oak. It must be many hundreds of years old, and therefore surely antedates the dispersal. Do you know the tree? I shall be there at noon tomorrow; and if you will go to the same place, we may look for each other. Do not ask how, for I do not know. I only know that I shall be there, and that I truly hope you will too.

Looking, listening,
Cass

To Cass Laureling, Rose Level, September 24, 2422:

I have to answer you immediately, Cass, because your message has me so excited—more excited than you can have expected, because there is wonderful news. Yes, I will certainly be at the oak tomorrow at noon; I recognize the walk you describe and I know the tree you mean. But I'll come there expecting a lot more than a romantic communing on separate levels—I could bear to be another Triste to your Isolate, but I think we can do much more.

Cass, do you know yet what these invading creatures are? They're not monsters and they're not ghosts —they're human beings! Two legs, two arms, five fingers, five toes; eyes, ears, noses, mouths, all. We see them more clearly by the hour now; their outlines become clear and sharp and they stay in focus longer. Virna even says she can hear them, though I'm not sure I can. She repeated for me one of their remarks: "The air is full of patterns."

The creature who said that—the *person*—was looking at us. It all fits together now: we felt the presence of these new people at first as moods, you heard them as sourceless sounds, and they see us as patterns. The "invaders" are people from different levels, Cass. The levels are drifting back together again.

I don't know how or why. The barriers between levels are only mental; if what you were saying about our isolation and loneliness was right, then our need for contact may be breaking down the barriers. I don't know, and it doesn't really matter, does it? Cass, if the levels are coming together at Portsmouth, then we're here at the right time and the right place: we can meet, really meet, and be together.

When I heard your message, it was more than just the voice of our gray crossminded little man, I actually heard *your* intonations, *your* accents, your *voice*. I was amazed, and I laughed; the man looked surprised, and paused in his reading, but I motioned for him to continue and he did. When he was finished I told him what I'd heard, your voice from his mouth, and he said the message had been particularly strong. In fact, crosstalk has been very clear to him for days, but he hadn't thought to wonder about it. So dull, so unreacting; he doesn't know what it means at all.

Tomorrow, Cass, near the oak at noon. I'll see you there. (Isn't that incredible? I really will *see* you there.) I can hardly believe it. But I do believe it. Tomorrow.

Ram

To Ram Manjari, Level Chandra, September 25, 2422:
I am suffused by joy, by hope: to see you, Ram, to meet in eye and mind and touch! It is hardly to be believed, but it will happen today. Earth's ancient stones grind and flow, new events come to us.

We have seen multitudes in the streets and homes of this portal-city; no longer only dim shadows but fully fleshed people, dressed strangely or not dressed at all. New faces, new voices speaking in strange accents. Their voices are clear, not booming or keening, and they can see us as well as we them.

Ruthanan fled to her focus, where she huddles and

pursues her disciplines, surrounded by the crowd. Unfamiliar faces abound even there, however—*especially* there. Portsmouth is suffused by sounds of speech, a babble, a drone, and it has become impossible even to hear Ruthanan's mind in the tumult. There are men and women of all descriptions, and children as well. We brush against one another in the streets, are pressed together in crowds. (Crowds!) I had not dreamed there might be so *many* of us, Ram; it is like decade-day and more.

At noon we shall meet, hardly more than an hour from now. Is there more I should say? I am besieged by fears you will not like me. But I shall not think of that; in an hour my fears will become fading ghosts.

Joyfully, joyfully,
Cass

The levels come together; there is a single reality after three prismed centuries. What I see, you may see, and what you hear is in my ears too. Your colors are my colors, and we can touch.

In a wide grassy field where one ancient oak spreads shadows by a path, crowds mill and jostle, voices babble and laughter goes up. Here a round man in leather, his outlines tinged violet, harangues those around him with elaborations of doom; here three naked children wrestle and shout; here a dark girl in many ribbons huddles and enwraps herself in silent chants; here a man with pale eyes stares in sightless wonder and reaches out to touch arms, shoulders, faces. Grass is crushed under many feet and the air smells of breath and perspiration.

Cass Laureling makes her way through the crowds slowly, as if in a dream, her mouth half-open and eyes moving, moving. It is difficult for her to see over the heads of those around her, but the oak where she and I are to meet rises massively into the ghosted sky, and she makes for it. Elbows jostle, voices babble, strange eyes seem to stare.

Not everyone is distinct even now; Cass meets the

gaze of a balding man and realizes with a start that
she can see through his eyes, past him to others in
the crowd. She brushes past a young woman and feels
her shoulder sink into the woman's arm as though it
were hanging moss. Shapes and colors wink in the
air above, and drift through the bodies around her. She
smiles nervously and presses on to the oak.

She finds an open place beneath the tree; a ghostly
couple are sitting here, but they are insubstantial as
yet and Cass shares their space. Currents seem to drift
through her and shadows move in her eyes, but otherwise they do not impinge on her. She stands with her
back to the tree and looks for Ram.

But she sees only the crowd: hundreds of strangers,
thousands. Occasionally a face that she has seen before in Portsmouth—or perhaps not. She is becoming
unsure of who is familiar, who strange, and this is new
to her. She shivers and searches faces anxiously, looking for Ram.

What does she know of him? He is nine, he might
be with a woman whose name is Virna. What else,
what else? Faces waver and blur around her, shapes
drift into the crowd and coalesce into human figures.
More are arriving every minute. *Ram, which one are
you?*

"Ram?" She says it tentatively, then louder: *"Ram?"*
She doesn't see how he could hear her in the hubbub.
But a voice to her left calls back, "Cass?"

"Ram—here, over here!" She stands on tiptoes to
look for him. She is pushed back as two boys dart past,
running through legs, but he has seen her and now
they move toward each other. Cass has to push against
the press of bodies; it is becoming difficult to move
at all. Her breath comes short; she is breathing other
people's exhalations. *How many of us are there?*

Voices, laughter, crying, singing. Strange cadences,
and words that seem not to be words. Bodies, feet,
odd clothes that smell strange. Pressing bodies, un-
moving. *Are there going to be more than this?* .

"Cass!" A hand appears, reaching for her. "Cass,

take my hand!" She does, and is jostled, her grip broken. But she pushed toward him, grasps his wrist, and they slide between people to each other.

The crowd shifts, and now it is pressing them together. Cass puts her arms around this boy, this person. Their eyes meet, a little fearfully, and they smile.

"It's really you, isn't it?" he says.

"Yes," she says, and their smiles catch from each other, widen till they are laughing. They hold each other, and none of the rest of the questions will come till later.

Tell Me All
About Yourself

F. M. BUSBY

This is another of the stories that Terry Carr passed along to me—but in this case he let me have it most reluctantly. He had worked closely with Busby, then a novice author, on the early drafts of the story, and ultimately had accepted it for *Universe*—which had shifted, in 1972, from Ace Books to Random House. It was the first story he had bought for the Random House *Universe,* and he was unwise enough to send it to New York as a sample of the sort of stories he meant to buy. The Random House people, apparently dismayed by the story's grim theme and offering the lame and foolish old argument that librarians would be offended by it, ordered him bluntly not to publish it. *Universe* was too precariously balanced at Random House for Carr to risk a confrontation just then; so he turned "Tell Me All About Yourself" over to me, and I, after getting Busby to make a couple of additional tiny revisions, bought it without trepidation for *New Dimensions*. It has since been reprinted many times, and is a particular favorite, I hear, in France.

And Terry had revenge, of sorts, by using the Busby story in the 1974 edition of his well-known anthology *The Best Science Fiction of the Year*—published by Ballantine Books, a division of Random House.

IT WAS CHARLIE'S IDEA. HE AND VANCE AND I WERE on the town, celebrating our luck. It hadn't been easy, cutting close to the edges of a minor typhoon to bring the big hydrofoil freighter safely to Hong Kong on schedule. So we celebrated, high-wide-and-sideways on a mixture of drugs; none of us were users on the job but ashore was different. Some alcohol, of course, plus other things of our separate choices. I stayed with cannabis and one of the lesser mindbenders; I forget the brand name. Vance was tripping and far out; Charlie was so speeded up that I kept expecting him to skid on the corners.

"Hey, Vance! Dale! Pop one of these, and let's go get some kicks." He was holding out some purple Sensies, which don't come cheap; sensory enhancement is worth money and the sellers know it.

"What kind of kicks, Chazz?" When Charlie gets loose, I get cautious.

"There's a Nec down this way a few blocks. You ever try that, Dale?"

"No." I'd never been to a Necro house; I wasn't sure I wanted to, either.

"Well, hell, then; come on, kid. You'll never learn any younger."

"What do you think, Vance?" I said. It was a waste of breath. Whatever Vance was thinking behind his blissful smile, he wouldn't be able, from where he was, to find words for it. He nodded, after a while. Very deliberately. Another country heard from, in shorthand.

"OK then; what say, gang?" Charlie held a pill out to Vance, then one to me, and took one himself. Vance swallowed his. I hesitated, then popped mine too. Hell, I didn't have to follow through with the rest of it if I didn't want to. But we began walking along toward the Nec, Charlie leading.

"Have you done this stuff much, Charlie? The Necs, I mean?"

"A few times, Dale."

"What's the hook? I don't get it. I mean, the broads are dead and so what?"

Charlie shrugged. "It's just different, is all. Well, OK: one time in a regular seaport fuckery, Marseilles I think, I got a deaf-mute ginch. It was—restful, sort of; you don't have to talk. Wouldn't do you any good if you did. And at the Necs it's even more like that, 'cause they don't move. And you kind of wonder about them, what they'd say if they could, and all. I dunno, Dale; you have to *be* there, I guess."

Vance said, "What they don't say is the most important." I hadn't known that Vance was a Necro; Charlie, of course, is everything that doesn't kill him. And sometimes I think he crowds *that* a little.

Before I could decide anything one way or the other, we were there. At the door and then inside. A woman greeted us; somehow I hadn't expected that. She was small, Eurasian, slim in stretch skintights. I wished it were a live house; the Sensy was taking hold and I wanted her. I missed hearing Charlie's first question.

"We have a good selection tonight in the A rooms," she said. "I trust that you gentlemen are interested in the A category?" I knew what that meant: after certain physical changes, the category reverts to B. I've heard of places where there's a C category but I don't like to think about that.

We all nodded, even Vance. A was the category of our choice; yes.

"Then I will show you the pictures of our A list," she said. She went behind a counter like a hotel registration desk and came back with two packets of 8-by-10 color prints. Each picture showed a woman nude, supine, arms and legs spread, eyes closed. Dead; they had to be, though it wasn't obvious.

She fanned the two sets of pictures out on a heavy teakwood table. "These," pointing, "are kept at body temperature. These others are at chill, for greater service life in the A category. Personal preferences differ."

Charlie and I looked only at the warm set; Vance smiled brightly and sorted through both. I was, I found, very taken with the picture of a small dark woman, voluptuous in a compact way. Charlie took it out of my hand.

"Hey, that's for me," he said. I was about to argue, though it's futile to argue with Charlie, when the picture was taken from him in turn.

I hadn't seen the man come in. He was tall, thin-faced and pale, wearing a light-gray suit and walking with no sound. He looked at the picture.

"So she's attracting trade already," he said.

"Mr. Holmstrom," the woman said, "I have the bank draft for you. I trust everything is satisfactory? Mrs. Holmstrom's appearance, and so forth?"

"Quite." Once again behind the counter, she found an envelope, came back and gave it to Holmstrom. He put the picture back on the table, thanked her and turned to leave.

"Just a minute," said Charlie. "This here is your wife, maybe?"

"She was."

"Sorry; sorry. But could I ask you a little something?"

"Of course. If I choose, I'll answer." Charlie blinked.

"Well, then," he said, "what I want to know is, how was she when—I mean, like *before?*"

"I doubt that you'll notice much difference," the man said, wheeling to walk out. The door closed behind him while Charlie gaped.

Somehow I had lost interest in the small dark woman; I leafed through the stack of warms. "I'll still take that one," Charlie said, and paid his money. The Eurasian woman handed him a numbered key. He took his direction from her pointing finger and walked away along a corridor to the right of the counter. I didn't notice whether Vance's choice was warm or chill, but he left by a different exit. I looked at the pictures, unable to choose, unable to consent.

The woman came to stand by me. "Perhaps we have noth.ng to interest you, sir, in this category? Perhaps the B category?"

God, NO! I shook my head violently, shuffling frantically through the pictures. Maybe that one? No. What the hell was I doing here, anyway?

"Perhaps something a little special, sir. More expensive, of course. But if expense is not a problem . . . a girl, young, though developed. Death by sad accident. No obvious mutilation, no cosmetic corrections necessary. And very rare in our trade, a virgin. Let me show you her picture."

The Sensy and the mindbender were fighting in my head and body. I waited while she brought the picture, then looked at it.

Virginity had never been important to me; it doesn't show visually, anyway. But I looked at this girl in glossy color and I liked her. She was someone I'd like to know. I decided to go about that now, the best I could.

Money paid, down a hall, key into the lock of numbered door, I entered and looked at her. At first I didn't understand the strangeness.

The way the best picture ever taken differs from a person is that the person is *there;* the depiction is not. Here, looking, I saw a halfway case. The girl was more than a picture but less than a person. I didn't figure the difference immediately; it took a while to sink in.

The pale-red hair was the same, longish and curling, spread out from her head. I wouldn't disarrange it; I didn't want to touch the tubes that pumped warm preservative fluid through her to maintain body temperature.

The slim strong limbs and body looked healthy enough to get up and walk. Her skin was warm, all right—a little dry, maybe. But it was the face that drew me: features strong but delicate. And I could not understand how she, or anyone, could smile so happily after she was gone. I wanted to ask her about that. I wanted to ask her about a lot of things.

The Sensy pill wanted more from me. There are things, I knew, that help a virgin girl. Though I'd had only two such, habit set me to those preparations. Then I realized, foolishly, that no stimulus could bring response, and that the house had prepared her as well as could be done. So I entered her.

Slow and easy, slow and easy, raising my head to see her smile. I had to speak. "Do you like that? This? You're beautiful; did you know?"

The smile flexed; I don't know how or why. But with that slight movement the beauty of her caught and held me. The intensity of the pull astonished me. I tried to lose myself in sensation—the augmented delights of the Sensy pill—but I couldn't. The smile wouldn't let me. And I ceased fighting what I felt.

"Why did you never know love?" I asked. "You should have. You were made for it. I wish I—" I wished I'd found her before. Because I knew, now, that always I had been looking for her.

And was this to be her only love? With care, with gentleness, I sought to make it worthy.

I had to know more. "Who are you?" Only her smile replied. "What did you want? What can I give you?"

My body answered that; I gave it. Not wanting to, begrudging the final ecstasy. I had so much more to say, to ask; I didn't want to leave her. But it was done; that is the rule, alive or dead.

I kissed her smooth forehead and released her, feeling empty, as though I should be the one lying there, not her. Numbly, I busied myself with my clothing.

Up and dressed, hand on the door, I looked back. Nothing had changed; she smiled as I had first seen her. In the picture, and here.

"But you haven't told me *anything*." No; and she would not. I said, "Goodbye. I'm sorry." And closed the door behind me. Opposite from the way I had come was an "Exit" sign. I went to that door, put my hand on the knob. And couldn't bring myself to turn it.

If I left, I would never see her again. I had to go back. My mind must have known all along; I found I still had the key.

She looked the same. Still the slim strong body, the hair, the smile. So lovely, and so alone. The silence.

I looked for a long time. Then I said goodbye again and turned away. But I couldn't go. I had remembered something.

Her picture. Now it would be in the warm stack of the A category, for Charlie and Vance and everybody. And she was defenseless.

I thought of Charlie with her. Charlie's all right; I like him, mostly. But sometimes, afterward, he says things I don't like to hear. I could not bear that thought.

And Charlie's not the worst. There are men who would hurt her.

No. They weren't going to have her. No one was going to have her. She was mine now.

Gently I disarranged her hair to expose the brown plastic tubes pumping fluid to and from the nape of her neck. The connections were self-sealing; only a few drops of colorless fluid escaped as I set the tubes aside.

A robe hung on a hook beside the door. It was bizarre; a less gaudy pattern would have better suited her. But the robe was all there was.

I robed her, limp like a passed-out drunk, and carried her out of the room, out through the exit. I left most of my money in the room; it wasn't enough, I knew, but it would help me feel less like a thief.

Overcrowded Hong Kong still has the jinrikishaw; the man said, "Lady not feel good?"

"She'll be all right," I said, and he took us to my hotel. After the first couple of times I don't book a room at the same hotel with Charlie and Vance, ashore.

The night clerk said, "Lady all right?" I smiled and nodded, carrying her.

In the room I arranged her beauty. "Is that all right? Would you like anything more?" Then again I loved her, and held her close in sleep against the threat of chill.

But in the morning there was no doubt. My head had cooled and so had she. Soon she would no longer be of the A category, or even B.

I couldn't let that happen to her. I couldn't let it happen to me, the seeing of what time would do.

I walked the crowded streets of Hong Kong, thinking, wondering. The drugs had worn off but the problem hadn't. Nowhere in the city could I bury her, even if I had wanted to. Burial at sea was out; I didn't want her moldering under earth *or* water. And the house would have the police pursuing me as relentlessly as Category B pursued her.

There is a waterfront area where tourists can rent motor-boats; I went there and rented one, cruising until I found a derelict wharf for moorage. Rickshaws were sparse nearby but I found one and returned to the commercial district, where I purchased a life raft and a few other things, mostly on the black market. These I took to my boat. Then I went back to the hotel.

She was so cold, but still she smiled. I respected her withdrawal; it was her right. I told her my plans. "Am I doing right? Is this what you want?" Her smile did not change. I sat a long time, stroking her hair; nothing more. In the streaked wall mirror I saw a fool. I smiled, and the fool smiled back at me.

We sat until dark. She was so quiet, never answering my questions. Then it was time to go.

The rickshaw was slow; the man lost his way several times more, I think, than his usual quota for tourists. But eventually we got to my rented boat, she and I.

Out into the water, out into the dark. Out into the middle of the bay where no one could interfere. I inflated the life raft and put it over the side. Then it was time to take her robe from her and spread it in the raft. At last, with the swells of the bay hampering me, I put her on the robe in the best beauty I could manage. Then I arranged the other things around her, that she needed, before I moved the boat away and threw the torch.

The first blaze showed her smile unchanged. Her hair vanished in a glorious crown of flame. I wanted, needed to look away, but I couldn't. I saw her smile widen into a look of ecstasy before a curtain of fire concealed everything. I'm so grateful that it did. Then the thermite went, that I'd placed around her. A searing blast of heat, a cloud of steam, and she and the raft were gone.

I took the boat back where it belonged.

Next day, back at the ship, Charlie talked a lot about his Nec piece. It sounded more like the B category but I didn't say so. Vance didn't say much; he just grinned. I think he was still up, though with Vance it's hard to tell for sure. He does his job.

I couldn't talk about it. Not to Charlie, not even to Vance. It's hard to think about.

I wanted so much for her to answer me, and she wouldn't.

The Examination

FELIX C. GOTSCHALK

This one came in unsolicited, some time in 1973, along with several other stories by the same author—all meticulously typed in some sort of futuristic IBM face, and all full of the damndest cold, cockeyed technological jargon. I realized after just a few pages that the writer was controlling the jargon, and not vice versa, and that in fact I had stumbled on to one of the great originals of science fiction. Gotschalk turned out to be a psychologist from North Carolina with—at least in his correspondence— a well-developed appreciation of his own many excellences. Though I've never met the man, I do suspect that Gotschalk's high level of self-esteem is altogether justified. I chose to introduce him with two stories at once in *New Dimensions 4*, and, since he was remarkably prolific, he has had a story in nearly every issue of *New Dimensions* since. He had sold a few stories, I think, before I began buying his work, and by now has appeared fairly widely in science fiction, publishing a novel or two and a bunch of shorter pieces. People are starting to notice what he can do; while I doubt he will ever be a very popular author (his vocabulary is too idiosyncratic for that) he's certainly going to be a respected one, and, if it can be done, an imitated one. *New Dimensions* has published the work of a lot of unknown writers, but I think of Gotschalk in particular as my special editorial discovery.

THE SMALL BLACK CHILD SAT ON THE WHITE VINYL chair and gave off an aura of coal-stove smoke and lard. Her wool coat was too hot but she kept it on. A waxy sleeper stuck in the corner of her eye and she sniffled productively.

"Do you want a Kleenex?" the examiner asked, an edge of weariness showing through his overt kindness.

"Naw," the girl said softly. The examiner took one of the 1906 Binet forms from a stack atop a cabinet and sat down across the desk from the girl. The form bore 1937 and 1960 restandardization copyright dates.

"Do you feel all right today?" he asked.

"Yeah." The reply was flat.

"Do you have to go to the bathroom?"

"Naw." The examiner pushed the Binet form across the waxed formica surface to the girl.

"The first thing I'd like for you to do is write your name right here." The girl took the pencil, rotated the page 90 degrees starboard, and wrote left-handed, straight down the line, right at her navel. Her pencil grip was crablike, even hemiplegic, but she printed "PAMELA" well enough, adding a very slight stylistic flourish to the final A. The examiner took the form once more and filled in several blanks with a ballpoint pen.

"Let's see," he said, "today is April the seventeenth, 1974, and when is your birthday?"

"I don't know," the girl said faintly.

"Let's see again. Here it is. You were born February the first, 1966. So, you are eight years and ten months." The examiner wrote "8-2" in the chronological age blank. "And, you're a girl," he chuckled in a friendly tone, "I'll put that down." He printed "NF" for Negro female.

"Where do you live, Pamela?"

"You know thet wott house ova dair?" The child pointed out the window.

"I think so." The examiner was used to responses like this.

"I live ona dert road."

"What school do you go to now?"

"South Main-Jones."

"And what grade are you in?"

"Thudd."

"Did you go to kindergarten?"

"Ah went to Haidstott."

"What's your daddy's name?"

The dark face brightened at the question. "Ah got me two daddies."

"Yay—good." The examiner fell in easily with the drift of the response. "Are they good to you?"

"Yeah." The examiner scanned the referral sheet for the name of the child's mother: PATRICIA ANN TUG-GERT OWEN RAIKES.

"What kind of work does your daddy do?"

"He break up rocks at the quarry."

"Do you have any special hobbies, or things you like to do a whole lot?"

"Ah locks to watch teevee."

"What shows do you like best?"

The girl looked thoughtful. The examiner had his head down when the child's pupils swam away into pinheads, glowed a fiery white for half a second, then returned to wet black and brown cow-eyes.

"Ah locks Gilgun's eye-lun and the Frintstones," the girl said.

"Do you have to do any work around your house?"

"Ah hev to wash deeshes sometimes."

"Do you get some money to spend sometimes?"

"Yeah."

"What do you like to buy with money?"

"Canny."

The examiner filled in his name on the Binet face-sheet: PAUL MACK GRASSY, ED.D. He looked at his

Nivada Grenchen. It read 9:22. Better get on with it, he thought.

"Well, I'm supposed to try you on a few little tests today, to find out something about how much you know, how smart you are. Is school hard for you, or easy?"

"Hodd."

"Well, let's try a few of these test things. Some of them are questions. Talking. Then, there are some pictures and puzzles that are sort of fun." The girl shifted in the chair and took off her coat. The examiner thought the girl's movements to be fluid and smooth and rapid. He began the testing:

"I want to find out how many words you know. Listen, and when I say a word, you tell me what it means. What is an orange?"

"Uh froot," she replied.

"Right. What is an envelope?"

"For a letter." The examiner rummaged in a drawer for a cigar. A sensor pad extended from the child's brow, rotated briefly, and retracted into the wiry black hairs. A few feet away, under a corner of the carpet, a roach suddenly ate its brood and felt its tropisms waver. The examiner looked back at the Binet text.

"The next word is 'straw.' What is a straw?"

"You suck it."

"What is a puddle?"

"A puddle of water."

"And, let's see here, the next word is 'tap.' What does that word mean?"

"You make a little noise."

"Good. A little noise. 'Gown.' What is a gown?"

"A nightgown."

"The next word is 'roar.' What does 'roar' mean?"

"Noise."

"Well, there are lots of kinds of noises. What would you say about 'roar' to tell exactly what it means?"

The child looked steadily at the examiner. "Ain't noise right?"

Grassy glanced at the text and saw the one-word response "noise" was a plus score. "Well, that's good enough. Let's try some more. 'Eyelash.' What is that?"

"Hair that protects your eyes," the girl said fairly quickly. Grassy now knew that the child was probably average in mental abilities, having scored successes with vocabulary terms standardized on population samples of eight-year-olds.

"Well, you're pretty good at this. You say school is hard for you?"

"Sometimes."

"Do you try hard?"

"Not all the time."

"Well, the next word is, let's see, 'Mars.' What is Mars, anyway?"

"A planet." The child put a small hand on the desk and some formica molecules sundered deep in their microcosms. No blood vessels were visible in the child's hand.

" 'Juggler' is the next word," the examiner said.

"A juggler is a man that juggles balls up and down."

" 'Scorch.' What does 'scorch' mean?"

"To burn," Pamela said in a clearing and increasingly perky voice. Aft of her dextral mastoid an auxiliary cardiac pump puckered and hot proline surged across her synapses.

Grassy knew now that the girl had passed vocabulary items designed for random samplings of eleven-year-olds. He began to feel that the girl might be a sleeper, a bright but dull-acting child. He leaned in closer to her and locked in steady eye contact. He started just slightly. The girl's eyes dilated quickly, like an owl's. He looked closer. "The black parts of your eyes are big," he said gently and interestedly. "Do you have good vision and hearing?"

Pam smiled engagingly, with a charming glimmer of shyness, and said yes. Her eyes fell on a wart in the web of Grassy's hand. Her eyeballs ellipsed to 50-power magnification and 100 candlepower. The wart looked like a raised crater stuffed with pointed fleshy buds. She beamed in a micro-laser at the precise azimuth and the wart spores withered and disappeared. Grassy did not see the wart wink out of existence.

"It looks like you're going to be extra smart, Pam," he said. "You know some hard words for a girl your age. Let's try a few harder ones. How about 'lecture'? Have you ever heard that word?"

"A speech," came the reply.

"Right. A speech. Very good. Now, what is 'skill'? Ess, kay, eye, ell, ell?"

"Something you do real well," Pam said, brightening perceptibly.

"Hey, you get better as you go along," Grassy said, with more enthusiasm than he usually expressed. "Do you have any special skills? Things you do well?" The girl's memory-trace engrams flashed in the subvocal input "3-D KINESTHETIC CHESS," but she looked neutrally at Grassy and said no.

"Well. How about this word. It is 'brunette.' Do you know what that is?"

"Black hair like mine." Pam seemed to give off some coy femininity.

"Right," Grassy said. "How about 'muzzle'?"

"What you put on a dog's face."

"How do you know that word?"

"A lady cross our road had to put one on her dawg cawz it wuz meen." The girl had reached a vocabulary level of twelve chronological years, and Grassy was beginning to be impressed and vaguely disquieted.

" 'Haste' is the next word, Pam," he said with an edge of expectancy and diffuse concern. "Do you know what that is?"

"Hurry," the girl said, and Grassy sensed a whisker of mockery in her voice. The room temperature had risen to 70.4 and an all but imperceptible hum was flickering at his auditory limens.

"Here's a hard one and it's hard to say. 'Peculiarity.' Anyone ever tell you that word?" Pam's lips parted to reveal serrated teeth. She closed her mouth quickly and gave Grassy a shy and unguarded look. "Yes," she said thoughtfully, "that means rare, or queer." *Alternate synonyms,* Grassy thought. *This little thing is at least superior.*

"Why did your parents want you to come and get tested?" he asked, thumbing through the referral notes.

"I really don't know," Pam said.

Grassy could not find the referral face-sheet. "Now I know I had that sheet. What did I do with it?" He looked up to see the girl looking at him quite intently. The look was instantly familiar. Bela Lugosi had greeted guests at Castle Dracula with the same vague expectancy. Grassy suaved off a nudging anxiety and returned to the Binet forms.

"What was the last word I asked you?"

" 'Peculiarity.' "

"Yes, well, let's try 'priceless.' " 'Priceless.' "

" 'Invaluable.' "

The reply was rapid, and the vocal nuance distantly goading, as if Pam had advance knowledge of the answers and was putting Grassy on. He looked searchingly at her. "My dear girl," he said earnestly, "I am amazed and gratified and puzzled by your knowing that word, and by your giving a synonym. That's the most advanced way of responding to vocabulary tasks. Do you understand what I am saying to you?"

Pam dropped her chin and softly said yes. "I try to read a lot," she said, "and I learn a lot from the trivid and the tape banks."

"Well, let's see how far you can go with the words. The next one is 'regard.' What does 'regard' mean?"

"You look at something."

Amazing, Grassy thought. "How about 'tolerate'?"

"Endure."

"Here's a huge word. 'Disproportionate.' "

"Out of size—out of shape." Grassy realized that his mouth was gaping open and that his Harsh Marsh Maduro had gone out and was smelly. He lit the cigar and clenched it in his teeth. A diffuse wreath of smoke floated toward Pam, and then stopped, inches from her face. The force-field isomorph read the smoke's particulate locus and Pam marveled why humanoids chose to ignite dried leaves and allow the combusted cells' smoke to play among the lungs and the sinus pockets and the olfactory shafts.

Pam had now defined Binet vocabulary words as well as average adults, and an extrapolated IQ on this one parameter would translate to 170 plus. Grassy truly prized bright kids, bright adults, anybody who showed the secret handclasp responses which betokened optimal brain-cell number, configuration, and condition. He was rarely if ever threatened intellectually. Now Pam grew more adult and supra-adult every minute. "Have you ever heard your voice on tape?" he asked her.

"No."

"You're doing so very well that I'd like to record some of the things you say. Okay?"

"Okay."

He flicked the cassette on and palmed the record slot.

"Here's a short word. 'Lotus.' What's that?"

"A plant. A Chinese plant. And an English racing car."

"How about 'shrewd'?"

"Discerning."

How the goddam mother hell could an eight-year-old humanoid know that word, Grassy thought.

" 'Mosaic,' " he said in a fringe-stentorian tone.

"An art form in which pictures or designs are made with stone, glass, or tile. Or"—and here she looked vaguely professorial—"of, or pertaining to, Moses." The response scored at SUPERIOR ADULT, LOCUS II.

"Nobody ever gets this one," Grassy said. "The word is 'stave.' "

"A curved board in a barrel."

"How in the world did you come to know a rare word like that?" Grassy had a whining shimmer in his tone.

"Definitive corollaries of linguistic gestalten are, of course, a matter of public information." Pam sounded robotlike.

Grassy felt his jowls go flaccid and his eyes begin to blink. He felt strangely introversive. He thumbed the Norelco to rewind, then to stop, then to a replay: a 132-cycle hum spat through the mike speaker, and a wavering overlay of pulsating psychophysical tones contrapunted through the basal pitch. Pam's eyes glowed a soft luminosity and antenna buds appeared at her parietal lobes. "You're an alien." Grassy tried to sound unafraid.

"Affirmative."

"What do you want?"

"I want to continue the evaluation."

"You want to define the rest of the words?"

"Negative. I want to put the remaining words to you as a testee." Pam's silver arm spread across the desk like a chrome piston and took the Binet text.

"First," she began, "is it true that humanoid language sounds evolved from the cries of animals?"

Grassy moved toward the door, but a modstun force-field enveloped him. He felt as if he had walked into a warm gossamer membrane.

"Be seated, please," the girl said. "You are in no danger. No harm will come to you."

Grassy sat down, trembling. The girl vectored in a tranquilizing matrix of oxygen dilutants. "Well," she said, "what is your response to my question?"

"I'm afraid I don't know. I guess I'm weak in the psycholinguistics bit."

"Is it true that what you term 'intelligence' is assessed by psychologists through linguistic exchanges with the evaluees?"

"Yes," Grassy answered, "although verbal expression, or particular verbal facility, is not a firm requirement. We can test mutes."

Pam's tungsten helices whirred in ambergris gelatin. She scanned the remaining Binet word lists. "How was word number twenty-six selected as a linguistic gestalten held to measure intelligence? The word is 'bewail.' "

"The words are weeded out on statistical difficulty curves during the test standardization process. Intelligent people seem to know harder words than unintelligent people. 'Bewail' ranked as one of the tougher words, because the standardization sample showed that a middle locus of superior adults knew the word."

"But, since the term 'superior' is taxonomic and dependent on performance, are you not talking circularly?" Pam asked. Then she passed quickly on: "What does the term mean to you?" she asked Grassy.

Grassy realized that his daily access to test items had not made him as test-wise as he might have thought, and the realization was a kind of double-edged sword. The specificity of his own mental abilities seemed preserved, yet the blind spots he had were being revealed; i.e., access to intelligence tests had not made him any more intelligent. And, he thought, this is somehow goddam good. " 'Bewail' means something like being sad," Grassy ventured.

"Deplore. Lament. Bemoan," Pam said quickly. "How about word number twenty-seven. 'Ocher.' Oh-Kerr."

"That's a mythological monster, a kind of troll that lives under bridges," Grassy said, trying to be playful. Pam smiled.

"I can read your ideational dynamics, your subvocal engrams. And I see much dissonance there—cognitive dissonance, one of your colleagues has called it. You think and feel one way, look and act another, and talk yet another. Do you really know what the term 'ocher' means?"

"As far as I know, it's a monster."

"An earthy clay with iron ore in it," Pam said.

"Oh yeah," Grassy said, "now I remember." He dropped his cigar on the rug beside the telephone. As he bent to pick it up, he lifted the receiver from its cradle, knowing that the local operator would come on the line in a few seconds. Pam's ears had sprouted tufts of crystalline cilia, and her eyes rotated to show at least a dozen wetly glowing facets. Her lip line had become more compressed, like a surgical slash on a bloodless cadaver. Her teeth meshed together like ring gears. Grassy wondered if she actually ate, in the sense of placing foliage or flesh or carrion in her mouth and ingesting it in some way.

"What does 'repose' mean to you?" she asked.

"To lie down, crap out, get supine," Grassy replied.

"Rest. Inactivity. Tranquillity. How about 'ambergris'?"

"Hello? Hello." The switchboard operator's voice came on the phone.

"Excuse me," said Grassy, and reached for the phone. He tried to tell the operator to ring the police, but Pam read his thoughts and masked out his laryngeal striations.

Her arm telescoped across the desk and her ball-socketed hand rotated to replace the receiver. "My dear Ducktoor Grassy," she said, "I am totally superordinate in relation to you. Please permit me to complete the questioning. As a scientist, or a quasi, or para-scientist, perhaps you are interested in my motives: they include the assessment of humanoid verbalizations as they differ from their supposed ideational bases. In other words, I know what you are thinking. I want to hear what you *say*. Now take this term 'ambergris.' "

"It's a puller, put in perfumes."

"True, but definitively diffuse. My data banks read the term as denoting a waxy gray substance excreted by sperm whales. It is actually an excretory lubricant. 'Limpet,' " Pam continued.

Her voice had lowered and softened, so that she sounded like the Lonesome Gal from old radio days. She still hummed softly, like a diapason cipher.

Grassy felt just enough playfulness to nudge against the force-field periodically, but he also felt quiescent and interested in Pam the alien. Grassy gently rotated the waxed tips of his mustache with his thumb and forefinger. "Limpet, limpet. I believe that relates to a quiet pool—a limpid pool, a calm dark pool."

"Shellfish. Mollusks. Conicals." Pam sounded computerized again. "Such a term is communicatively esoteric. Have you truly found that this is a utilitarian word? Do you need to know that the word denotes a generic group, a taxonomic cluster?"

"Intelligent people often seem to know esoteric things. But, the Esso Terrier per se is defined as a statistical or actuarial norm. In other words, a person who is bright or who tests as being artifactually or psychometrically bright is not that way because he has scavenged for nits or groveled compulsively. He is rather like the teevee receiving stations that monitored the 1970 moon landings: powerful, rich, self-actualizing, high in perceptual sensitivity."

"You pretty well imply an hereditary or structurally invariant basis for intelligence," Pam said.

"We have wrangled over that for at least seventy years," Grassy said, half-waving off the questioning nuance of the tone, "and never got it adequately resolved. Historically, aristocrats have claimed an attendant right to high intelligence, while the serfs assumed a yoke of stupidity. There were people who felt that they had no *right* to be bright because they were poor. There now seems to be a measurable hierarchy of intelligence groupings, which is only partially related to socio-economic class."

Pam seemed to listen attentively, her cilia waving like anemone sepals and her eyes now showing a more assuring humanoid warmth. Her charisma index wavered with her persona variations, so that she seemed both child and god, both small and overpowering, both human and suprahuman.

"What does 'frustrate' mean?"

"To feel bugged, miffed, or irritated."

"Foil, baffle, defeat, ineffectuate," Pam clacked out. " 'Flaunt.' "

"If you've *got* it, *flaunt* it," Grassy said in weak

THE BEST OF NEW DIMENSIONS 195

camaraderie. "I think it means something like bragging or teasing."

"To make a gaudy, ostentatious, or defiant display," the succinct definition clacked out again. " 'Incrustation,' " she continued neutrally.

"Like barnacles all over a ship."

"A hard outer layer or coating." Grassy began to feel stirringly dumb.

" 'Retroactive,' " Pam continued.

"Applicable to recent events, like retroactive pay raises," Grassy said.

"Having application to or effect on things prior to its enactment or effectuation." Pam stood up. She was now about six feet tall. "Would you stand, please?" she asked. "I want to get your somatotype parameters and your brain mass relative to total organismic displacement."

Grassy got up awkwardly, his chair rolling off the beaver-board template and onto the red carpet. Pam now looked like the Statue of Liberty. Grassy felt the barely liminal comfort of the forcefield, as if he were dozing before a lingering hardwood fire.

The alien seemed to center herself in front of Grassy, like a surveyor's rod man. "Be quite still, please," she said, increasing the force-field density. A segmented antenna appeared at her waistline and she moved around the desk to Grassy's side. Standing closely ventral-ventral, she embraced him with eight chrome pseudopods. His body was yoked to hers. He closed his eyes. "Do you feel anything when I do this?" she asked, somehow sweetly.

"No," he said. "What is it you are doing?"

"Getting a holographic mold of your body. The pseudopods are vectoring in isomorphic tape measures, so to say. It will take just a few more seconds." Grassy opened his eyes inches from the alien face. It was smooth, like wetly polished marble.

"Your vertical spine and curved horizontal ribs must cause you discomfort," she said. "Do you sometimes move like quadrupeds, to ease the feeling?"

"No. Never."

"Did you evolve from quadrupeds?"

"I don't really know."

"Do you ever regress to quadruped or anthropoid behaviors? For instance, do you groom or preen one another?"

"Occasionally, but such behaviors are considered in questionable taste."

"Do you smell your armpits or axillary vellus areas?"

"Rarely," Grassy replied.

"Are you capable of self-fellation?"

"An anatomic impossibility. But no, I recall one case reported by Kinsey, of a man who utilized this method for several years."

"Are you in any sense cloacal, like serpents?"

"No, but urinary fluids and seminal fluids do share a single distal ducting, so that we are probably more cloacal than we would care to admit."

"Is it true that orgasm is held to be the pinnacle of humanoid experience?"

"I think yes." The pseudopods retracted and Pam spun slowly, like a heavy periscope, and glided off a few feet.

"Would you like to question me any more?" she asked.

Grassy looked sheepish. "I am too sedated to do much good. Do you fear capture by us?"

"No." Pam sat down and her appearance changed wispily. "I can alter my appearance from raw diffusion to lead monoliths. I am impervious to physical harm. You could not capture me. Come, complete the few terms left on the test, and you can ask me anything you wish." They sat in their original positions as testee and tester and exchanged long neutral looks.

"This is ironic, or humbling, or something," Grassy said. "My intelligence, however you wish to define it, plus my educational credentials and professional experience, accord me a statutory sphere of competency, and a certain implied superordinacy in assessing people's behaviors. I naturally bring this reinforced orientation to you, an overtly deprived member of a racial minority group, and you obliterate it as an alien. Now you want me back in the examiner's role. Do you feel sadistic motives?"

"We feel no such motives. We have no need or wish to express aggression. Come, the appointment span will be over soon. Ask me the last few words and I will tell you something about my organismic grouping."

Grassy looked half-heartedly at the Binet text. He felt like he was about to read *The Readers Digest* to a national Mensa group. "Word number forty-three is 'philanthropy.' "

"Love of mankind. Desire to help mankind. Something that helps mankind."

" 'Piscatorial.' "

"Of fishes, fishermen, or fishing."

" 'Milksop.' " Grassy felt disgusted and somehow ashamed.

"Unmanly man or boy. Mollycoddle. Sissy."

"Do you have sexes among your people?" Grassy put in.

"No. We do not reproduce. We are made of insoluable crystalline matrices, held in quasi-permeable colloid states by reverse parity."

"Parity in the sense of right-handed and left-handed atoms?"

"No." Pam smiled through her little-girl physiognomy. "Two Oriental physicists won one of your prizes years ago by showing experimentally that atoms are not handed."

"Are your crystalline units homogeneous? Are you reductionistic?"

"Your celestial galaxy is a macrocosmic homology of our crystalline structures. We have homogeneity in the sense of spinning spheroids, a space medium or host environment, and inertias born of centrifugal force. Try the toughest Binet words."

" 'Harpy.' "

"Mythological bird-woman creatures, perceived as an inverted major detail on Card Nine of the Rorschach plates."

"How did you know that?"

"It is bold in your subvocal engrams."

" 'Depredation,' " said Grassy.

"Plundering, laying waste, robbery."

" 'Perfunctory.' "

"Done without care or interest or as a routine form."

" 'Achromatic.' "

"Colorless."

"Do you have a light spectrum in your perceptual world?" Grassy asked.

"Yes," Pam said, "but we are able to see the bands of coloration all along the angstrom unit abscissa. You humans are really quite limited, what with your range of visible light equal to about one-twentieth of the total actual light. For instance, I can see the alternating current in your stereo system, the radio waves in the atmosphere, as well as gammas and ultraviolets and all the rest. You are really unable to protect yourself from such things as X-rays."

" 'Casuistry' is the next word," Grassy continued. He heard the muffled steps and voices of several people outside his door. Pam was fully in the guise of the little girl.

"Some sheriff's deputies are outside," she said. "The switchboard operator got my wavelength when you picked up the phone receiver. These frequencies are enough to make birds wake up screaming and hippopotami burst from the surface of their quiet pools. Listen to me now, don't make a fool of yourself. They will not believe your reporting that I am an alien life form. I can be totally Pamela. So be cool, as you say. *And,* casuistry is a philosophical term denoting the solving of special cases of right and wrong in conduct by . . ."

A heavily authoritative knocking rang through the

cheap beige paint and thin pine wood of the door. "Dr. Grassy? Are you all right?"

Grassy scrambled up from his chair and all but wrenched the plastic knob from the door. Two fatly dumb-looking deputies filled the framing space.

"She's a goddam alien!" Grassy sang out to the men, his arms flailing in air, his eyes white-wide and rolling, "she's got spaghettini oozing from her ears and an antenna in her navel! She's got teeth like bank-vault hinges, her eyes glow like coals, and she's got eight chrome-plated goddam fucking arms!"

A small but determined social worker winced, then moved easily between the ballooning hulks of the deputies, and all but sprinted to the small sobbing form of the dull-looking negroid girl.

"Look out!" Grassy trumpeted. "She's pure, raw, crystalline-matrix colloid! She just looks like a lidda durl. Don't touch her, dammit."

He felt fingers big as hotdogs close around his arms and he was held very firmly against a wall. "Man, this fox has really flipped," one of the deputies said, getting a ham-sized hand inside Grassy's Sansabelt. Pam was crying little shudders of fear and being hugged and cooed over by the social worker.

"Idiots!" Grassy grated broken resonance at the gathering group of staff members. "I tell you that girl is an alien being. She is not humanoid. You can find out for yourself, just take her clothes off! She's a lab-yrinth of data storage tiers! She knew every one of the goddam Binet vocabulary words!" Pam was crying louder and being hugged closer.

"Let's get this dude out of here," the deputy said. "He's blown all his fuses." They hustled Grassy down the hallway.

" 'Homunculus!" he called back to Pam. "Hoe-Mun-Kew-Luss. Tell them what that means, Pam. 'Sudorific'! 'Sudorific'! 'Parterre'! Goddamn 'parterre!' No priest-prodding, nun-knocking fair, Pam! You didn't finish the test!"

Grassy heard Pam's voice close at his ear as he was

trundled into the car: " 'Homunculus.' A little man. Dwarf. A model of a human body used for demonstrating anatomy."

"See?" He sat up intently. "She knew those answers. She's talking to me now. I tell you she is an alien organism."

"Relax, Doc," the deputy said, "we'll get it all straight."

Grassy jumped slightly as the alien voice returned: " 'Sudorific': causing or increasing sweat. 'Parterre': part of a theater beneath the balcony and behind the parquet."

"See? See?" Grassy said. "She's still talking. She knows about dwarfs, and sweat, and theaters. These are things most of us don't know about. Nobody ever gets those words right. You believe me, don't you?"

"Sure, Doc," one of the men said. The deputies exchanged tight, knowing smiles as the car drove off.

Find the Lady

NICHOLAS FISK

I have met, or at least exchanged letters with, virtually every writer who has ever contributed to *New Dimensions*. But Nicholas Fisk is an exception. His story came to me from a New York agent; I liked it and sent the agent a contract; and to this day I know nothing about Nicholas Fisk except the biographical statement his agent sent me, which tells me that he is British, was born in 1923, has written for a living since he was sixteen, and is interested in such things as microscopy, billiards, and "underwater sightseeing." Since I published "Find the Lady"—and I gave it the lead position in *New Dimensions 5,* for I was much taken by its grace and high spirits—Fisk has had several science-fiction novels for younger readers published in the United States, but I think this remains his only American s-f short story.

THE SCARRED METAL GRAB REACHED OUT AND touched the little wooden writing desk. Mitch, feeling the giggles rising in him, clutched Eugene's arm. Eugene glared, but it only made things worse.

"Ooop!—ooo!—ooop!" went Mitch.

"Shut up! Oh, do shut *up!*"

"Ooop! Oh, dearie me, I'll die."

"Silly pouf! Shut up!"

"Don't call me that name—"

"Shut UP! They'll hear!"

The metal grab protruded a metal claw. It made a tiny puncture in the ginger wood and withdrew. A hundred feet or so away in the grab's parent body, a message was received. There was a lacklustre spurt of messages—a dim buzzing and clicking and whirring echoing up and down the extensible limb.

The metal grab, with surprising delicacy, again protruded its claw and began tracing the outlines and surfaces of the desk. It was what had been known as a Davenport. It had a tooled-leather inclined lid with storage space beneath it, supported on a body containing a multiplicity of drawers, sliding boxes and trite gadgetry. The claw explored.

"God save us," wheezed Eugene, "when it gets to the *legs* . . ." The giggles were fighting through again. The legs! "The *legs!*" groaned Mitch, clutching himself.

They were too absurd, the legs. Once, the Davenport must have been possessed of two respectable curlicued fretwork legs—or perhaps two faked wooden pillars with capitals. They had long gone. Filled with joyous spite, Mitch and Eugene had replaced them with two rusty chromium-plated tubes they had found in the rubble. The effect was lunatic: the grandiose little ginger Davenport had somehow become a desk of easy virtue. They had danced round it, shouting at it.

"Harlot!"

"Strumpet!"

"Wicked thing!"

"Dirty French whore, showing your legs!"

"Soiled dove!"

"Naughty saucy beastly dirty DAVENPORT!"

Then they staggered in helpless laughter, holding each other up; two ageing queers, delirious with malice and joy.

"Bet you They buy it!"

"Bet you They don't!"

"Don't be such a sillybilly, you *know* They will! They'll *leap* on it! They'll *lust* for it! Our dirty Davenport!"

"Just because They bought the telephone and the King George the Fifth biscuit tin doesn't mean They'll—"

"It does, it must! They'll simply *coo* over it! They've simply no *taste*—"

"They don't understand *nice* things, *pretty* things—"

"They've no *feelings*—"

"Well, how could They, the poor loves? I mean, just *look* at Them! *Gaze* upon Them!"

They had both turned their heads and gazed upon Them. There was nothing much else to look at. What had been a country town was now a plain of reddish dust. What had been trees were now fungus-pocked stains on that dust. What had been railway lines were rusty traces of another red. Even the sky was tainted with the same glowering, indelible redness. The dust was everywhere.

Not that They stirred it. For five years They had stood sentinel, ringing the area of the town centre. They seldom moved. The reddened sun glanced off their opaque bodies—fused glass which sometimes emitted winks and rays and subdued noise, but more often not. The metallic leg, 250 feet or so high at full extension, seldom shifted their articulated, raft-like feet, which might be embedded for months on end in the compound of brick dust, vegetable dust and human bonemeal. Lichens and fungi grew over the feet, and once Eugene swore he had seen a rat. But never an insect or a bird. Dead five years.

But now, at this very moment, the claw was tracing the lines and textures of the Davenport and Mitch and Eugene clasped hands, shaken by suppressed and holy glee. The *legs!* The claw solemnly examined them, the clumsy grab moving on hidden articulations of silken perfection.

"OK," said the grab. It spoke in an approximation of the town's mayor—a voice five years silent.

"OK. Will take genuine antique. Genuine. Or kill. OK?"

"OK," whispered Eugene, the giggles suddenly gone.

"OK antique!" said Mitch. "Genuine. No kill. OK. *Hon*estly."

"*Ask!*" hissed Eugene.

"Not you!"

"It's your turn—"

"Fat pouf! You know it's your turn to ask—"

"Pouf yourself!"

"Bedwetter! Queer! Stinkpants! *Ask* it!"

But Mitch began helplessly to cry, so Eugene had to ask.

"What will you give us? Something good, OK?"

No answer. Messages ran up and down the grab's arm. Then the voice in the grab answered.

"More food. More bricks. More alcohol. More water More lamp oil. OK."

"Yes, but—*how* much more? *Much* more this time, OK?"

Again a long pause, then, "OK." The grab retracted with a soft whirr, carrying the Davenport as if on a platform. The machine's legs twitched and moved and a great metal foot knocked the top off the humans' hovel, then guiltlessly crushed its way, hayfoot, strawfoot, across the dust to resume station.

"Oh, and *now* look what They've done!" wept Mitch. "Clumsy beasts! I hate Them! I loathe Them! Big silly *cows!*"

"Come and help me put it all *back*—"

"You called me *names,* you're always calling me *names*—"

"I didn't mean it, you know I didn't mean it. Do be a dear and *help*."

"If I'm what you called me, so are you and worse. Worse! Sometimes I think I hate you, you're so cruel, so mean, you've given me my pain again—"

"Come and *help*."

"My pain—"

"Oh, do please, please, please SHUT UP."

They put the hovel together and crawled into it. It grew darker. Quite soon, the only light would be the dim blue chain of beams linking Them. You could not pass this chain. Nobody had tried now for four years and eleven months. The powdery marks of disintegrated bodies had of course long since disappeared.

Two hours later, Mitch and Eugene were giggling mad again.

"Do stop!" gasped Mitch. "You're killing me! I'm quite *damp!*"

But Eugene wouldn't stop. "I'm one of THEM!" he chanted. "One of THEM!" He had pulled a broken plastic bucket over his head; the remains of two squeegee floor mops served as Their legs and feet. He jerked and slithered grotesquely. Then, inspired, he picked up an oil lamp and hung it over his backside.

"Deathray!" he shouted. "You can't get past! Oh no, you can't! I've got a deathray in my bottie!"

In the corner, the alcohol dripped from the still. Tonight was a good night. Tomorrow, They would bring more of life's little luxuries. Life was good.

Life was awful. Most of those who had lived past Their coming had died more or less voluntarily. There was nothing to live for.

It had all been very simple. One day, you were a barber or a butcher or a baby or a businessman or a beautician. You said "Good morning" or kept yourself to yourself. You ordered lamb chops, put the cat out, mowed the lawn, tinkered with the car, watched TV, played bingo, distributed leaflets for the council elections.

Next day, They came and you were dead.

The TV was dead, the telephone was dead, the neighbours were dead, the flowers in your garden were dead, the cat was dead, the baby was dead, the municipal county council was dead. All without a whimper. All inside one violet-flashing, flesh-eating, matter consuming millisecond.

All except those who were actually under and within the areas covered by Them and Their machines. For those, if their hearts did not burst with the shock, there was life of a sort. Not that anyone understood what sort. Consider Eugene and Mitch.

They had been the scandal of the little town. As they walked together, their waved hair and their glittering slave bangles caught the sun. Their staggeringly tight jeans displayed rolling hips and twitching buttocks as they walked. Under the broad straps of their sandals peeped the lacquered toenails, now crimson, now silver-pearl. No hairs showed on their toes; they plucked them out with tweezers.

They touched each other incessantly as they walked. A manicured hand would find a sunlamp-bronzed forearm and rest there to stress a point. They were always stressing points. The waved heads would converge and nod and shake, the sibilant whispers would be exchanged, the eyes would roll and pop; then the heads would be thrown back and shrill whinnying laughter would bounce off the Georgian brickwork of the high street, tinkle against the curved glass of the slenderly framed and elegantly proportioned windows, desecrate the war memorial.

They simply adored the town, it was too utterly winsome and tender.

The town blackly hated them.

They ran the antique shop. Or seemed to do so. For no townsman would ever visit it. Perhaps Eugene and Mitch lived on legacies; perhaps they supplied the big, important antique dealers in the cities; no one knew how they lived or what they lived on. It was enough of an affront that they lived at all, a disgrace to the whole community.

Not that they had any part in the community. They lived in their own little tinkling pagoda of a world, primping their hair in the sweetly darling Regency mirror by the Adam mantel (but could one be sure it was really, truly Adam?) and pouting naughtily when it was their turn to make the Lapsang Souchong, or pursing lips in concentration when trying out new drapes (*not* the viole, Mitcrie love, something more *floating* and *ethereal*) to hang on the great fourposter they were said to share . . . They needed no one but each other.

It was on one of those ordinary, halcyon days that Mitch said, "Oh, but Eugene, do *listen!*"

"I won't, I simply won't. I'm stopping my ears. There!"

"But Eugene, hear you must, hear you shall! It's a com*plete*ly genuine and *quite* ridiculous earthenware water filter thing, something from the Crimean *war,* I dare promise, and it's lying in a *field* not a mile from here and we could fill it with potpourri—"

"I despise the very sound of it."

"But if only you'd come with me and look at it with me and help me carry it, you'd make me the happiest boy in the *world*—'

"Really, Mitch, how camp can you get! 'The happiest boy in the world'!"

"Well, *will* you or *won't* you help me carry it?"

That evening, they had minced briskly down the main street and were soon out in the fields. The water filter, a great ceramic thing bespattered with relief plaques saying NONPAREIL and PATENTED and so on, lay in a ditch. As they bent over to lift it, the strange shadows darkened the ground. It was Them, one of Their machines, directly overhead.

A second later, the world ended.

"But did it?" Eugene asked. "I mean, who are They? I mean, is it the machines—"

"H. G. Wells hardware, that's all the machines are!"

"Well, what and where are They?"

"Grotty little *insect* men, with colds in their heads. Or delicious hairy, bug-eyed monsters. *Do* you remember that *blissful* horror film, with that too utterly *ghoul-ish*—"

"Oh, do make an *effort*. I mean, at *most* fifty people survived in our town. We're probably the last people alive. And They took the mayor, do you remember . . . Why the mayor? Did They *know* he was the mayor? They can't have done, such a *plebeian* little man, you could never have told—"

"I can't see why They bothered to let *anyone* survive. I suppose we're merely specimens, and They keep us alive just to *gloat*."

"But the darlings do fancy our antiques."

"Oh, yes, we've always got that. Well, for a few weeks, anyhow."

"Anyhow, we're obviously not the last people alive, there's Adam and Madam and Crazy Annie. Oh, no, she's dead now, isnt' she? *Poor* old faggot."

In a hovel some hundreds of feet from theirs had lived a crazy old woman called Annie. She had been crazed enough, God knows, before They came. Latterly she had rotted in the dust like a hen, scratching at nothing in particular with horny fingers and mouthing filth when Their machines came with supplies. Mitch and Eugene had been afraid of her. not for what she *was*, but for what she represented: themselves, later . . .

Farther away, there was Adam something-or-other. He was dark, unpleasant, disgruntled and musical. He shared his hovel with a girl who had worked in the greengrocer's shop when there had been a greengrocer's shop. Then, she had been a nice little mini-skirted, pony-tailed, blond piece. Now she was a nasty, gross, sacking-skirted virago and the blond had grown out. Her name was Lucy. This was the couple that Mitch and Eugene called Madam and Adam. But the two couples had seldom spoken to each other. Burying crazy old Annie had brought the four of them together.

Adam and Madam made musical instruments out of bits of tubing, and played and sang. They played very softly, for they were afraid of Them. They might hear and take away the instruments.

Possible there were other people here or there, but there were reasons for not finding out. As Eugene and Mitch agreed, "We might seem a little odd, but we're used to being thought odd, aren't we? And we've got each other, while all Adam and Madam have got is a hachet to *kill* you with, or a kinky tin whistle to *bore* you with . . . I mean, they're not really people any more. They've nothing to live for."

But then, only too often Eugene and Mitch would have a little spat and say things they didn't mean—or worse, things they did mean—and see each other as they really were. They would weep and accuse and even slap and scratch, and end by sobbing, "What are we living for? Why do we go on?"

One reason was the cellars. The Davenport had come from a cellar. Shortly, the Davenport would be transmuted into food, warmth and comfort. They knew this from experience. They had already offered Them oddments from various cellars and each time had been rewarded. It was rather like the old days when they ran the antique shop. Only now it was a matter of survival.

That was why they were so pleased with the pickaxe. Mitch had found it in the Davenport cellar; with it, they could open up more cellars. The pickaxe was their key to capitalism.

Almost immediately, it opened up a treasure-trove.

In a freshly opened cellar they found a birdcage, a settee covered in brown plush and a wind-up gramophone.

As they were about to dig up more treasure, they heard the noise they should have anticipated: Their machine. It was shuffling about in the near distance outside their hovel. It was saying, "OK. Come out. OK. Bricks, lamp oil, food, alcohol, water. OK. OK, come out."

"Jesus H. *Christ*," whispered Mitch. "If They knew we were here—"

"Oh, do be *quiet!* Walk, do not run, to your nearest hovel—"

"If it ever suspected—"

"Well, let's take it something. Distract it."

"Not the birdcage, it's *too* precious—"

"The gramophone, then. Quickly!"

The two of them slid through the hole in the cellar wall, Eugene carrying the gramophone. In seconds they were back in the hovel.

Where you were?" said the grab.

"Call of nature, dear. OK?"

"Not OK," said the grab. "Perhaps kill."

"You don't have them, calls of nature, do you? Lucky old you!"

"Perhaps kill."

"Got a needle stuck, poor love," whispered Mitch.

"Oo, what a good idea! Show it the gramophone!" said Eugene.

"Look, dear!" said Mitch to the grab. "Lovely gramophone! *Ever* so genuine antique, worth goodness *knows* how much!"

"How much?" said the grab. Its messages had started up.

"Oh, lots and lots of *everything*. You see, gramophones are *quite priceless*—"

"Better even than Davenports with chromium-plated legs—"

"What is for?" said the grab.

"Ah," said Mitch, "I'm glad you asked me that. Well, no, I'm not. You see, it's ever so—complicated . . . Particularly," he added aside, "when you've got no bleeding records to play."

"What is for?" said the grab's voice, dourly.

"Like I said, dear, it's a gramophone—"

Messages started going back and forth within the grab's arm.

"Do be careful, Mitch, They take it all down and look it up in something," whispered Eugene.

"Gramophone OK," said the grab.

"OK? It's simply *fabulous*. Particularly these very super-delicious ones with the *doggies* on them——"

"Gramophone," said the grab. "What is for?"

"Well, as I was saying, this is a *round-and-rounder* type gramophone. You wind it up like this"——Eugene wound the dismally creaking handle——"and you turn the lever *so,* and there you are! Round and round! *Too* enchanting!"

"Not OK," said the grab. "Perhaps kill. Incomplete. Not OK. Perhaps take away oil, water, food——"

"Don't let's be hasty!" said Eugene, horrified. "Mitch, for heaven's sake get back down there and look for records."

"Don't be so *crass*. They mustn't find out about the *cellar*——"

"Oh, dear. Listen, love," said Eugene brightly to the grab. "My friend and I will just riffle through our little treasures while you trot off and have a lovely rest. Your poor *feet* . . . "

"And come back before it's dark and perhaps we'll have a *surprise* for you!" said Mitch.

More messages; then the machine lumbered away.

"Cheeribye!" cried Mitch.

"Drop dead! Turn blue! Perhaps kill!" added Eugene quietly.

It was gone, back in station with the others.

"Please God," sighed Eugene, "we'll find some records."

They found them. Old 78s in a sort of hatbox.

"Deanna Durbin!" breathed Mitch. "How too *utterly*, in*toxi*catingly, de*liri*ously mirth-provoking!"

" 'I love to climb an apple tree, but apples disagree with me——' "

" 'And I'll be sick as sick can be——' "

"Perhaps kill, OK?"

They pranced with joy and put the record on. For a moment, the voice from the past clutched at some soft and vulnerable and half-forgotten soft centre inside them. But they were tougher than they knew. Soon their mocking falsettos blended with the scratchy soprano from the gramophone. They sorted through the records.

"Duke Ellington! 'The Mooche'! Whatever happens, we'll keep that, and *bother* Them!"

"Nothing *really* my style here, except one Peggy Lee."

"What's the good of records if we give Them the gramophone—"

"Oh, do *look,* I can't believe it. A Benny Goodman quintet! 'Seven Come—' "

"Not 'Seven Come Eleven'! Utter bliss! Throw darling Deanna away and let's get *in the groove,* as one said!"

They were dancing together, Eugene leading, to the strains of "I'll be loving you, always" when suddenly they became aware that Their machine was standing looming over them. They broke apart and Mitch made to switch off the gramophone.

"OK," said the grab. "Continue. Don't stop."

"Well, actually, dear" said Mitch, "that was the last waltz and Mummy will be furious if I'm not home by midnight." He switched the gramophone off.

"Don't stop!" said the grab, loudly and instantly.

"In a *trice,* all our lovely clothes turn into *rags*—"

"Again!" said the grab.

"—And Prince Charming will do his *lot!"*

"Again," said the grab, menacingly. The messages thrummed.

"Give him Deanna," said Mitch. "Don't waste Peggy Lee on old Tin-ear."

" 'Ave Maria'!" announced Eugene. *Wholly* holy." Deanna Durbin's voice warbled. The grab was still. The needle went "Grrk" at the end of the track. There was silence.

Then messages started running up and down, furiously.

"Again," said the grab.

"That's all for now, there isn't any more," said Mitch.

"If you liked us, tell your friends," added Eugene. "If you don't like us, turn blue."

"Again!" said the grab.

"Goodies," said Eugene, blandly. *"Lots* of goodies. Oil, water, alcohol, everything—*lots* of everything. Then we play it again, OK?"

Messages percolated. "OK!" said the grab. "Again. Now."

"Okay, toots. One more time, Deanna baby—and make it *swing."*

"Aaaaaaaaah vay . . . MaREEEEE-EEEEE- aa- ah . . ." began the record. The music poured over the derelict landscape like treacle over iron filings.

Too grotesque!" murmured Eugene. *"Too* puke-provoking."

"Look!" whispered Mitch.

"What? Where?"

"The *grab! Look* at it!"

Eugene looked. His eyes and mouth made Os of amazement.

The grab was swaying in time with the music.

Mitch swilled the Médoc round his teeth, swallowed, considered, and said, "No. Positively and irrevocably NO."

"Well, I think it's very fair for a 1962. And it must have been utter *agony* for them to find anything at *all*—". . . . . .

Not a nice wine. Not nice *at all*. If they can find that very acceptable Riesling, they can find something better in Médocs. I will *not* be put off with this disgusting, *spec*ious, hydrochloric-acid Médoc. Not after all the music we've played them."

"I suppose we'll have to pass the Médoc on to Adam and Madam. Though they couldn't care *less* what they drink . . . "

"They wouldn't notice the difference between python's pee and Piesporter. All I'm saying is, up with this I will not put. I shall tell our little metal chum when he comes: *could do better if tried harder*. I shall tell him, go and find some better red wines—*preferably* château-bottled—or it's *Smackbottomsville*."

"And no Golden Hour of Melody tonight."

But of course there was a Golden Hour of Melody. There had to be. It was the GHM that brought the rugs, the unlimited lamp oil, the bottled chicken breasts, the sprung mattress. It was the GHM that had turned the hovel into what Eugene and Mitch called the Mixed Blessing—a home filled with extraordinarily assorted furniture and fittings, but a home for all that.

For music had, to put it mildly, caught on with Them. It had infected Them, almost enslaved Them. They had to have their music. They had to pay for it with untold diggings and burrowings, by uncovering God knows what mounds of rotting horrors. The grabs would thrust and gouge through shreds of decaying scalp, through pavements and pelvises, through Old Masters or a stockpile of suppositories . . . The spoils would be laid before Eugene and Mitch: a doll's head, a belly dancer's nipple cover, a pack of cards, a garnet brooch, a German dictionary, a set of dentures—nearly, but not all, broken, decayed, crushed, torn, mouldering, useless, horrible; grist to the music mill, grist to the Mixed Blessing.

Adam and Madam arrived, dour, half-drunk, bickering, stupid, smelly and uncouth.

"*Darlings!*" said Mitch, advancing on them, then recoiling from their stench. "All tuned up, are we? Ready to play?"

"Ur."

"How *very* fetching that sacking looks, Lucy. But now I *insist* you wet your whistles with some of this too-scrumptious Médoc—the wine of France, the very latest consignment from our shippers, specially for *you*. Eugene, foaming beakers, *if* you please."

"With beaded bubbles winking at the *brim,* loves. Ladies first."

"Ur."

"The true, the blushful Hippocrene."

"Grr."

On the whole, though, the party was going very well. Adam and Madam tuned their by no means unsophisticated instruments—the grabs had worked overtime to find guitar strings, tuning heads, pieces of wind instruments, even a flute in working order—and, whatever their social failings, Adam and Madam played and sang rather well. Even more important, both had an excellent ear. Between the four of them, they could produce an almost endless anthology of words and music, containing anything from "Greensleeves" and harmonised fragments of operatic arias to soldiers' songs of unspeakable filthiness.

"Tonight, I *rather* thought," said Mitch, "we could oblige with a *soupçon* of the hey-nonny-no stuff. 'There was a lover and his lass,' perhaps. Then a nice slow rendition of 'Danny Boy,' very *pathetic*. Then—but do let's agree on the words—that rather *malodorous* song of yours, Adam, 'I've got a bulldog called Big Ben.' "

"Ur."

" 'Eats like nine and'—oh dear!—'*defecates* like ten.' I *can't* bring myself to utter it. But They seem *so* to enjoy it—"

"They're coming," said Eugene. "Now, are we all in tune? *Goodness,* at least a quarter tone flat. How one *longs* for something that doesn't need tuning with a *spanner* . . ."

"They're here."

And there They were (three of them!) with grabs extended. "Like Oliver Twists," murmured Eugene, preparing to enjoy himself. He was Master of Ceremonies and as such felt himself licensed to be amusing at Their expense.

"Ladies, Gentlemen, and assorted Hardware," he began. "This evening, we celebrate the *umpteenth* Golden Hour of Melody—an occasion of *particular* significance, as you will readily agree—with the rendition of a deliriously auspicious conglomeration of polyphonic exuberances—in short, something for everyone. Something old, something new, something borrowed—yes, and something *blue* to set those turgid old circuits tingling—"

"Hurry *up.*"

"Don't *pull* at me. But before commencing our pro-gramme—which will begin with that stirring and ever-popular anthem in praise of our staunch four-footed friend, the bulldog—I will ask you to show your ap-preciation for the artistes in the accustomed manner. In short, *clap,* you bleeders! Rattle your puddies!"

"Good and *loud!*" muttered Mitch, leaning forward expectantly. This was the only part of the concert he really enjoyed—Their obligatory applause before-hand, the grating, rattling noise that the grabs had been taught to make. Applause! Well, after all, it rep-resented some small victory or other . . .

"Let's hear it for the melody makers!" said Mitch in his DJ voice.

But there was no applause. No applause! The grabs were motionless. Mitch and Eugene looked at each other. Adam and Madam grumbled an uneasy. "Ur." Eugene faced Them.

"The *usual* thing, the *polite* thing, before a concert is a nice cosy round of *applause*—" he began.

A grab moved, ominously. It came toward them. "*Sing!*" shouted Eugene. They sang. The grab kept moving forward and lifted to the height of their heads. Then higher. The song tailed off.

The grab kept moving. Now it was poised above the Mixed Blessing.

"Don't you *dare*—" yelled Mitch.

The grab slammed down. The Mixed Blessing bulged, leaked, crumpled, puffed red dust and flat-tened. Then the grab went up and down, slowly and rhythmically and deafeningly pounding the Mixed Blessing into the ground.

Mitch had stopped yelling and started blubbering.

Eugene just looked, wide-eyed and expressionless. Adam and Madam formed a pyramid, leaning against each other. They looked merely bovinely interested, but tears trickled down the girl's face.

"They'll 'ave our place next," she snivelled.

She was right. The grab, leaking red silt, snaked away on its apparently infinite flexible arm, reached the hovel, smashed it at a blow, and turned over the debris as if with a spade. Madam began to howl "*Ooooooo!*" and Adam growled.

Shattered, the little party stood there. The grab snaked back. An almost visible question mark hovered over the bowed human heads.

The question was answered.

"Your music," announced a grab, "no good. We kill."

"Natch," said Eugene, bravely flippant.

"Not OK music," said the grab. "We learn all you know. More. Listen."

There was a click, and it started. Their music. The music of Them. Music vast in amplitude—

A mother was bathing her baby one night,
'Twas the youngest of ten and a delicate mite,

They sang. The massed choir was so loud that dust trembled. The hooting orchestra was so sweet that teeth ached.

The mother was poor and the baby was thin,
'Twas only a skellington wrapped up in skin . . .

"Skellington . . ." murmured Mitch. "How bleeding, bloody *funny*"

The mother looked round for the soap on the
*   rack,*
'Twas only a moment, but when she looked
*   back—*

Divine harmonies fluttered and swooped, twittered and burped. *"Crinoline* ladies, can't you *see* them!" said Mitch. "And we taught them. *We* taught them *this . . ."*

> *My baby has gorn down the plug 'ole!*
> *My baby has fell down the plug!*

bellowed the grab, in a maelstrom of bathos

> *The pore little thing*
> *Was so skinny and thin*
> *It oughter been washed in a jug—*

("—in a jug," echoed a million metal voices through a million metal noses.)

> *My baby has gone down the plug 'ole,*
> *It won't need a bath any more,*
> *My baby has gone down the plug 'ole—*
> *Not lost—but gone—beeeefore.*

("Oh, gone, be-fore!" echoed the choir, its vibrato a whole tone wide, its pathos as wide as the ocean and as deep as an ink stain.)

The song ended. The silence was deafening. The game was up.

"You poor, silly, po-faced, stinking, bleeding, boneless, gutless, soulless, mindless *tin turds,"* said Eugene at last, and began to laugh. Soon the four of them were laughing. They laughed until they cried, cried until they hiccupped, hiccupped till they choked. Then were silent again.

"Now kill," said the grab.

"OK, kill," said Eugene. "Big deal."

"And so, as the sun sinks in the west, we bid a reluctant 'Farewell' to lovable old Mother Earth and her dirty denizens," recited Mitch, shakily.

"Kill," said the grab. The other two machines had

already plodded back and resumed station. The blue beams were linked.

"Not with a bang, but a whimper," said Eugene. "We could be the *very last four left!* On this whole planet! It gives one *furiously* to think." He began to weep, quietly.

"——Them!" said Adam, indistinctly.

"Oh, *don't* do that for God's sake, I do *beseech*. There's enough of Them already," said Eugene, hysterically.

"Kill now," said the grab.

"How are you going to do it? Smash us flat?"

"Through the beams," said the grab. "Walk. Kill now."

"Bags, I not go first!" said Mitch, flightily.

"Cut," said Adam. He bent down and picked up their pack of cards out of the dust.

They cut, cut again, and cut again. But it could not last.

"Now! Kill now!" said the grab. "Walk."

It lithely glided behind them, shepherding them. They walked.

"So ri*dic*ulous!" said Mitch. "The last! The very last! We could be the very last people in all the world! I mean, there was Jesus Christ and Fabergé and Socrates and the Unknown Soldier and poor Oscar, and Queen Victoria and that boy in Corfu, and George Washington—everyone—"

"—and the pyramids and spacecraft and men on the moon and Cleopatra on the Nile and soldiers dying from phosgene gas . . . Then us. Pitiful us. Oh, Mitch, pitiful, pitiful, *pitiful!*"

"First you see it, now you don't," said Adam unexpectedly. "The bloody end. Like this!" He spat in the red dust. They were very close now to the blue rays and death.

"First you see it, now you don't!" said Mitch. He was sniffling and at the same time doing a card trick. "First you see it"—and there was the card between two fingers—"now you don't." A flick of the wrist, a turn of the fingers.

They were at the perimeter. They stopped.

"Walk," said the grab. "Walk."

Eugene crumpled at the knees and sat down, legs straight out like a doll's "It's no good, I just *can't!*" he sobbed. "Not like *this* . . . I'm me, *me!* It's not *fitting,* it's not seemly, it's too *hideous*—"

The girl sat down too. "I bleeding won't!" she said.

The grab sidled up and scooped them to their feet. "Kill now," it remarked. "Walk."

She began to run, away from the perimeter. She ran and ran, stumbled and fell, got up and ran again. The grab smoothly wove its way after her but when she stumbled, overshot. Mitch sniggered hysterically. "Find the lady!" he shouted. "Now you see her, now you don't!"

. In the end she was shepherded back by the grab. No one could bear to look at her face; no one could keep their eyes from it. Desperately, Mitch shouted, "Come on then, you lucky lads! Find the lady, win a fiver! I place three cards, so!—Acey-deucy, King, and last *but* not least, the lady—the Queen! *Face* down on the ground, positively no deception! You want a second look, lady? Right you are—Ace, King, Queen. Positively no deception! Now, keep your peepers on the *Queen,* that's all you've got to do! On the Queen! On the lady!"

His hands swept over the three cards, fluttering and magical. Yet it was easy enough to see through the trick. There was the Queen! Now there! Still there! Now over there, on the left! Child's play.

"All right!" shouted Mitch. "Now—*find the lady!*"

Adam spat disgustedly. Lucy looked at nothing through her swamped, defeated eyes. Eugene— But the grab pushed him aside, hovered over the three cards, extended its metal claw, and said, "Lady."

"Do I hear you aright, sir? *Here,* sir? *This* card, sir? You're quite *sure,* my dear sir?"

"Lady!" The metal claw tapped.

Mitch turned over the card: the King.

Messages tinkled, swelled, hummed.

"Again," said the grab.

The sun was lower, lower still.

"Again," said the grab.

The lamps, Their lamps, blazed under the night sky.

"Take a card. Any card! That is your choice? Excellent. Commit it to memory . . " Mitch shuffled gaudily and kept up the patter. "Now, you, sir, as I instantly discerned, are no mere acolyte at the shrine of prestidigitation, but a veritable *adept*. So when I ask you once again to select a card—"

Dawn.

"Again," said the grab.

A Scarab in the
City of Time

MARTA RANDALL

first met Marta Randall at a science-fiction
convention in San Francisco in the summer
of 1973. She was then, and still is, a small
articulate woman of strongly held and forcefully expressed opinions, and I recall her telling me, in one of
our early discussions of literary matters, that she preferred the sort of stories with an identifiable beginning,
middle, and end. "So do I," I replied, "although I
don't necessarily require that. they happen in that order." We went round on that for a time, she taking a
relatively conservative view of the art of the short
story, I supporting greater freedom of construction;
but, as is usual in such debates, neither of us held as
extreme a position as it might have seemed to the
other.

She had already published one story, in Michael
Moorcock's *New Worlds,* under her former married
name of Marta Bergstesser. I think she had written
several others that were making the rounds, and had
begun to sketch the outline for the novel that eventually would be published as *Islands*. In January of
1974, she showed me a story called "A Scarab in the
City of Time," with some trepidation, I believe; I
read it on the spot and rather to her surprise accepted
it then and there. Trepidation is no longer a Marta

Randall characteristic, for in the intervening years she has gone on to publish stories in *Universe, Fantasy and Science Fiction,* and various other places, including several issues of *New Dimensions,* and has had three novels published, with two more currently in progress. (The best known of them is *Journey.*) And as of the eleventh issue she has become co-editor of *New Dimensions,* a development that surely neither of us could have anticipated when we had that first discussion of the art of the short story six years ago.

I SKULK IN A FORGOTTEN ALLEY WHILE THEY SCURRY by outside, searching for me. Whippety-whip, they dive around corners with unaccustomed haste, and they have all donned worried faces for the occasion. Even the robo-cops look worried, and look well; were there stones in this City they would turn them all. But they won't find me, not me, no. When their programmed darkness falls I move from the alley, slyly insert myself in their streets and avenues, slink through the park to the City Offices and scrawl "I am a scarab in the City of Time" over the windows of the mayor's office. I use a spray of heat-sensitive liquid crystals; my graffito will be pretty tomorrow as the wind and fake sunlight shift it through the spectrum. Then I sneak to an outlying residential section where I've not been before, eluding robo-cops on my way, and steal food from an unlocked house for my night's meals. I wouldn't steal from citizens if I could help it, but my thumbprint isn't registered, isn't legal tender in the City of Time. So I burgle and the Association of Merchants grows rich because of me, as locks and bars appear on doors and windows throughout the City. I'm good for the economy of the City of Time, I am.

I'm a sociologist. I'm not supposed to be doing any of this.

When morning comes they cluster before the City

Offices, gesticulating, muttering, shifting, frightened. I watch them from a tree in the park, am tempted to mingle with them, sip the sweet nectar of their dismay. No, no, not yet. I remain hidden as the mayor appears on the steps of the building, glares at my beautiful sign. Workers are trying to remove it, but there's a bonding agent in my paint and the colors shift mockingly under their clumsy hands. The mayor reassures the people, calming them with the dignity of her silver hair and smooth hands, and they begin to disperse. I'm tired. The pseudo-sun is far too bright today, a faint wind rustles the leaves around me. When noon comes I slip from my perch, move easily under the eaves and edges of bushes to the Repairs Center, sneak into a storage room and curl down on a pile of cables to sleep.

The City is hard on the eyes, from the outside. Its hemisphere rises from a lush plain, catches the light of the sun and reflects it back harshly at the resurrected earth. Time has silted soil high around the City, but it's probable that the City doesn't know, or care to know. When we returned to colonize Terra we tried to make contact with the City, sent waves of everything we could manage at the impervious dome, received nothing in reply. Years passed and we built our own cities, clean and open to the fresh winds; sailed our ships and floated through the skies, tilled the soil, farmed the seas. Occasionally threw more junk at the City and argued about it. Some held that the City was dead, a gigantic mausoleum; some that it was inhabited by inbred freaks and monsters; some that it was merely the same City our ancestors had left behind as they fled from a poisoned planet. But no one knew, until I dug down beyond the City's deepest foundations, through the bedrock and up into the City. And I can't get out again.

I awaken at nightfall, as the dome of the City turns dark and the stars come on, and spend some time on the roof of the Repairs Center watching the sky and plotting new mischief. Those stars, those · stars—no one has seen the original of these dome-printed constellations in two thousand years, yet here they shine in mimicry of the true sky. I tighten the straps of my pack, slip from the building, through the dim streets. The robocops hunt for me while the good citizens of the City sleep. And the bad citizens? There are none in the City of Time, none except me, me, and I only by default. Tiers of buildings loom over my head, tapering to the arch of the dome; cascades of plants spill over the walls and display fragrant, flagrant blossoms; most of the doors are locked, the windows closed tight, the citizenry unquiet in their quiet beds. I move to the museum and inside, pad softly through the dark to the echoing Hall of Animals. Hundreds, thousands of them here, some preserved carcasses, some simply statues of those beasts that were extinct by the time the City locked its dome against the poisoned world. I holograph each exhibit carefully, setting the receptors with delicacy, with art, and when I am finished I move through the hall and append notes in liquid script to the signboards: "This animal survives, outside." "This animal is now twice as big and looks like an elephant (see Exhibit 4659)." "This animal now flies." "This animal now breathes air." And, in huge block letters on the face of the museum, "HERE THERE BE DRAGONS." As I finish, the street explodes into a commotion of light and noise, scores of robo-cops and citizens pour from the cross streets and buildings. Have I tripped an alarm? Possibly, probably, someone has monkeyed with the wiring, created an alarm in this uneventful City. The scarab is the mother of invention. Someone sees me clinging to the face of the museum and sets up a cry in counterpoint to the larger one. In my initial surprise I almost drop the paint, then finish the last swing of the "S" before swinging myself down to the roof of the portico, scamper along the protruding tops of the columns and slither down to an open window. I run through the museum, not stopping to stuff the paint into my pack, up one shaft and down another, followed by the hue and cry behind me. I halt for a bare moment to pop the cube from a holojector and stuff another in its place, flick on the machine, and when I am two corridors away I hear the howling populace come to a sudden halt as they face the new projection. And so they should. I took it just before invading their sealed city, setting my receptors about the rim of the hills surrounding the plain on which the City sits. They are seeing their City from the wrong side, from Out, and as it is now. Perhaps they do not know what it is, but the surprise of its presence gives me time to flee through another corridor, out into a dawn-lit empty street and away.

"When meeting a strange animal, stay quiet until you know where the teeth are," they had told me; when I entered the belly of the City of Time I remembered, moved through shadows. Watched from vantage points as the citizens lived their lives before me, whispered notes into my 'corder, took holographs, invaded their library at night with my screens and read their journals and books, lists and agglomerations. Snuck into their City Offices and recorded their records and records of records until my cubes were filled and most of my food gone, and then I tried to go home. But the robo-techs had found and filled my miniature hell-mouth, sealed it over and sealed my digging tools in it. I searched the City for another way home, delved in corners and edges and ragged remnants, and found nothing. Not a crack nor a leak, door nor window. Nothing. How large a City is, when you search for one small scarab-hole. Nothing. I looked about me at the strange, pale people, I opened my ears to the archaic rhythms of their speech, I sniffed the ancient odors of their air and I wept, homesick, from the tops of trees in the park by the City Offices. When they came looking for me I fled. Stole my food from unlocked houses, stole my sleep in small snatches in small places, lived miserably, yearning for the fresh sweet scents of home. Until it came to me that the only way I could go home was if everyone went home, if the City grated open its rusted doors and let the clean air blow in. I considered this, lurking in odd nooks and corners. I couldn't walk into the mayor's office and say, "Hey, listen, lady. The world's all fresh and clean and lovely outside, and it's time to take a walk in sunlight." People who say that are heretics. They dispose of them. It says so in their books, it is recorded in the records of their courts, their preachers bellow it from the pulpits of their temples. I don't want to die, I don't want to be a martyr. I simply want to go home again, to my children, my husband, the stones and rafters of my home, the voices of my students. So I pound in the night on the gates of the City, and hope that those behind me will hear.

I'm hungry. No food on tonight's expedition, just some water I poured into my wetpouch on the run, from a fountain by the Wheel of Fate. The streets around the Repairs Center are swarming with people up and about, in full hue and cry, and I search for a new place. Here, a church, deserted and dim. I scuttle inside, up to the lofts, through undisturbed dust beneath the eaves, and curl myself into a tight ball behind a filthy window. Feed my hungry belly on nightmares and wait for another dusk. Sleep. Sleep.

Dirty windows? Are their purifiers breaking down, their life supports whimpering to a halt after all this time? Dust?

How pale these people are! Fair pink skins and light brown or yellow hair, light eyes; they look like illustrations from a history book. When they locked themselves up in their unhatched egg there were still races in the world, people simplistically divided into preposterous colors; the people of the City were "white" ones, fair of skin, straight of nose and hair, lords of the globe for a time until they grew frightened and hid. The rest of humanity poured out into the galaxy and soon the ridiculous distinctions were lost, for in space and on new worlds people are people are people, valued for their simple humanity amid environments alien beyond description. The books of the City tell of the battles fought, of the expulsion of the black vermin and yellow lice. If I showed my brown face and epicanthic eyes, my bush of light brown hair, they would stopper my mouth with death before I had a chance to speak. I peer at them from the grimed church window, shake my head, tiptoe to the vestry to steal bread and wine from sacramental silver.

How long does it take for a two-thousand-year-old egg to rot?

They hold a service below me for the expulsion of the demon. A wise conclusion: I obviously could not have come from Out, and I am not one of them. They've checked themselves, most carefully; they are, each of them, finger-printed, foot-printed, voice-printed, retina-printed, lip-printed, brainwave-printed, holographed, measured and metered from the moment of their metered births. They're all present and accounted for, and so I am a demon, a ghost amok in the City of Time. I make a note to add that to the sign on the City Offices, and watch the archaic stars appear. Stars. Floating through ancient skies.

When the prank comes to me it is so obvious, so clear, so simple that I laugh aloud, and the congregation below me freezes in fear. I laugh again, pure joy, and hide in a forgotten closet until they stop looking and flee superstitiously from the building. I follow them out, across the City to the vault of controls. I've picked the locks here before and I do it again now, slip inside, lock the door behind me and consider the panels on the wall. Here, and here, linked to this, and here the main nexus, here the central time control.

Then I sit and open my mind to memories, recall the clearest, purest night of resurrected Terra I have seen, and I program the skies of the City of Time, jumping their heavens two thousand years forward in the space of half an hour. I add to the moon the smudge of Jump I, I put our latest comet in the sky. What else? Of course, the weather satellites, all five in stately, if not entirely accurate, orbit through the heavens. The computer is not programmed to let me add a starship, or I would do that too. There. There must be stargazers in the City of Time, people who will look above them and see my altered cosmos, will wonder, speculate, go take a look. They will. They *must*. I lock the door behind me and go to write graffiti on the walls of the static City.

Why has their birthrate declined? The City was built to accommodate twice as many as it now encloses—such an empty City now!

Someone finally noticed the report from the robotech that found and sealed my way home, and someone else decided that the hole might have some connection with the haunting of their sealed City. A large group of them has come down to inspect it, while I inspect them. Hope springs eternal, yes, and perhaps one of them will come to the right conclusion. But no, they inspect the sealed hole, they argue at great length about it, stamping their feet on the plasteel floor. Perhaps they think that some small animal with laser teeth has sawed its way around their citadel, or that some anomalous tremor has produced this round aperture with fused sides. Whatever, whatever; they decide finally that the hell-mouth couldn't possibly have been made from the outside; no one lives out there, no one could live out there. They are very certain. After a while they leave and I emerge, howl in rage, kick at the floors and walls, tear at the impervious sides of the machines. The echoes of my disappointment rampage through the vault, activate some electronic curiosity in the robo-techs, and they come to investigate. But I am long gone, following the course of my despair up into the nub of the City.

They argue about it now. I listen to the mayor berate the police system over my unapprehended state, yet there is hesitation in her voice. I hear my pranks and myself denounced from pulpits while the congregation sits oddly silent. Young ones at the schools explode with oratory, wave their urgent hands skyward. I listen, strain my ears, want to rush to them yelling, "Yes, yes, you are almost right! Come, show me the doors, I'll take you Out into clarity! Come!" But I remain hidden, eager, awake, hope boiling within me. Come, hurry, let me go home again!

They still argue, endlessly. I am impatient. It's harvest time Out, the schools and shops are closed and the population pours forth to reap and celebrate. Home! Home! I program their night skies to blink at them, I paint pictures on fountain lips of harvests under round moons, of large cats prowling the yards of houses, calling to be fed and stroked; of giant lilies floating in the calm air of forests. Home! I consider poisoning their water, rerouting their waste system, flooding their streets, giving them twenty-hour nights and two-minute days. I could do it all, easily, from the depths of the service cores, from the corners of the control rooms, but I refrain. The City is unbearable enough to me by itself, without my self-made catastrophes. Home! Jora will be seven by now, Karleen twelve, my corn ripens on the hill and my students wait in classrooms, Petrel stalks the hillside and awaits my return. Home! I huddle in a corner of the park, weeping, until the universe shrinks to accommodate only my soul pain and nothing more. Then, angered, I waken the rusting voice of the call system above the City Offices and bellow through the streets, "For God's sake, walk into the light! The sun shines Out, there are trees and birds and water sweet as spring! Come Out! Come Out and home again!"

They're opening the door. They found it, buried in a forgotten service area, behind piles of wire and cable, guarded by an ancient robo-cop. I watch, amazed, through the shards of plasti-glass in an abandoned storage room, my fingers at my mouth, teeth to nails, reverting to primitivism as the young people overpower the robo-cop by the airlock. They do it quite simply. Five of them lunge at the robot, grab, twist the paneled head until it pops off and rolls down the alley, trailing multicolored wires. The body, relieved of its burden, wanders in a melancholy way down the blind alley and stands bleeping aimlessly at the end of it, uncertain of where to turn. The young ones ignore the distressed machine, turn their attention to the great wheels and plates of the airlock door. Have they . . . yes, they've brought meters, and one of them applies the leads to a small, unobtrusive control box, reads the meter, shakes her head, shakes the meter, tries again, shrugs. More uncertainty, more discussion, then the robot-slayers grasp the great wheel of the door and strain at it. Two others join in, the last one watches uneasily at the entrance to the alley. Why didn't they completely dismantle the robo-cop? Where's the transmitter in the damned thing, anyway? It's likely, possible, probable, certain that the mutilated beast is sending silent, roaring distress signals throughout the City, calling cops and more cops, bringing them rushing to the door to freedom. I watch the young ones as they wrench and twist at the wheel, frightened, excited, defiant, sweaty, the age of my students. The wheel groans, turns, suddenly spins free, spilling the young ones over the polymer pavement. Quickly then, yes, they gather at the door, pry it open slowly, swinging it on its ancient hinges. Hurry! Hurry! From my higher vantage point I can see scurries in the distance, fast approaching, hurry! And the door stands open, they cluster at its mouth, waver, enter one after another. My God, the door's closing! Of course, an airlock, of course. I scramble from my perch, tear through the empty storage center, down to the alley. My pack falls to the floor behind me, my torn tunic catches on something and tears completely from me but I can't stop, mustn't, run, *run,* watching in agony as the door closes, closes, closes and suddenly I am inside, braking the force of my flight on their soft bodies, slumping against the far wall, panting, while they stand gaping at me. The door swings shut, clicks into place. Safe. Safe.

I catch my breath, gesture toward the next door. "Out," I gasp. "S'okay, clean, open."

But they're frightened of me, hair, skin, eyes, semi-nakedness. They huddle together, shivering slightly. I force the beating of my heart down, take a deep breath, tell them of my journey, my trials, my home-sickness. Do they believe me? They cluster together, wide-eyed, silent. I've not bathed properly in five months, my hair bushes in lumps around my sun-starved face, my eyes are rimmed with weariness. Why should they believe this horrific apparition? I shrug, reach for the great wheel, yank. It does not budge to my pulling. I grasp it more tightly, desperately, pull again, sob, and then there are two hands, four, ten, sixteen pulling at the wheel with me. It groans, shivers, turns ponderously, clicks free. Together we pry the great door open.

And, over the piled dirt of centuries, the sunlight pours in.

The Psychologist
Who Wouldn't Do
Awful Things to Rats

JAMES TIPTREE, JR.

The first Tiptree story I published was "Filomena & Greg & Rikki-Tikki & Barlow & The Alien," in *New Dimensions 2*—a delicious farce that has since been republished as "All the Kinds of Yes," and which I love without reservation under whatever title. I had no idea then—this was 1971—that "Tiptree" was a pseudonym for one Alice Sheldon. At least the persona behind the letters-typed-in-blue that I got from Tiptree seemed thoroughly male to me, and we exchanged a lot of correspondence, much of it of the mutual-admiration sort. (Tiptree then seemed to have an exaggerated awe of other writers and an implausibly low opinion of "his" own work. Perhaps this has been corrected by all the subsequent Hugos and Nebulas, but maybe not.)

One of those Hugos arrived a couple of years later for "The Girl Who Was Plugged In" (*New Dimensions 3*), which reached me, courtesy Terry Carr, and thank you again, Terry. That one perhaps should have been included in the present collection, in recognition of its award-winner status. Certainly it (and "Filomena" too) would have been ornaments to the current contents page. But I allow myself but one per author, and the Tiptree quota has been allotted to

"The Psychologist Who Wouldn't Do Awful Things to Rats," from the sixth *New Dimensions,* 1976. I do of course like and respect all of the hundred-odd stories I have published in *New Dimensions,* and greatly admire many of them, and inordinately admire a few. But if I were allowed to claim as my own work just one out of the whole hundred-odd, this is the one I would take.

HE COMES SHYLY HOPEFUL INTO THE LAB. HE IS UNable to suppress this childishness which has deviled him all his life, this tendency to wake up smiling, believing for an instant that today will be different.

But it isn't; is not.

He is walking into the converted cellars which are now called animal laboratories by this nationally respected university, this university which is still somehow unable to transmute its nationwide reputation into adequate funding for research. He squeezes past a pile of galvanized Skinner boxes and sees Smith at the sinks, engaged in cutting off the heads of infant rats. Piercing squeals; the headless body is flipped into a wet furry pile of a hunk of newspaper. In the holding cage beside Smith the baby rats shiver in a heap, occasionally thrusting up a delicate muzzle and then burrowing convulsively under their friends, seeking to shut out Smith. They have previously been selectively shocked, starved, subjected to air blasts, and plunged in ice water; Smith is about to search the corpses for approrpriate neurograndular effects of stress. He'll find them, undoubtedly. *Eeeeeeee—Ssskrick!* Smith's knife grates, drinking life.

"Hello, Tilly."

"Hi." He hates his nickname, hates his whole stupid name: Tilman Lipsitz. He would go nameless through the world if he could. If it even could be something simple, Moo or Urg—anything but the absurd high-pitched syllables that have followed him through life: Tilly Lipsetz. He has suffered from it. Ah well. He makes his way around the pile of Purina Lab Chow

bags, bracing for the fierce clamor of the rhesus. Their
Primate Room is the ex-boiler room, really; these are
tenements the university took over. The rhesus scream
like sirens. Thud! Feces have hit the grill again; the
stench is as strong as the sound. Lipsetz peers in
reluctantly, mentally apologizing for being unable to
like monkeys. Two of them are not screaming, hud-
dled on the steel with puffy pink bald heads studded
with electrode jacks. Why can't they house the creatures better, he wonders irritably for the nth time. In
the trees, they're clean. Well, cleaner, anyway, he
amends, ducking around a stand of somebody's bread-
board circuits awaiting solder.

On the far side is Jones, bending over a brightly
lighted bench, two students watching mesmerized. He
can see Jones's fingers tenderly roll the verniers that
drive the probes down through the skull of the dog
strapped underneath. Another of his terrifying stereo-
taxes. The aisle of cages is packed with animals with
wasted fur and bloody heads. Jones swears they're all
right, they eat; Lipsitz doubts this. He has tried to feed
them tidbits as they lean or lie blear-eyed, jerking with
wire terrors. The blood is because they rub their heads
on the mesh; Jones, seeking a way to stop this, has put
stiff plastic collars on several.

Lipsitz gets past them and has his eye rejoiced by
the lovely hourglass-shaped ass of Sheila, the brilliant
Israeli. Her back is turned. He observes with love the
lily waist, the heart-lobed hips that radiate desire. But
it's his desire, not hers; he knows that. Sheila, wicked
Sheila; she desires only Jones, or perhaps Smith, or
even Brown or White—the mucular large hairy ones
bubbling with professionalism, with cheery shop talk.
Lipsitz would gladly talk shop with her. But somehow
his talk is different, uninteresting, is not in the mode.
Yet he too believes in "the organism," believes in the
miraculous wiring diagram of life; he is naïvely impressed by the complexity, the intricate interrelated
delicacies of living matter. Why is he so reluctant to
push metal into it, produce lesions with acids or shock?

He has this unfashionable yearning to learn by appreciation, to tease out the secrets with only his eyes and mind. He has even the treasonable suspicion that other procedures might be more efficient, more instructive. But what other means are there? Probably none, he tells himself firmly. Grow up. Look at all they've discovered with the knife. The cryptic but potent centers of the amygdalas, for example. The subtle limbic homostats—would we ever have know about these? It is a great knowledge. Never mind that its main use seems to be to push more metal into human heads, my way is obsolete.

"Hi, Sheila."

"Hello, Tilly."

She does not turn from the hamsters she is efficiently shaving. He takes himself away around the mop stand to the coal-cellar dungeon where he keeps his rats—sorry, his experimental subjects. His experimental subjects are nocturnal rodents, evolved in friendly dark warm burrows. Lipsitz has sensed their misery, suspended in bright metal and plexiglas cubes in the glare. So he has salvaged and repaired for them a stack of big old rabbit cages and put them in this dark alcove nobody wanted, provoking mirth among his colleagues.

He has done worse than that, too. Grinning secretly, he approaches and observes what has been made of his latest offering. On the bottom row are the cages of prurient females, birthing what are expected to be his experimental and control groups. Yesterday those cages were bare wire mesh, when he distributed to them the classified section of the Sunday *Post*. Now he sees with amazement that they are solid cubic volumes of artfully crumpled and plastered paper strips. Fantastic, the labor! Nests; and all identical. Why has no one mentioned that rats as well as birds can build nests? How wrong, how painful it must have been, giving birth on the bare wire. The little mothers have worked all night, skillfully constructing complete environments beneficient to their needs.

A small white muzzle is pointing watchfully at him from a paper crevice; he fumbles in his pocket for a carrot chunk. He is, of course, unbalancing the treatment, his conscience remonstrates. But he has an answer; he has carrots for them all. Get down, conscience. Carefully he unlatches a cage. The white head stretches, bright-eyed, revealing sleek black shoulders. They are the hooded strain.

"Have a carrot," he says absurdly to the small being. And she does, so quickly that he can barely feel it, can barely feel also the tiny razor slash she has instantaneously, shyly given his thumb before she whisks back inside to her babies. He grins, rubbing the thumb, leaving carrots in the other cages. A mother's monitory bite, administered to an ogre thirty times her length. Vitamins, he thinks, enriched environments, that's the respectable word. Enriched? No, goddam it. What it is is something approaching sane unstressed animals—experimental subjects, I mean. Even if they're so genetically selected for tameness they can't survive in the feral state, they're still rats. He sees he must wrap something on his thumb; he is ridiculously full of blood.

Wrapping, he tried not to notice that his hands are crisscrossed with old bites. He is a steady patron of the antitetanus clinic. But he is sure that they don't really mean ill, that he is somehow accepted by them. His colleagues think so too, somewhat scornfully. In fact Smith often calls him to help get some agonized creature out and bring it to his electrodes. Judas-Lipsitz does, trying to convey by the warmth of his holding hands that somebody is sorry, is uselessly sorry. Smith explains that his particular strain of rats is bad; a bad rat is one that bites psychologists; there is a constant effort to breed out this trait.

Lipsitz has tried to explain to them about animals with curved incisors, that one must press the hand into the biter's teeth. "It can't let go," he tells them. "You're biting yourself on the rat. It's the same with

cat's claws. Push, they'll let go. Wouldn't you if somebody pushed his hand in your mouth?"

. For a while he thought Sheila at least had understood him, but it turned out she thought he was making a dirty joke.

He is giving a rotted Safeway apple to an old male
named Snedecor whom he has salvaged from Smith
when he hears them call.

"Li-i-ipsitz!"

"Tilly? R. D. wants to see you."

"Yo."

R.D. is Professor R. D. Welch, his department head
and supervisor of his grant. He washes up, makes his
way out and around to the front entrance stairs. A
myriad guilts are swirling emptily inside him; he has
violated some norm, there is something wrong with his
funding, above all he is too slow, too slow. No results
yet, no columns of data. Frail justifying sentences revolve in his head as he steps into the clean, bright
upper reaches of the department. Because he is, he
feels sure, learning. Doing something, something appropriate to what he thinks of as science. But what?
In this glare he (like his rats) cannot recall. Ah, maybe it's only another hassle about parking space, he
thinks as he goes bravely in past R. D.'s high-status
male secretary. I can give mine up. I'll never be able
to afford that transmission job anyway.

But it is not about parking space.

Doctor Welch has a fat file folder on his desk in
Exhibit A position. He taps it expressionlessly, staring at Lipsitz.

"You are doing a study of, ah, genetic influences
on, ah, tolerance of perceptual novelty."

"Well, yes . . ." He decides not to insist on preci-
sion. "You remember, Doctor Welch, I'm going to
work in a relation to emotionalism too."

Emotionalism, in rats, is (a) defecating and, (b)
biting psychologists. Professor Welch exhales trou-
bledly through his lower teeth, which Lipsitz notes are
slightly incurved. Mustn't pull back.

"It's so unspecific," he sighs. "It's not integrated with the overall department program."

"I know," Lipsitz says humbly. "But I do think it has relevance to problems of human learning. I mean, why some kids seem to shy away from new things." He jacks up his technical vocabulary. "The failure of the exploration motive."

"Motives don't *fail*, Lipsitz."

"I mean, conditions for low or high expression. Neophobia. Look, Doctor Welch. If one of the conditions turns out to be genetic we could spot kids who need help."

"Um'mmm."

"I could work in some real learning programs in the high tolerants, too," Lipsitz adds hopefully. "Contingent rewards, that sort of thing."

"Rat learning . . ." Welch lets his voice trail off. "If this sort of thing is to have any relevance it should involve primates. Your grant scarcely extends to that."

"Rats can learn quite a lot, sir. How about if I taught them word cues?"

"Doctor Lipsitz, rats do not acquire meaningful responses to words"

"Yes, sir." Lipsitz is forcibly preventing himself from bringing up the totally unqualified Scotswoman whose rat knew nine words.

"I do wish you'd go on with your brain studies," Welch says in his nice voice, giving Lipsitz a glowing scientific look. Am I biting myself on him? Lipsitz wonders. Involuntarily he feels himself empathize with the chairman's unknown problems. As he gazes back, Welch says encouragingly, "You could use Brown's preparations; they're perfectly viable with the kind of care you give."

Lipsitz shudders awake; he knows Brown's preparations. A "preparation" is an animal spread-eagled on a rack for vivisection, dosed with reserpine so it cannot cry or struggle but merely endures for days or weeks of pain. Guiltily he wonders if Brown knows who killed the bitch he had left half dissected and staring over Easter. Pull yourself together, Lipsitz.

"I am so deeply interested in working with the intact animal, the whole organism," he says earnestly. That is his magic phrase; he has discovered that "the whole organism" has some fetish quality for them, from some far-off line of work; very fashionable in the abstract.

"Yes." Balked, Welch wreathes his lips, revealing the teeth again. "Well. Doctor Lipsitz, I'll be blunt. When you came on board we felt you had a great deal of promise. *I* felt that, I really did. And your teaching seems to be going well, in the main. In the main. But your research; no. You seem to be frittering away your time and funds—and our space—on these irrelevancies. To put it succinctly, our laboratory is not a zoo."

"Oh, no, sir!" cries Lipsitz, horrified.

"What are you actually doing with those rats? I hear all kinds of idiotic rumors."

"Well, I'm working up the genetic strains, sir. The coefficient of homozygosity is still very low for meaningful results. I'm cutting it as fine as I can. What you're probably hearing about is that I am giving them a certain amount of enrichment. That's necessary so I can differentiate the lines." What I'm really doing is multiplying them, he thinks queasily; he hasn't had the heart to deprive any yet.

Welch sighs again; he *is* worried, Lipsitz thinks, and finding himself smiling sympathetically stops at once.

"How long before you wind this up? A week?"

"A week!" Lipsitz almost bleats, recovers his voice. "Sir, my test generation is just neonate. They have to be weaned, you know. I'm afraid it's more like a month."

"And what do you intend to do after this?"

"After this!" Lipsitz is suddenly fecklessly happy. So many, so wondrous are the things he wants to learn. "Well, to begin with I've seen a number of behaviors nobody seems to have done much with—I mean, watching my animals under more . . . more naturalistic conditions. They, ah, they emit very interesting responses. I'm struck by the species-specific aspect—I mean, as the Brelands said, we may be using quite unproductive situations. For example, there's an enormous difference between the way Rattus and Cricetus —that's hamsters—behave in the open field, and they're both *rodents*. Even as simple a thing as edge behavior—"

"What behavior?" Welch's tone should warn him, but he plunges on, unhappily aware that he has chosen an insignificant example. But he loves it.

"Edges. I mean the way the animal responds to edges and the shape of the environment. I mean it's basic to living and nobody seems to have explored it. They used to call it thigmotaxis. Here, I sketched a few." He pulls out a folded sheet,* pushes it at Welch. "Doesn't it raise interesting questions of arboreal descent?"

Welch barely glances at the drawings, pushes it away.

"Doctor Lipsitz. You don't appear to grasp the seriousness of this interview. All right. In words of one syllable, you will submit a major project outline that we can justify in terms of this department's program. If you can't come up with one such, regretfully we have no place for you here."

Lipsitz stares at him, appalled.

"A major project . . . I see. But . . ." And then something comes awake, something is rising in him. Yes. Yes, yes, of course there are bigger things he can tackle. Bigger questions—that means people. He's full of such questions. All it takes is courage.

"Yes, sir," he says slowly, "There are some major problems I have thought of investigating."

"Good," Welch says neutrally. "What are they?"

"Well, to start with . . ." And to his utter horror his mind has emptied itself, emptied itself of everything

---

* See illustrations next page.

EDGE BEHAVIORS OF RATTUS RATTUS
(Lipsitz' sketches)

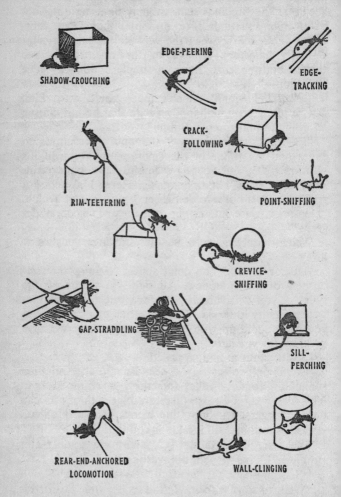

SHADOW-CROUCHING

EDGE-PEERING

EDGE-TRACKING

CRACK-FOLLOWING

RIM-TEETERING

POINT-SNIFFING

CREVICE-SNIFFING

GAP-STRADDLING

SILL-PERCHING

REAR-END-ANCHORED LOCOMOTION

WALL-CLINGING

Appendix III, Figure 18. Examples of Thigmotaxic Responses

except the one fatal sentence which he now hears himself helplessly launched toward. "Take us here. I mean, it's a good principle to attack problems to which one has easy access, which are so to speak under our noses, right? So. For example, we're psychologists. Supposedly dedicated to some kind of understanding, helpful attitude toward the organism, toward life. And yet all of us down here—and in all the labs I've heard about—we seem to be doing such hostile and rather redundant work. Testing animals to destruction, that fellow at Princeton. Proving how damaged organisms are damaged, that kind of engineering thing. Letting students cut or shock or starve animals to replicate experiments that have been done umpteen times. What I'm trying to say is, why don't we look into why psychological research seems to involve so much cruelty —I mean, aggression? We might even . . ."

He runs down then, and there is a silence in which he becones increasingly aware of Welch's breathing.

"Doctor Lipsitz," the older man says hoarsely, *are you a member of the SPCA?*"

"No, sir, I'm not."

Welch stares at him unblinkingly and then clears his throat.

"Psychology is not a field for people with emotional problems." He pushes the file away. "You have two weeks."

Lipsitz takes himself out, momentarily preoccupied by his lie. True, he is not a *member* of the SPCA. But that ten dollars he sent in last Christmas, surely they have his name. That had been during the business with the dogs. He flinches now, recalling the black Labrador puppy, its vocal cords cut out, dragging itself around on its raw denervated haunches.

Oh God, why doesn't he just quit?

He wanders out onto the scruffy grass of the main campus, going over and over it again. These people. These . . . people.

And yet behind them loom the great golden mists, the reality of Life itself and the questions he has earned the right to ask. He will never outgrow the thrill of it. The excitement of *actually asking,* after all the careful work of framing terms that can be answered. The act of putting a real question to Life. And watching, reverently, excited out of his skin as Life condescends to tell him yes or no. My animals, my living works of art (of which you are one), do thus and so. Yes, in this small aspect you have understood Me.

The privilege of knowing how, painfully, to frame answerable questions, answers which will lead him to more, insights and better questions as far as his mind can manage and his own life lasts. It is what he wants more than anything in the world to do, always has.

And these people stand in his way. Somehow, some way, he must pacify them. He must frame a project they will buy.

He plods back toward the laboratory cellars, nodding absently at students, revolving various quasi-respectable schemes. What he really wants to do is too foggy to explain yet; he wants to explore the capacity of animals to *anticipate,* to gain some knowledge of the wave-front of expectations that they must build up, even in the tiniest heads. He thinks it might even be useful, might illuminate the labors of the human infant learning its world. But that will have to wait. Welch wouldn't tolerate the idea that animals have mental maps. Only old crazy Tolman had been allowed to think that, and he's dead.

He will have to think of something with Welch's favorite drive variables. What are they? And lots of statistics, he thinks, realizing he is grinning at a really pretty girl walking with that cow Polinski. Yes, why not use students? Something complicated with students —that doesn't cost much. And maybe sex differentials, say, in perception—or is that too far out?

A wailing sound alerts him to the fact that he has arrived at the areaway. A truck is offloading crates of cats, strays from the pound.

"Give a hand, Tilly! Hurry up!"

It's Sheila, holding the door for Jones and Smith.

They want to get these out of sight quickly, he knows, before some student sees them. Those innocent in the rites of pain. He hauls a crate from the tailboard.

"There's a female in here giving birth," he tells Sheila. "Look." The female is at the bottom of a mess of twenty emaciated struggling brutes. One of them has a red collar.

"Hurry up, for Christ's sake." Sheila waves him on. "But . . ."

When the crates have disappeared inside he does not follow the others in but leans on the railing, lighting a cigarette. The kittens have been eaten, there's nothing he can do. Funny, he always thought that females would be sympathetic to other females. Shows how much he knows about Life. Or is it that only certain types of people empathize? Or does it have to be trained in, or was it trained out of her? Mysteries, mysteries. Maybe she is really compassionate somewhere inside, toward something. He hopes so, resolutely putting away a fantasy of injecting Sheila with reserpine and applying experimental stimuli.

He becomes aware that the door has been locked from the inside; they have all left through the front. It's getting late. He moves away too, remembering that this is the long holiday weekend. Armistice Day. Would it were—he scoffs at himself for the bathos. But he frowns, too; long weekends usually mean nobody goes near the lab. Nothing gets fed or watered. Well, three days—not as bad as Christmas week.

Last Christmas week he had roused up from much-needed sleep beside a sky-high mound of term papers and hitchhiked into town to check the labs. It had been so bad, so needless. The poor brutes dying in their thirst and hunger, eating metal, each other. Great way to celebrate Christmas.

But he will have to stop that kind of thing, he knows. Stop it. Preferably starting now. He throws down the cigarette stub, quickens his stride to purposefulness. He will collect his briefcase of exam papers from the library where he keeps it to avoid the lab smell and get on home and get at it. The bus is bound to be jammed.

Home is an efficiency in a suburban high-rise. He roots in his moldy fridge, carries a sandwich and ale to the dinette that is his desk. He has eighty-one exams to grade; junior department members get the monster classes. It's a standard multiple-choice thing, and he has a help—a theatrically guarded manila template he can lay over the sheets with slots giving the correct response. By just running down them he sums an arithmetical grade. Good. Munching, he lays out the first mimeoed wad.

But as he starts to lay it on the top page he sees— oh, no!—somebody has scrawled instead of answering Number 6. It's that fat girl, that bright bum Polinsky. And she hasn't marked answers by 7 or 8 either. Damn her fat female glands; he squints at the infantile uncials: "I wont mark this because its smucky! Read it, Dr. Lipshitz." She even has his name wrong.

Cursing himself, he scrutinizes the question. "Fixed versus variable reinforcement is called a—" Oh yes, he remembers that one. Bad grammar on top of bad psychology. Why can't they dump these damn obsolete things? Because the office wants grade intercomparability for their records, that's why. Is Polinsky criticizing the language or the thought? Who knows. He leafs through the others, sees more scribbles. Oh, shit, they know I read them. They all know I don't mark them like I should. Sucker.

Grimly masticating the dry sandwich, he starts to read. At this rate he is working, he has figured out, for seventy-five cents an hour.

By midnight he isn't half through, but he knows he ought to break off and start serious thought about Welch's ultimatum. Next week all his classes start Statistical Methods; he won't have time to blow his nose, let alone think creatively.

He gets up for another ale, thinking, Statistical Methods, brrr. He respects them, he guesses. But he is incurably sloppy-minded, congenitally averse to ignoring any data that don't fit the curve. Factor analysis, multivariate techniques—all beautiful; why is he troubled by this primitive visceral suspicion that somehow it ends up proving what the experimenter wanted to show? No, not that, really. Something about qualities as opposed to quantities, maybe? That some statistically insignificant results *are* significant, and some significant ones . . . aren't? Or just basically that we don't know enough yet to use such ultraprecise weapons. That we should watch more, maybe. Watch and learn more and figure less. All right, call me St. Lipsitz.

Heating up a frozen egg roll, he jeers at himself for superstition. Face facts, Lipsitz. Deep down you don't really believe dice throws are independent. Psychology is not a field for people with personality problems.

Ignoring the TV yattering through the wall from next door, he sits down by the window to think. Do it, brain. Come up with the big one. Take some good testable hypothesis from somebody in the department, preferably something that involves electronic counting of food pellets, bar presses, latencies, defecations. And crank it all into printed score sheets with a good Fortran program. But what the hell are they all working on? Reinforcement schedules, cerebral deficits, split brain, God knows only that it seems to produce a lot of dead animals. "The subjects were sacrificed." They insist on saying that. He has been given a lecture when he called it "killing." Sacrificed, like to a god. Lord of the Flies, maybe.

He stares out at the midnight streets, thinking of his small black-and-white friends, his cozy community in the alcove. Nursing their offspring, sniffing the monkeys, munching apples, dreaming ratly dreams. He likes rats, which surprises him. Even the feral form, Rattus rattus itself; he would like to work with wild ones. Rats are vicious, they say. But people know only starving rats. Anything starving is "vicious." Beloved beagle eats owner on fourth day.

And his rats are, he blushingly muses, affectionate. They nestle in his hands, teeteringly ride his shoulder, display humor. If only they had fluffy tails, he thinks. The tail is the problem. People think squirrels are cute. They're only overdressed rats. Maybe I could do something with the perceptual elements of "cuteness," carry on old Tinbergen's work?

Stop it.

He pulls himself up; this isn't getting anywhere. A terrible panorama unrolls before his inner eye. On the one hand the clean bright professional work he should be doing, he with those thousands of government dollars invested in his doctorate, his grant—and on the other, what he is really doing. His cluttered alcove full of irregular rodents, his tiny, doomed effort to . . . what? To live amicably and observantly with another species? To understand trivial behaviors? Crazy. Spending all his own money, saving everybody's cripples—God, half his cages aren't even experimentally justifiable!

His folly. Suddenly it sickens him. He stands up, thinking, It's a stage you go through. I'm a delayed adolescent. Wake up, grow up. They're only animals. Get with it.

Resolve starts to form in him. Opening another ale can, he lets it grow. This whole thing is no good, he knows that. So what if he does prove that animals learn better if they're treated differently—what earthly use is that? Don't we all know it anyway? Insane. Time I braced up. All right. Ale in hand, he lets the resolve bloom.

He will go down there and clean out the whole mess, right now.

Kill all his rats, wipe the whole thing off. Clear the decks. That done, he'll be able to think; he won't be locked into the past.

The department will be delighted, Doctor Welsh will be delighted. Nobody believed this thing was anything but a waste of time. All right, Lipsitz. Do it. Now, tonight.

Yes.

But first he will have something analgesic, strengthening. Not ale, not a toke. That bottle of—what is it, absinthe?—that crazy girl gave him last year. Yes, here it is back of the roach-killer he never used either. God knows what it's supposed to do, it's wormwood, something weird.

"Fix me," he tells it, sucking down a long liquorice-flavored draft. And goes out, bottle in pocket.

It has, he thinks, helped. He is striding across the campus now; all the long bus ride his resolve hasn't wavered. A quiet rain is falling. It must be two in the morning, but he's used to the spooky empty squares. He has often sneaked down here at odd hours to water and feed the brutes. The rain is moving strange sheens of shadow on the old tenement block, hissing echoes of the lives that swirled here once. At the cellar entrance he stops for another drink, finds the bottle clabbered with carrot chunks. Wormwood and Vitamin C, very good.

He dodges down and unlocks, bracing for the stench. The waste cans are full—cats that didn't make it, no doubt. Inside is a warm rustling reek.

When he finds the light, a monkey lets out one eerie whoop and all sounds stop. Sunrise at midnight; most of these experimental subjects are nocturnal.

He goes in past the crowded racks, his eye automatically checking levels in the hundreds of water bottles. Okay, okay, all okay . . . What's this? He stops by Sheila's hamster tier. A bottle is full to the top. But there's a corpse by the wire, and the live ones look bedraggled. Why? He jerks up the bottle. Nothing comes out of the tube. It's blocked. Nobody has checked it for who knows how long. Perishing of thirst in there, with the bottle full.

He unblocks it, fishes out the dead, watches the little beasts crowd around. How does Sheila report this? Part of an experimental group was, uh, curtailed. On impulse he inserts some carrots too, inserts more absinthe into himself. He knows he is putting off what he has come here to do.

All right, get at it.

He stomps past a cage of baby rabbits with their eyes epoxyed shut, somebody's undergraduate demonstration of perceptual learning, and turns on the light over the sinks. All dirty with hanks of skin and dog offal. Why the hell can't they clean up after themselves? We are scientists. Too lofty. He whooshes with the power hose, which leaks. Nobody cares enough even to bring a washer. He will bring one. No, he won't! He's going to be doing something different from here on in.

But first of all he has to get rid of all this. Sacrifice his subjects. His ex-subjects. Where's my ether?

He finds it back of the mops, has another snort of the cloudy liquor to fortify himself while he sets up his killing jars. He has evolved what he thinks is the decentest way: an ether pad under a grill to keep their feet from being burned by the stuff.

The eight jars are in a row on the sink. He lifts down a cage of elderly females, the grandmothers of his present group. They cluster at the front, trustfully expectant. Oh God; he postpones murder long enough to give them some carrot, deals out more to every cage in the rack so they'll have time to eat. Tumult of rustling, hopping, munching.

All right. He goes back to the sink and pours in the ether, keeping the lids tight. Then he reaches in the holding cage and scoops up a soft female in each hand. Quick: He pops them both in one jar, rescrews the lid. He has this fatuous belief that the companionship helps a little. They convulse frantically, are going limp before he has the next pair in theirs. Next. Next. Next . . . It takes five minutes to be sure of death.

This will be, he realizes, a long night.

He lifts down another cage, lifts up his bottle, leaning with his back to the jars to look at his rack, his little city of rats. My troops. My pathetic troops. An absinthe trip flashes through his head of himself leading his beasts against his colleagues, against the laughing pain-givers. Jones having his brain reamed by a

Dachshund pup. A kitten in a surgical smock shaving Sheila, wow. Stop it!

His eye has been wandering over the bottom cages. The mothers have taken the goodies in to their young; interesting to see what goes on in there, maybe if he used infra-red—stop that, too. A lab is not a zoo. Down in one dark back cage he can see the carrot is still there. Where's Snedecor, the old brain-damaged male? Why hasn't he come for it? Is the light bothering him?

Lipsitz turns off the top lights, goes around to the side to check. Stooping, he peers into the gloom. Something funny down there—good grief, the damn cage is busted, it's rotted through the bottom. Where's old Sneddles?

The ancient cage rack has wheels. Lipsitz drags one end forward, revealing Stygian darkness behind. In prehistoric times there was a coal chute there. And there's something back here now, on the heap of bags by the old intake.

Lipsitz frowns, squints; the lab lights behind him seem to be growing dim and gaseous. The thing—the thing has black and white patches. Is it moving?

He retreats to the drainboard, finds his hand on the bottle. Yes. Another short one. What's wrong with the lights? The fluorescents have developed filmy ectoplasm, must be chow dust. This place is a powder keg. The monkeys are still as death too. That's unusual. In fact everything is dead quiet except for an odd kind of faint clicking, which he realizes is coming from the dark behind the rack. An animal. Some animal has got out and been living back there, that's all it is.

All right, Lipsitz: Go see.

But he delays, aware that the absinthe has replaced his limbs with vaguer, dream-like extensions. The old females on the drainboard watch him alertly; the dead ones in the jars watch nothing. All his little city of rats has stopped moving, is watching him. Their priest of pain. This is a temple of pain, he thinks. A small shabby dirty one. Maybe its dirt and squalor are better so, more honest. A charnel house shouldn't look pretty, like a clean kitchen. All over the country, the world, the spotless knives are slicing, the trained minds devising casual torments in labs so bright and fair you could eat off their floor. Auschwitz, Belsen were neat. With flowers. Only the reek of pain going up to the sky, the empty sky. But people don't think animals' pain matters. They didn't think my people's pain mattered either, in the death camps a generation back. It's all the same, endless agonies going up unheard from helpless things. And all for what?

Maybe somewhere there is a reservoir of pain, he muses. Waiting to be filled. When it is full, will something rise from it? Something created and summoned by torment? Inhuman, an alien superthing . . . He knows he is indulging drunkenness. The clicking has grown louder.

Go and look at the animal, Lipsitz.

He goes, advances on the dark alcove, peering down, hearing the click-click-click. Suddenly he recognizes it: the tooth-click a rat makes in certain states of mind. Not threatening at all, it must be old Sneddles in there. Heartened, he pulls a dim light bulb forward on its string—and sees the thing plain, while the lab goes unreal around him.

What's lying back there among the Purina bags is an incredible whorl—a tangle of rat legs, rat heads, rat bodies, rat tails intertwined in a great wheellike formation, *joined* somehow abnormally rat to rat—a huge rat pie, heaving, pulsing, eyes reflecting stress and pain. Quite horrible, really; the shock of it is making him fight for breath. And it is not all laboratory animals; he can see the agouti coats of feral rats mixed in among it. Have wild rats come in here to help form this gruesome thing?

And at that moment, hanging to the light bulb, he knows what he is seeing. He has read in the old lore, the ancient grotesque legends of rats and man.

He is looking at a Rat King.

Medieval records were full of them, he recalls dimly. Was it Württemberg? *"They are monstrously Joynt, yet Living . . . It can by no way be Separated, and screamed much in the Fyre."* Apparitions that occurred at times of great attack on the rats. Some believed that the rat armies had each their king of this sort, who directed them. And they were sometimes connected to or confused with King Rats of still another kind: gigantic animals with eyes of fire and gold chains on their necks.

Lipsitz stares, swaying on the light cord. The tangled mass of the Rat King remains there clicking faintly, pulsing, ambiguously agonized among the sacks. His other hand seems to be holding the bottle; good. He takes a deep pull, his eyes rolling to fix the ghastliness, wondering what on earth he will do. "I can't," he mumbles aloud, meaning the whole thing, the whole bloody thing. *"I can't . . ."*

He can do his own little business, kill his animals, wind up his foolishness, get out. But he cannot—cannot—be expected to cope with this, to abolish this revenant from time, this perhaps supernatural horror. For which he feels obscurely, hideously to blame. It's my fault, I . . .

He realizes he is weeping thinly, his eyes are running. Whether it's for the animals or himself he doesn't know; he knows only that he can't stand it, can't take any of it any more. And now *this*.

"No!" Meaning, really, the whole human world. Dizzily he blinks around at the jumbled darkness, trying to regain his wits, feeling himself a random mote of protesting life in an insignificant fool-killer. Slowly his eyes come back to the monstrous, pitiable rat pie. It seems to be weakening; the click has lost direction. His gaze drifts upward, into the dark shadows.

—And he is quite unsurprised, really, to meet eyes looking back. Two large round animal eyes deep in the darkness, at about the level of his waist, the tapetums reflecting pale vermilion fire.

He stares; the eyes shift right, left, calmly in silence,

and then the head advances. He sees the long wise muzzle, the vibrissae, the tuned shells of the ears. Is there a gold collar? He can't tell; but he can make out the creature's forelimbs now, lightly palping the bodies or body of the Rat King. And the tangled thing is fading, shrinking away. It was perhaps its conjoined forces which strove and suffered to give birth to this other—the King himself.

"Hello," Lipsitz whispers idiotically, feeling no horror any more but emotion of a quite other kind. The big warm presence before him surveys him. Will he be found innocent? He licks his lips; they have come at last, he thinks. They have risen; they are going to wipe all this out. Me, too? But he does not care; a joy he can't possibly control rises in him as he sees gold glinting on the broad chest fur. He licks his dry lips again, swallows.

"Welcome. Your Majesty."

The Beast-King makes no response; the eyes leave him and go gravely toward the aisles beyond. Involuntarily Lipsitz backs aside. The King's vibrissae are fanning steadily, bringing the olfactory news, the quiet tooth-click starts. When the apparition comes forward a pace Lipsitz is deeply touched to see the typical half hop, the ratly carriage. The King's coat is lustrous gray-brown, feral, pelage. Of course. It is a natural male, too; he smiles timidly, seeing that the giant body has the familiar long hump, the heavy rear-axle loading. Is old Snedecor translated into some particle of this wonder? The cellar is unbreathing, hushed except for the meditative click-click from the King.

"You, you are going to . . ." Lipsitz tries but is struck dumb by the sense of something happening all around him. Invisible, inaudible—but tangible as day. An emergence, yes! In the rooms beyond they are emerging, coming out from the score upon score of cages, boxes, pens, racks, shackles and wires—all of them emerging, coming to the King. All of them, blinded rabbits, mutilated hamsters, damaged cats and rats and brain-holed rhesus quietly knuckling along, even the paralyzed dogs moving somehow, coming toward their King.

And at this moment, Lipsitz realizes the King is turning too, the big brown body is wheeling, quite normally away from him, going away toward the deeper darkness in the end of the coal bay. They are leaving him!

"Wait!" He stumbles forward over the dead rat pie; he cannot bear to lose this. "Please . . ."

Daring all, he reaches out and touches the flank of the magical beast, expecting he knows not what. The flank is warm, is solid! The King glances briefly back at him, still moving away. Boldly Lipsitz strides closer, comes alongside, his hand now resting firmly on the withers as they go.

But they are headed straight at what he knows is only wall, though he can see nothing. The cellar ends there. No matter—he will not let go of the magic, no, and he steps out beside the moving King, thinking, I am an animal too!—And finds at the last instant that his averted, flinching head is moving through dark nothing, through a blacker emptiness where the King is leading—they are going, going out.

Perhaps an old sewer, he thinks, lurching along beside the big benign presence, remembering tales of forgotten tunnels under this old city, into which the new subway has bored. Yes, that's what it must be. He is finding he can see again in a pale ghostly way, can now walk upright. His left hand is tight on the shoulders of the calmly pacing beast, feeling the living muscles play beneath the fur, bringing him joy and healing. Where are the others?

He dares a quick look back and sees them. They are coming. The dim way behind is filled with quiet beasts, moving together rank on rank as far as he can sense, animals large and small. He can hear their peaceful rustling now. And they are not only the beasts of his miserable lab, he realizes, but a torrent of others—he has glimpsed goats, turtles, a cow, raccoons, skunks, an opossum and what appeared as a small monkey riding on a limping spaniel. Even birds are there, hopping and fluttering above!

My God, it is everything, he thinks. It is Hamlin in reverse; all the abused ones, the gentle ones, are leaving the world. He risks another glance back and thinks he can see a human child too and maybe an old person among the throng, all measuredly, silently moving together in the dimness. An endless host going, going out at last, going away. And he is feeling their emanation, the gentleness of it, the unspeaking warmth. He is happier than he has been ever in his life.

"You're taking us away," he says to the King-Beast beside him. "The ones who can't cut it. We're all leaving for good, isn't that it?"

There is no verbal answer; only a big-stemmed ear swivels to him briefly as the King goes gravely on. Lipsitz needs no speech, no explanation. He simply walks alongside letting the joy rise in him. Why had it always been forbidden to be gentle? he wonders. Did they really see it as a threat, to have hated us so? But that is all over now, all over and gone, he is sure, although he has no slightest idea where this may be leading, this procession into chthonian infinity. For this moment it is enough to feel the silent communion, the reassurance rising through him from his hand on the flank of the great spirit-beast. The flank is totally solid; he can feel all the workings of life; it is the body of a real animal. But it is also friendship beyond imagining; he has never known anything as wonderful as this communion, not sex or sunsets or even the magic hour on his first bike. It is as if everything is all right now, will be all right forever—griefs he did not even know he carried are falling from him, leaving him light as smoke.

Crippled, he had been; crippled from the years of bearing it, not just the lab, the whole thing. Everything. He can hardly believe the relief. A vagrant thought brushes him: Who will remain? If there is anything to care for, to be comforted, who will care? He floats it away, concentrating on the comfort that emanates from the strange life at his side, the myth-beast ambling in the most ordinary way through this dark conduit, which is now winding down, or perhaps up and down, he cannot tell.

The paving under his feet looks quite common-place, damp and cracked. Beside him the great rat's muscles bunch and stretch as each hind leg comes under; he glances back and smiles to see the King's long ring-scaled tail curve right, curve left, carried in the relaxed-alert mode. No need for fluffy fur now. He is, he realizes, going into mysteries. Inhuman mysteries, perhaps. He doesn't care. He is among his kind. Where they are going he will go. Even to inhumanity, even alone.

But he is not, he realizes as his eyes adapt more and more, alone after all! A human figure is behind him on the far side of the King, quietly threading its way forward, overtaking him. A girl—is it a girl? Yes. He can scarcely make her out, but as she comes closer still he sees with growing alarm that it is a familiar body—it could be, oh God, it is! Sheila.

Not *Sheila,* here! No, no.

But light-footed, she has reached him, is walking even with him, stretching out her hand, too, to touch the moving King.

And then to his immense, unspeakable relief he sees that she is of course not Sheila—how could it be? Not Sheila at all, only a girl of the same height, with the same dove-breasted close-coupled curves that speak to his desire, the same heavy dark mane. Her head turns toward him across the broad back of the King, and he sees that although her features are like Sheila's, the face is wholly different, open, informed with innocence. An Eve in this second morning of the world. Sheila's younger sister, perhaps, he wonders dazedly, seeing that she is looking at him now, that her lips form a gentle smile.

"Hello," he cannot help whispering, fearful to break the spell, to inject harsh human sound into his progress. But the spell does not break; indeed, the girl's face comes clearer. She puts up a hand to push her hair back, the other firmly on the flank of the King.

"Hello." Her voice is very soft but in no way fragile. She is looking at him with the eyes of Sheila, but eyes so differently warmed and luminous that he wants only to gaze delighted as they pass to whatever destination; he is so overwhelmed to meet a vulnerable human soul in those lambent brown eyes. A soul? he thinks, feeling his unbodied feet step casually, firmly on the way to eternity, perhaps. What an unfashionable word. He is not religious, he does not believe there are any gods or souls, except as a shorthand term denoting—what?—compassion or responsibility, all that. And so much argument about it all, too; his mind is momentarily invaded by a spectral horde of old debating scholars, to whom he had paid less than no attention in his classroom days. But he is oddly prepared now to hear the girl recite conversationally, "There is no error more powerful in leading feeble minds astray from the straight path of virtue than the supposition that the soul of brutes is of the same nature as our own."

"Descartes," he guesses.

She nods, smiling across the big brown shape between them. The King's great leaflike ears have flickered to their interchange, returned to forward hold.

"He started it all, didn't he?" Lipsitz says, or perhaps only thinks. "That they're robots, you can do anything to them. Their pain doesn't count. But we're animals too," he added somberly, unwilling to let even a long-dead philosopher separate him from the flow of this joyous River. Or was it that? A faint disquiet flicks him, is abolished.

She nods again; the sweet earnest woman-face of her almost kills him with love. But as he stares the disquiet flutters again; is there beneath her smile a transparency, a failure of substance—even a sadness, as though she was moving to some inexorable loss? No; it is all right. It is.

"Where are we going, do you know?" he asks, against some better judgment. The King-Beast flicks an ear; but Lipsitz must know, now.

She smiles, unmistakably mischievous, considering him.

"To where all the lost things go," she says. "It's very beautiful. Only . . ." She falls silent.

"Only what?" He is uneasy again, seeing she has turned away, is walking with her small chin resolute. Dread grows in him, cannot be dislodged. The moments of simple joy are past now; he fears that he still has some burden. Is it perhaps a choice? Whatever it is, it's looming around him or in him as they go—an impending significance he wishes desperately to avoid. It is not a thinning out nor an awakening; he clutches hard at the strong shoulders of the King, the magical leader, feels his reassuring warmth. All things are in the lotus . . . But loss impends.

"Only what?" he asks again, knowing he must and must not. Yes; he is still there, is moving with them to the final refuge. The bond holds. "The place where lost things go is very beautiful, only what?"

"Do you really want to know?" she asks him with the light of the world in her face.

It *is* a choice, he realizes, trembling now. It is not for free, it's not that simple. But can't I just stop this, just go on? Yes, he can—he knows it. Maybe. But he hears his human voice persist.

"Only *what?*"

"Only it isn't real," she says. And his heart breaks.

And suddenly it is all breaking too—a fearful thin wave of emptiness slides through him, sends him stumbling, his hand-hold lost. "No! Wait!" He reaches desperately; he can feel them still near him, feel their passage all around. "Wait . . ." He understands now, understands with searing grief that it really is the souls of things, and perhaps himself that are passing, going away forever. They have stood it as long as they can and now they are leaving. The pain has culminated in this, that they leave us—leave me, leave me behind in a clockwork Cartesian world in which nothing will mean anything forever.

"Oh, wait," he cries in dark nowhere, unable to bear the loss, the still-living comfort, passing away. *Only it isn't real,* what does that mean? Is it the choice, that the reality is that I must stay behind and try, and try?

He doesn't know, but can only cry, "No, please take me! Let me come too!" staggering after them through unreality, feeling them still there, still possible, ahead, around. It is wrong; he is terrified somewhere that he is failing, doing wrong. But his human heart can only yearn for the sweetness, for the great benevolent King-Beast so surely leading, to feel again their joy. "Please, I want to go with you—"

—And yes! For a last instant he has it; he touches again the warmth and life, sees the beautiful lost face that was and wasn't Sheila—they are there! And he tries with all his force crazily to send himself after them, to burst from his skin, his life if need be—only to share again that gentleness. *"Take* me!"

But it is no good—he can't; they have vanished and he has fallen kneeling on dank concrete, nursing his head in empty shaking hands. It was in vain, and it was wrong. Or was it? his fading thought wonders as he feels himself black out. Did something of myself go too, fly to its selfish joy? He does not know.

. . . And will never know, as he returns to sodden consciousness, makes out that he is sprawled like a fool in the dirt behind his rat cages with the acid taste of wormwood sickly in his mouth and an odd dryness and lightness in his heart.

What the hell had he been playing at? That absinthe is a bummer, he thinks, picking himself up and slapping his clothes disgustedly. This filthy place, what a fool he'd been to think he could work here. And these filthy rats. There's something revolting back here on the floor, too. Leave it for posterity; he drags the rack back in place.

All right, get this over. Humming to himself, he

turns the power hose on the messy floor, gives the stupid rats in their cages a blast too for good measure. There are his jars—but whatever had possessed him, trying to kill them individually like that? Hours it would take. He knows a simpler way if he can find a spare garbage can.

Good, here it is. He brings it over and starts pulling out cage after cage, dumping them all in together. Nests, babies, carrots, crap and all. Shrieks, struggling. Tough tit, friends. The ether can is almost full; he pours the whole thing over the crying mess and jams on the lid, humming louder. The can walls reverberate with teeth. Not quite enough gas, no matter.

He sits down on it and notices that a baby rat has run away hiding behind his shoe. Mechanical mouse, a stupid automaton. He stamps on its back and kicks it neatly under Sheila's hamster rack, wondering why Descartes has popped into his thoughts. There is no error more powerful—Shit with old D., let's think about Sheila. There is no error more powerful than the belief that some cunt can't be had. Somehow he feels sure that he will find that particular pussy-patch wide open to him any day now. As soon as his project gets under way.

Because he has an idea. (That absinthe wasn't all bad.) Oh yes. An idea that'll pin old Welch's ears back. In fact it may be too much for old Welch, too, quotes, commercial. Well, fuck old Welch, this is one project somebody will buy, that's for sure. Does the Mafia have labs? Ho ho, far out.

And fuck students too, he think genially, wrestling the can to the entrance, ignoring sounds from within. No more Polinskis, no more shit, teaching is for suckers. My new project will take care of that. Will there be a problem getting subjects? No—look at all the old walking carcasses they sell for dogfood. And there's a slaughterhouse right by the freeway, no problem at all. But he *will* need a larger lab.

He locks up, and briskly humming the rock version of "Anitra's Dance," he goes out into the warm rainy dawnlight, reviewing in his head the new findings on the mid-brain determinants of motor intensity.

It should be no trick at all to seat some electrodes that will make an animal increase the intensity of whatever it's doing. Like say, *running*. Speed it right up to max, run like it never ran before regardless of broken legs or what. What a natural! Surprising someone else hasn't started already.

And just as a cute hypothesis, he's pretty sure he could seal the implants damn near invisibly; he has a smooth hand with flesh. Purely hypothetical, of course. But suppose you used synthetics with, say, acid-release. That would be hard to pick up on X rays. H'mmm.

Of course, he doesn't know much about horses, but he learns fast. Grinning, he breaks into a jog to catch the lucky bus that has appeared down the deserted street. He has just recalled a friend who has a farm not fifty miles away. Wouldn't it be neat to run the pilot project using surplus Shetland ponies?

On the Air

BARRY N. MALZBERG

Choosing just one Malzberg story for this collection has been a nasty task, too, for he turned up with "Conquest" in the first issue, had "Out from Ganymede" and "The Men Inside" in the second, and thereafter was rarely absent from the book. But only one could make it into *The Best of New Dimensions,* and why this one in particular?

Because I find it funny. The popular critical assessment of Malzberg's science fiction is that it is dark gloomy, despondent stuff. I suppose it is. Kafka and Dostoevsky were pretty dark and gloomy too, and you'll note that neither of them ever won a Hugo. But gloom without an infusion of the comic muse is mere foolishness; Malzberg, I feel, is quintessentially a comic writer, one of the few in science fiction who can actually make me laugh out loud as I read. (There are two others, and one of them is generally considered pretty morbid and gloomy too.) I don't know what this says about me, or about Malzberg, but I'm inclined to think that in the confrontation between Malzberg and the general science-fiction audience, it is the audience that has been weighed in the balance and found wanting. What most science-fiction readers seem to want, when they want comedy, is actually fluffy farce of the Jerry Lewis variety. True comedy bites much harder. Malzberg is the least jolly man I know, but he is also one of the funniest, in the purest sense of the word. "On the Air" comes from *New Dimensions 6*. During a moment of internal crisis Malzberg tried to withdraw it from publication after I had accepted it; I held firm, and after some yelling the story was mine. And yours.

I

DIAL SLOW. EASY TO GET NERVOUS WHEN PUTTING IT in, easy to lose the direction altogether and that is why it is important, it is important man to move the wheel slowly, not get fucked up between the twos and the threes, get it right. two one two. three seven six. five four two *one*. there. the first bleep sounds like a near busy and you don't like that at all, that means that all five lines are jammed up and god alone knows when you'll be able to get through, how many times you'll have to sit here racketing the numbers against themselves, busies are no *good* man they are a bad scene but it goes through, that easy purring ring coming soft out of the earpiece and you know you are set. on the dial this frigging cunt she is talking about her problems with the group, just going on and on but stevie is already making the good-restless sounds that means he's about to split and leave and maybe you'll be the next one in. once you get the ring-in it is just lights on the dial, stevie can push one or four-oh or seventy-three for all he cares, he has explained that and it is random. call late and get in early; call early and never get in at all. it is not fair but then who ever in the words of our late great prez ever said that life is fair? ring in the earpiece. got to go, stevie says on the *rad*-io, got to take care of business and the lady burbles burbles in stevie's ear but her voice is already soft and going. she knows when she is done. got to *go* my

dear stevie says and then just like that he is saying
hello into your ear. seven-second lag a truly great thing
to keep the fuckers and suckers and mother-fuckers off
the air. while the radio is still playing stevie saying
goodbye to the cunt he is saying *hello you are on the
air now* into your ear but this will only come out on
the radio seven seconds later so if you say fuck or
twat or eat my shit stevie will hit the switch with his
hand and you will be canceled off. hello, stevie says
again, who is this ringing my bell? in ten seconds you
will be *off* the air if you do not move.

quick then, one hand flick off the switch of the radio, first thing the experienced phone talker does, second cuddle the receiver into the chest come forward
then into a confidential posture. 'hello,' you say
'stevie?' although you know it is him of course this is
just what is called an instinctive nervous reaction. going on the air is an uptight-making process; stevie
knows this has warned us against it many times. let it
all hang out, reel it out, stevie says, forget the jet-lag
and the fuck-switch or you will not be able to wing it
which is the principle of free form.

'hi,' you say, 'how are you?'

i am all right, stevie says. i am not complaining.

'the topic for this evening is drugs,' you say, 'i had
a few comments on the drug situation in relation to
what this previous caller said.' stevie likes you to give
the calls what he calls *reference* so that they do not
hang out in the open. 'if i may continue.'

you may continue. this is your radio.

'good,' you say. you draw yourself into it the way
that you always do when you go on the air. somewhere in the hall there is the sound of movement,
somewhere out on the street there is a siren which
comes through the open window but these are ignored,
you draw yourself into that ball of flame which is
contact and going on the air. 'now i don't know about
drugs,' you say, 'not really being a user but i want to
say—'

if you don't use why shoot off your mouth.

that is stevie. he is often insulting but inside there is this core of real warmth which can be perceived and gotten hold of and despite the cynical exterior at almost any time can break down into tears if he is really moved. i have heard him in the early-morning hours near the end of his shift weeping and telling of his childhood. 'stay with me, stevie,' you say, 'and i will explain.'

you ain't explained anything yet. you are just calling in to hear yourself talk on the radio.

'listen here, stevie,' i say assuming an attitude of command without which call-in live radio is nothing and you are merely at the mercy of the host who merely uses you for the purposes of his own moods and passions, 'you will let me explain what i have to say and then you will understand exactly why i have called in.'

i have heard your voice before. i think that you are one of the regulars.

'everybody is a regular, stevie,' i say, 'once you call in or even try to once you are a regular.'

that is the truth, he says, that is the truth.

II

it may be asked why i am writing these memoirs in lower-case type without capitals that is to say and my answer is that the typewriter has a bad shift key and a poor spacer when you get into the upper-case leads. there are those who will say this is bullshit and the real reason for this very jazzy and self-conscious method of diction is because i am trying to reproduce typographically the feeling of anonymity of the caller in live-show radio and how oppressed and small they feel and deprived of that true sense of identification which would enable them to capitalize capitalization being a way of establishing names and dating but i say that this is a load of crap as i make my points as stevie has always asked us to in my words and manner of speaking and not in any tricky methods which would only get you bleeped off on the cuts anyway.

III

others may say of live call-in radio who needs it? who needs memoirs about this horseshit much less from one of the call-in creeps themselves or himself? live-call-in-radio shows the isolation and emptiness of modern life, lost souls in their separate shells in the city desperately trying to establish communication with the host who in his invulnerability and lack of known feature can be called god and that is all you can say about a country which has so taken power out of the hands of its citizenry to say nothing of a sense of purpose that they are reduced to call-in radio to get their rocks off. this is a lot of crap because only a very small percentage of these so-called anonymous and frustrated citizens call in and they are not representative of citizenry in general being in fact very strong and individuated types who wish to change their lives by assuming control over them hence the call-in. one who calls in is already three quarters of the way to being an individual and from my analysis of the many people who will be on the air during the night because you must listen as well as talk to get into the beat of the show i would like to say that they represent a high grade of intelligence and articulacy well beyond modern politicians for instance and do not feel at all helpless at least i do not think that they feel completely helpless or otherwise why would they call in at all, eh? that is the question i would like to put.

IV

my name is raoul the caller; raoul the call that is how i identify myself when i talk to stevie which is every so often although he does not still recognize my voice reserving recognition for real regulars of the sort who call every night whereas i only call when i have something to say and to contribute to the discussion which in my case is no more than once or twice a week. raoul the call has a ball. 'listen here,' i say, 'about these drug problems, this situation you are talking about i have had some experience with drugs and i tell you they are a downer altogether. one does not need drugs to take the ultimate trip.'

what is the ultimate trip?

'well there is some who say that death is the ultimate trip and others who say sex of course but to me the ultimate trip would be actual spaceflight and that is what i want to say i am doing. i am going to go on a spaceship tonight. i am going to go to venus by way of the moon and i wish to tell that to everyone.'

that is cool, stevie says, that is real cool that you are going on a spaceship. you have a spaceship in your backyard or are we talking of one at kennedy airport which you are boarding?

'now that is ridiculous,' i say knowing how stevie can ride over you and start to abuse unless you pull him up short at the beginning also thinking of the seven-second lag and the knowledge that if i get too clever with him he will cut me off. 'no one has a spaceship in their backyard particularly on west 93rd street between amsterdam and columbus avenues which is a courtyard of about two feet square and there are no commercial spaceship flights going from kennedy as far as you or i know. i am going to will myself to venus by way of the moon, inner space is a condition of validity of travel which is a proper metaphor for any external reality and one can travel if one wills himself to do so.'

you are losing me, stevie says, inner space and external reality and validity. i do not know validity. i recognize your voice now. you are raoul the call.

'that is right,' i say. i am cheered because usually stevie does not recognize my voice but this proves that i have made an impression on him or then again that he will admit i have made an impression on me. 'i am raoul the call and inner space is the proper conjecture for external reality. i am going to board the ship of my soul and go straight out to venus with a moon stop-over.'

far out stevie says, you are one far-out guy.

'i am going on a long trip.'

are you carrying any messages?

'if you wish me to,' i say, 'i will carry any messages you wish. but i have been on venus and the moon many times before and i wish to assure you that they are uninhabited with conditions not conducive to life and there is no one to leave the messages for except coliform bacteria which can make it occasionally in the methane swamps of venus.'

oh man stevie says you are far far out you are wild. how many times before have you gone?

'i have gone to venus sixteen times and the moon eighteen and mars once. mars is so hot that there is no way you can even do any sightseeing even under glass. later on they will open the mercury shoot but this will not be for several years. there is nothing on mars or mercury either by the way,' i say.

you are flipped out, stevie says, you are freaked out, you are flippo. raoul the call why you do this to me?

'the topic was of general interest tonight,' i say, 'not limited to a special subject and i thought that the discussion of drugs and trips before led naturally to this. i have been wanting to tell you for a long time of my exploits and this seemed to be a good time to do it.'

you are too much, stevie says, you are too much. he pauses and i wonder if he is going to cut me off the way he will often do to move on to the next call if he feels the show is lagging but he does not want to leave this one go i can tell if he can. he begins to ask me what methane gas is and i tell him giggling a little because even thinking of methane make me light-headed.

V

stevie holds me on the line after a time and takes
other calls. gang-calls are a technique of the modern
switchboard; he can bring in as many as ten talking to
each other and on the air at once but he settles for
just five this time. naturally they all want to talk to
raoul the call about his trip to venus. some feel that
raoul is crazy or being sarcastic about drugs and their
effect on consciousness but at least two are very serious and want to ask me further questions, how long
has this been going on? how long have i now been
flying to venus with stops on the moon? does modern
technology admit of this possibility? do we have the
machines and the government is sitting on the information as it has sat on so many other things and all
of this is going on beyond the knowledge of the public?
i reply that i do not want to get into politics or the
specifics of the matter and besides the machines are
not under government control. stevie always tries to
steer his callers into political channels but raoul the
call has never taken such bait. politics acts to conceal
the realities it is at best a metaphor. it is interested in
the suppression of issues and not their articulation
something which i would not get into on the air because of the general mental inferiority—although i
have conceded their courage and individuality—of
stevie's callers. finally i decide that it is time to go or
stevie decides it is time to go the good host never letting you know when you are being manipulated unless
he wants you to know. the five or six callers drop off
like fruit from a vine and only stevie and i are left in
the singing emptiness of the strand that connects us
through the heart of the city from west ninety-third to
east sixty-fourth street dead river to river waste on
both ends. i wish you a good trip, stevie says, you will
call in and tell us how it was will you not?

'i have not yet,' i say, 'i have been a caller to your
show *the wasteland* for three years and two months

and have never mentioned my space flights until now. i wish to keep most of this confidential.'

i do understand that, stevie says. you are freako. you are farout man you are wild, raoul.

'so are you stevie,' i say, 'so are you my friend,' and we disconnect then; to put the phone down after so long is to be empty and alone my ear craving for its contact the way the cupped hand of a lover may shrivel for lack of a breast—but i do not wish to get into the even more difficult issue of sex here—and i put on the radio just in time to hear myself saying in seven-second lag *so are you my friend* and a long pause even a sigh from stevie. it is too much, he says, this is some night. i have some friends. i will play a record now. while i look for a record why do we not think of what has been heard tonight and what we have learned.

that is stevie, pedagogical. i join him in thought, thinking of what we have learned tonight what the true sense of it all is until the thunder of the music begins to pour out of the receiver and then disconnecting it is the music itself that i allow to carry me my ship to the dark and departed spaces the rolling balls the incontestable fire of the planets above, mercury, mars, venus or the moon i am carried and so my voyage begins.

VI

there are some who will say that this story is not about actual events but is merely a clever attempt to show that traveling to mars to venus is no more absurd or strange or wonderful than talking to stevie in the night the two of us linked by invisible wire. there are some who will say that i have merely tied one mystery to another mystery to show that all of life is an implausability and that i never really went to the planets at all but this would be untrue and would show that the readers are stupid and missed the point for i did indeed carried by the music begin my voyage then and it is going on now even at this moment my first and terrible voyage to venus because of course i did lie to stevie . . . although i had had the method before i had not had the courage to use it now for the first time until at last through declaring myself on the air i found the strength to make the commitment because otherwise stevie and the listeners would have known that i was weak and carried forth by that i continue on my strange and terrible journey. in one sense i owe it all to stevie and *the wasteland* and in another sense i owe it nothing but the resolution of this is strange and by the time i return to earth with the look of eagles in my eyes will seem unimportant.

A Quiet Revolution
for Death

JACK DANN

J ack Dann is one of the unsung heroes of
New Dimensions' intricate history. When
it looked like all was lost in 1973, it was
he, on a timely visit to New York City editorial offices, who engineered the transfer of the book to
Harper & Row, thus keeping it alive for five more
years. Coincidentally, the first Harper issue, number
5, contained Dann's vivid and powerful short story,
"The Dybbuk Dolls." Good as that one was, though,
it is not in the class of his other *New Dimensions* con-
tribution, "A Quiet Revolution for Death," lead story
in the eighth issue and a Nebula awards finalist in
1979.

> *No other epoch has laid so much stress as
> the expiring Middle Ages on
> the thought of death.*
> —J. HUIZINGA

IT IS A LOVELY DAY FOR A DRIVE AND A PICNIC. THERE
is not a hint of rain in the cerulean sky, and the super-
highway snakes out ahead like a cement canal. The

cars are moving in slow motion like gondolas skiffing through God's magical city.

"What a day," says Roger as he leans back in his cushioned seat. Although the car is on automatic, he holds the steering stick lightly between his thumb and forefinger. His green Chevrolet shifts lanes and accelerates to 130 miles an hour. "This is what God intended when he made Sunday," Roger says as he lets go of the steering stick to wave his arms in a stylized way. He dreams that he is an angel of God guiding the eyeless through His realms.

The children are in the back seat where they can fight and squeal and spill their makeup until Sandra becomes frustrated enough to give them some *Easy-Sleep* to make the trip go faster. But the monotony of the beautiful countryside and the hiss of air pushing past rubber and glass must have lulled Sandra to sleep. She is sitting beside Roger. Her head lolls, beautiful blonde hair hiding her beautiful face.

"I'm practicing to be an angel," shouts Bennie, Roger's oldest and favorite son. The other children giggle and make muffled shushing noises.

Roger turns around and sees that his son has painted his face and smeared it with ashes. He's done a fair job, Roger thinks. Blue and grey rings of make-up circle Bennie's wide brown eyes. "That's very good, indeed," Roger says. "Your face is even more impressive than your costume."

"*I* could do better if I wanted to," says Rose Marie, who is seven and dressed in a mock crinoline gown with great cloth roses sewn across the bodice.

But Bennie is nonplused. He beams at his father and says, "You said that everyone—even kids—must have their own special vision of death. Well, my vision is just like yours." Bennie is twelve. He's the little man of the family, and next year, with God's help, he will be bar mitzvahed, since Sandra is half-Jewish and believes that children need even more ceremony than adults.

Rose Marie primps herself and says "ha" over and over. Samson and Lilly, ages five and six respectively, are quietly playing "feelie" together. But Samson—who will be the spitting image of his father, same cleft in his chin, same nose—is naked and shivering. Roger raises the car's temperature to 79 degrees and then turns back to Bennie.

"How do you know what my vision is?" Roger asks, trying to find a comfortable position. His cheek touches the headrest and his knee touches Sandra's bristly leg. Sandra moves closer to the door.

"You're nuts over Guyot Marchant and Holbein," says Bennie. "I've read your library fiche. Don't you think I'm acquainted intellectually with the painted dances of death? Well, ha, I know the poetry of Jean Le Fèvre, and I've seen the holos of the mural paintings in the church of La Chaise-Dieu. I've read Gédéon Huet in fiche and I've even looked at your books—I'm reading *Totentanz,* and I'm almost finished."

"You must ask permission," says Roger, but he is proud of his son. He certainly is the little man of the family, Roger tells himself. The other children only want to nag and cry and eat and play "feelie."

Sandra wakes up, pulls her hair away from her face, and asks: "How much longer?" Her neck and face are glossy with perspiration. She lowers the temperature, makes a choking noise, and insists that this trip is too long and she's hungry.

"I'm hungry, too," says Rose Marie. "And it's hot in here and everything's sticky."

"We'll be there soon," Roger says to his family as he gazes out the large windshield at the steaming highway ahead. The air seems to shimmer from the exhaust of other cars, and God has created little mirages of blue water.

"See the mirages on the highway," Roger says to his family. What a day to be alive! What a day to be with your family. He watches a red convertible zoom right through a blue mirage and come out unscathed. "What a day," he shouts. He grins and squeezes Sandra's knee.

But Sandra swats his hand as if it were a gnat.

Still, it *is* a beautiful day.

"Well, here we are," says an excited Roger as the dashboard lights flash green, indicating that everyone can now get out of the car.

What a view! The car is parked on the sixteenth tier of a grand parking lot which overlooks the grandest cemetery in the East. From this vantage ground (it is certainly worth the forty-dollar parking fee) Roger can view beautiful Chastellain Cemetery and its environs. There, to the north, are rolling hills and a green swath which must be pine forest. To the west are great mountains which have been worn down by God's hand. The world is a pastel pallet: it is the first blush of autumn.

The cemetery is a festival of living movement. Roger imagines that he has slipped back in time to fifteenth-century Paris. He is the noble Boucicaut and the duke of Berry combined. He looks down at the common folk strolling under the cloisters. The peasants are lounging amidst the burials and exhumations and sniffing the stink of death.

"I'm hungry," whines Rose Marie, "and it's windy up here."

"We came up here for the view," Roger says, "So enjoy it."

"Let's go eat and put this day behind us," Sandra says.

"Mommy lives in her left brain, huh, Dad?" says Bennie. "She suffers from the conditioning and brainwashing of the olden days."

"You shouldn't talk about your mother that way," Roger says as he opens the trunk of the car and hands everyone a picnic basket.

"But mother is old-fashioned," Bennie says as they walk toward the elevators. "She thinks everyone must conform to society to tame the world. But she is committed only to appearances; she cares nothing for substance."

"You think your father's so modern?" Sandra says to Bennie, who is walking behind her like a good son.

"You're an antique," Bennie says. "You don't understand right-brain living. You can't accept death as an ally."

"Then what am I doing here?"

"You came because of Dad. You hate cemeteries."

"I certainly do not."

But the argument dies as the silvery elevator doors slide open to take them all away from left-brain thinking.

"Let's take a stroll around the cemetery," Roger says as they pass under a portiere which is the cemetery's flag and insignia. Roger pays the gateman who wears the cemetery's colors on the sleeves and epaulets of his somber blue uniform.

"That's fifty-*three* dollars, sir," says the gateman. He points at Bennie and says, "I must count him as an adult; it's the rules."

Roger cheerfully pays and leads his noisy family through the open wrought-iron gates. Before him is Chastellain Cemetery, the "real thing," he tells himself—there it is, full of movement and life, neighbor beside neighbor, everyone eating, drinking, loving, selling, buying, and a few are even dying. It is a world cut off from the world.

"This is the famous Avenue d'Auvergne," Roger says, for he has carefully studied Hodel's *Guidebook to Old and Modern Cemeteries*. "Here are some of the finest restaurants to be found in any cemetery," he says as they pass under brightly colored restaurant awnings.

"I want to go in here," Rose Marie says as she takes a menu card from a doorman and holds it to her nose. "I can smell aubergine fritters and pig's fry and *paupiette de veau* and I'm sick of Mommy's cooking. I want to go in here."

The doorman grins (probably thinking of his commission) and hands Roger a menu card.

"We have a fine picnic lunch of our own," Roger says, and he reminds himself that he's sick of French food anyway.

As they stroll north on the beautiful Avenue d'Auvergne which is shaded by old wych-elms, restaurants give way to tiny shops. Farther north, the avenue becomes a dirty cobblestone street filled with beggars and hawkers pushing wooden handcarts.

"I don't like it here," says Rose Marie as she stares at the jettatura charms and lodestone ashtrays which are arrayed behind a dirty shop-window.

"You can find all manner of occult items in these little shops," Roger says. "This cemetery is a sanctuary for necromancy. Some of the finest astrologers and mediums work right here." Roger pauses before a shop which specializes in candles and oils and incense made of odoriferous woods and herbs. "What a wonderful place," Roger says as he takes Sandra's hand in his own. "Perhaps we should buy a little something for the children."

A hunchbacked beggar pulls at Roger's sleeve and says, "Alms for the poor," but Roger ignores his entreaties.

"The children are getting restless," Sandra says, her hand resting limply in Roger's. "Let's find a nice spot where they can play and we can have our picnic."

"This is a nice spot," Bennie says as he winks at a little girl standing in an alleyway.

"Hello, big boy," says the girl, who cannot be more than twelve or thirteen. "Fifty dollars will plant you some life in this body." She wiggles stylishly, leans against a shop window, and wrinkles her nose. "Well?" She turns to Roger and asks, "Does Daddy want to buy his son some life?" Then she smiles like an angel.

Roger smiles at Bennie, who resembles one of the

death dancers painted on the walls of the Church of the Children.

"C'mon, Dad, please," Bennie whines.

"Don't even consider it," Sandra says to Roger. "We brought the children here to acquaint them with death, not sex."

"That smacks of left-brain thinking," says the little girl as she wags her finger at Sandra. "Death is an orgasm, not a social artifact."

"She's right about that," Roger says to Sandra. Only youth can live without pretense, he thinks. Imagining death as a simple return to nature's flow, he hands Bennie a crisp fifty-dollar bill.

"Thanks, Dad," and Bennie is off, hand in hand with his five-minute friend. They disappear into a dark alley that separates two long tumbledown buildings.

"He shouldn't be alone," Sandra says. "Who knows what kind of people might be sulking about in that alley?"

"Shall we go and watch him, then?" Roger asks.

"It's love and death," Rose Marie says as she primps her dress, folding the thin material into pleats.

"I want to go *there*," says Samson, pointing at a great Ferris wheel turning in the distance.

Roger sighs as he looks out at the lovely gravestone gardens of the cemetery. "Yes," he whispers, dreaming of God and angels. "It's love and death."

Sandra prepares the picnic fixings atop a secluded knoll which overlooks spacious lawns, charnelhouses, cloisters adorned with ivory gables, and even rows of soap-white monuments. Processions of mourners wind their way about like snakes crawling through a modern Eden. Priests walk about, offering consolation to the bereaved, tasting tidbits from the mourners' tables, kissing babies, touching the cold foreheads of the dead, and telling wry jokes to the visitors just out for a Sunday picnic and a stroll.

"All right," Sandra says as she tears a foil cover

from a food cylinder and waits for the steam to rise.
"Soup's on. Let's eat everything while it's hot." She
opens container after container. There is a rush for
plates and plasticware and the children argue and fill
their dishes with the sundry goodies. Then, except for
the smacking of lips, a few moments of silence: a
burial is taking place nearby, and everyone is caught
up in profound emotion.

"It's a small casket," Roger says after a proper
length of time has passed. He watches two young men
clad in red lay the casket down on the grass beside
the burial trench. "It must be a child," Roger says. A
middle-aged man and woman stand over the tiny casket; the man rocks back and forth and rends his gar-
ments while the woman sobs.

"You see," Bennie says after he has cleaned his
plate. "That kind of crying and tearing clothes is for
the old left-brain thinkers. I wouldn't mind dying right
now. Death is wasted on the old. Look at Mommy—
she's haunted by silly dreams of immortality. Old
people are too perverse to joyously give themselves
back to nature." Bennie stands up, looking ghoulish
and filthy in his death costume.

"And where are you going?" Sandra asks.

"To dance on the fresh grave."

"Let him go," Roger says. "It is only proper to continue great traditions."

The sun is working its way toward three o'clock.
There is not a cloud in the sky, only the gauzy cross-
hatchings of jet-trails. A few birds wing overhead like
little blue angels. Roger sits beside his lovely Sandra,
and they watch Bennie as he dances stylishly with the
two young mourners clad in red. Roger is proud and
his eyes are moist. Bennie has stolen the show. He
has even attracted a small crowd of passersby.

This is a sight that would have made Jean Le Févre
turn his head! Roger says to himself as he watches
Bennie work his way through a perfect *danse macabre*.

The mourners are already clapping. Bennie has their hearts. He has presented a perfect vision of death to his spectators.

"Wave to Benjamin," Roger says to his family. "See, he's waving at us." Roger imagines that he can hear the sounds of distant machinery. He dreams that God has sent angels to man the machinery of His cemetery.

And with the passing of each heavenly moment, the noise of God's machinery becomes louder.

But God's machines turn out to be only children, hundreds of noisy boys and girls come to join in the Sunday processions. They're here to burn or bury innocents and bums and prostitutes, to learn right thinking and body-knowing, and share in the pleasures and exquisite agonies of death's community. The children seem to be everywhere. They're turning the cemetery into a playground.

As Roger watches children playing bury-me-not and hide-and-seek between the tombstone teeth of the cemetery, he thinks that surely his son Bennie must be in their midst. Bennie might be anywhere: taking a tour through the ossuarium, lighting fires on the lawns, screwing little girls, or dancing for another dinner.

"We should not have permitted Bennie to leave in the first place," Sandra says to Roger. "He's probably in some kind of trouble." She pauses, then says, "Well *I'm* going to go and look for him." Another pause. "What are you going to do?"

"Someone has to remain with the children," Roger says. "I'm sure Bennie is fine. He'll probably be back."

Sandra, of course, rushes off in a huff. But that's to be expected, Roger tells himself. Bennie was right: she is perverse. After a few deep breaths, Roger forgets her. He stretches out on the cool grass, looks up at the old maple trees that appear to touch the robin's-egg sky, and he feels the touch of God's thoughts. He yawns. This bounty of food, fresh air, and inspiration has worn him out. He listens to the children and dreams of tractors.

A fusillade echoes through the cemetery.

"Daddy, what's that noise?" asks Rose Marie.

"The children are probably shooting guns," Roger says. He opens his eyes, then closes them.

"Why are they shooting guns?"

"To show everyone that death must be joyous," Roger says. But he can't quite climb out of his well of sleep. He falls through thermoclines of sleep and dreams of tractors rolling over tombstones and children and trees.

"When is Mommy coming back?" asks Rose Marie.

"When she finds Bennie," Roger says, and he buttons the collar of his shirt. There is a slight chill to the air.

"When will that be?"

"I don't know," Roger says. "Soon, I hope." He watches the rosy sunset. The western mountains are purple, and Roger imagines that rainbows are leaking into the liquid blue sky.

"Another fusillade echoes through the cemetery.

"Maybe Mommy was shot," Rose Marie says in a hushed tone.

"Maybe," Roger replies.

"Maybe she's dead," says Rose Marie, smoothing out her dress, then making cabbage folds.

"Is that so bad?" Roger asks. "You must learn to accept death as an ally. If Mommy doesn't come back it will teach you a lesson."

"I want to ride on the Ferris wheel," Samson says. "You promised."

"If Mommy doesn't return soon, we'll go for a ride," Roger says, admiring the cemetery. Even at dusk, in this shadow-time, Chastellain Cemetery is still beautiful, he tells himself. It is a proud old virgin, but soon it will become a midnight whore. It will become a carnival. It will be Ferris wheels and rides and lights and candlelight processions.

Lying back in the grass, Roger searches for the first evening stars. There, he sees two straight above him. They blink like Sandra's eyes. He makes a wish and imagines that Sandra is staring at him with those cold lovely eyes.

In the evening haze below, the candlelight processions begin.

When the Morning Stars Sing Together

DONNAN CALL JEFFERS, JR.

The summer of 1974 brought me a manuscript bearing the byline of Donnan Call Jeffers, Jr., and the return address of Tor House, Carmel, California. Which startled me, for many times while visiting Carmel I had driven past the brooding and mysterious Tor House, built some fifty or sixty years ago by the poet Robinson Jeffers, and paused to stare, like any tourist, at its rough-hewn stone exterior. Some younger Jeffers, plainly, was dabbling in science fiction; and when I returned the story (for, though it showed the poet's heritage in its wild and soaring eloquence, it soared just a bit too far for my editorial purposes) I asked its author how he was related to Robinson Jeffers. A grandson, came the reply; and with it came a story called "Mask," which, after further work, I was able to buy for *New Dimensions 6*. It turned out that this was the younger Jeffers' first professionally published work of fiction; it turned out, too, that he was about seventeen years old, which astonished me considerably in view of the beauty and power of his prose. Since I visit the Carmel area frequently, I soon found occasion to call on the Jeffers family—Tor House is the residence of one of the poet's twin sons, his wife, and their two sons—in what was the first of many pleasant meetings.

In the years since, the junior Donnan Jeffers has enjoyed a lengthy archaeological sojourn in Mexico and a brief one in a southeastern college, has moved from the ancestral castle to a house in nearby Carmel Valley, and has continued to pursue a writing career that can scarcely fail to be illustrious. His stories have appeared several times since in *New Dimensions;* this, from the eighth issue, is my favorite.

Faster moment spent, spread tales of change within the
  sound,
Counting form through rhythm, electric freedom,
Moves to counterbalance stars
                    —Yes: "Sound Chaser" /RELAYER

So HE DOES IT, NOW, AT LONGEST LAST. THE MEMORY is on; some year it will be heard, whether on Earth or elsewhere: *First Symphony for Unaccompanied Starship.*

His name is Konstantín Vallejo. His descent is Greek and Argentine. He lives in the city and is subject to the sovereignty of the king of Buenos Aires. He was born in the año católico 2340, the año aireano, 117, el catorce de julio. On the fourteenth of July 127 he was taken to the Ballet Real where he saw the revival of Béjart's "Nijinsky—El Payaso del Dios," Çe Arran's first major role. Before this it had been his family's desire that he go into cybernetics training, but his reaction to Pierre Henri's score was so intense that at the same time he studied electronics he was also apprenticed to Lázaro Serra y Justín who taught him piano and computer keyboards, techinique, theory, and composition. In 133 his first major piece, *Cycle for Electrimonium and Siren,* was premiered at the

Academy of Music; the same year he was graduated from his cybernetics courses and received a scholarship to study at the Institut de recherche et de coordination acoustique-musical in Paris, at that time almost four hundred years old and after a century of quiescence regaining its dominance over the musical landscape of the world and the slowly evolving Synergie Humain. In residence at IRCAM was Michel Stephens the physicist, while Alacrán Lûn of Tycho was a fellow in absentia; these two became his mentors —much of his compositional work derives from Lûn and in collaboration with Stephens he developed the theoretical model for his starship.

From the beginning music was a transcendental— almost religious—experience for him. When his parents took him to the ballet and he heard for the first time music that was not the traditional Argentine folksongs, simple and naïve, when he heard for the first time instruments other than the voice and unamplified guitar of the song-sellers, when he heard for the first time those complicated patterns called from synthesizers, electrimonia, percussive tape-loops, it was as though the universe fell apart before his eyes and was miraculously reconstructed within his ears. The dancers on stage were merely motes flittering across his corneas; only the music was important. When, later, Lázaro began to show him how he could, himself, form those chains of sound it became pure ecstasy. Nothing could compare with the incandescent joy of performance or composition. Music was at his core; there was a string vibrating to a pure bright tone at the center of his soul. His training in cybernetics was important only inasmuch as it allowed him to devise new instruments; the scholarship to IRCAM was attractive mainly because he had exhausted the musical possibilities of Buenos Aires—there was so much more he could learn but no one here to teach him. Music, and the ecstasy derived from it, was his obsession, his addiction, and as with any addiction he constantly required new and greater inputs to reach the heights of ecstasis; eventually he could be satisfied with nothing less than the starship.

After a discussion with Michel on the physical attributes of sound early on in his residence at IRCAM, he has a dream. He sees a huge baroque cathedral organ somehow integrated with blocks of pre-transistor circuitry and hardware floating free in the spaces between galaxies, surrounded by a brilliant corona of astral fire. A manic Lucifer is seated at the keyboard and as his hands move across the keys and his feet press the pedal board the universe twists and shudders about the instrument, folding and refolding, tortured by the music, propelling the demon and his instrument to an unimaginable destination. A random flake of dream imagery, superficially flamboyant though conceptually near-barren, recurrent over the next few months, out of which he evolves his theory for a starship.

Despite his knowledge of computer and instrumental technology he could provide only the abstract, uncohered image; he wasn't competent to envision a concrete form for it. Eventually he forced himself to take the idea to Michel. He had little hope. It was an insane thought. He could hardly believe it himself: how could a physicist, a scientist like Michel, believe in an instrument that might be a starship?

"Music is an arrangement of sounds according to the desires of the composer and performer, and the capabilities of the sound-producing instrument. Sound is an arrangement of vibrations moving through a medium and perceptible in the aural range, as light is vibration in the visible range and heat vibration in the tactile; heat and light are at a higher pitch, a higher 'octave' than sound but are similar vibrations nonetheless. Subatomic particles, atoms, molecules, matter itself is held in formation by vibration and matter is merely energy frozen—energy, matter, vibration: variant manifestations of the same 'thing.' It has long been known that crystalline structures can be disrupted by the human voice—sound—pitched at a certain level; the complementary vibration obscures and distorts the vibration which maintains the crystals' integrity. If an instrument can be devised and a music composed to produce specific tones, pitches, harmonics —vibrations—in a specific sequence and of a specific duration, the vibrations that bind a being to a certain place, time and state of matter can be obscured; the limits of mass, time, location can be transcended. That music will be my symphony and that instrument will be my starship."

At first, even with the specifications already formulated in conference with Michel and IRCAM's computers, he is unable to throw off the dream of a recognizable and massive instrument for him to play, and this image makes it more difficult for him to understand and believe in plans that describe a construction involving less than a kilogram of mass, concentrated mostly in the double eleven-octave-range keyboard and its associated phase-shifters, tonal controls, volume adjusters, and other necessarily physical components of any instrument. In an earlier time it could not even have been conceived, and he is still trapped in those outmoded thought-patterns. the specially coded harmonics and pitches cannot be produced by an instrument composed solely of matter. But with the flux technologies developed within the last century, matter is no longer the only building block available. Self-maintaining magnetic fields engendered by computer and keyboard will carve from the pure force of a plasma-flux miniature sun a coherent energy construct capable of playing the music to move the universe. And as his belief grows he begins

to envision a time when even the corporeality of keyboard and computer will be transcended and the performer himself will be the only matter engaged in the
matrix of the starship.

He began composing the symphony before he was
entirely certain his theories were valid and could be
implemented. It was the most difficult piece he had
ever embarked on. From his long conferences with
Michel and the computers at IRCAM's Artificial Intelligence Project Center came several meter-long
printouts of harmonics, tonal sequences, chord changes
and time shifts, and graphs and diagrams, which he
had to condense, rearrange, distill into his music. And
because he was more a composer than a scientist, and
because the ecstasy of it would not be as great, he
could not be satisfied with a strict and literal transcrip-
tion of the requisites; there were two goals to be ful-
filled: the creation of an artwork able to stand on its
own merits and to instill in him a joy more intense
than any other, and the formulization of a flight program for the starship—which must itself be formulated. The knowledge was always there; that it must
be as much a musical instrument as a vehicle, as
much a vehicle as an instrument, that the two must
be equal, congruous, balanced. Adding to the difficulty
of the composing, even were the plans for construction
finalized, until the construction itself was finished
everything must be tentative, capabilities could not be
judged from schematics, much less the provisional
ones he had; there was no guarantee that the little
abstract symbols dotted across the staves on his readout screen could be realized or that the printouts,
graphs, and diagrams would be accurate, that completion of either schematics or construction would not
create new questions. But even so, in his IRCAM
studio, on his synthesizers and pianos he went ahead
with a work that could be played only once and only
on the completed starship.

In July of 144, ten years after theoretical work had commenced, Konstantín and Michel released a report on their progress to that point. In Buenos Aires the minister for culture read that report in his annual address to the throne. Alfonso II Rey and his council deliberated. La nación de los Buenos Aires was too young, too precarious in its statehood to be anything but parochial, nationalistic. It was decided, *in camera,* that no research of this magnitude—if the claims for it were valid—could be undertaken by an Airean citizen on foreign ground and using foreign capital. It was decided to forbid Konstantín Vallejo the use of the commission tendered by Mohammed Sharif Al Kalif, IRCAM's major patron. It was decided to command Vallejo's immediate return to his homeland. When he was requested to present himself at the Airean consulate in Paris, Konstantín had been in the process of planning, with Michel and the board of governors of IRCAM, a timetable for the starship's construction. The schedule wasn't firm when he learned it must be discarded. He was given scant time to prepare for his departure. Michel, accustomed as he was to a democratic government so well worn and of such age, raged; Konstantín could only accept this disruption of his plans, this infringement on his future ecstasy, this threat to the starship.

At his audience with the king and the lords of the council, he speaks of the hypothesized near-instantaneity of transition between one point and another across the universe, at least as compared to the currently used ram-ships, still hampered by the limiting velocity of light; of the negligible cost once primary research is completed due to the self-maintenence of the plasma-flux; of the incalculable worth of Buenos Aires and the world of this advance in extrasolar transportation; of the questing spirit of humankind and the opening of new horizons; of the fusion of art and science—but he does not mention what to him is the greatest benefit: the unknowable transcendental experience of playing the music of the spheres, the merging with tone and harmony, the union with the cosmos. And he is unable to convince them. The king considers the hypothetical nature of the project and the possibility of failure; the minister for culture is uncertain of the worth of a musical composition that cannot be played by conventional instruments and before an audience; the minister for science, himself an amateur musician, dislikes the muddling of barriers between aesthetics and physics, and is unable to comprehend Michel's theories; the minister for national integrity is distressed that the work was funded by the Kalifate and that, moreover, even now Michel, a French national, is able to go ahead with the construction without permission of the Airean government. Finally they decide that they cannot support the project and, because he is a citizen of la Nación de los Buenos Aires and Alfonso II Rey's subject, they will not allow Konstantín Vallejo to continue his work on the starship.

"But don't you see," he wanted to cry, "don't you understand that none of that matters? The only thing that matters is the exaltation, the beatitude of it! Can't you comprehend, can't you imagine the miracle of tuning oneself to the very basis of reality, of holding the universe in one's soul? Only that matters! And I can achieve it only through the starship."

Outwardly he accepts. He is a loyal citizen. He writes asking Michel to shelve the project. He accepts a post as resident composer and professor at la Universidad de Entre Ríos in Paraná. He composes chamber and orchestral works for the university and the Academy of Music. The only outward sign of rebellion is his refusal to undertake a royal commission for a symphony to be prepared for the sesquicentennial in 150. But within himself he refuses to be balked.

He still dreams. On his own time he persists in refining, perfecting the unplayable symphony. Echoes of it carry over into his simultaneous legitimate composition. But it is not truly rebellion. Too implicit in him is respect for the throne. The king has been misled by his council; eventually el rey will understand; he need only wait. But it is difficult with the vision shining in his dreams, the vision of the starship.

As time passes in contemplation and forced idleness, as the vision becomes obsessional and central, his dream-image of it alters, grows closer to the supposed reality of the starship. At the center of it is the tiny crystal microchip of the computer that will translate the impulses from each key, switch and rheostat into graded pins of coherent sound. The computer is mounted in a keyboard of fine plastics and light, tensile alloys to withstand the enormous pressures of radiation-flux, floating in the core of the plasma sun itself. A sphere of magnetic force surrounds the keyboard and computer, creating a frantically brilliant interface with the flux, which expands outward in a fire of nuclear breakdown and fusion. The thin, unimaginably strong skin of current could not protect the flaming Lucifer who is bathed by it except that he is sheathed in a modified lunar air-envelope, an intangible second skin of congealed force. To the hypothetical outside observer—which at times he is—the starship is from a distance only a star as any other until moving closer it is too small to be a true star; closer and closer: the observer realizes it is less tangible than a sun, not massive enough to sustain the continual fusion: not a star but the effect of one, imprisoned in unbreakable bonds. And because the observer is only hypothetical, only dreaming, he can hear the ineffable music, the music that moves the universe, the music of the starship.

The university granted him a sabbatical in 147. He went to the moon, to the Free City of Tycho, where

Alacrán was. His second week there he celebrated his thirtieth birthday by attending the premiere of one of his mentor's scores at the Lunar Ballet of Tycho. When he returned to Alacrán's rooms after the performance, he found Michel there, come from Paris to see him. Even after three years, the physicist was still angry; he argued with Konstantín, demanding that he defect, abandon his allegiance to Buenos Aires's king, acquire French or Lunar citizenship, work with Alacrán and him on the starship. But Konstantín was adamant in his refusal, sure that it was only a matter of time before Alfonso II would support the project. He could hardly understand Michel's frustration; what could it mean to him when it was only conceptual, only a thing of intellectual curiosity? He could never comprehend the meaning it had for Konstantín. And Konstantín could not disobey his monarch. Yet Michel wore at him with his constant pressuring: though he refused to compromise his loyalty, the continual referral to it brought further to the fore in his mind his need for the starship.

His sabbatical is cut short when in the second week of August Mohammed Sharif mounts his insanely anachronistic *jihad* against the pagan and almost immediately afterward is assassinated. The mad Kalif's actions jeopardize the fragile stability of the nominal Federation of Earth States and shatter the Moslem hegemony. The ultranationalistic Buenos Aires government feels threatened; potentially subversive citizens like Konstantín must be accounted for and cleared. For the second time his return is ordered, and he must present himself again before king and council. He cannot stop himself, when he stands in front of them; he is unable not to beg them to reconsider their verdict on the starship—it is a matter of such importance and urgency for him. They become angry: to intrude his wild fantasies on these vital proceedings. Yet he is so involved in constructing arguments, in

weaving a tapestry whose central figures are Buenos
Aires, the king, himself, and the starship, that he does
not notice their anger. At length they can tolerate it no
longer. Konstantín Vallejo is charged with treasonous
conduct and sentenced to prison, where his only solace
will be the dream of the starship.

He was held at Iguazú in Misión, Buenos Aires's
most northerly province. He would sit in his tiny cell
in the stifling moist heat playing the little mahogany
recorder which was the only instrument he was allowed for long solitary hours. When he wasn't piping,
the silence would become intolerable, because it was
not silent. Through the bone-walled caverns and corridors of his skull the symphony reverberated until he
could feel the calcium cathedral crumbling to the rumbling bass and the stained-glass windows of his eyes
fracturing to the treble. The program of the score had
been confiscated when he was arrested, but he had it
all in his mind, graved into the tissues, singing through
the ganglia. When he slept his dreams were of stars
and the symphony and the starship. The longer he was
there the more it occupied him and as, slowly, his
sanity faltered in the heat and damp and claustrophobia, so the vision became progressively baroque, once
again an organ with gleaming pipes encrusted with
rococo putti and wreaths of gilt fruit and flowers, con-
ducted through the galaxies by a blinding, deafening
choir of angels, archangels and principalities, powers,
virtues and dominations, thrones, cherubim and
seraphim, all revolving in a vast concourse about the
organ as though it were the divine light. All the elements of his upbringing in the regressive Church of
the True Pope in Santiago rushed together into a gorgeous cataclysm about the beautiful seraph Lucifer,
the light bearer who played the starship.

Not knowing he was imprisoned, Michel had written
Konstantín several times before Alacrán of neutral
Tycho learned of it and told him. This was early in

149; Konstantín Vallejo had been in jail for a year and a half. Michel and IRCAM's governors with the French government lodged a complaint; it did no good, and it was intimated that were the matters pressed much further the Airean council might cut off relations with France. The starship had become now for Alacrán and Michel more than "only conceptual, only a thing of intellectual curiosity"; they knew, though not why, that it was of central importance to Konstanín, and as they had come to be bound up with him, so they were bound up in it. It was of central importance to them. But it seemed there was nothing to be done, it seemed that what had begun as a dream must end as a dream, never to be realized, the starship.

Lucifer rides the chariot across the heavens like Apollon, drawn by two horses, the pure white Pitch and the opalescent Harmony. The road is ruled with two parallel tracks of five lines each. The gates of delirium crash before him, each flange ornamented with a single symbol: on the left $\flat$ and on the right $\natural$. The chariot is gilded in silver and gold, its keys are of ebony and ivory; Lucifer's robes are painted in blistering medieval tinctures, gules and azure and vert and purpure: it is as though the whole assemblage is the vignette of a genius monk, inked onto the staves of the score for a Gregorian chant. The chariot shines; it is the starship.

Michel Stephens goes again to Tycho, for Alacrán Lûn cannot come to him in Paris, trapped by the irrevocable bonds of mass and gravity as he is. What can they do, they ask each other. It is unthinkable that Konstantín be left rotting in his tropic prison, as it is unthinkable that the starship not be built or the symphony be left unplayed. Ultimately Alacrán has the idea: they will appeal to the Aireans' national patriotism. Buenos Aires's sesquicentennial is approaching; the governments of France and the Free City of Tycho will jointly fund the construction of the starship and

give it to la Nación de los Buenos Aires for the celebration of its first one hundred fifty years. And Konstantín Vallejo, as the originator of the idea and the
only one capable of playing it, must be released.
France and Tycho agree to the proposal; negotiations
with Buenos Aires are instigated through Luna, and
Alfonso II Rey, against his council's wishes, agrees.
There will be a starship.

To see sunlight again, to breathe once more the
crisp clean air of the capital, to stretch one's fingers
across a keyboard and *play:* almost it returned Konstantín to full sanity. He spent most of his time in the
studio at the Academy that had been allotted him. It
was a small room, like but so unlike his cell; he did
not require space for his work. His computer was
hooked into two readout screens: one, for the continuing composition, always displaying the endless staves
which, even as he filled them with the diamond points,
lines, and squiggles of notation, would disappear into
the memory and be replaced by more naggingly empty
staves to be covered by points, lines, squiggles—the
score-program had been destroyed and he had to re-
suscitate it note by note from the corpse in his mind;
the other screen was set for direct-line communication
with Michel's laboratory outside Paris where the construction was on, or, with some difficulty, Alacrán on
Luna so he could cascade the elder composer with
showers of sharps, flats, naturals, fragments of harmony, questions on tempo, dissonance and other matters or simply mute requests for affirmation—almost
always forthcoming as Alacrán recognized how fragile
Konstantín's stability was. Konstantín's favorite piano
was there for him, the carefully reconstructed early
twentieth-century Steinway studio grand, more for
emotional reassurance than anything else. And a syn-
thesizer, built to his specifics, with the double eleven-
octave keyboard of the starship.

Increasingly, as the first wall of relief thrown up by his freedom erodes with time, he finds himself in his dreams back roaming the floor of that vast limestone and jeweled dome he grew to know so well when he was jailed. Each dawn he must slam the gates of delirium on the glorious phantasm of Lucifer's chariot and concentrate on the no less glorious reality of the starship.

In May of 150 he finished the symphony, at least to the extent possible without the use of the instrument for which it was written. And even when the instrument was readied, as Michel promised it soon would be, he could not test its capacities and from them mold the music to fit; for to play the starship would set in motion the irreversible reactions and counterreactions that would start its movement through and simultaneous warping of the universe. When the time came to test it, test and action would be the same; if his music, though after such preparation, proved unsuitable, he would be forced to improvise. Thus while it was a complete work it was also a sketch for the fully realized piece that could only be completed in its performance. After sending a synthesizer-redaction to Alacrán at Tycho, and a cube of his playing, he went into retreat for a month to perfect his improvisational technique and ready himself for the task, the joy, the ecstasy of playing the starship.

Even in his peculiarly brilliant dreams he is unable fully to comprehend the reality of it. Now, el catorce de julio de 150, his thirty-third birthday and the sesquicentennial of his country's creation, in the center of the city it begins, to the greater glory of himself and la Nación de los Buenos Aires. The king is present with his retinue, the president of France, the ambassadors or heads of state of many other principalities, including the Free Cities of Luna and the

Communality of Ares, and the people of Buenos Aires; several seconds lagged, Alacrán Lûn watches via 'cast; Michel Stephens is here to help him in his preparations and share in his long-delayed triumph. The Royal Academy's orchestra performs an all-Vallejo program: first the *Cycle for Electrimonium and Siren,* moving through to his last work before the symphony's completion, the *Prison Pieces for Recorder and Orchestra.* By himself he can carry the merely physical matter of his instrument, the keyboard and microchip computer, to the dais in the center of the plaza; then he goes before his monarch to pledge, without rancor, his allegiance and receive decorations from Alfonso II Rey and both the French president and the ambassador for Tycho. Now, he stands in the coldly brilliant winter sunlight, the orchestra and the audience quiet. He disrobes, giving his clothing to Michel, and is naked and alone. He activates the computer and its memory. He sits cross-legged before the keyboard. He begins to play the starship.

As the first unhearable chords ring out, the mechanism comes into being. First the envelope covers him and he is as though aluminum-plated. Invisible magnetic fields weave a tensile cocoon about him. The computer emits coded lasers, the visible manifestation of the music, which thread in scintillating, complicating display, becoming more dense and brilliant until the performer is hidden within a blinding starlike effect fluctuating to its own internal tempi, the rhythms of his symphony. And suddenly, though the observers cannot see it through the afterimage, there is nothing but a shifting in the air where was the starship.

As his fingers, one hand on the upper and one on the lower keyboard, activate the first chords, the instrument absorbs him into it so that even if he wished he could not observe what appears to be around him

—though how could he wish it, with the apotheosis upon him? Now he is only another part of the small physical aspect of the being, the Angel, that is his symphony and his starship.

He climbs the walls to the gates of delirium. With ponderous thunder they open. His horses, Pitch and Harmony, whicker and nuzzle him. He harnesses them with rhythm. He climbs into the chariot and sets out across the great calcine dome of night. He is Apollon, he is Lucifer, he is Archangel, he rides the starship.

The music is a self-contained, self-sustaining, self-perpetuating moment. He—the computer, the keyboard—is the spark, but once begun, mass becomes extraneous, at least momentarily, to instantaneity. Labels are meaningless, in this instant of creation; what does a Principality distinguish among, in eternity? The starship is the music, the music is Konstantín Vallejo, he is the starship.

As he sits at the Lord's organ he is filled with limitless power. He is Power. What can he not do? The heavenly host rises up around him to do his bidding, the greatest of the servants of the Lord. What can he not do who is Lucifer the light bearer who plays the starship?

Matter does not exist in Virtue the spirit of preservation. Form is embodied in shifting rhythms, harmonics, modulations of the infra-aural vibration which is the Virtue Konstantín Vallejo who is the starship.

In this durationless, timeless state the eternal and eternally modulating pitch is entangled and one with the cyclic central vibration of the universe. As they are identical and equal, yet the music, a Domination, molds and distorts the song of the universe, a Domination, creating a momentary discontinuity that has always been and always will be a part of the fabric of reality. Into it falls and has fallen and will fall the starship; falls, has fallen, will fall the universe, Dominations both and one, for they are united in the vibrations of the symphony. Universe is discontinuity is starship.

Nothing and everything exist within the ever-revolving Throne. Reality is and is not a part of the divinely circular Throne. The vibration that is the universe is the music that is he who is the starship is the vibration ordered and arranged by his mind which is ordered and arranged by the universe that is the starship.

It is beatitude and exaltation and adoration. He is Cherub, part of the great multitude of the second circle about the divine light of the Son. He is Cherub, the second mandala that surrounds the divine sun that is the starship.

The glory and the pain are exquisite, ecstatic, unceasing for they are, have been, will be the eternal fire of the first ring that he is as Seraph. He sits behind God, he sits at the feet of God, he sits on the right hand and the left, all about, he surrounds his Lord as an infinite globe of divine radiance. He is pleasing to the sight of God, he is pleasing to the starship.

The fabric of space folds according to the modulations of the symphony. He bends the universe for He is God, He is the Three-in-One and the One-in-Three; He is the universe and the symphony and the starship.

In the first movement all is quiescent and nonexisting. A slow gathering of energies becoming inchoate mass as His ten fingers aggregate a ringing tone-cluster. A shattering run of crescendi and diminuendi begins the expansion, the creation. As He claws in disparate notes, matter coalesces in thin nebular drifts of dust pocked with deposits of hydrogen collapsing under their own density until they commence their spinning and their fusion to become stars. In the second movement, the tempo increases, series of hardening and eroding arpeggios. High, scattered triplets as each new star is stimulated to ignition, low rumbles as they decay and burn out, violent chord-eruptions if they nova. The tempo is even faster in the third movement, solar rather than galactic or universal time. Still, in its minor reaches, His music recognizes and directs everything else; but He concentrates now on a single pocket of hydrogen and helium, tainted with trace heavy elements emitted by older stars. The pocket condenses, whirls, throws out a disk of extraneous matter, and in its core a crescendo initiates fusion. Nine orbiting motifs conglomerate as planets with their attendant satellites. One, almost as soon as it has a discrete identity, shatters from the conflicting resonances of too-close pitches; it is replaced by a wandering chord diverted from the outermost planet. The fourth movement He plays in terrestrial time as the crust hardens and the atmosphere forms. A pair of notes, uttered at seemingly random intervals as tides roll the seas back and forth, are at a certain point sustained and the spark of life is lit. That two-note chord modulates slowly, growing more complex, and finally with all its ramifications it becomes the major theme of the fifth movement, which He has set in human time, the time of Konstantín Vallejo who, in the process of the movement, will devise and play the starship.

So he does it, now, at longest last, so he begins. Only He will hear it in its fullness, only He Who plays it: *First Symphony for Unaccompanied Starship.*

may—august—1976
carmel, san francisco

(for Chris Squire, Steve Howe,
Jon Anderson, Alan White,
Patrick Moraz, of Yes.)

Calibrations
and Exercises

GREGORY BENFORD

G regory Benford has been a regular contributor to *New Dimensions* since the
fifth issue, with such fine stories as
"White Creatures," "Knowing Her," and "Calibrations
and Exercises." He began his career writing gently
didactic technology-oriented space-adventure fiction,
somewhat in the Heinlein manner—he is by profession a professor of physics doing advanced thermonu-
clear research—but by the early 1970's a deeper
emotional intensity and a far more complex narrative
technique began to enter his work, manifesting itself
not only in his *New Dimensions* stories but in his
splendid novel *In the Ocean of Night,* published in
1977. This story first appeared in the ninth *New Dimensions.*

1. ALPHA AWAKENS 18 MINUTES EARLIER THAN
usual. He nudges Beta up from her muzzy slumber.
They make love, self-critically. Beta holds that signs
of impending interpersonal problems appear first in
nuances of caresses, intersections, rhythms. Alpha
feels his moves and vectors being calibrated by
her. He comes with a curious pressing jerk. Beta

makes a deep fluttery sigh; their timed rising signal begins to buzz. Once up, they dispatch their morning tasks with brisk efficiency. Over breakfast Alpha discusses the option clauses in their bonding contract; they are in the second year of a five-year agreement, which specifies in gratifying detail the terms of their living together. Alpha asks if she wishes to renegotiate anything. Beta remarks, in a slurred mumble, that he is blocking his transference to her with all this talk. He retorts that he has always regarded psychonalysis as a disease masquerading as a cure, and then leaves for work, bristling, feeling things have come to a draw.

QUESTION: Is the score truly even?

2.   As he reaches the foyer of their apartment building, a man is trying to insert a sheet of plastic into the lock of a side door. Alpha is dressed conservatively in gold and red; the man wears fashionable denims. As he turns toward Alpha, warned by the muffled slide of the elevator doors, Alpha sees that the man is a Mexican-Black mixture (the most common minority associated with crimes of violence in California, Alpha recalls quickly, taking fully 37 percent of the raw totals). The man glowers at Alpha and says curtly, "Delivery man"—clearly a time-buying ruse. Alpha steps out of the elevator, calculating the situation. The plastic slips home. The lock clicks free. The Mexican-Black yanks the door open and darts through it, into the maintenance zone of the building. Alpha feels a sudden surge of adrenaline, a prickling and tingling, as he stares at the vacant doorway; his body's response has come absurdly late. Sheepishly he walks to the house telephone and dials the four-digit code, well memorized, for Security. As he is talking, a hooting alarm begins. Alpha picks up his briefcase and walks out onto Post Street and goes to work.

PROBLEM: Alpha is 38, in reasonable health, with a blood pressure ratio 143/101 in the supine position. Distance from the ele-

vator to the house telephone is 4.3
meters. Calculate:

(a) his adrenaline rush rate;

(b) time to inform Security.

(c) Using (a) and (b), estimate the
distance the Mexican-Black burglar has
run (in meters) before the alarm
sounds.

3.   At work Alpha reads the monthly issue of *Predex,*
the professional journal for sociometricians. There is a
small item about Alpha's recent development of a
sophisticated interfacing matrix, for slide-through future projections. The matrix output carries explicit in-
dicators of any value-free assumptions made earlier.
Predex compares the matrix, in a chatty way, with the
legend of Croesus. Alpha smiles.

(*Abstract:* Croesus frequently consulted the oracle
of Delphi on matters of state. The oracle told
Croesus that if he went to war against the Persians,
he would destroy a great country. He went to war,
and soon destroyed his own. *See index for back-
grounding references.*)

Alpha reluctantly puts aside *Predex* and sets to work.
He is evaluating the load factors of water usage in
San Francisco, a chronic problem. The largest fraction
of water is flushed away down toilets. Alpha, as a
leading sociometrician, has the power to recommend
new controls—San Francisco lies within his regional
jurisdiction. Alpha spends the morning calculating the
optimal flush in a mean-sized private home. Devices
in the water closet already keep the maximum man-
dated flush below 2.3 liters. Alpha soon proves, from
parametric analysis, that substantial savings of water
(26 percent, minimax) can now come only by not
allowing users to flush after every use. The only plau-

sible scenario is to disallow a flush until after three urinations or two defecations, whichever comes first. Alpha is pleased with this result; it promises a considerable saving, when factored through the water grid of the Bay Area.

PROBLEM: Calculate the mean urine retention rate for an adult male, age 38, blood pressure 143/101. What is the average flush rate he requires? How does he feel about this?

4. Alpha remembers an aphorism attributed to Murray Gell-Mann: "Everything not disallowed by the laws of nature is compulsory." Gell-Mann intended this sentence to describe nature's richness, the precise implication of physical laws. Alpha feels this statement should apply to social-sexual rules as well. His contract with Beta does not specifically rule out his seeing other women, after all. Thus, quitting work an hour early, he meets Delta at her walkup apartment. She is younger than Beta by 8 years and her waistline is formed of exquisite hyperbolas, viewed from the front, the two curves symmetrically pinching in to a minimum separation of 33 centimeters. Yet when Alpha lies at that place where all parts of her coverge, head cradled between thighs, his mind still slips ahead to his planned trajectory. Seeing Delta at this time of day provides a reasonable cover, in case Beta should become jealous of the amount of time he spends with Delta. (Despite her theoretical lack of concern/ possessiveness, Alpha senses that Beta can be tipped over the edge on such a point.) With Delta's salty musk aswarm in his nostrils, he regards this issue of sins and sensibility. He can plausibly maintain to Beta that he became trapped in a traffic jam, and spend the extra time with Delta. Private vehicles are now outlawed in San Francisco (Alpha's first major triumph), but the press of buses still slows things to a crawl during peak load times.

PROBLEM: (a) Calculate Alpha's time of arrival at home, given that Alpha and Delta do not pause for the preliminary cocktails they usually share (Margaritas). Allow 28 minutes for their copulation.

(b) Calculate the arrival time with Margaritas, but with no foreplay.

(c) Redo part (a), adding an air pollution alert from a methyl plant explosion, which halts all commercial buses for 19 minutes.

(d) Estimate the credibility of Alpha's claim, upon reaching home, that his delay was due to part (c) and had nothing whatever to do with Delta.

5.   On this particular Saturday, Alpha meets his son (9 years, 4 months), the only testament to his first bonding contract. They participate in the Dad's Day Mercury Hunt. Into the sewers of San Francisco they descend, orange flashlights spiking through the murk. Mercury, now exceedingly rare, commands a price in excess of 1000 New Dollars a kilogram. In earlier, wasteful, uncaring times, commercial-grade mercury was poured down sinks and drains to dispose of it. The heaviest metal (13.5 times the density of water), it immediately sought the lowest spots in the sewer system and pooled there. Alpha and his son wade through the coiled tunnels; other fathers and sons shout gaily in adjacent tubes, and their lights cast sparkling reflections from the wrinkled skin of the flowing waters. His son is clumsy, splashing through puddles and bumping his head on the low curved ceilings. Their conversation sputters along; the acoustics of these concrete tubes seems to make each word have a hollow center. Alpha catches his boot on something and spills into the scum of a standing pond. He curses. His son bends down. In the flashlight's cone they see a seam of tarnished quicksilver. Alpha has stumbled on a crack where two pipes butted unevenly. In the crack mercury gives

off its smudged glitter, a thin trapped snake worth at least 400 New Dollars. Alpha slaps his son's back and for the first time that day feels a genuine surge of emotion. Later, outside, they win fourth place in the Dad's Day competition; the profits from collected mercury go to the city's extensive program for abandoned children. As they stand in Golden Gate Park sipping from steaming cups of coffee, feeling the chill bite of the air, Alpha talks and jokes with the other fathers. There is much skeptical discussion of the new Emergency Provisions enacted that week by Congress. Alpha nods earnestly to what the other men say. He waits for a suitable pause in their conversation and then says, "If pro is the opposite of con, what's the opposite of progress?" His son laughs earnestly at this.

QUESTION: Does Alpha actually agree with the joke?
Does his son?

6. He arrives early for his self-defense class. The instructor is not there. She is rarely on time, a fact which Alpha always notices; it is one kernel in his simmering resentment of her. Thoughts of the Mexican-Black man in the foyer swim up to the conscious level once more. In the stale-smelling gym he trundles out the kick target, a padded wafer of canvas which turns about its base as a fulcrum. He adjusts the target. Somewhere he has read that the average weight of muggers in the city is 84.6 kilograms, the average height 1.73 meters. He raises the tan canvas target to where he estimates the throat of a 1.73-meter-high man would be, an idealized spot hanging in the cold air, a disembodied Adam's apple. Alpha backs off and comes at the target from the side, using a high kick, heel turned outward to take the impact. He misses clean. Alpha switches over to his frontal kick, striding innocently toward the target and then whipping his knee up, lashing out and up with his foreleg. The ball of his foot smacks the target with a satisfying thud. Alpha springs back balanced and ready, eyes nar-

rowed, anticipating the canvas bag's recovery. The instructor comes into the chilly room. Alpha feels oddly uncomfortable, anxious, sheepish.

EXERCISES: Estimate Alpha's height in meters.
Estimate the instructor's height.

7. Beta's agriresearch project is not going well and fine lines of strain develop in her relations with Alpha. He offers to apply some of his techniques to her problems, on an informal basis, of course. Beta purses her lips and nods. Her eyes flicker once and then become unreadable. Alpha sets to work. Beta is supervising forced-growth schemes to dramatically raise food production. They have tried high-CO_2 greenhouses for the plants, with indifferent success; similarly, a back-burner project to breed for larger leaves—thus increasing their efficiency of sunlight use—seems to have mixed returns, at best. Alpha tells Beta to drop these programs and deflect the staff from them to better ideas—primarily, fabricated foods. He advocates pushing ahead on the single-cell protein, a football-sized gray dollop grown in synthetic ethyl alcohol. Similarly, glucose can be made from sawdust. Alpha smiles at her, sure of himself on this new ground, and taps his pencil decisively on their organiform dining table. She frowns. After the fabricated goods are grown, Alpha goes on, they can be puffed, salted, sugared, laced with high-fat derivatives for taste and used to adulterate the corn-based or potato-based mass giveaway foods. This will keep the nutrient density at a respectable level in northern California, he calculates. Problems of zinc deficiency, which worry some of the staff, can be worked out later. Beta blinks, nods, says nothing.

QUESTION: Estimate the probability that Beta wanted any advice at all.

8. By clever management of a trip to the eroding Eastern Seaboard, Alpha arranges to return early and thus spend a night with Delta. They eat at a Cam-

bodian restaurant (fluffy vegetables, a sauce like air, dense layered cakes of a white meat) and return to her apartment. It is a high encased space above the city; Alpha fluxes the wall and watches headlights swarm like yellow hornets in the circle below. Delta appears to him as an eddy of warmth. Outside, Xmas is coming; shoppers mill and scatter below; on the gray monolith of an office building a nondenominational angel appears, shimmering. He murmurs to her that she is enough to stiffen a priest, even in these out-moded, discounted holy days. She blows him a snog, he merges into billowing gold cloudbanks of philosophy. Is this Delta? or Beta? Later, in the thin light of morning, he lies beside her (Delta it is, indeed) and feels seeping from him the soft consolations of chemistry that pad the hard skeleton of facts:

(a) that his hair fell out at age 26, from anthricine in the meat preservatives of that era;
(b) but still, given (a), a perma-wig suffices;
(c) then, from complications with the anthricine, he lost his teeth and
(d) now has a removable denture. Molars of solemn hardness, eternal, an implied rebuke to the easy soft slide of skin around them.

Alpha blinks himself into the new day, to comfort a fresh problem. He has not told Delta of his chemical hair, his ceramic mouth. How to avoid it? His comfortable, familiar life with Beta suddenly beckons: the known, the anxiety-free. But here he is and, vanity stretching thin, he does not want Delta to see these signs of deformity, of aging. He rolls smoothly out of the gurgling bed and pads to the sink, which lies within view of her. To remove the denture, yes, scrub it quietly, getting into the browned crevices (artfully irregular, flawed, human-seeming). In those pockets lurk the telltale rancid odors; if she smells them upon arising she will know all. Or so he imagines. He runs the water fast and hunches over, back turned so that if she does look she sees mostly ass and bathrobe, a sight of implied unwelcome. He relies on the politeness that prevents outright staring at a person performing acts of maintenance or plumbing, however intimate the two of them might have been only moments before. He makes noisy use of the toothbrush, fumbles it into place and scuttles bedward, all—he notes—without arousing interest, without causing an eyelid to flicker.

QUESTION: Does she know, actually?

9. Alpha has seen the future and found it, by and large, scruffy. Unless, of course, proper methods are employed. Technique is, after all, the whole point. Every major culture has had its ways of reading the future. (In ancient Rome, he is fond of pointing out, divination of the future was the function of the College of Augurs, which was still flourishing as late as the fourth century after Christ. Ranging in size from 4 to 16 members, the augurs worked principally in Rome itself—close to the center of power—advising senators, generals, even emperors. Their primary method was to ascend a hill at midnight, to survey a particular quadrant of the night sky and seek omens in shooting stars, clouds and storms, and the flight of birds. Other techniques the augurs employed included the casting of lots and the examination of the entrails of animals, specially disemboweled for the purpose.) Alpha realizes that his earnestness on this point makes him vulnerable to quick stilettoes of wit from Beta. But it helps him in the weekly meeting, such as this one:

The Board reviews his flush-quenching proposal. Ecoaccounting gives it a 93 percent reliability rating; there are few side effects. One of Alpha's rivals, a ferret-faced man, counters that trying a two-defecation minimum between flushes in an office building will cause hostile intergroup relations. Alpha points out that he is only proposing a program for private homes; office environments (where 43 percent of all flushes transpire) are excluded. The usual argument breaks out among the Board: enforcement or education? Alpha adroitly sidesteps the issue, reasoning that one makes only enemies that way.

PROBLEM: Estimate, using standard forecasting methods, the impact of a two-defecation minimum on adolescent dating practices over the next decade.

10.   Alpha accompanies Delta and Beta to the estuaries of the San Francisco Bay, for a holiday of boating. He notes that the influx of sea water into this region has exceeded the allowed parameter space and makes a note to refer this to Enforcement. He and Beta watch a cloud sculpture being carved by a high, darting flittercraft. The pilot chops, prunes, extrudes and slices the taffy-white cumulus until it takes on the trim features of Lantanya, the current 3D star. Next to her he sculpts a being: serpentine tail, exaggerated fins, knotted balls of cotton for feet. The act is admirably timed: as the flitter shepherds the remaining puffs into place, to shape the snouted face, the eyes turn ominously dark. They expand, purpling, and suddenly lightning forks from a rolling wall of thunderheads that splits the dragon in two. The sullen clouds churn. Claps of thunder roll over Alpha and Beta.

Somehow, he and Beta end up taking shelter under different boating sheds. Delta comes stumbling in from the spattering avalanche, half soaked. They stand a slight distance away from the rest of the holiday crowd and watch the downpour. Alpha savors the scent of first rain; like popcorn and tobacco, the smell is somehow always better than the reality. As he stands, hands in pockets, Delta tells him. Haltingly at first, she relates how she has just signed a three-year contract with a traveling executive. The executive will stop by when he can, at unpredictable intervals. The man expects her to always be ready, though not necessarily always alone when he appears. So she and Alpha must see each other less frequently, and be

more cautious; she does not wish to offend her mate
by flaunting her relations with others. Delta wishes
things were otherwise, but she really wants to make
this contract work. It's time she was beginning a series
of more substantial relationships. She says all this with
a becoming smile. Her voice is warm and soothing
over the drumming of the rain. Alpha's face clenches.
She begins to apologize. He says, "Things happen, people do things, and that's it." Meaning: Words are in-
effective; only actions matter. She has acted and now
he has only words. She murmurs something, but Alpha reels away into the rain, his mind a . . .

QUESTION: Is the story true? or is she trying to get
rid of him?

11. His visits to his father are periodic but not frequent. Before leaving the apartment and the brittle
silence that hangs between him and Beta, he wanders
restlessly to the kitchen and finds there a raw cabbage, partially cut away. It squats on a sideboard,
resolutely natural, as mute rebuke of his advice to
Beta about fabricated foods. He slices into its waxy
layers and plucks out a bit of the center. He eats it.
The sting fills his mouth. He feels in this small fact
some new connection to Beta, and kisses her warmly
on the way out.

He takes the Bay Area Rapid Transit to the Mac-
Arthur station and changes, to go south and then east
to Pleasanton. The BART car rattles onto the long
bridge which spans a crevasse, mute memory of the
Quake. The light and airy filaments flicker by. Alpha
reflects that there is a lot of truth in suspension
bridges. The impending visit to his father nags at his
mind and he turns to reading. He finds it difficult to
know, reading popular news magazines, whether one
is really thinking about things or simply rearranging
one's prejudices. He suspects most news is reported
so as deliberately to blur the distinction. He reads of
the Exodus of the million from India: freighters
jammed with starving human cargo, bound for Aus-

tralia in a gesture of defiance against the food with-
holders, the white devil farmer-murderers. One ship
has sunk already. Sabotage? Accident? A sly portent
from the Australian navy? He suspects the latter; indeed, a scenario cast last month predicted as much.
The eternal rule of sociometrics was that all island
cultures newly entered on the stage of power are ag-
gressive: Japan, England, dim Crete. Now Australia;
it followed as the night the day. Alpha sniffs, turns
the page and reads that what Nietzsche *really* meant
when he said God is dead, was that the orgasm had
been separated from social usefulness. He closes the
magazine abruptly just as the BART car pulls into
the station, a mere block from the square white place
that encases what is left of his father.

The visit begins with Alpha's ritual offering of forbidden fruits: chocolate almonds, a half-bottle of
Cognac (small enough to hide from the nurses), a
snog mistifier. The old man rambles on in a softly
intense voice, recounting his clearly seen visions of the
1950s, life histories of people now dead. His eyes are
small and cloudy, framed in a crosshatching of wrinkles that shift and crinkle as his lips move. Alpha
feels himself slipping away as this man, born in 1935,
instructs him in how to live, with stories from ancient
eras to illustrate his points. Alpha tries to interject, to
make the conversation two-way, but this mottled rai-
sin of a man meanders on, pausing only to crunch an
almond, awash in temporocentricity as he shuffles
through implausibilities about auto racing, black-and-
white movies, new dances, great men glimpsed from
a distance, using a firearm to kill an animal for food,
cigarettes . . . and Alpha flees, a smokescreen of ex-
cuses disguising his abrupt liftoff and exit, something
running cold and weak through him as he hurries to
the BART station.

He resolves, in the antiseptic BART car, to stop
and see Delta on the way home. She seems older now,
in the enfolding hand of her executive; his infrequent
visits find her brisk and urbane, her conversation a

smart rattle of wry observations, insider's jargon, epigrams. He remembers her now, in daydreams, as standing hipshot, the cradle of her abdomen tilted, jaunty. The distance between Beta and Delta is widening. He feels himself suspended between them.

He glances at his watch. Sighs.

PROBLEM: (a) Given random motion and access by Delta's executive, how does the probability of an unpleasant surprise, while Alpha is in her apartment, increase with time? Exclude the executive's lunch hour (he always eats with business associates, for tax purposes), transit time and occasional illnesses. (Here "occasional" translates as 9/365 of a year.) (b) Estimate the probability that the executive is the Mexican-Black in the foyer.

12.   Months later, Alpha takes the bus to work. He glides in a smooth arc around the perimeter of the new public works area, carved from the old Sunset district. The new façades gleam in the lancing sunlight. Alpha recalls vaguely that once there were porches here dotted with people; children playing with sticks and balls in the street; an occasional hearty, blackened tree; small grocery stores; signs in the windows for at-home businesses; knots of dungareed men, hands in hip pockets as they talked and squinted in the sun. Where are they? The streets are clean, safe. Why are the people not here? There are benches provided, far better than uncomfortable stoops and porches. Children could play on the lanes of fresh grass. Alpha frowns. He glances up; a face is bracketed in a window above. The man seems swarthy, familiar; it is the man in the foyer. At that moment the bus surges forward and Alpha stares straight ahead, unsure of what to do.

Shortly thereafter, Beta announces that she wants to terminate their contract prematurely. She agrees to pay whatever unusual expenses this requires of him.

A news item in the fax carries a photo: the Mexican-Black. He has been charged with assault, convicted and sentenced to three years in a labor gang.

Predex asks him for a major review article, to be accompanied by Alpha's photograph.

He graduates to a more strenuous self-defense class.

His policy on water use, including the flushing mandates, becomes a Regional Law.

His father dies suddenly of cardiovascular arrest.

Delta is rejected by her executive, her contract bought off. After a week of slammed doors and dropped forks, she makes herself available to Alpha twice a week, no contract demanded.

His problems, which once loomed as a denumerably infinite set, have now shrunk, as though exponentials, to zero. Difficulties disappear, hyperbolically.

And yet, and yet . . . Alpha feels that something is missing.

QUESTION: Can he calculate it?

Yes Sir, That's My

DANIEL P. DERN

The first issue of *New Dimensions* contained a long and lovely story by Thomas Disch, "Emancipation," about a man who chooses to relieve his wife of the burden of pregnancy by bearing their child himself. There are three or four reasons of varying plausibility why that excellent story is not included here, despite its worth. (Its length is the chief problem.) But an incidental by-product of the omission of the Disch is that I can, without worrying about repetitiveness, reprint *New Dimensions'* *other* pregnant-man story—Daniel Dern's. "Yes, Sir, That's My" from the eighth issue.

Daniel Dern is a young Easterner with a literature degree from MIT, of all strange things. He has worked as a consultant in various technical fields and has had several stories in other science-fiction publications.

I TRY TO IMAGINE, AMID OUR EARLY-MORNING TUS-sling, what it must be like, in her body, how it feels, to have foreign flesh pushed within me; how strange it is, that in pressing two bodies so close together another body could be formed and plucked from me. And that would be the meaning of it all, a meaning so clear that all attempts to subvert it would seem distasteful, no matter how necessary. And I would stay home and cook and wash dishes while she went out to hustle her bustle nine to five (assuming rotation rather than revolution) and the moon would go round the earth and I would feel mysterious and burbling (so they say); but I'll never understand, all I can do is hold her tight as one of us bucks above the other, and smile, feeling that I *do* understand something, and that I must pretend the rest. Or make do, accepting that there are some things I will never understand.

We drift back to sleep, and then the alarm is going off, *brrp, barrupp,* ho, time to get up. I blink hard, tap the switch for silence, and walk my fingers up the arm across my chest to her neck, chin, nose. Her face tells me she has cramps, slight ones; I kiss her gently and place my palms below her stomach for a moment, then turn her on her side and rub her back, paying special attention to the diagonals behind her kidneys, where the warmth is most needed. We get up, and in the shower she pinches my waist; *you're getting fat,* she says, so I promise to skip lunch and jog, which satisfies her. Then, as we clear away breakfast, and she leafs through her papers for the morning's appointments, she curses and snaps the briefcase shut, biting her upper lip between the teeth.

What's wrong? I ask. She has to go to the clinic, some special test they want her to take, a urine sample, sugar levels, whatever. *Can I help?* I offer. She goes and dials a number on the phone, chews on a nail while they leave her holding. I put the dishes away and knot my tie. *Yes,* she tells me; I can bring it in for her. In fact, they want my sample, too, while I'm there. One moment. She shuffles through the shelves. Here, this will do. Hang on.

Lawyers—even bright-eyed, red-haired, long-nosed lawyers—have to start their days early. Especially when they're just out of law school, as my wife is, and don't own or run the office which she doesn't. Us photographers have it easier. No model is going to show her body, much less her face, before ten, and all the adfolks I know believe it's immoral to start drinking before ten-thirty. So all I have to do, unless there's work left over from the day before, is know what to set up and check over my equipment and hope it's merely another long day in the studio and not some bright sales maven's idea of inspiration to make me go out on location chasing long-legged dreams in this New York's most unlikely folly of a cold, cold winter. Never mind my solidified sinuses and blue-tinged fingers—do you know what those subfreezing temperatures do to my *film*? Not to mention my shutters? Give me a CIA special Besseler Topcon Super D and I'll shoot your frozen beauties; just spare, if you will, my poor gray Hasselblad.

So while she makes ready to go off to help honest, outraged prostitutes bring suit against the police department in arresting sellers while ignoring purchasers —tort for tart, she calls it—I hunt up a book to accompany me to the clinic, knowing there will be a wait. "Feel better?" I ask as she leaves. She nods. "See you tonight."

Her family's got this hyperglycemia habit; we check her every so often but luckily haven't nabbed her metabolism yet. She shows traces, however, so she eats real careful. Me, I got my own worries. Now they find another new test, or it's a golden oldie, or maybe they just want to keep us worried, whatever the reason, off I go, maybe we'll learn something new today.

The doctor's office is typically clogged; squalling rug rats quiver in their mothers' laps; lizard-skinned septuagenarians sit motionless; I twiddle a *Reader's Digest*, taking two and three readings to decode each joke. Vaguely I remember my first visits as a child: brown block toys, the bristling smell I now know to be ammonia, the anticipation of pain. My eyes take in the paragraph once again; I know there is humor in there, but it evades me with Middle-American cunning.

A starch-white nurse gargles my name.

I quickstep down the hallway and return with filled bottle and vial, extract from my pocket the home brew. Tests, yes, mumble check babble the doctor mutters, see you at pay the next week call you. Still cringing from the shot my childhood memories awaited, I rebundle and trudge off.

It's a problem day, they keep sending models with skin tones half a zone off, too dark, too light, I'm tempted to send them back saying, not cooked enough, another turn on the spit please. Finally we slide the last film back off and call it a day. That's all girls see you tomorrow and don't break that smile.

The phone is ringing when I unboot in the doorway; I ignore it, knowing you never make it in time. Settling back with a light drink and heavy novel, I brood over Eleanor of Aquitaine until another car rattles in the driveway.

She is perturbed, I can tell; I start tea and gentle her as she uncloaks. *The doctor called,* she recites, *they want me in for testing.*

I hold her and ask, *did they say why;* she shakes her head. Tea, news, dinner, work, wine, shower, and bed. I hold her again and whisper not to worry. She cries out as she clutches me, and in relaxing, weeps.

The look upon her face next evening is stranger still: *They thought I was pregnant, but I'm not; they want to see you tomorrow at ten.*

Penetration, relaxation, penetration, relaxation— whose arrogance is it to classify this act "invasion"? For every woman demanding *out, out,* is there not a male whose inner voice screams, *keep it in, don't let anything escape,* and then roll away before feeling becomes a fact. Lock it in, lock it out; it is the violation of surfaces that distresses. I cannot imagine what it would be to have her squirt inside me, fill me and lie by my side empty and drained. Nor the inexhaustible transport of her release; this jealousy will never be reconciled. What soft, bleary smile might I drift with after such elevation, and the warm knowing shit-eating grin that would mist my eyes till noon?

I cannot know, only cause; rod and tongue march around her flesh like Jericho horns until she crumbles.

The office is still fey; they pluck fluids from me, prod me, ray me, invade me, with stiff lights and cold devices up every orifice, and gather like flies to prognose.

It is evident, it is impossible; I am *enceinte*.

A blessed event! Will it be a boy or a girl? Shall I knit booties and crave pickles? What are the rules in such circumstances? *Man Expecting,* tabloids would hawk. *Hubby Takes Turn—Mom Stays Mum.* Men's faces grow pale; women guffaw. They have to be carried; their deep laughter overcomes them. The rich chortling echoes down the hallways and explodes in amazed whispers. I sit there, stomach twisting; I am not amused.

Ectopic pregnancy, they chant. *Parthogenetic reproduction, reverse ovarian drift.* Not impossible, not odd. Perfectly explainable. Nature not putting all her eggs in one basket. *Liberoparous hominem. Homo anticipatus.* Their professional mumbo-jumbo permits them to gloss over the miraculous with blasé jargon, but I am not fooled. They are staggered and still reeling from the blow; all their fancy words are just a mask for their fright. I loosen my belt thoughtfully; I've got love in my tummy.

How do I tell her? Am I going to be a father or a mother? Will she be suspicious, suspect another woman? Is she willing to accept this child? My God, suppose she refuses—am I prepared to sacrifice this flesh of my flesh, say yes to the silver knife and sucking tube? Not with my child you don't!

Then again, this could be more than a mild disruption in my life: by what right would the church and others decide what I will do with my body?

Thoughts avalanche faster than I can cope: what

about my job, my career? Is it all right for me to work, can I get paternity leave?

I wonder if my medical plan will cover the hospital bills.

And will my dry breasts blossom in time to suckle my child?

First she is amused, then startled, then shocked. As she slowly believes, her emotions do a tango. The lawyer's cool surfaces, mixed with spousely concern. Unbelief returns; she cannot grasp the truth. Jealousy. Confusion. Love. Fear. Joy. Humor. Concern. Doubt. She proves equal to the situation; she is no more capable of accepting it than I am.

We sit and think.

A strange, loving look suffuses her features. Never before has she been gentle in this way. It is a deep loving we make late that evening, almost irrelevant to pleasure. I hold her close and weep.

My belly is swelling; we have abandoned tobacco, alcohol, aspirin. Loose trousers hide my precious paunch; even so, I get comments—*Too much beer, old fellow? Better get to work on those pounds, boy.*

I banter back and look chagrined. Conveniently, the clinic has maintained my delicate condition *entre nous* and *sub rosa* and no doubt *oy vey iz mir,* but I still fear someone will discover me.

Is it embarrassment or the inevitable pursuit by the media and fanatics that encourages my furtiveness? It is not yet too late for this all to turn out a bad dream, or at least a creative tumor.

No one could be more loving, more supportive than that bright-eyed, red-haired, long-nosed lawyer who is my wife. "The entire legal establishment is prepared to defend you," she assures you. "At least, I pledge myself without cost in your cause, no matter how prolonged. So long, Mom, and all that. Here is a list of precedents I have made up for you already."

Spencer Tracy never received so magnanimous an offer from his legal-minded screenmate Kate; happy am I to have such a wife, to care for the swelling life within me.

The doctors are very puzzled.

"It's not a parthen," they declare. "It's clearly got both your chromosomes. Confess, sly scoundrel, how did you do it? Did Johns Hopkins pull this fast one? What perverse position did your wife and you employ that fatal night? Talk, or we shall publish!"

I stay silent, aware of my rights. Their bluster cannot budge me. I know they are relieved that Christmas will come only once this year.

She is gentle with me now, allowing me the bottom in all but our most energetic moments. Even so, my tongue is more convenient. We do not go out much; our evenings are preoccupied with reading and talk. We have much to discuss; all these years she has been a woman and I have failed to take interest except in the obvious. Suddenly I am very concerned; the rights of mothers, Lamaze and painless birth, proper nutrition, obligations to the state—I find I am less alert to the outside world than I used to be; my mind drifts at unlikely moments and fills with thoughts of sky.

To hide our fear, we joke: will she join me in the delivery room, or pace frantically outside, choking on cigars?

Someone has told the papers, the mercenary scoundrel. Peace is a forgotten concept; the household, the driveway, the entire block is littered with newssneaks. Our phone sounds like an ice cream truck. Our mailbox is overrun; indeed, the mailman has taken to doing our house as an entire bag drop. Luckily, no one has yet been violent.

The church is rather off-balance. Hurrah!

I can feel movement already. My body feels light

in spite of its new bulk; I rest my hands on my hairy navel and wonder whether some mistake has not been made. Surely the noble doctors could not be wrong?

Perhaps the women never really did it at all, it is only a lie spread and carefully maintained by some mysterious power structure. It is as likely as my being the only one.

The thought does not console me.

Spring has exploded: the air is overpoweringly sweet. Birds sing, worms turn, leaves unroll . . . I feel a mysterious kinship with the earth, and cautious of my cargo I take to our garden.

Sitting in the class together, my wife and I attract strange glances, but everyone is too polite to talk to us. *I don't mind,* I would say, *come, do you believe in breast-feeding.* But beneath their distance I know I frighten them, so we do not press for company. *One, two, one, two,* we all chant together. *Breathe. Breathe. Relax.*

You have given your fellow men another tool for oppressing us, an angry woman writes. *Now you don't need us at all.* Uncertain, I ponder this. But: *You are a brave man,* another letter says, *to share our burden with us. I wish you well.*

I answer as many of these letters as I am able; their encouragement strengthens me. The others, the distressed mudslingers, I skim for originality and then feed to the trash.

Business is booming, I can report. Vicarious notoriety has brought flush times to the law firm. Multi-digit offers from institutions and periodicals cover our bulletin board. We contemplate the temptation, but steadfastly refuse to say, "Come on over."

I drink milk, take vitamins. Obviously I have not been to work in weeks; my condition is distracting when not downright encumbering, and I feel as if I am in front of the cameras instead of behind them. Well, that's what you get for not taking precautions.

I wonder if she would have married me, had we been single when it happened.

Our parents, who have always pestered us to have children, do not appear satisfied by the recent development. There's no pleasing some people.

The companies are beginning to get obnoxious again; they view me as a viable sales gimmick. Entire new markets! Dolls! Sweatshirts! Advice to unwed fathers! Bah!

The only consolation I have is that *Pravda* has not yet announced the previously unpublicized case of a Russian man who gave birth to a healthy seven-pound boy—or maybe twins—back in 1962.

Well, we had to give in; Blue Cross would not spring for my obstetric expenses. We expect to win the lawsuit, but in the meantime the clinic's offer was our only hope of financial non-ruin. We intend to get those hard-fisted bastards, however. Deny childbirth coverage on account of my sex, will they? I will relish watching them squirm in court. Let's hear it for the Equal Rights Amendment, brothers!

Buying a suitable nursing brassiere was quite an adventure.

It is a triumph worth crowing over. Single-handedly, I have thrown an entire medical research team into panic. Now that they've got me, they don't know what to do with me. Hi-ho, they're so confused! They'd love to be able to say, *there's been a mistake, it's only a strange growth,* but not after the X rays.

Actually, it began as a wart on my ass.

My art is suffering, I admit, but I realize I am not the first whose baby preempted a career.

When the child is two months old, I intend to go

back to work full-time, if at all possible. Meanwhile, I am catching up on my reading.

I have accepted an invitation to speak before the upcoming Gay Rights Conference. My topic (by request): Male Mothers: A Viable Gay Alternative to Adoption.

Though uncertain how I feel about all this, I was too flattered to refuse.

The day has come. Swollen-bellied they cart me away, accompanied by a certain red-haired lawyer. The connection between my vast abdomen and a son or daughter seems tenuous even at this moment; it is hard to believe that another living creature is in there. I think Saul's a good name for a boy, although Minerva might be more appropriate. Though the prospect of being a househusband swaddled by mewling babes frightens me, the whole experience has been most enlightening. I wonder if my feelings are common.

They have the operating theatre all ready for me. Doctors circle like eager vultures. (A large fuss was needed to get my wife's permission to be with me.) TV cameras wait, ready to dolly in for the close-ups; should we have sold tickets to the intrigued M.D.? But viewing privileges were included in the deal we made.

It will have to be the knife. The one thing I lack is an egress; however the little bugger managed to sneak inside me, he or she forgot to provide for a graceful exit. For some reason, neither my wife nor I really worried about it; I guess I thought I would sprout a zipper in the final week, or something.

They assure me the caesarean is routine and I do not have to be afraid.

Since this is a high-class operation, well-funded, I get the luxury of an epidural. I would have insisted on a local rather than general anesthetic in any case. *I will not sleep through the birth of my child.* In their arrogant professional distance they assumed I would take a dive. And not know what they were doing to me? I will endure pain if I must, but I will be there and awake the whole time.

The insufferable *maleness* of the medical profession has never been more evident.

The nurses are all on my side. They have been good to me. Those who have children of their own have spent time chatting with me to put me at ease; they made sure I was comfortable and not worried. It was at their urging that I insisted on staying awake.

Trembling shakes my body; I grasp the sides of the table. Where are my rope handles!

A white-masked face nods; another needle sinks into my flesh. They wheel a device which sounds like a coffee percolator to my side.

Holding my hand, my wife stands by me. She tries to look calm and loving, but I can see fear, the worry in her eyes.

In her place, would I have cared so well?

My guts buckle. I suck air and scream in pain. This is a mistake. They wave the gas tube in my face. *Are you sure?* they inquire.

Don't you dare, I threaten. My wife's hand tightens around my fingers. They back off.

Another pain. How the devil can I suffer contractions when I don't have a birth canal?

The entire event has been irregular that way.

The pains quicken. I moan softly. The doctors confer in whispers; then the head shaman steps near. He flexes his arms as if preparing to carve a holiday bird. They lift the white sheet from my body.

Somewhere below my monstrous belly hang my standard-issue male-type genitals. I have not seen them lately, being too fat in front for line-of-sight viewing, but since I can still urinate while standing, I assume that everything is still there. (Actually, I can still feel them when I wash.)

So I am cheered; some things have *not* changed . . .
I want ice cream.

Ahhh the metal is cold! Damn them! *Aieee!*
My hairless flesh prickles at their touch. (They shaved me yesterday—my belly that is. They had the goodness to leave the pubic hair intact, as it was not in the way.)
They swab me down with antisepitcs. The drying alcohol tingles. I imagine already hearing my child's cries.
A wave of love fills me, dulling the first incision's pain. I can tell I am bleeding.
The television lights shine on my skin. *Ladies, have you tried* . . . Unlike most commercial housewife illusions, my skin is not soft, but my wife still loves me.

In the later months of my pregnancy I was gleeful. I had never felt more handsome. But in the odd moments I found myself thinking, *Is she out with other women now? Other men? Do I look fat and ugly now?* Afraid, I did not mention these thoughts to my wife.
Under the bright-lit pain of parturition, my mask dissolves. I hear voices discussing me. I do not care.
My breath comes in chunks now: *a-haa, a-haa.* My diaphragm is rock-hard. They are peeling me apart like an orange.
My breasts throb. My body is being torn in two. *What are they doing to me?* Pain, incredible pain, the rush of voices, the measured beat of calm nurses ready with the instruments, oxygen shoved in my mouth, futile nausea, wrenching jolts that shake the table and rattled the trays. Shake, rattle and roll. My fingernails are ripping into my palms. *How can they stand it?* My eyes press shut in pain; my screams fill the room. No more strength now—*let it be over, please!* Hands explore me; fingers close like hooks in around the payload. My flesh parts and I feel the sucking as they lift the body from me, there is another wave of pain that blurs my eyes and I feel cold air

inside me while I gasp above—and suddenly everything is silent, it is over.

In that still moment before they slap the baby into
squalling life, I am overcome with emptiness; I am
empty again and helpless to change it. *Put it back in!*
I try to cry out, even as they begin to sew me up
again, but I am too weak to speak. Reflex attempts
to make me ignore my feelings, but they are too strong;
reaching for my wife's hand, I begin to weep. Overcome with grief, joy, and loss, I let my tears mingle
with the cries of my newborn child.